# GIANT DAYS

## VOLUME FOURTEEN

Published by

BOOM! BOX

ROSS RICHIE................................................................CEO & FOUNDER
JOY HUFFMAN.....................................................................................CFO
MATT GAGNON...............................................................EDITOR-IN-CHIEF
FILIP SABLIK.............................PRESIDENT, PUBLISHING & MARKETING
STEPHEN CHRISTY..............................................PRESIDENT, DEVELOPMENT
LANCE KREITER...................VICE PRESIDENT, LICENSING & MERCHANDISING
ARUNE SINGH.......................................VICE PRESIDENT, MARKETING
BRYCE CARLSON..................VICE PRESIDENT, EDITORIAL & CREATIVE STRATEGY
KATE HENNING................................................DIRECTOR, OPERATIONS
SPENCER SIMPSON.....................................................DIRECTOR, SALES
SCOTT NEWMAN.............................MANAGER, PRODUCTION DESIGN
ELYSE STRANDBERG.........................................MANAGER, FINANCE
SIERRA HAHN...............................................EXECUTIVE EDITOR
JEANINE SCHAEFER.......................................EXECUTIVE EDITOR
DAFNA PLEBAN.................................................SENIOR EDITOR
SHANNON WATTERS..........................................SENIOR EDITOR
ERIC HARBURN................................................SENIOR EDITOR
MATTHEW LEVINE.....................................................EDITOR
SOPHIE PHILIPS-ROBERTS...............................ASSOCIATE EDITOR
AMANDA LaFRANCO........................................ASSOCIATE EDITOR
JONATHAN MANNING......................................ASSOCIATE EDITOR
GAVIN GRONENTHAL.......................................ASSISTANT EDITOR

GWEN WALLER....................................................ASSISTANT EDITOR
ALLYSON GRONOWITZ...........................................ASSISTANT EDITOR
RAMIRO PORTNOY................................................ASSISTANT EDITOR
SHELBY NETSCHKE...............................................EDITORIAL ASSISTANT
MICHELLE ANKLEY...............................................DESIGN COORDINATOR
MARIE KRUPINA.................................................PRODUCTION DESIGNER
GRACE PARK.....................................................PRODUCTION DESIGNER
CHELSEA ROBERTS.............................................PRODUCTION DESIGNER
SAMANTHA KNAPP.........................................PRODUCTION DESIGN ASSISTANT
JOSÉ MEZA......................................................LIVE EVENTS LEAD
STEPHANIE HOCUTT...........................................DIGITAL MARKETING LEAD
ESTHER KIM...................................................MARKETING COORDINATOR
BREANNA SARPY............................................LIVE EVENTS COORDINATOR
AMANDA LAWSON...............................................MARKETING ASSISTANT
HOLLY AITCHISON.............................................DIGITAL SALES COORDINATOR
MORGAN PERRY.................................................RETAIL SALES COORDINATOR
MEGAN CHRISTOPHER.........................................OPERATIONS COORDINATOR
RODRIGO HERNANDEZ.........................................OPERATIONS COORDINATOR
ZIPPORAH SMITH...............................................OPERATIONS ASSISTANT
JASON LEE.....................................................SENIOR ACCOUNTANT
SABRINA LESIN................................................ACCOUNTING ASSISTANT

BOOM! BOX™

GIANT DAYS Volume Fourteen, October 2020. Published by BOOM! Box, a division of Boom Entertainment, Inc. Giant Days is ™ & © 2020 John Allison. Originally published in single magazine form as GIANT DAYS No. 53-54, As Time Goes By No. 1. ™ & © 2019 John Allison. All rights reserved. BOOM! Box™ and the BOOM! Box logo are trademarks of Boom Entertainment, Inc., registered in various countries and categories. All characters, events, and institutions depicted herein are fictional. Any similarity between any of the names, characters, persons, events, and/or institutions in this publication to actual names, characters, and persons, whether living or dead, events, and/or institutions is unintended and purely coincidental. BOOM! Box does not read or accept unsolicited submissions of ideas, stories, or artwork.

BOOM! Studios, 5670 Wilshire Boulevard, Suite 400, Los Angeles, CA 90036-5679. Printed in China. First Printing.

ISBN: 978-1-68415-605-4, eISBN: 978-1-64668-017-7

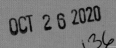

# GIANT DAYS™

CREATED + WRITTEN BY
## JOHN ALLISON

ART BY
## MAX SARIN

COLORS BY
## WHITNEY COGAR

LETTERS BY
## JIM CAMPBELL

COVER BY
## MAX SARIN

SERIES DESIGNER
## GRACE PARK

COLLECTION DESIGNER
## MARIE KRUPINA

EDITOR
## SOPHIE PHILIPS-ROBERTS

SENIOR EDITOR
## SHANNON WATTERS

# CHAPTER
# FIFTY-THREE

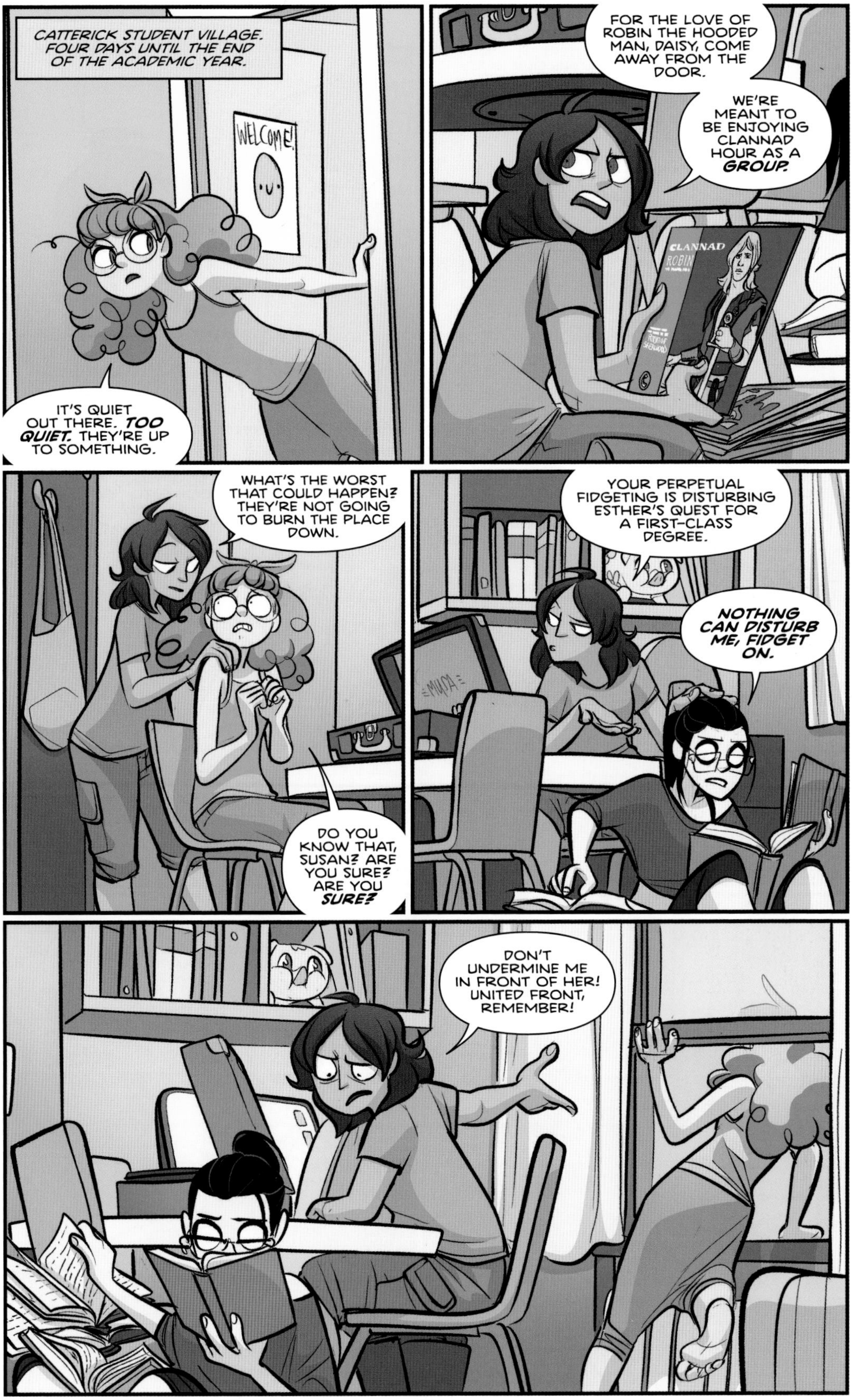

CATTERICK STUDENT VILLAGE. FOUR DAYS UNTIL THE END OF THE ACADEMIC YEAR.
WELCOME!
IT'S QUIET OUT THERE. TOO QUIET. THEY'RE UP TO SOMETHING.
FOR THE LOVE OF ROBIN THE HOODED MAN, DAISY, COME AWAY FROM THE DOOR.
WE'RE MEANT TO BE ENJOYING CLANNAD HOUR AS A GROUP.
CLANNAD
ROBIN
WHAT'S THE WORST THAT COULD HAPPEN? THEY'RE NOT GOING TO BURN THE PLACE DOWN.
DO YOU KNOW THAT, SUSAN? ARE YOU SURE? ARE YOU SURE?
YOUR PERPETUAL FIDGETING IS DISTURBING ESTHER'S QUEST FOR A FIRST-CLASS DEGREE.
NOTHING CAN DISTURB ME, FIDGET ON.
DON'T UNDERMINE ME IN FRONT OF HER! UNITED FRONT, REMEMBER!

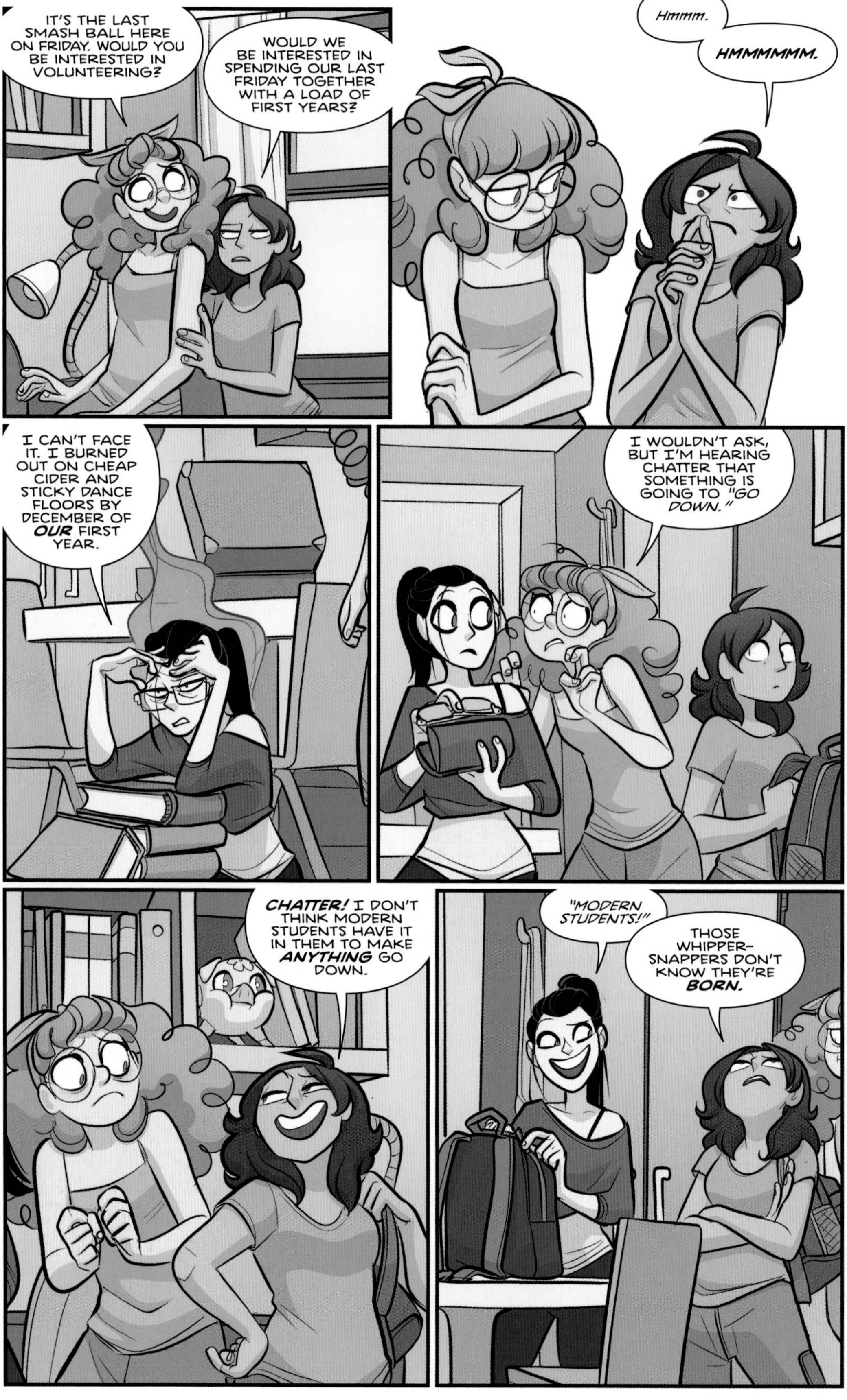
IT'S THE LAST SMASH BALL HERE ON FRIDAY. WOULD YOU BE INTERESTED IN VOLUNTEERING?
WOULD WE BE INTERESTED IN SPENDING OUR LAST FRIDAY TOGETHER WITH A LOAD OF FIRST YEARS?
Hmmm.
HMMMMMM.
I CAN'T FACE IT. I BURNED OUT ON CHEAP CIDER AND STICKY DANCE FLOORS BY DECEMBER OF OUR FIRST YEAR.
I WOULDN'T ASK, BUT I'M HEARING CHATTER THAT SOMETHING IS GOING TO "GO DOWN."
CHATTER! I DON'T THINK MODERN STUDENTS HAVE IT IN THEM TO MAKE ANYTHING GO DOWN.
"MODERN STUDENTS!"
THOSE WHIPPER-SNAPPERS DON'T KNOW THEY'RE BORN.

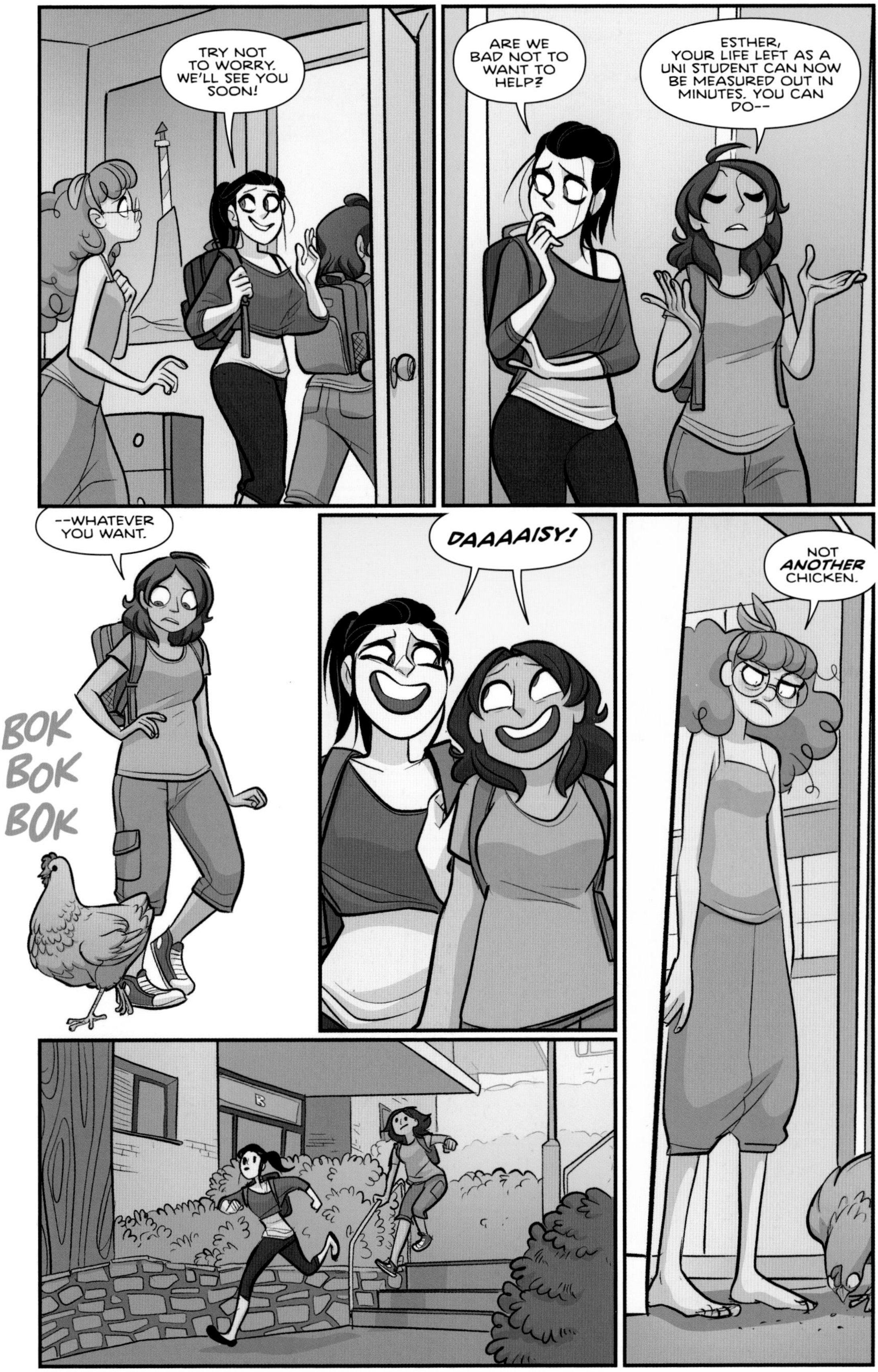
TRY NOT TO WORRY. WE'LL SEE YOU SOON!
ARE WE BAD NOT TO WANT TO HELP?
ESTHER, YOUR LIFE LEFT AS A UNI STUDENT CAN NOW BE MEASURED OUT IN MINUTES. YOU CAN DO--
--WHATEVER YOU WANT.
BOK BOK BOK
DAAAAAISY!
NOT ANOTHER CHICKEN.

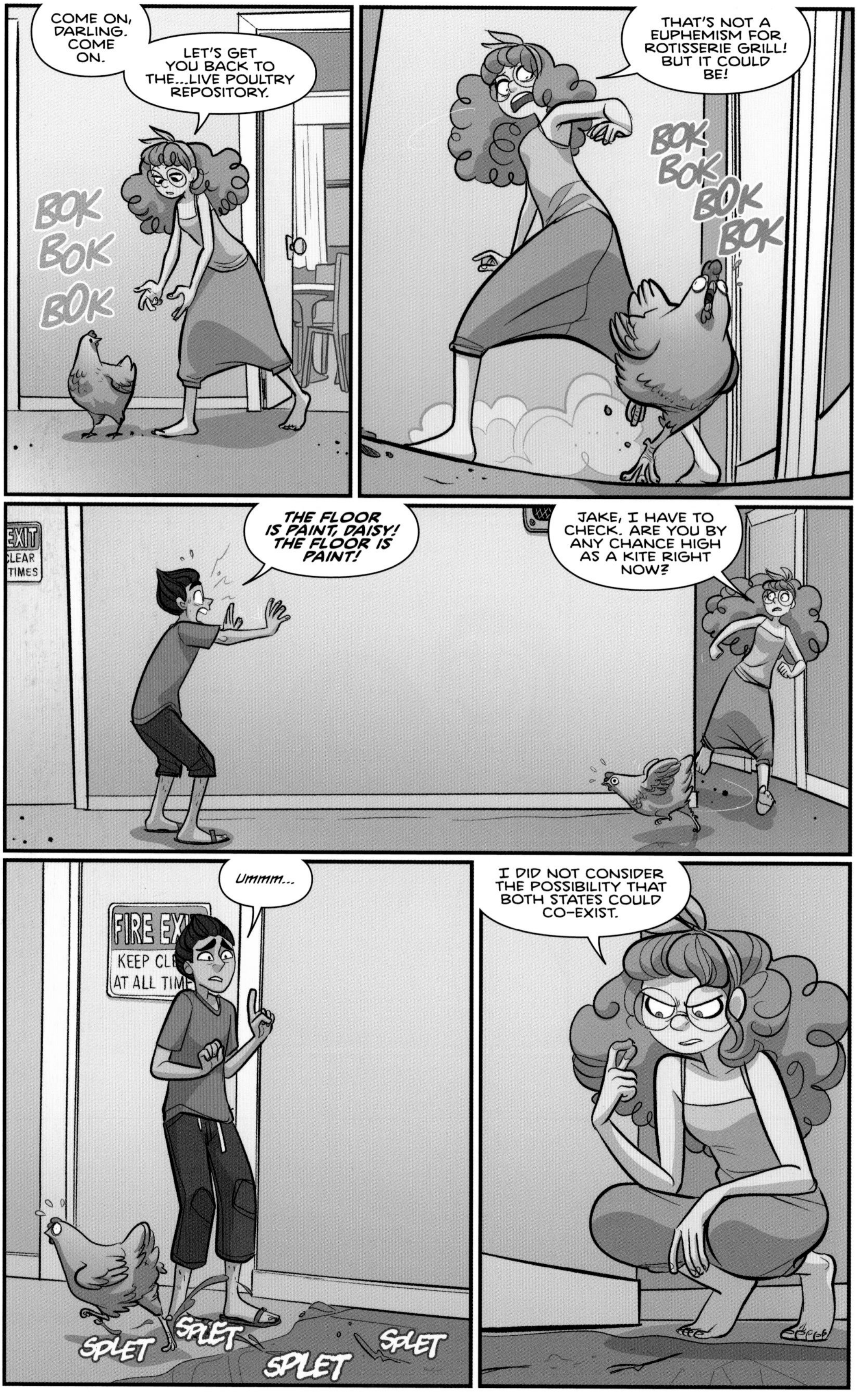
COME ON, DARLING. COME ON.
LET'S GET YOU BACK TO THE...LIVE POULTRY REPOSITORY.
BOK BOK BOK
THAT'S NOT A EUPHEMISM FOR ROTISSERIE GRILL! BUT IT COULD BE!
BOK BOK BOK BOK
EXIT
CLEAR
TIMES
*THE FLOOR IS PAINT, DAISY! THE FLOOR IS PAINT!*
JAKE, I HAVE TO CHECK. ARE YOU BY ANY CHANCE HIGH AS A KITE RIGHT NOW?
FIRE EX
KEEP CLE
AT ALL TIM
*Ummm...*
SPLET SPLET SPLET SPLET
I DID NOT CONSIDER THE POSSIBILITY THAT BOTH STATES COULD CO-EXIST.

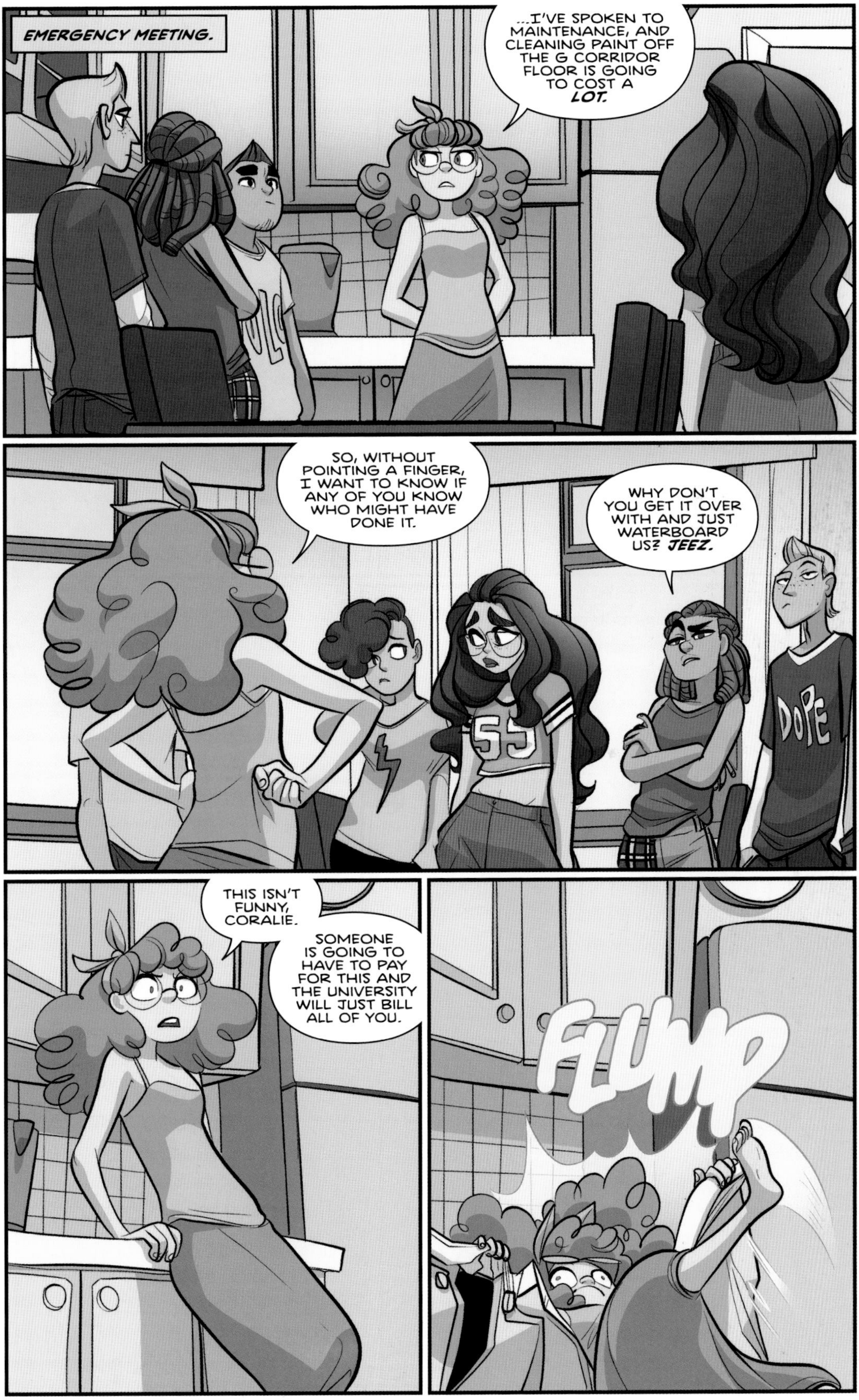
EMERGENCY MEETING.
...I'VE SPOKEN TO MAINTENANCE, AND CLEANING PAINT OFF THE G CORRIDOR FLOOR IS GOING TO COST A LOT.
SO, WITHOUT POINTING A FINGER, I WANT TO KNOW IF ANY OF YOU KNOW WHO MIGHT HAVE DONE IT.
WHY DON'T YOU GET IT OVER WITH AND JUST WATERBOARD US? JEEZ.
DOPE
THIS ISN'T FUNNY, CORALIE.
SOMEONE IS GOING TO HAVE TO PAY FOR THIS AND THE UNIVERSITY WILL JUST BILL ALL OF YOU.
FLUMP

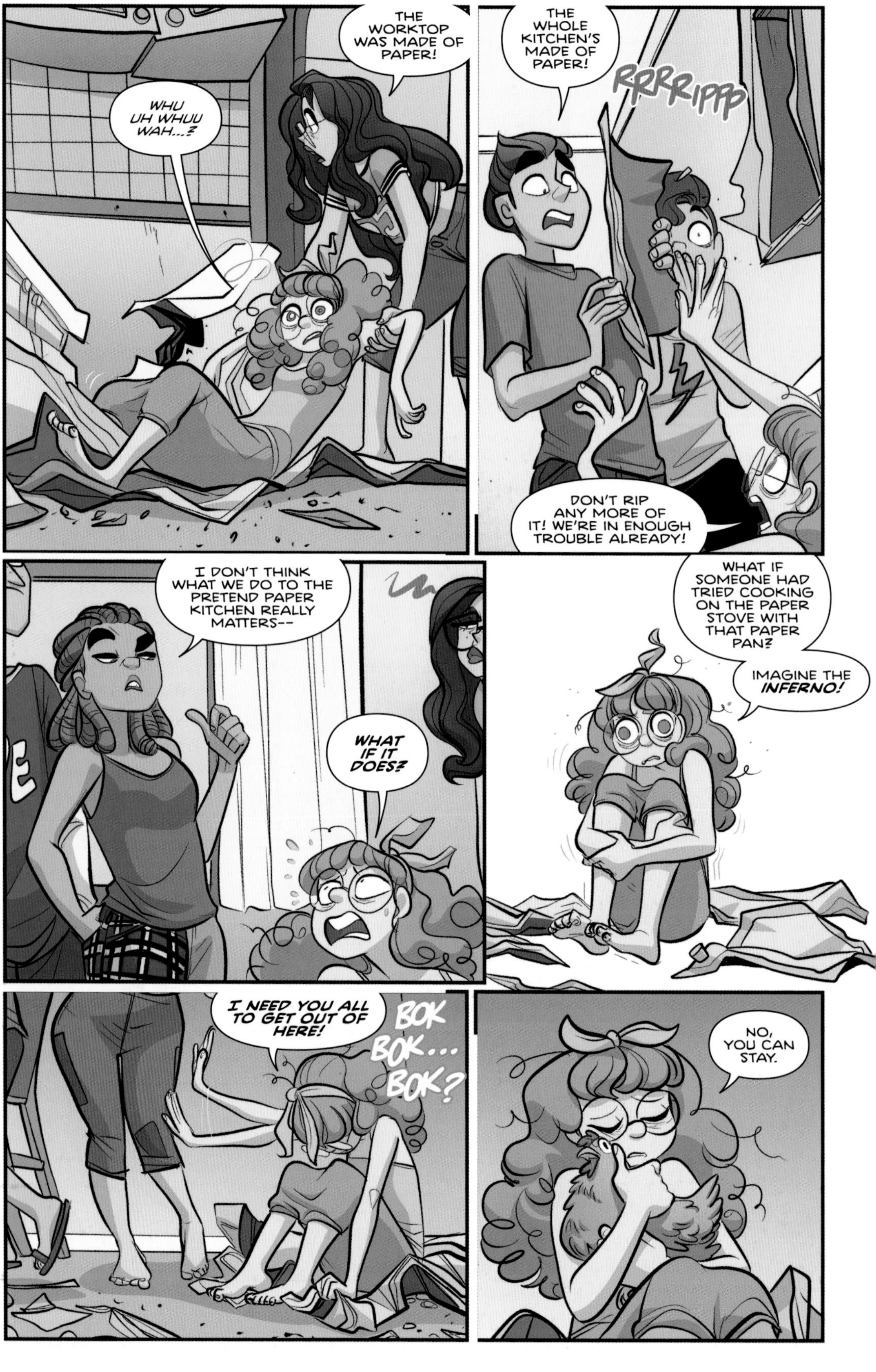

THE WORKTOP WAS MADE OF PAPER!
WHU UH WHUU WAH...?
THE WHOLE KITCHEN'S MADE OF PAPER!
RRRRIPPP
DON'T RIP ANY MORE OF IT! WE'RE IN ENOUGH TROUBLE ALREADY!
I DON'T THINK WHAT WE DO TO THE PRETEND PAPER KITCHEN REALLY MATTERS--
WHAT IF IT DOES?
WHAT IF SOMEONE HAD TRIED COOKING ON THE PAPER STOVE WITH THAT PAPER PAN?
IMAGINE THE INFERNO!
I NEED YOU ALL TO GET OUT OF HERE!
BOK BOK... BOK?
NO, YOU CAN STAY.

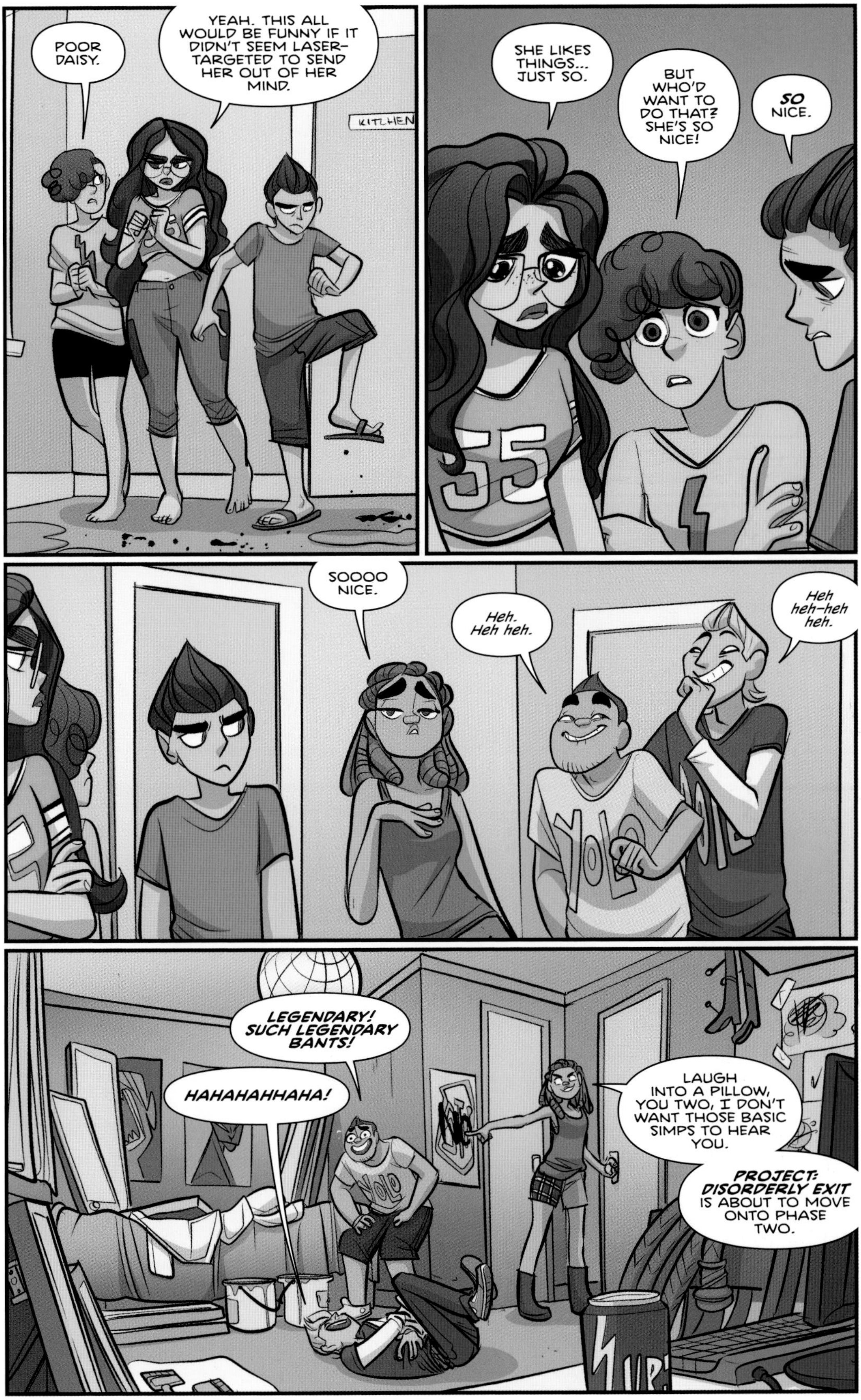
POOR DAISY.
YEAH. THIS ALL WOULD BE FUNNY IF IT DIDN'T SEEM LASER-TARGETED TO SEND HER OUT OF HER MIND.
KITCHEN
SHE LIKES THINGS... JUST SO.
BUT WHO'D WANT TO DO THAT? SHE'S SO NICE!
SO NICE.
SOOOO NICE.
Heh. Heh heh.
Heh heh-heh heh.
LEGENDARY! SUCH LEGENDARY BANTS!
HAHAHAHHAHA!
LAUGH INTO A PILLOW, YOU TWO, I DON'T WANT THOSE BASIC SIMPS TO HEAR YOU.
PROJECT: DISORDERLY EXIT IS ABOUT TO MOVE ONTO PHASE TWO.

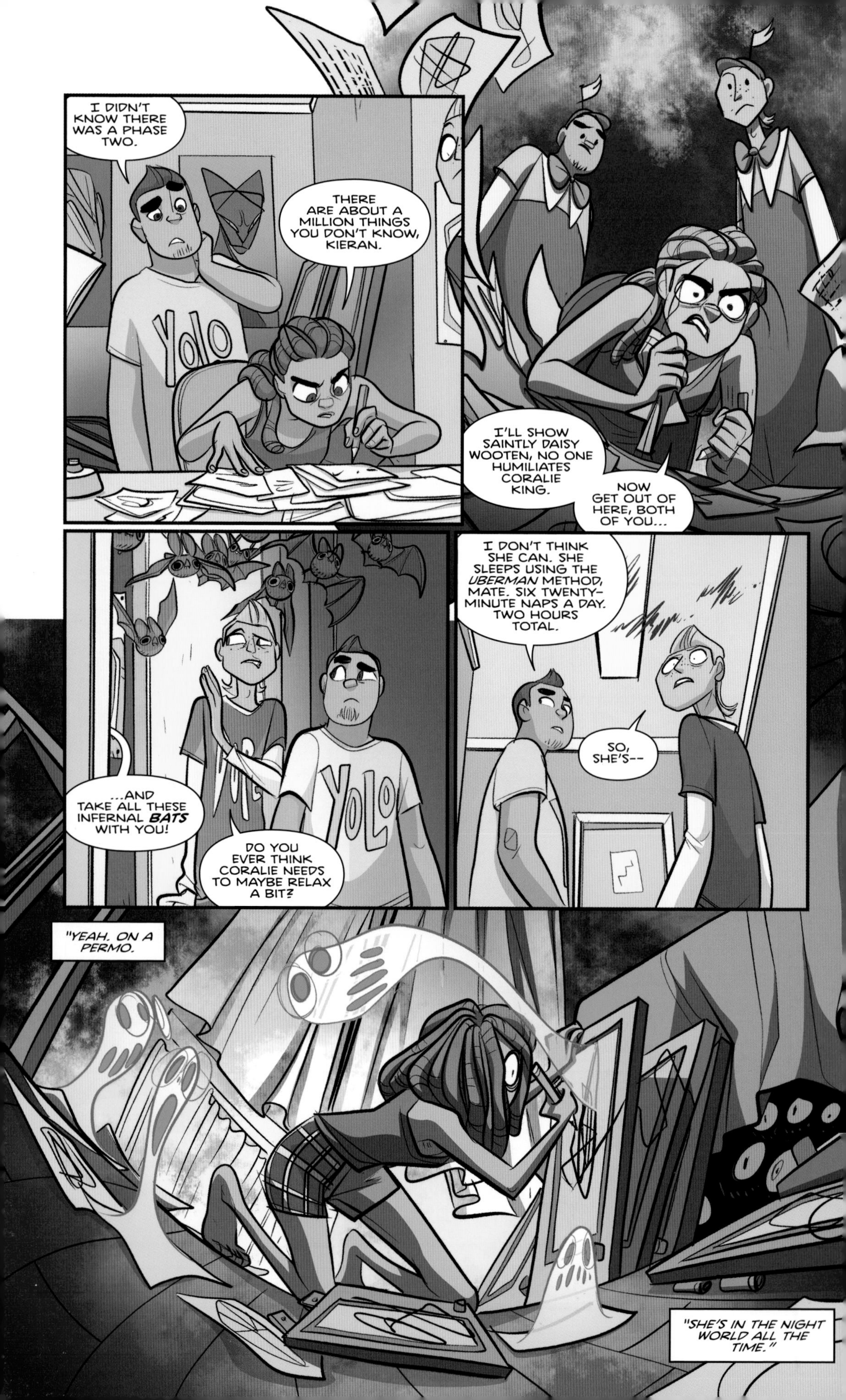
I DIDN'T KNOW THERE WAS A PHASE TWO.
THERE ARE ABOUT A MILLION THINGS YOU DON'T KNOW, KIERAN.
I'LL SHOW SAINTLY DAISY WOOTEN, NO ONE HUMILIATES CORALIE KING.
NOW GET OUT OF HERE, BOTH OF YOU...
...AND TAKE ALL THESE INFERNAL *BATS* WITH YOU!
DO YOU EVER THINK CORALIE NEEDS TO MAYBE RELAX A BIT?
I DON'T THINK SHE CAN. SHE SLEEPS USING THE *UBERMAN* METHOD, MATE. SIX TWENTY-MINUTE NAPS A DAY. TWO HOURS TOTAL.
SO, SHE'S--
"YEAH. ON A PERMO.
"SHE'S IN THE NIGHT WORLD ALL THE TIME."

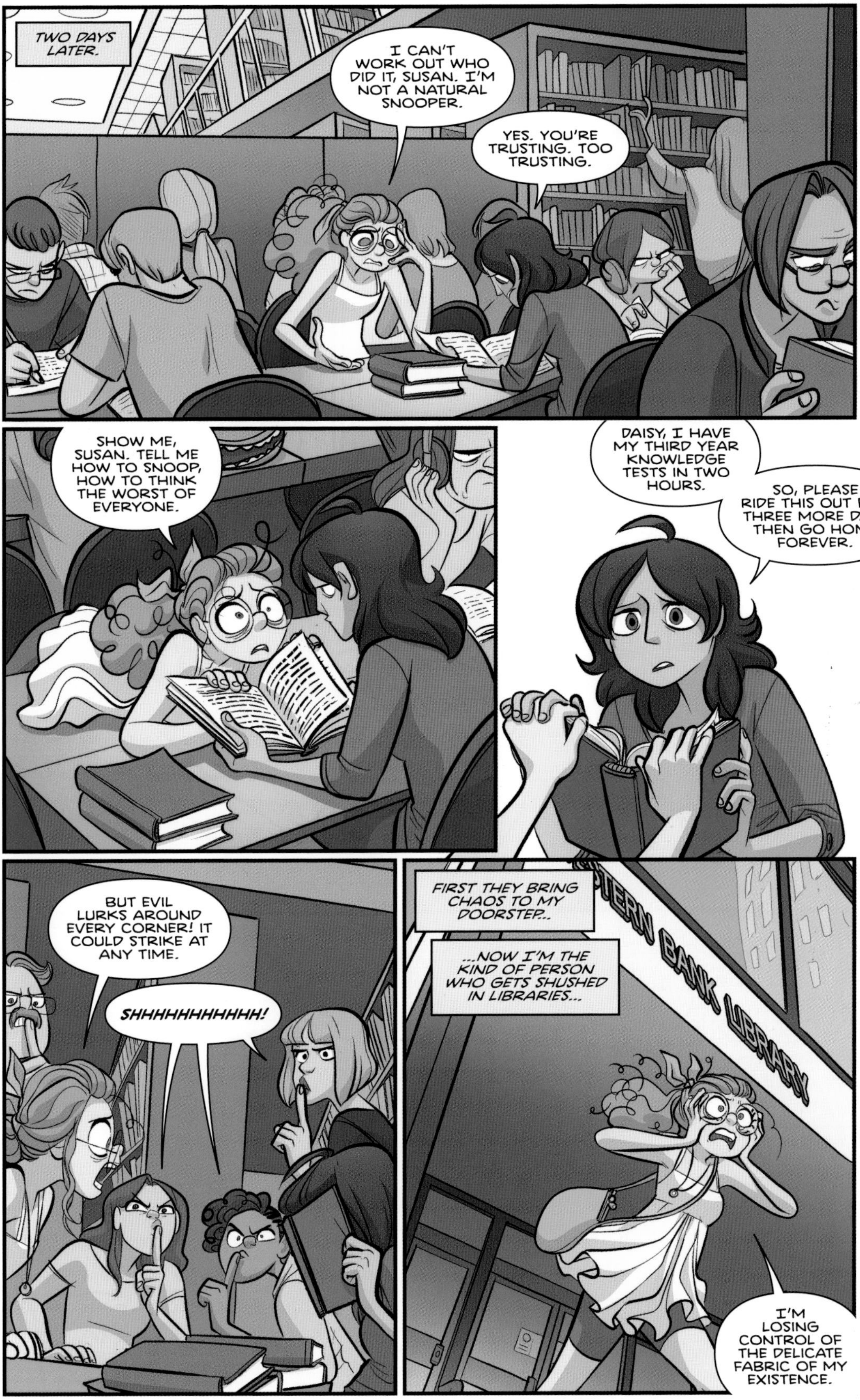
TWO DAYS LATER.
I CAN'T WORK OUT WHO DID IT, SUSAN. I'M NOT A NATURAL SNOOPER.
YES. YOU'RE TRUSTING. TOO TRUSTING.
SHOW ME, SUSAN. TELL ME HOW TO SNOOP, HOW TO THINK THE WORST OF EVERYONE.
DAISY, I HAVE MY THIRD YEAR KNOWLEDGE TESTS IN TWO HOURS.
SO, PLEASE RIDE THIS OUT FOR THREE MORE DAYS THEN GO HOME FOREVER.
BUT EVIL LURKS AROUND EVERY CORNER! IT COULD STRIKE AT ANY TIME.
SHHHHHHHHHHH!
FIRST THEY BRING CHAOS TO MY DOORSTEP...
...NOW I'M THE KIND OF PERSON WHO GETS SHUSHED IN LIBRARIES...
BANK LIBRARY
I'M LOSING CONTROL OF THE DELICATE FABRIC OF MY EXISTENCE.

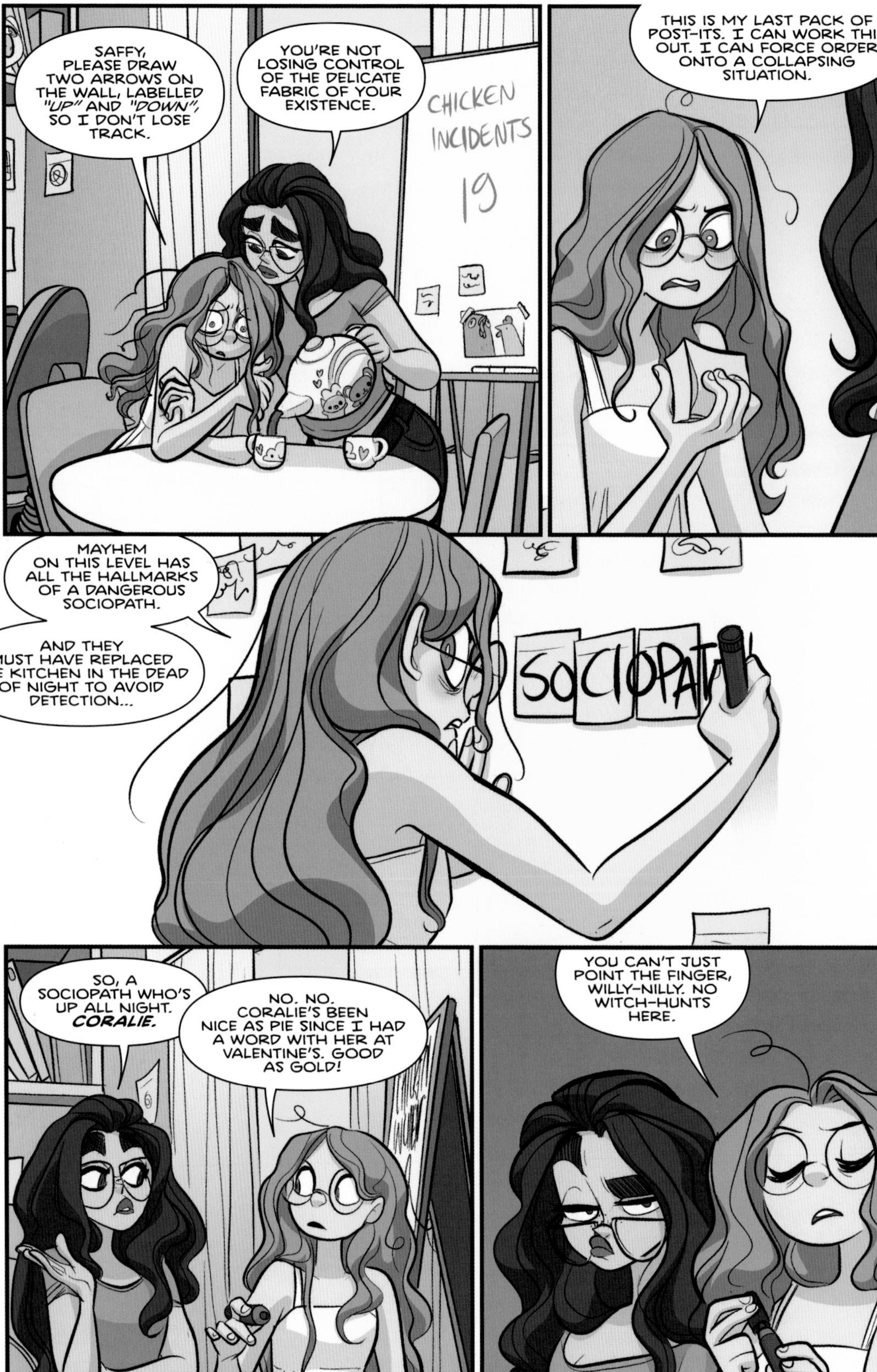
SAFFY, PLEASE DRAW TWO ARROWS ON THE WALL, LABELLED *"UP"* AND *"DOWN"*, SO I DON'T LOSE TRACK.
YOU'RE NOT LOSING CONTROL OF THE DELICATE FABRIC OF YOUR EXISTENCE.
CHICKEN INCIDENTS
19
THIS IS MY LAST PACK OF POST-ITS. I CAN WORK THIS OUT. I CAN FORCE ORDER ONTO A COLLAPSING SITUATION.
MAYHEM ON THIS LEVEL HAS ALL THE HALLMARKS OF A DANGEROUS SOCIOPATH.
AND THEY MUST HAVE REPLACED THE KITCHEN IN THE DEAD OF NIGHT TO AVOID DETECTION...
SOCIOPAT
SO, A SOCIOPATH WHO'S UP ALL NIGHT. ***CORALIE.***
NO. NO. CORALIE'S BEEN NICE AS PIE SINCE I HAD A WORD WITH HER AT VALENTINE'S. GOOD AS GOLD!
YOU CAN'T JUST POINT THE FINGER, WILLY-NILLY. NO WITCH-HUNTS HERE.

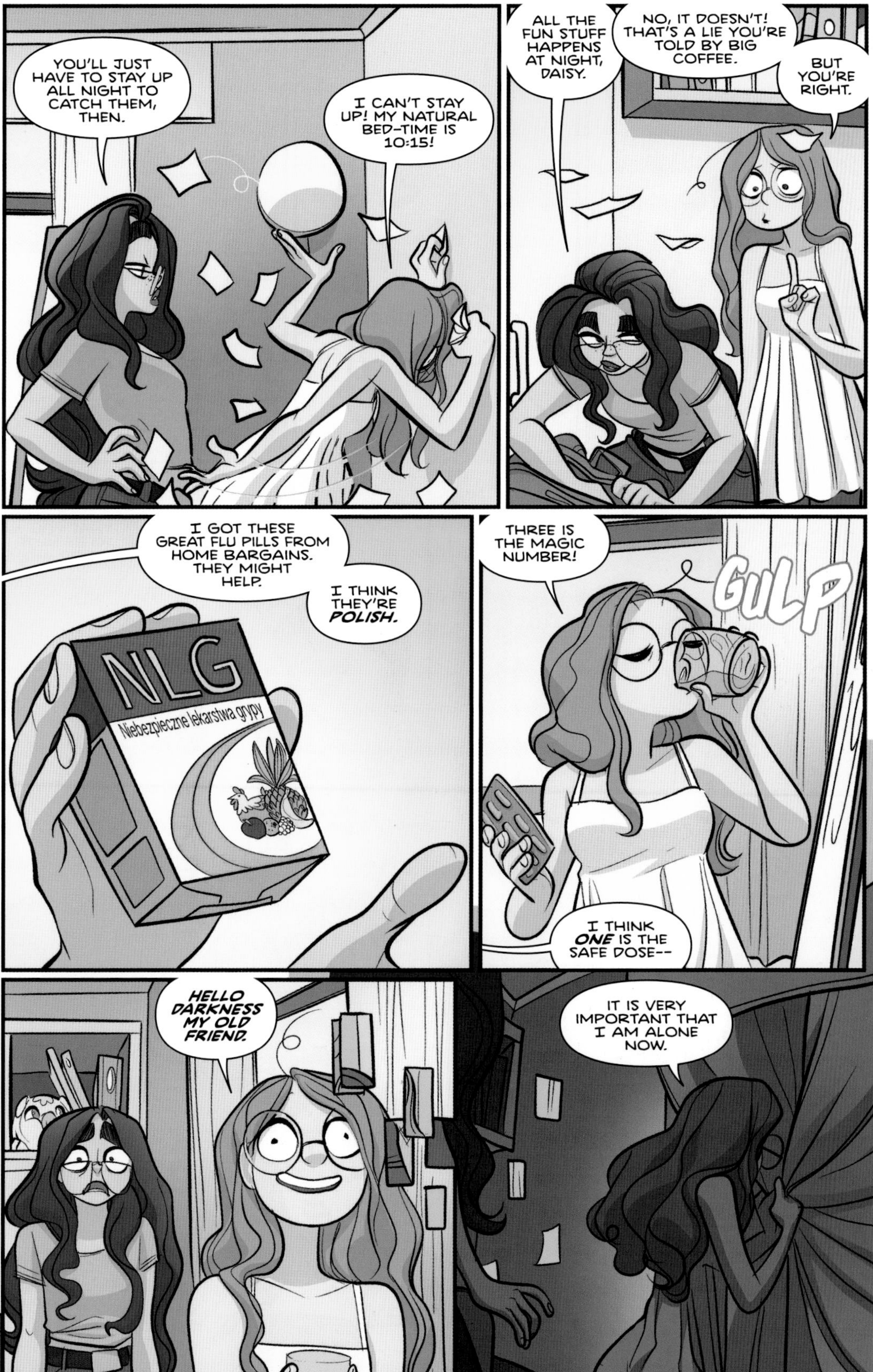
YOU'LL JUST HAVE TO STAY UP ALL NIGHT TO CATCH THEM, THEN.
I CAN'T STAY UP! MY NATURAL BED-TIME IS 10:15!
ALL THE FUN STUFF HAPPENS AT NIGHT, DAISY.
NO, IT DOESN'T! THAT'S A LIE YOU'RE TOLD BY BIG COFFEE.
BUT YOU'RE RIGHT.
I GOT THESE GREAT FLU PILLS FROM HOME BARGAINS. THEY MIGHT HELP.
I THINK THEY'RE POLISH.
NLG
Niebezpieczne lekarstwa grypy
THREE IS THE MAGIC NUMBER!
GULP
I THINK ONE IS THE SAFE DOSE--
HELLO DARKNESS MY OLD FRIEND.
IT IS VERY IMPORTANT THAT I AM ALONE NOW.

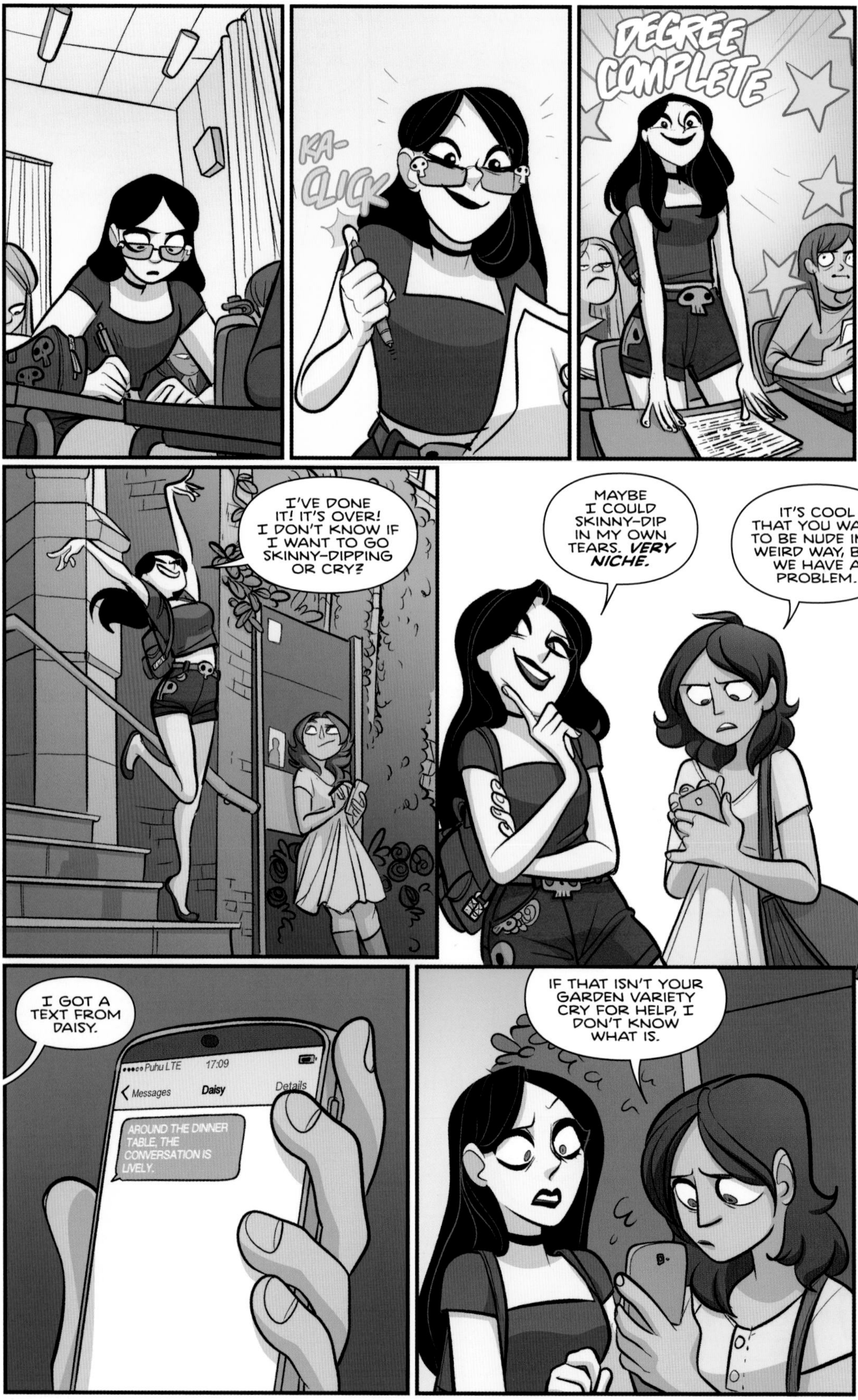

KA-CLICK
DEGREE COMPLETE
I'VE DONE IT! IT'S OVER! I DON'T KNOW IF I WANT TO GO SKINNY-DIPPING OR CRY?
MAYBE I COULD SKINNY-DIP IN MY OWN TEARS. VERY NICHE.
IT'S COOL THAT YOU WANT TO BE NUDE IN A WEIRD WAY, BUT WE HAVE A PROBLEM.
I GOT A TEXT FROM DAISY.
Puhu LTE
17:09
Messages
Daisy
Details
AROUND THE DINNER TABLE, THE CONVERSATION IS LIVELY.
IF THAT ISN'T YOUR GARDEN VARIETY CRY FOR HELP, I DON'T KNOW WHAT IS.

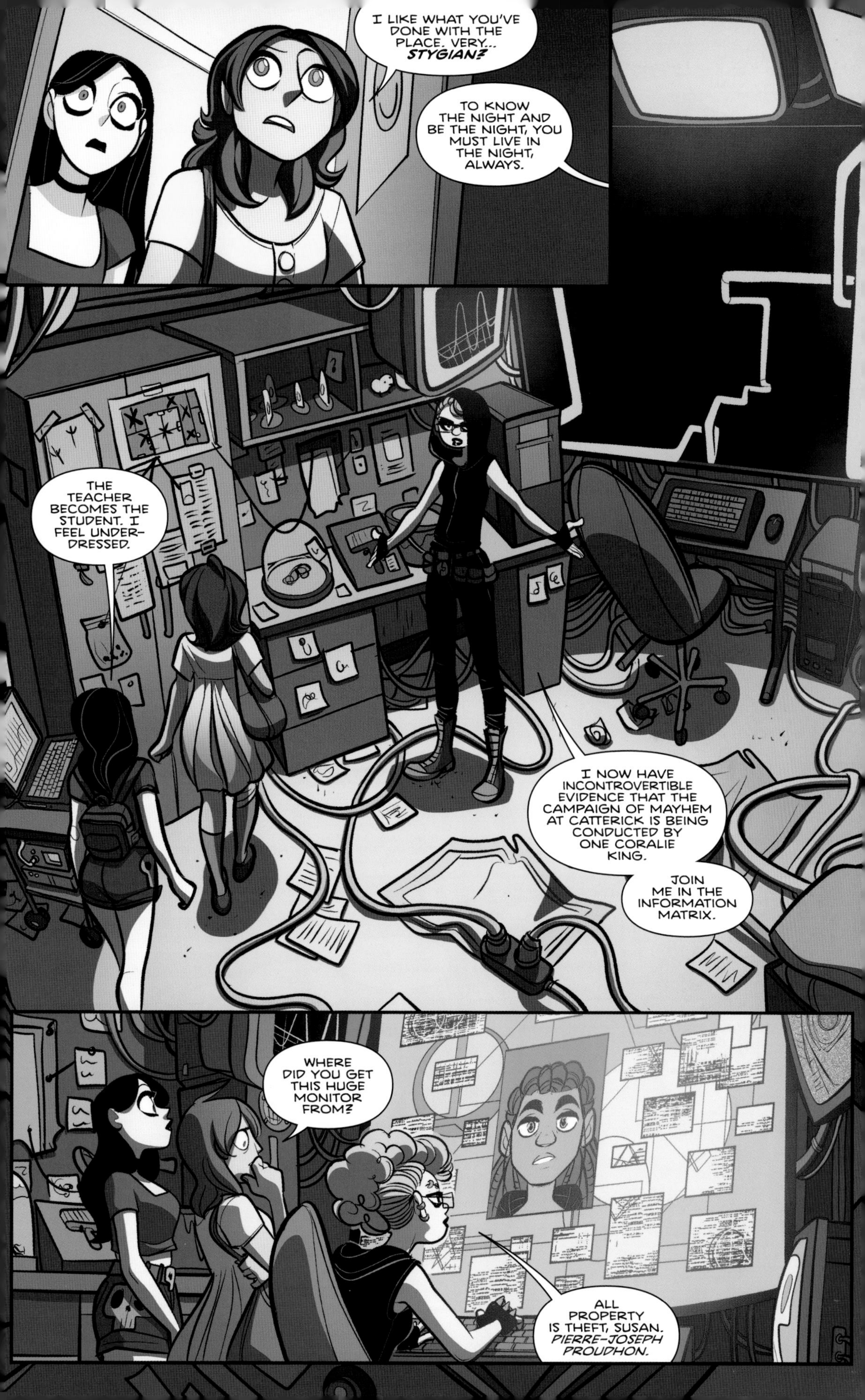

I LIKE WHAT YOU'VE DONE WITH THE PLACE. VERY... *STYGIAN?*
TO KNOW THE NIGHT AND BE THE NIGHT, YOU MUST LIVE IN THE NIGHT, ALWAYS.
THE TEACHER BECOMES THE STUDENT. I FEEL UNDER-DRESSED.
I NOW HAVE INCONTROVERTIBLE EVIDENCE THAT THE CAMPAIGN OF MAYHEM AT CATTERICK IS BEING CONDUCTED BY ONE CORALIE KING.
JOIN ME IN THE INFORMATION MATRIX.
WHERE DID YOU GET THIS HUGE MONITOR FROM?
ALL PROPERTY IS THEFT, SUSAN. *PIERRE-JOSEPH PROUDHON.*

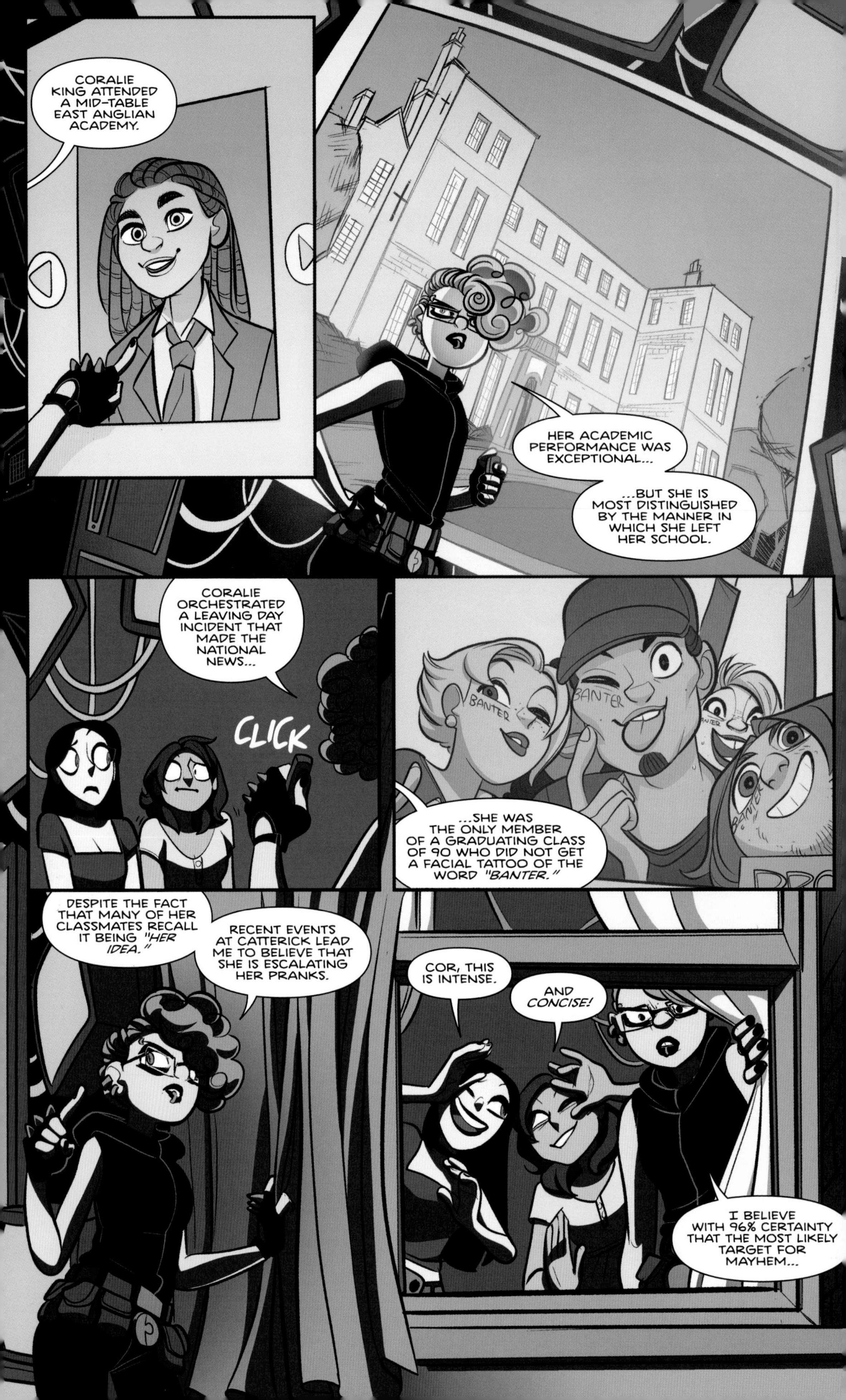
CORALIE KING ATTENDED A MID-TABLE EAST ANGLIAN ACADEMY.
HER ACADEMIC PERFORMANCE WAS EXCEPTIONAL...
...BUT SHE IS MOST DISTINGUISHED BY THE MANNER IN WHICH SHE LEFT HER SCHOOL.
CORALIE ORCHESTRATED A LEAVING DAY INCIDENT THAT MADE THE NATIONAL NEWS...
CLICK
BANTER
BANTER
...SHE WAS THE ONLY MEMBER OF A GRADUATING CLASS OF 90 WHO DID NOT GET A FACIAL TATTOO OF THE WORD *"BANTER."*
DESPITE THE FACT THAT MANY OF HER CLASSMATES RECALL IT BEING *"HER IDEA."*
RECENT EVENTS AT CATTERICK LEAD ME TO BELIEVE THAT SHE IS ESCALATING HER PRANKS.
COR, THIS IS INTENSE.
AND *CONCISE!*
I BELIEVE WITH 96% CERTAINTY THAT THE MOST LIKELY TARGET FOR MAYHEM...

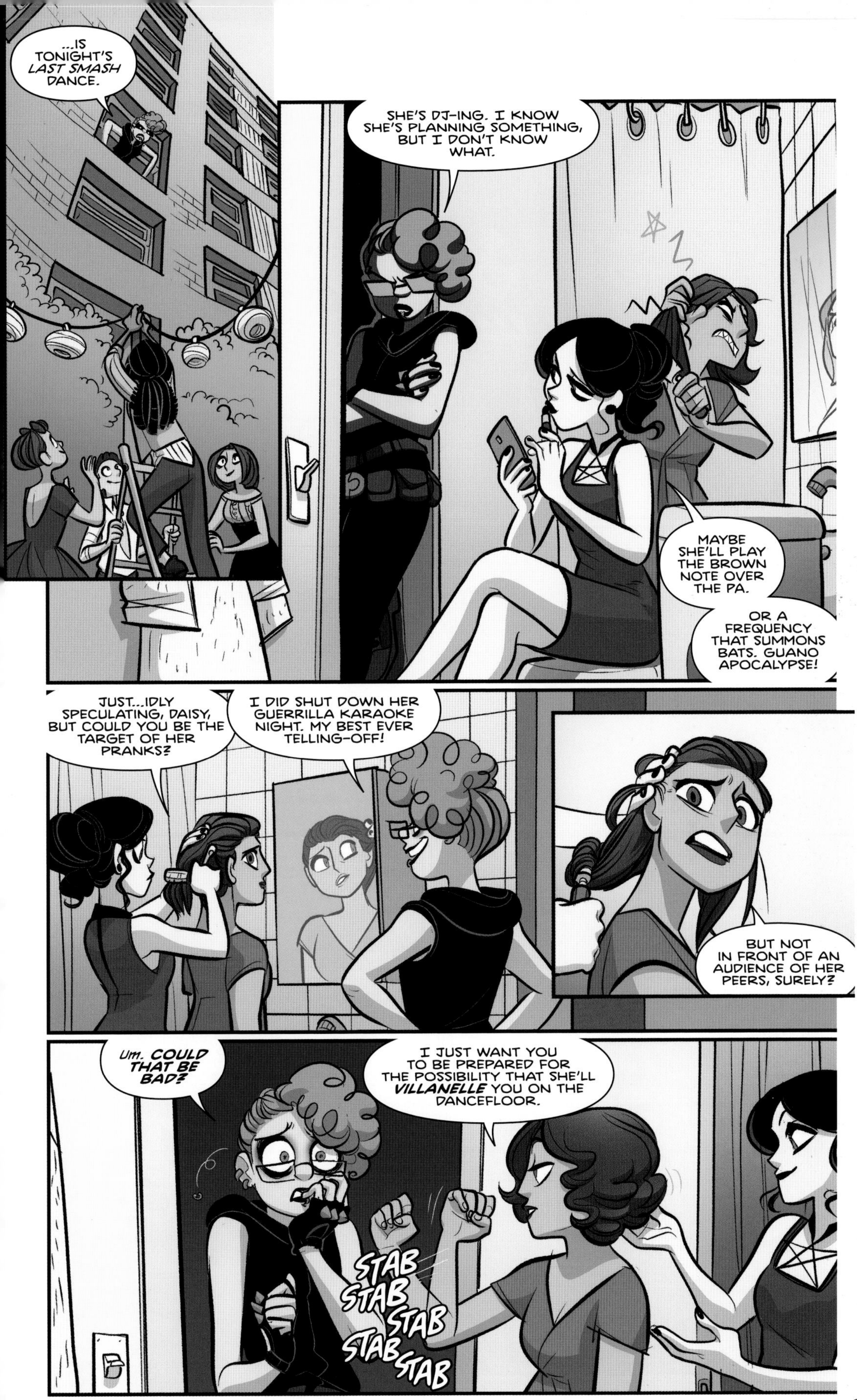

...IS TONIGHT'S *LAST SMASH* DANCE.
SHE'S DJ-ING. I KNOW SHE'S PLANNING SOMETHING, BUT I DON'T KNOW WHAT.
MAYBE SHE'LL PLAY THE BROWN NOTE OVER THE PA.
OR A FREQUENCY THAT SUMMONS BATS. GUANO APOCALYPSE!
JUST...IDLY SPECULATING, DAISY, BUT COULD YOU BE THE TARGET OF HER PRANKS?
I DID SHUT DOWN HER GUERRILLA KARAOKE NIGHT. MY BEST EVER TELLING-OFF!
BUT NOT IN FRONT OF AN AUDIENCE OF HER PEERS, SURELY?
*Um.* ***COULD THAT BE BAD?***
I JUST WANT YOU TO BE PREPARED FOR THE POSSIBILITY THAT SHE'LL ***VILLANELLE*** YOU ON THE DANCEFLOOR.
STAB STAB STAB STAB STAB


136

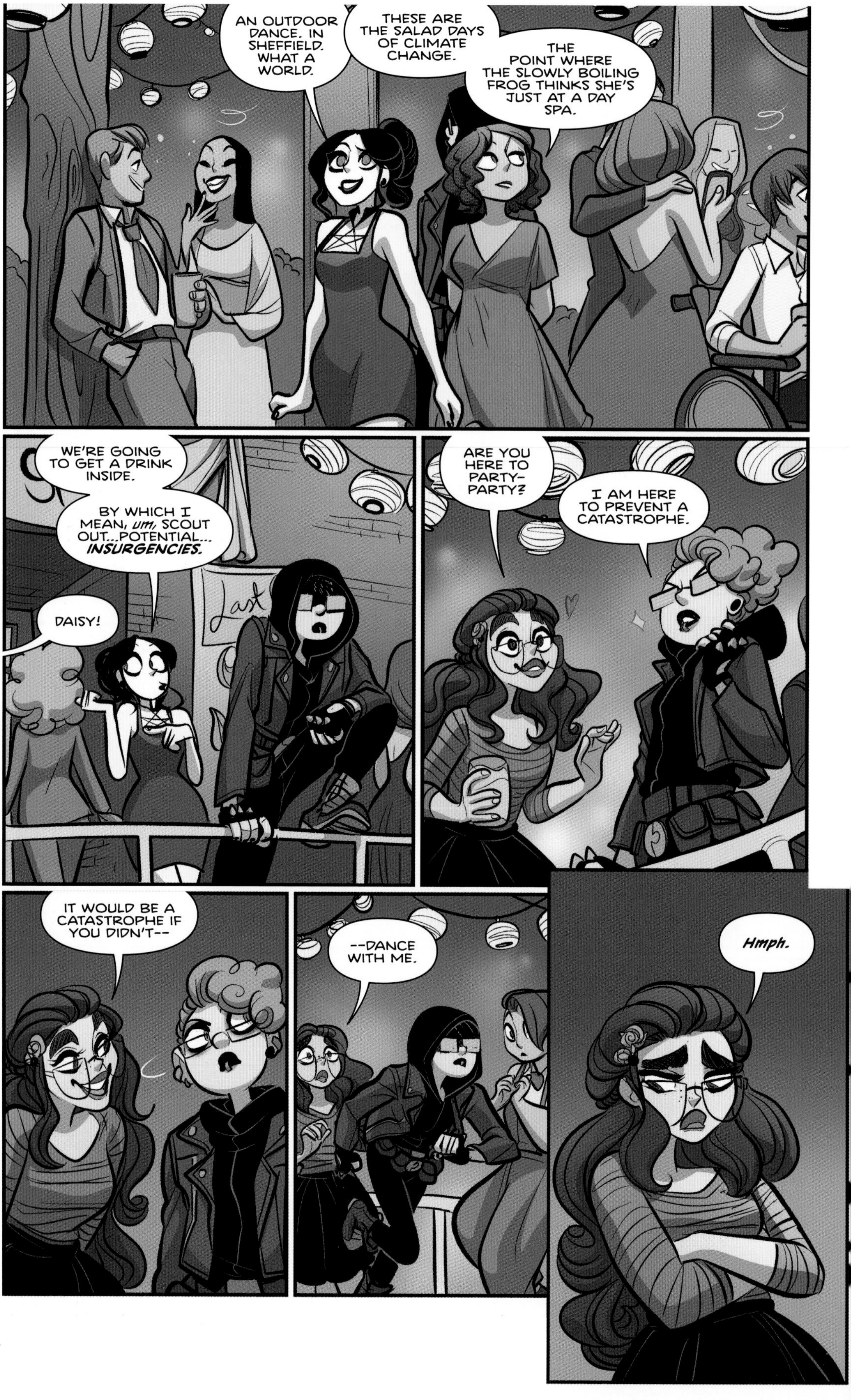
AN OUTDOOR DANCE. IN SHEFFIELD. WHAT A WORLD.
THESE ARE THE SALAD DAYS OF CLIMATE CHANGE.
THE POINT WHERE THE SLOWLY BOILING FROG THINKS SHE'S JUST AT A DAY SPA.
WE'RE GOING TO GET A DRINK INSIDE.
BY WHICH I MEAN, *UM,* SCOUT OUT...POTENTIAL... ***INSURGENCIES.***
DAISY!
ARE YOU HERE TO PARTY-PARTY?
I AM HERE TO PREVENT A CATASTROPHE.
IT WOULD BE A CATASTROPHE IF YOU DIDN'T--
--DANCE WITH ME.
*Hmph.*

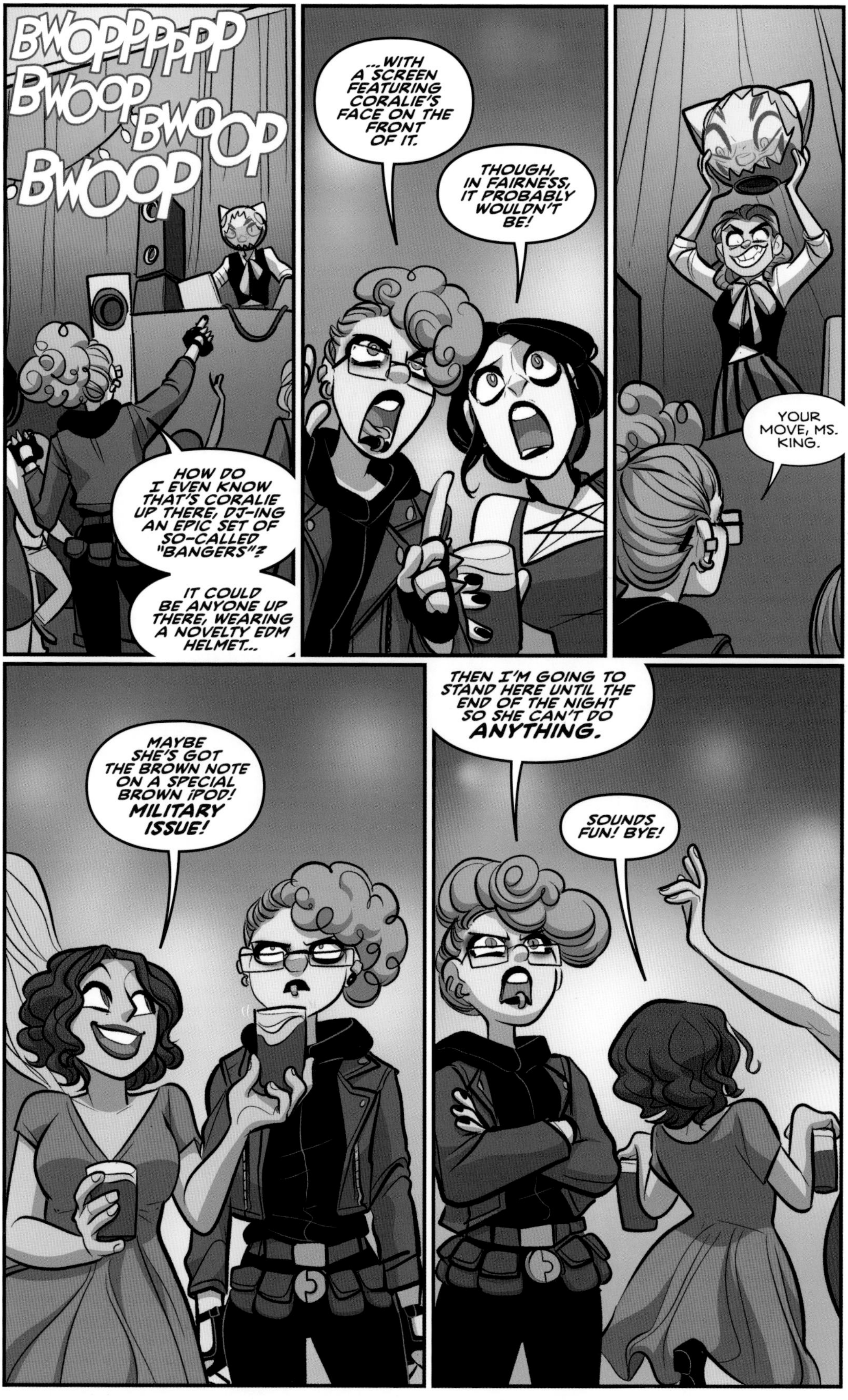
BWOPPPPPP
BWOOP BWOOP
BWOOP
HOW DO I EVEN KNOW THAT'S CORALIE UP THERE, DJ-ING AN EPIC SET OF SO-CALLED "BANGERS"?
IT COULD BE ANYONE UP THERE, WEARING A NOVELTY EDM HELMET...
...WITH A SCREEN FEATURING CORALIE'S FACE ON THE FRONT OF IT.
THOUGH, IN FAIRNESS, IT PROBABLY WOULDN'T BE!
YOUR MOVE, MS. KING.
MAYBE SHE'S GOT THE BROWN NOTE ON A SPECIAL BROWN iPOD! MILITARY ISSUE!
THEN I'M GOING TO STAND HERE UNTIL THE END OF THE NIGHT SO SHE CAN'T DO ANYTHING.
SOUNDS FUN! BYE!

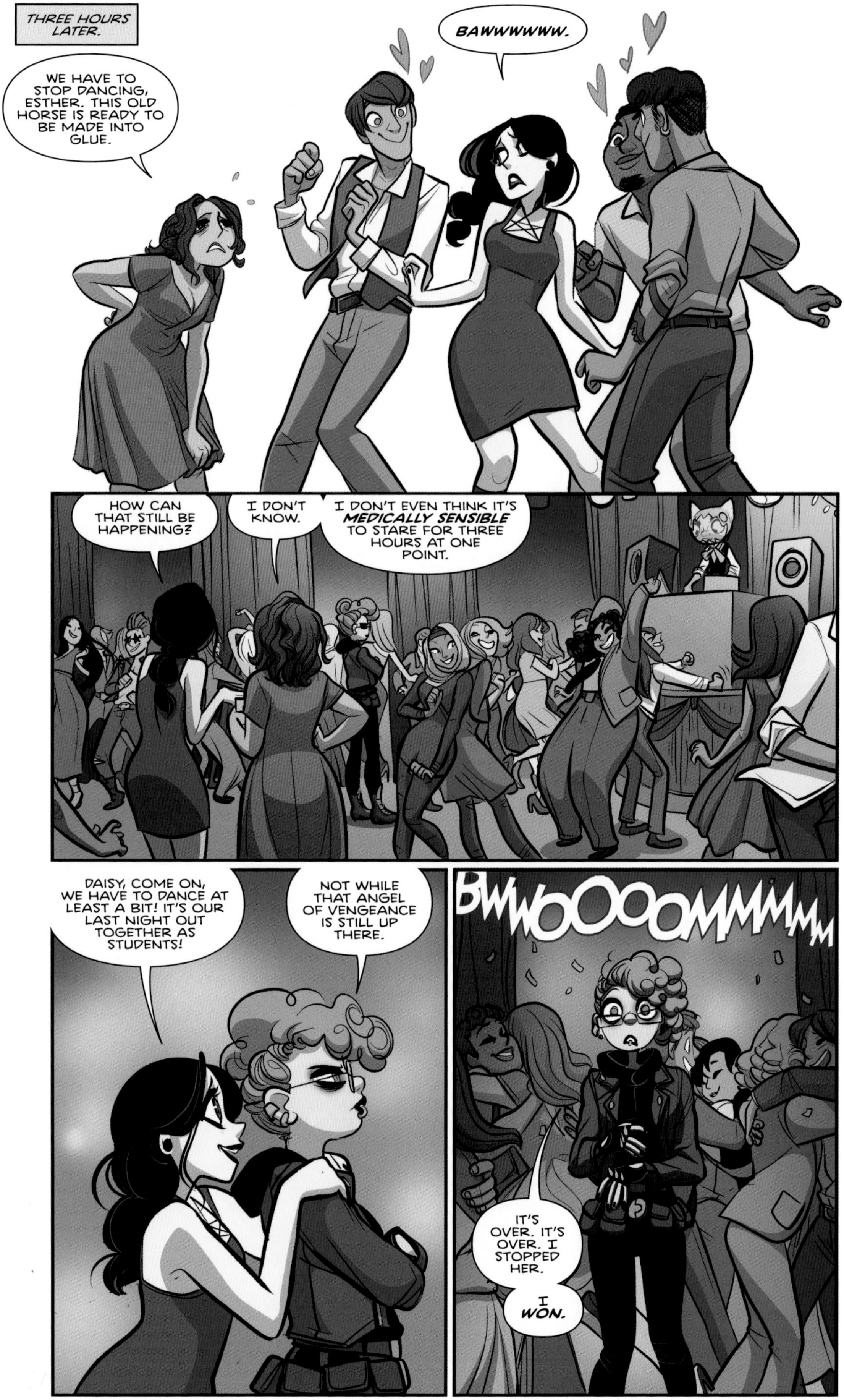
THREE HOURS LATER.
WE HAVE TO STOP DANCING, ESTHER. THIS OLD HORSE IS READY TO BE MADE INTO GLUE.
BAWWWWWW.
HOW CAN THAT STILL BE HAPPENING?
I DON'T KNOW.
I DON'T EVEN THINK IT'S MEDICALLY SENSIBLE TO STARE FOR THREE HOURS AT ONE POINT.
DAISY, COME ON, WE HAVE TO DANCE AT LEAST A BIT! IT'S OUR LAST NIGHT OUT TOGETHER AS STUDENTS!
NOT WHILE THAT ANGEL OF VENGEANCE IS STILL UP THERE.
BWOOOOOMMMMMM
IT'S OVER. IT'S OVER. I STOPPED HER.
I WON.

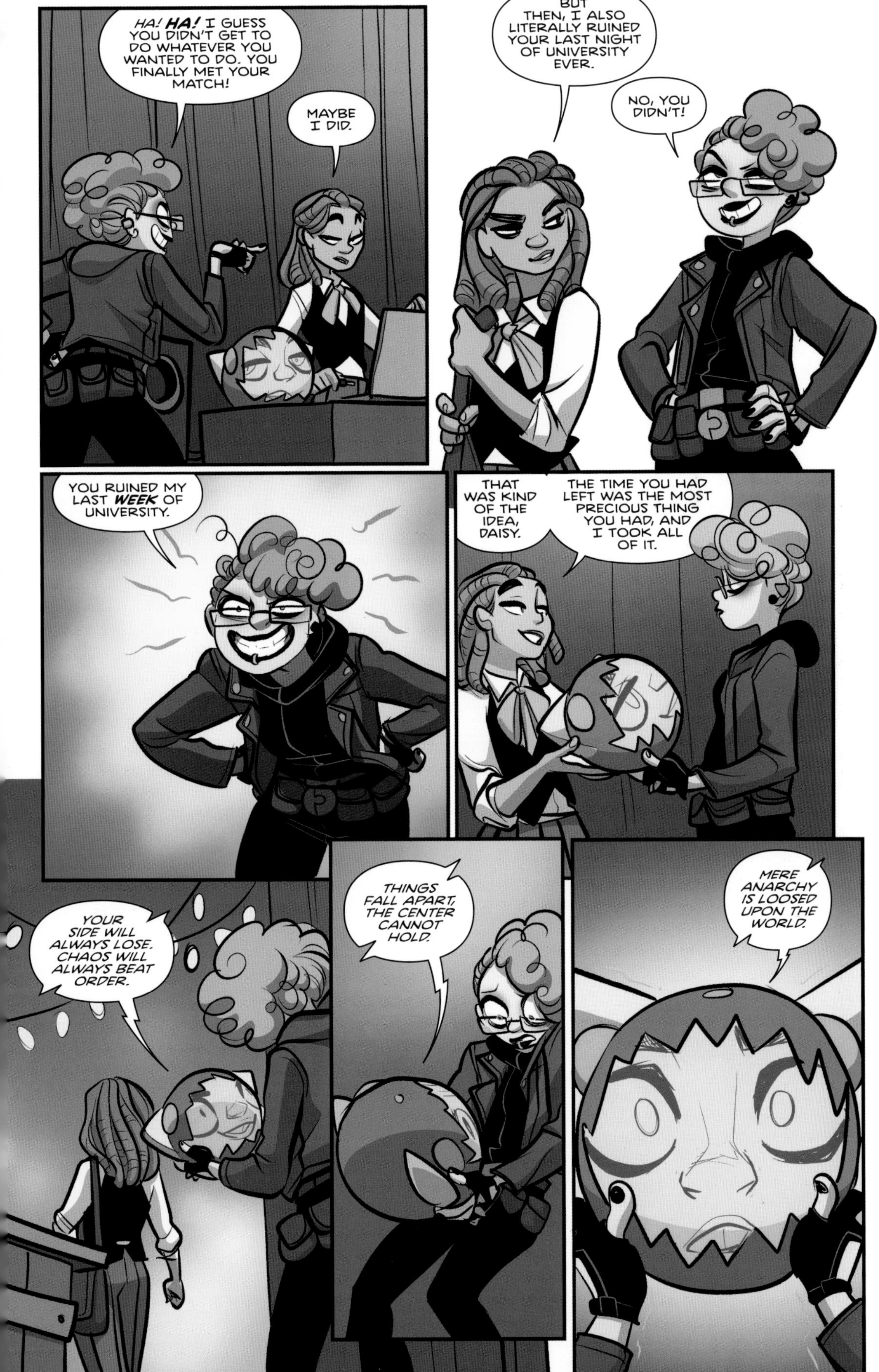
HA! HA! I GUESS YOU DIDN'T GET TO DO WHATEVER YOU WANTED TO DO. YOU FINALLY MET YOUR MATCH!
MAYBE I DID.
BUT THEN, I ALSO LITERALLY RUINED YOUR LAST NIGHT OF UNIVERSITY EVER.
NO, YOU DIDN'T!
YOU RUINED MY LAST WEEK OF UNIVERSITY.
THAT WAS KIND OF THE IDEA, DAISY.
THE TIME YOU HAD LEFT WAS THE MOST PRECIOUS THING YOU HAD, AND I TOOK ALL OF IT.
YOUR SIDE WILL ALWAYS LOSE. CHAOS WILL ALWAYS BEAT ORDER.
THINGS FALL APART, THE CENTER CANNOT HOLD.
MERE ANARCHY IS LOOSED UPON THE WORLD.

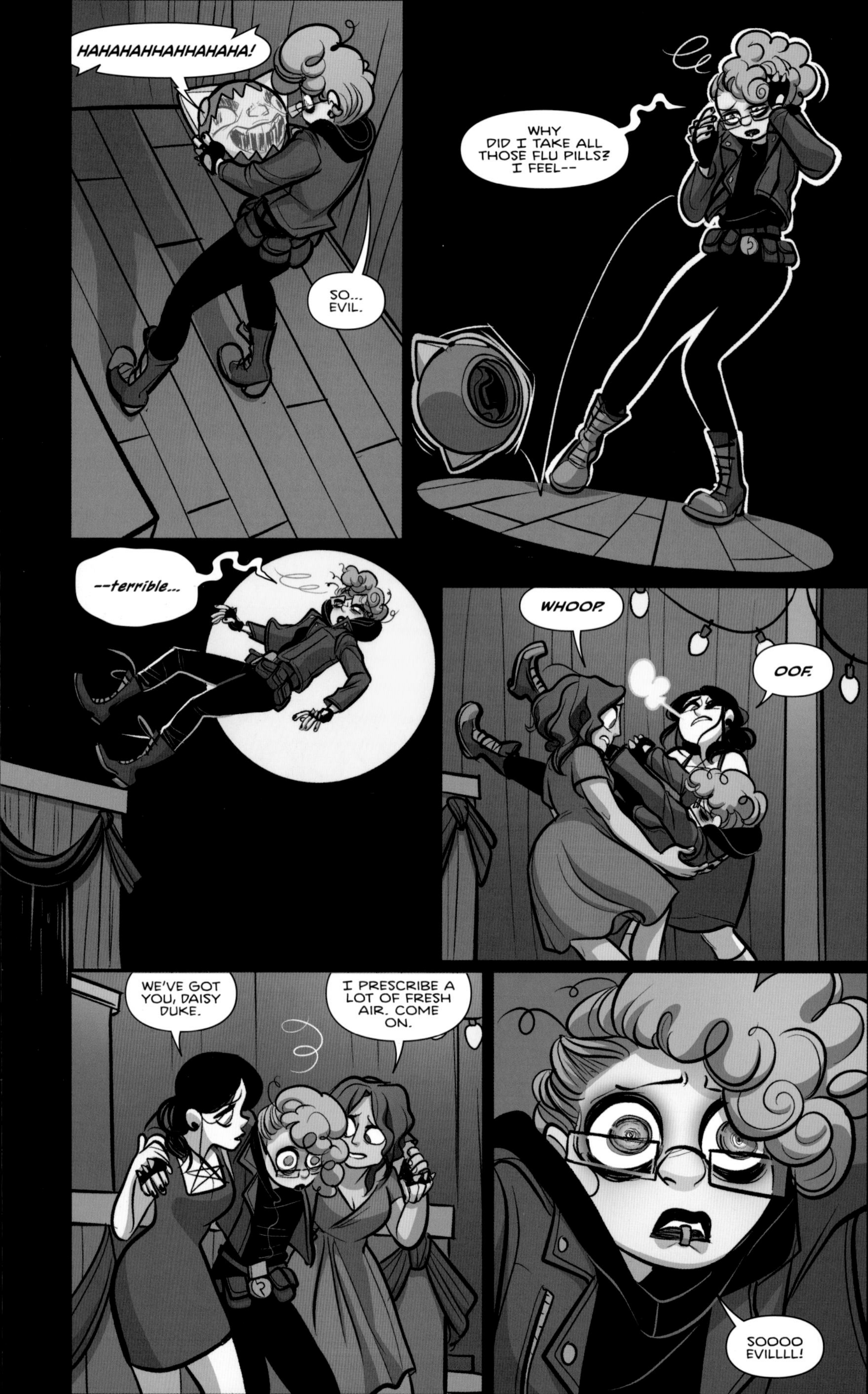
HAHAHAHHAHHAHAHA!
SO... EVIL.
WHY DID I TAKE ALL THOSE FLU PILLS? I FEEL--
--terrible...
WHOOP.
OOF.
WE'VE GOT YOU, DAISY DUKE.
I PRESCRIBE A LOT OF FRESH AIR. COME ON.
SOOOO EVILLLL!

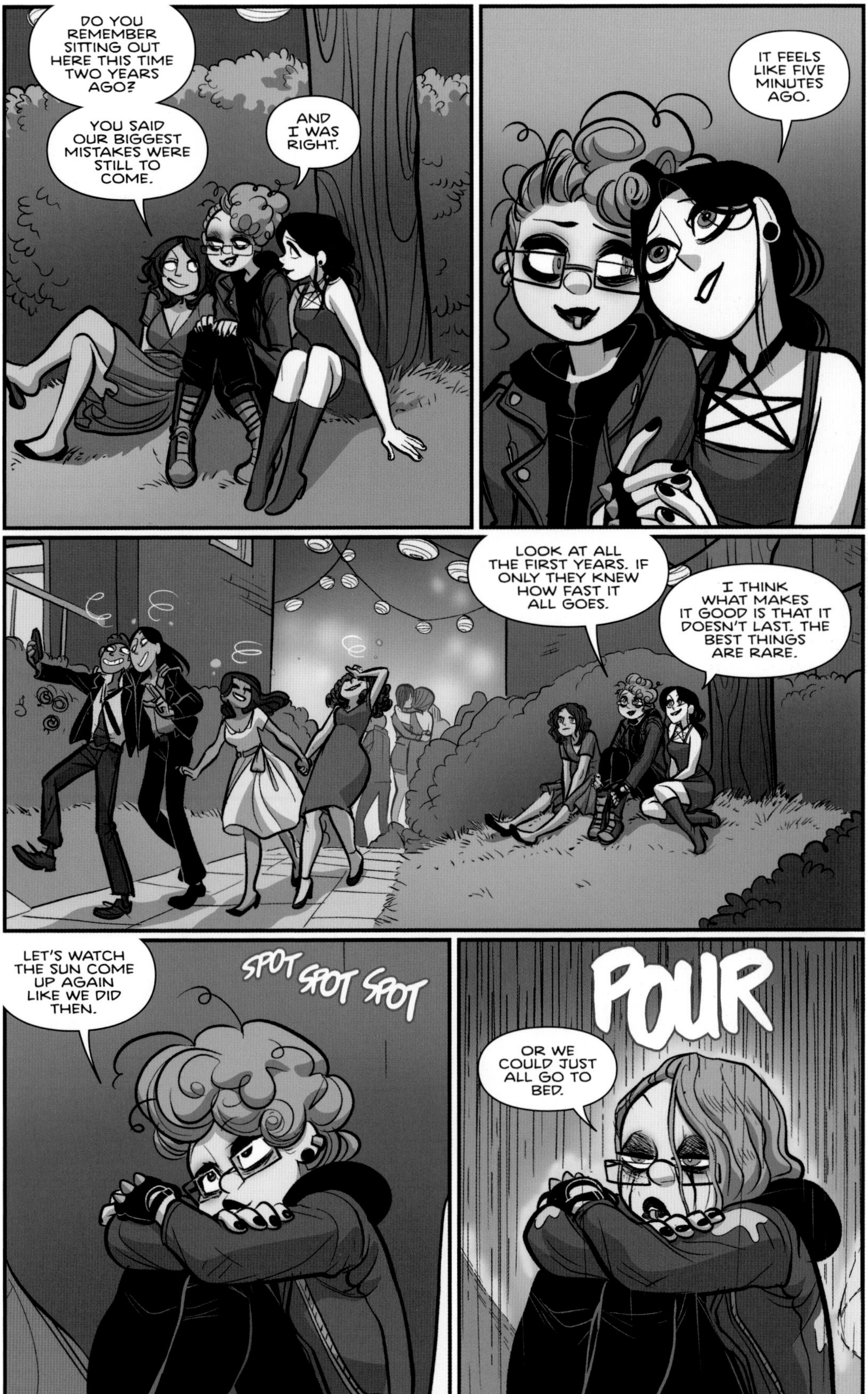
DO YOU REMEMBER SITTING OUT HERE THIS TIME TWO YEARS AGO?
YOU SAID OUR BIGGEST MISTAKES WERE STILL TO COME.
AND I WAS RIGHT.
IT FEELS LIKE FIVE MINUTES AGO.
LOOK AT ALL THE FIRST YEARS. IF ONLY THEY KNEW HOW FAST IT ALL GOES.
I THINK WHAT MAKES IT GOOD IS THAT IT DOESN'T LAST. THE BEST THINGS ARE RARE.
LET'S WATCH THE SUN COME UP AGAIN LIKE WE DID THEN.
SPOT SPOT SPOT
POUR
OR WE COULD JUST ALL GO TO BED.

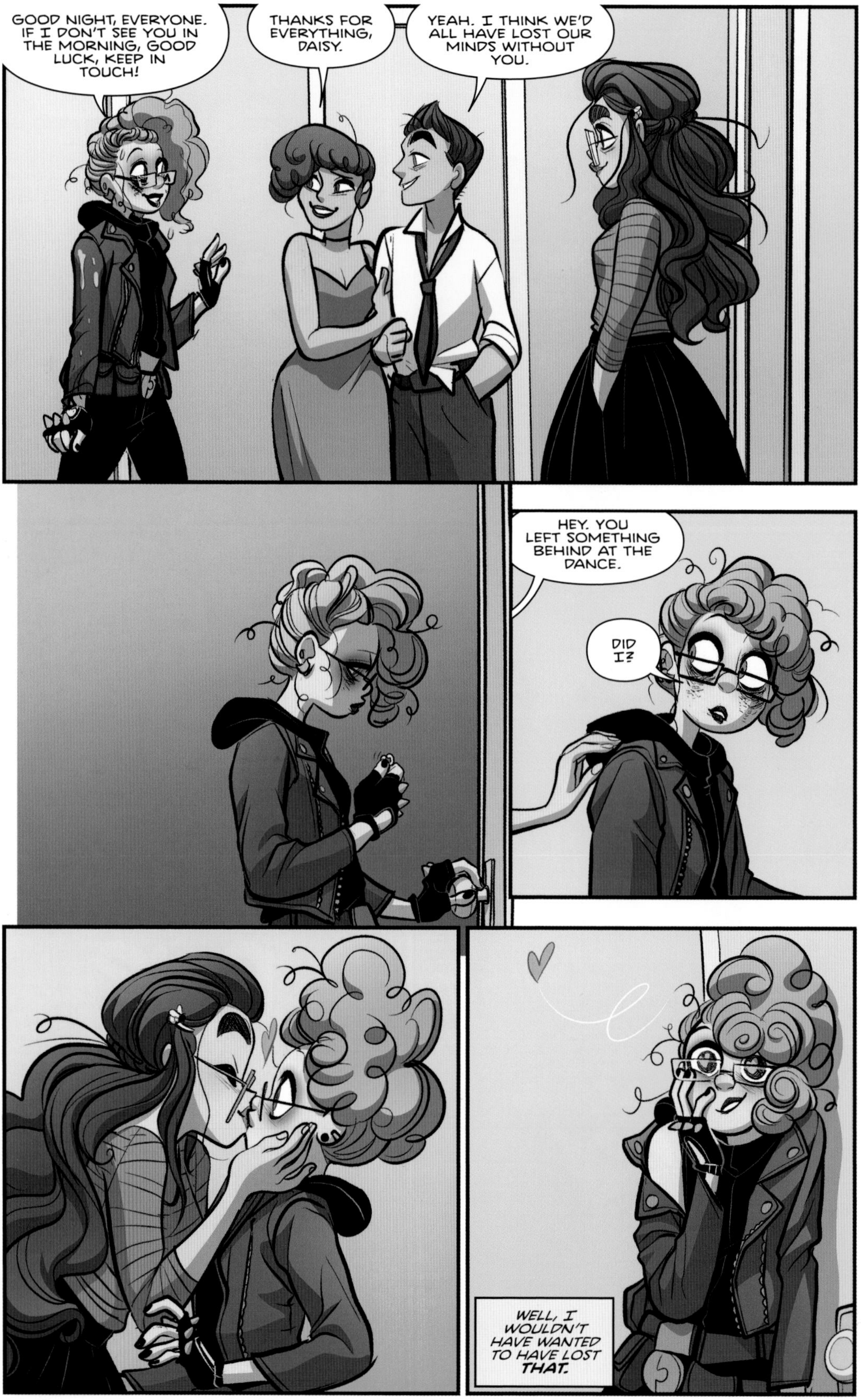
GOOD NIGHT, EVERYONE. IF I DON'T SEE YOU IN THE MORNING, GOOD LUCK, KEEP IN TOUCH!
THANKS FOR EVERYTHING, DAISY.
YEAH. I THINK WE'D ALL HAVE LOST OUR MINDS WITHOUT YOU.
HEY. YOU LEFT SOMETHING BEHIND AT THE DANCE.
DID I?
WELL, I WOULDN'T HAVE WANTED TO HAVE LOST *THAT.*

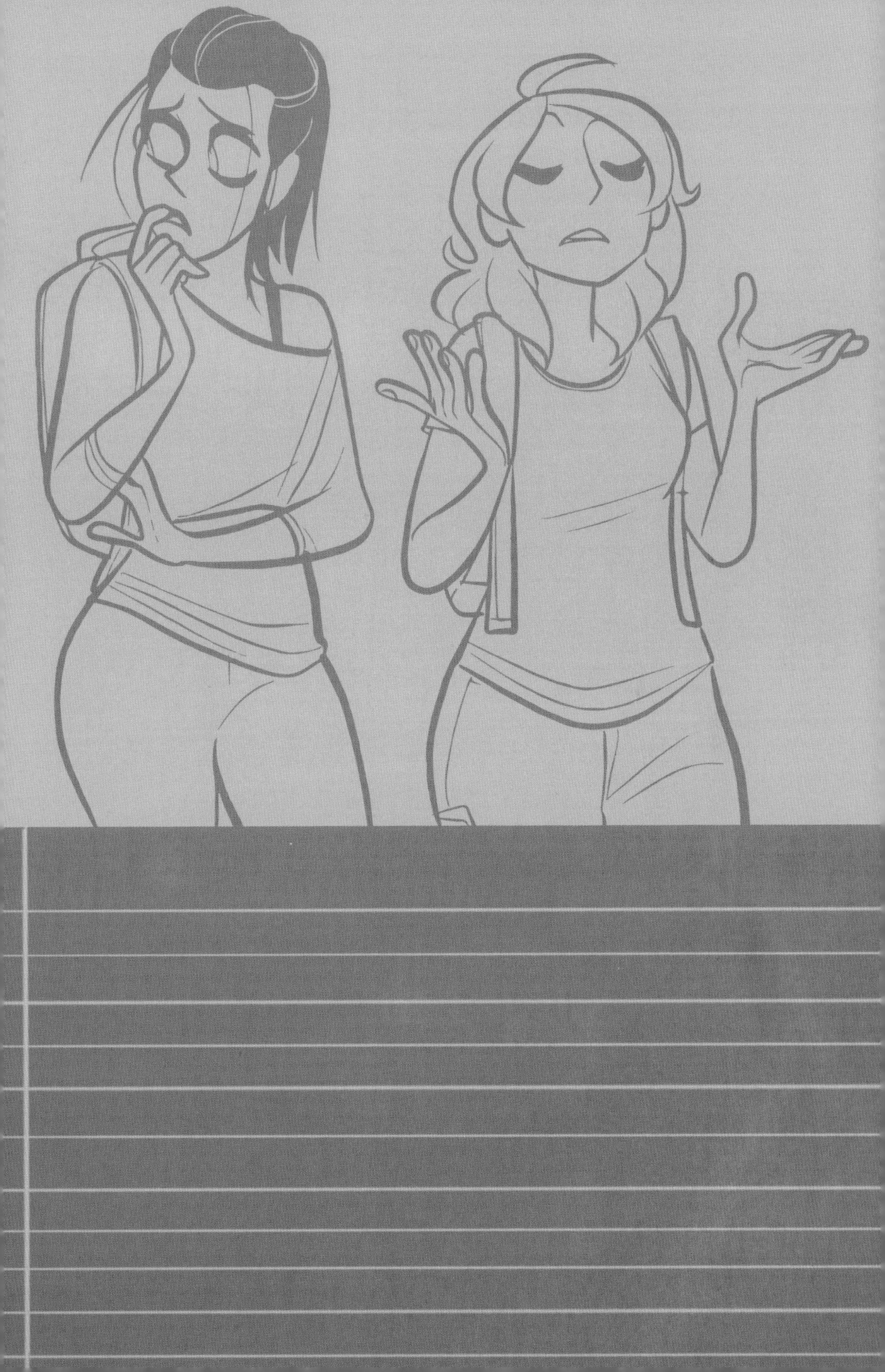

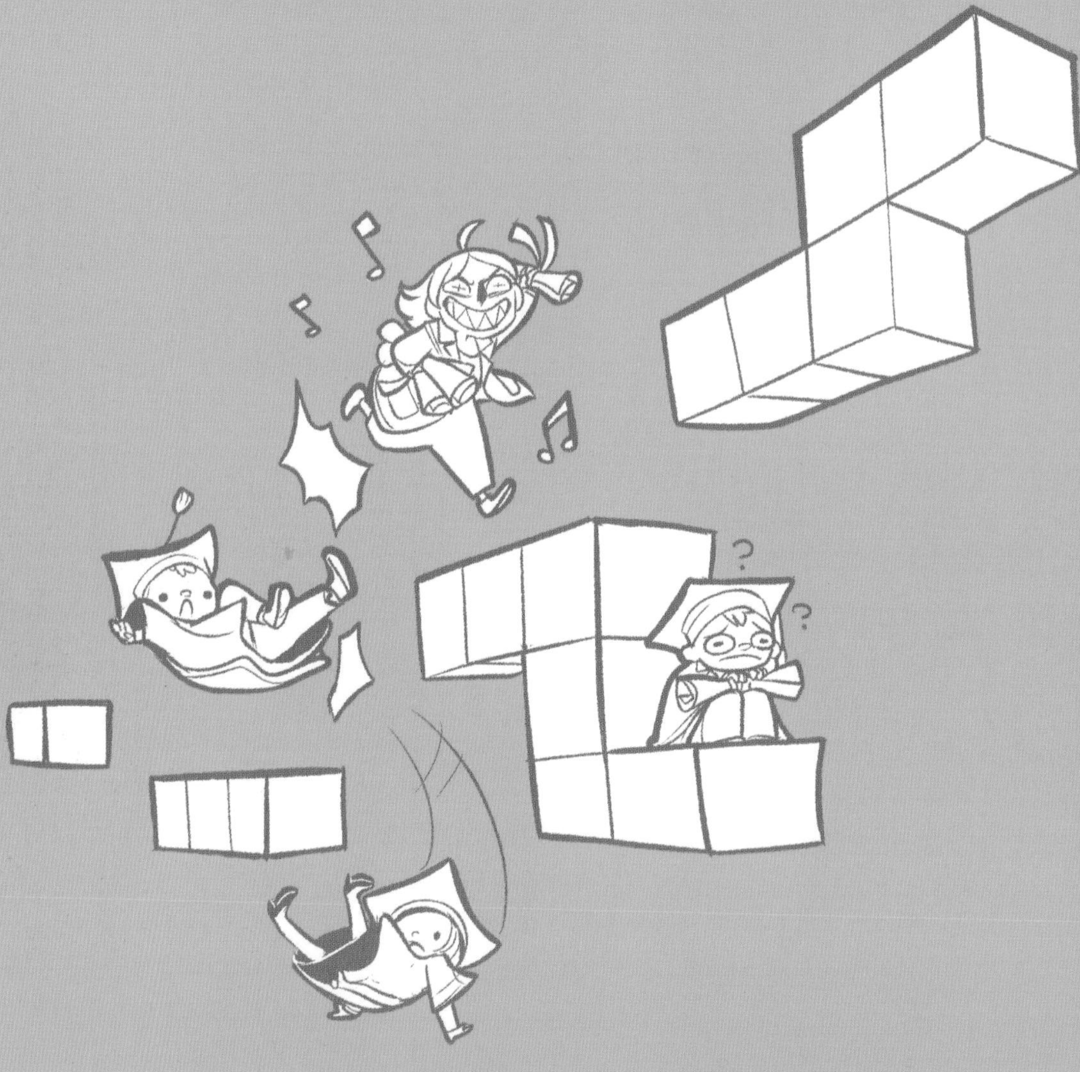

# CHAPTER FIFTY-FOUR

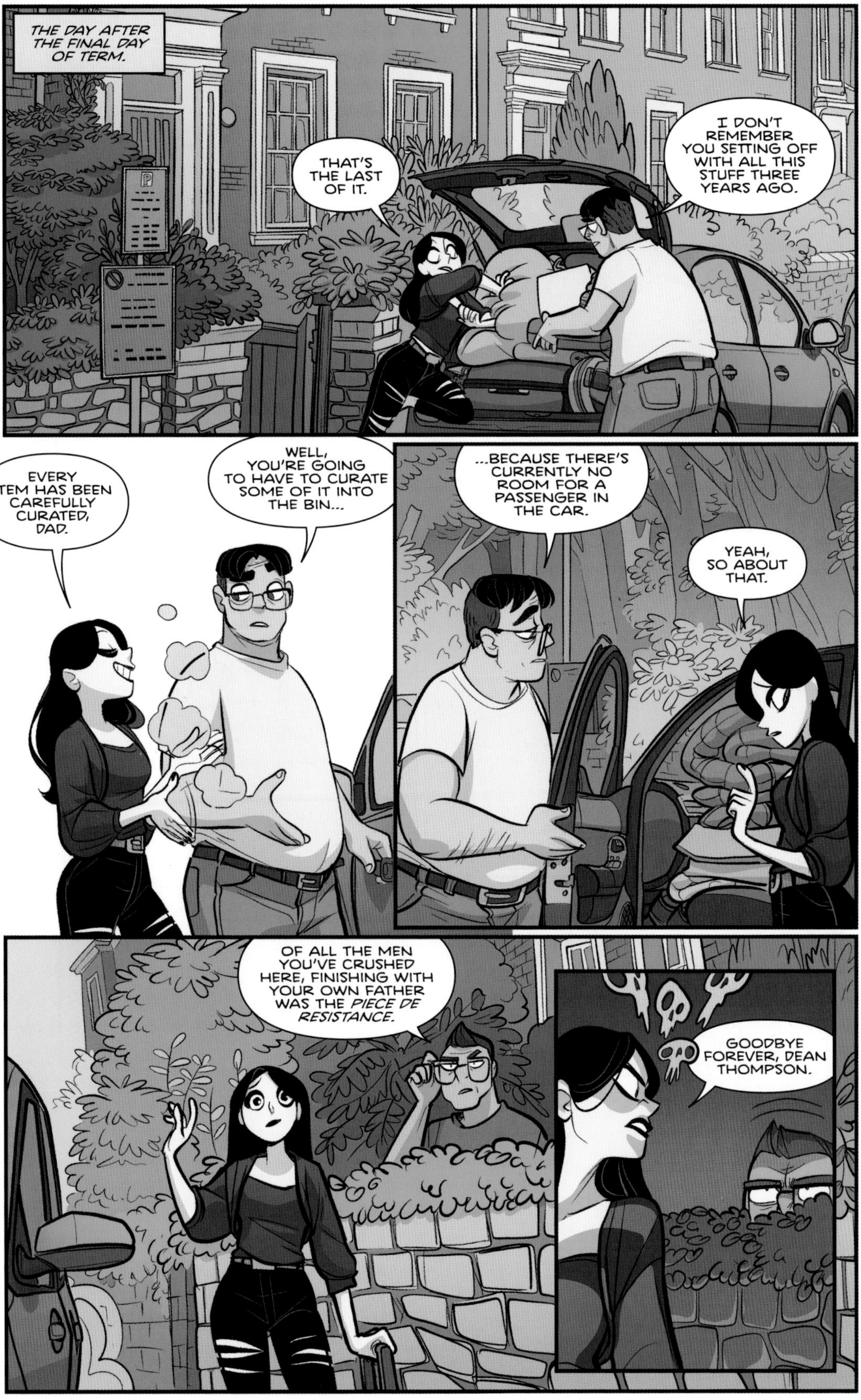
THE DAY AFTER THE FINAL DAY OF TERM.
THAT'S THE LAST OF IT.
I DON'T REMEMBER YOU SETTING OFF WITH ALL THIS STUFF THREE YEARS AGO.
EVERY ITEM HAS BEEN CAREFULLY CURATED, DAD.
WELL, YOU'RE GOING TO HAVE TO CURATE SOME OF IT INTO THE BIN...
...BECAUSE THERE'S CURRENTLY NO ROOM FOR A PASSENGER IN THE CAR.
YEAH, SO ABOUT THAT.
OF ALL THE MEN YOU'VE CRUSHED HERE, FINISHING WITH YOUR OWN FATHER WAS THE *PIECE DE RESISTANCE.*
GOODBYE FOREVER, DEAN THOMPSON.

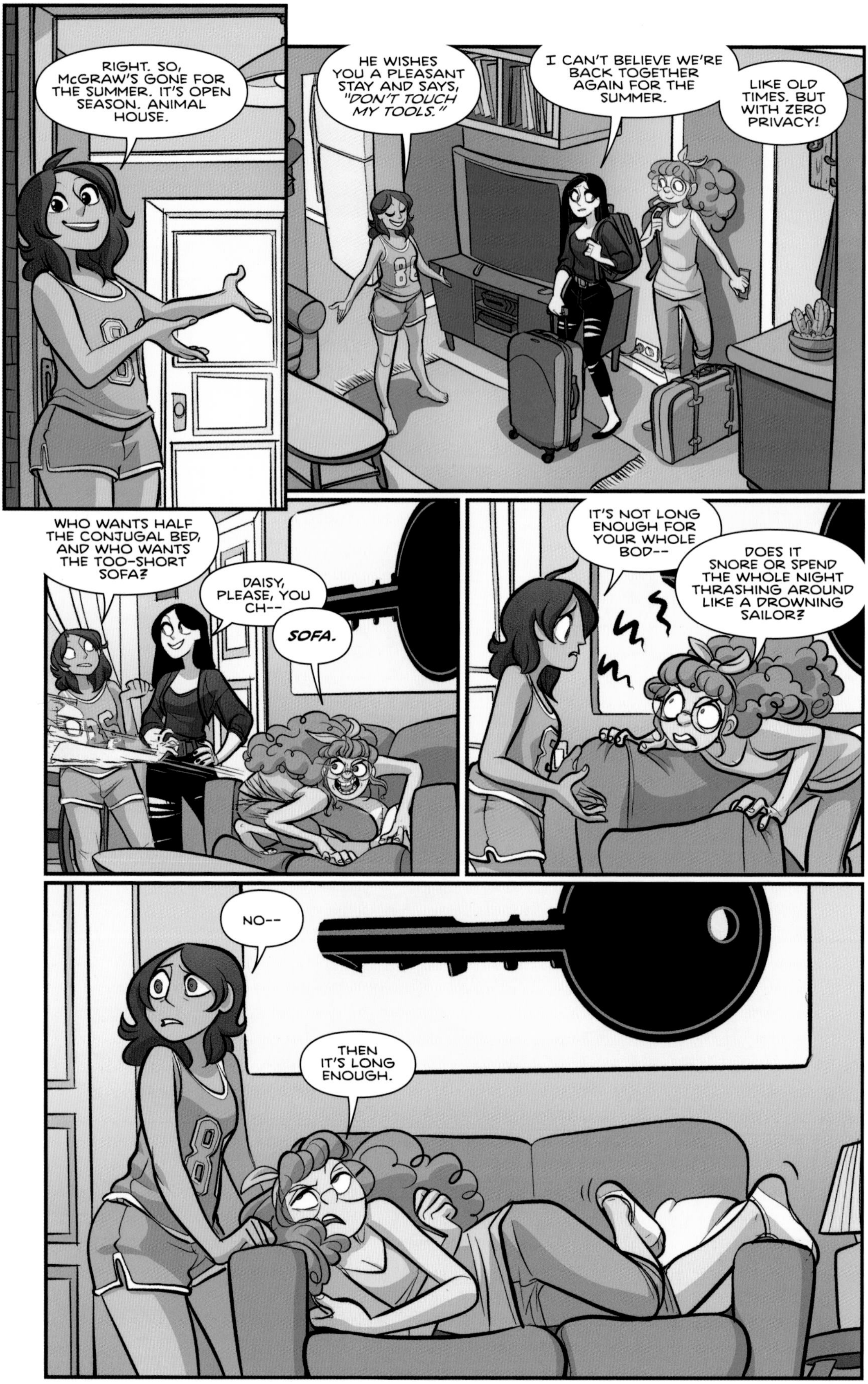
RIGHT. SO, McGRAW'S GONE FOR THE SUMMER. IT'S OPEN SEASON. ANIMAL HOUSE.
HE WISHES YOU A PLEASANT STAY AND SAYS, "DON'T TOUCH MY TOOLS."
I CAN'T BELIEVE WE'RE BACK TOGETHER AGAIN FOR THE SUMMER.
LIKE OLD TIMES. BUT WITH ZERO PRIVACY!
WHO WANTS HALF THE CONJUGAL BED, AND WHO WANTS THE TOO-SHORT SOFA?
DAISY, PLEASE, YOU CH--
SOFA.
IT'S NOT LONG ENOUGH FOR YOUR WHOLE BOD--
DOES IT SNORE OR SPEND THE WHOLE NIGHT THRASHING AROUND LIKE A DROWNING SAILOR?
NO--
THEN IT'S LONG ENOUGH.

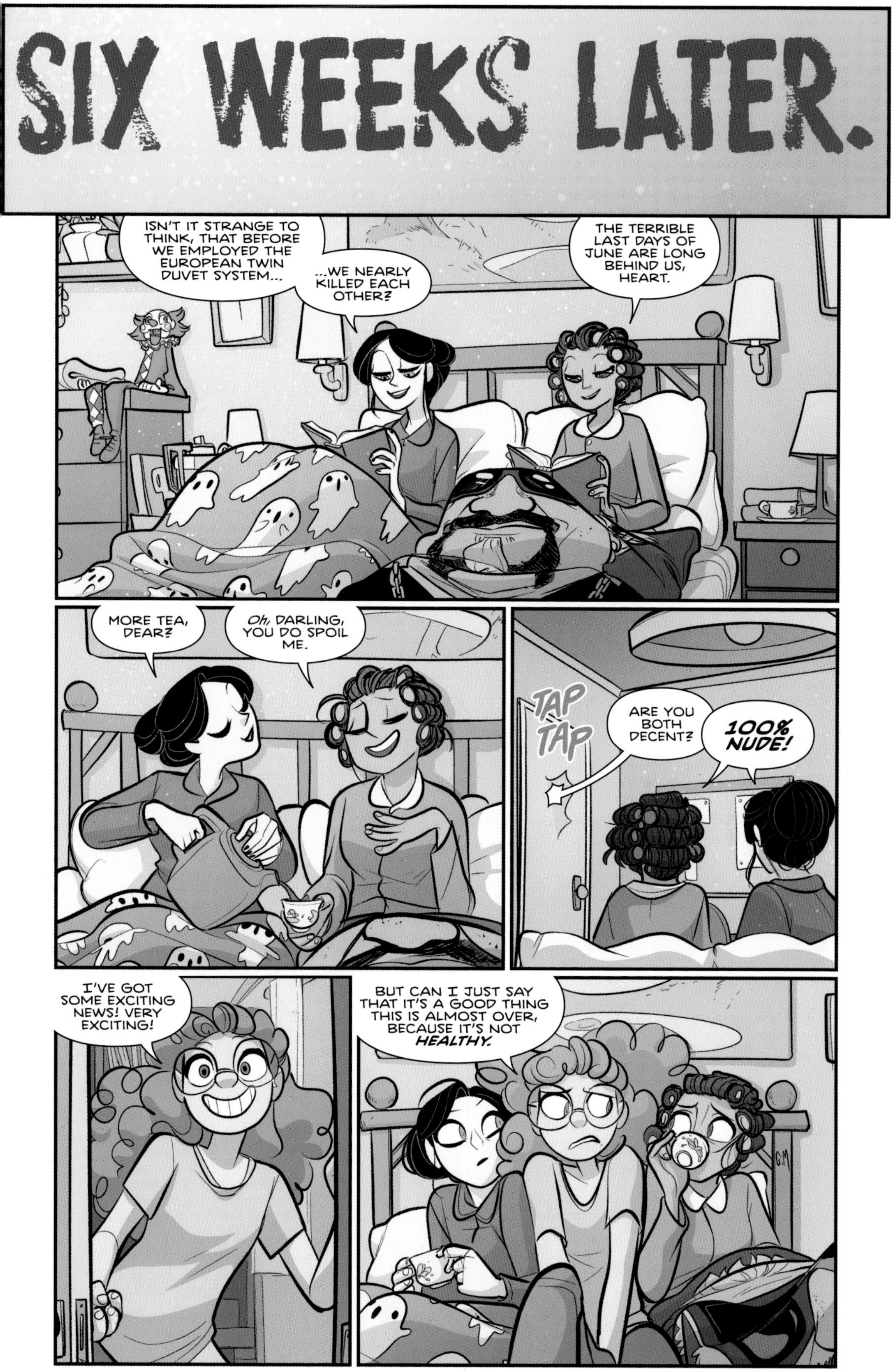
SIX WEEKS LATER.
ISN'T IT STRANGE TO THINK, THAT BEFORE WE EMPLOYED THE EUROPEAN TWIN DUVET SYSTEM...
...WE NEARLY KILLED EACH OTHER?
THE TERRIBLE LAST DAYS OF JUNE ARE LONG BEHIND US, HEART.
MORE TEA, DEAR?
*Oh,* DARLING, YOU DO SPOIL ME.
TAP TAP
ARE YOU BOTH DECENT?
100% NUDE!
I'VE GOT SOME EXCITING NEWS! VERY EXCITING!
BUT CAN I JUST SAY THAT IT'S A GOOD THING THIS IS ALMOST OVER, BECAUSE IT'S NOT ***HEALTHY.***

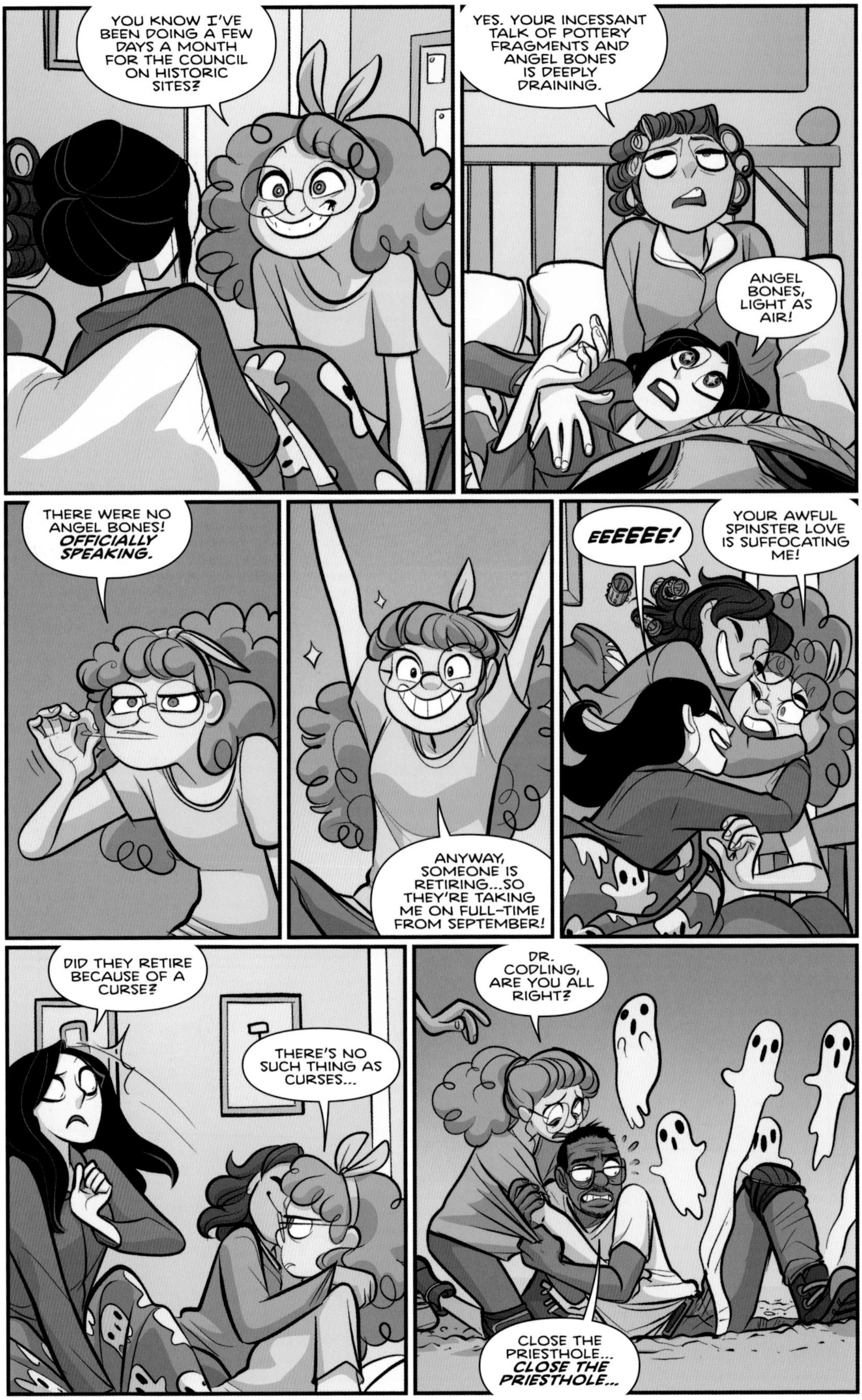

YOU KNOW I'VE BEEN DOING A FEW DAYS A MONTH FOR THE COUNCIL ON HISTORIC SITES?
YES. YOUR INCESSANT TALK OF POTTERY FRAGMENTS AND ANGEL BONES IS DEEPLY DRAINING.
ANGEL BONES, LIGHT AS AIR!
THERE WERE NO ANGEL BONES! OFFICIALLY SPEAKING.
ANYWAY, SOMEONE IS RETIRING...SO THEY'RE TAKING ME ON FULL-TIME FROM SEPTEMBER!
EEEEEE!
YOUR AWFUL SPINSTER LOVE IS SUFFOCATING ME!
DID THEY RETIRE BECAUSE OF A CURSE?
THERE'S NO SUCH THING AS CURSES...
DR. CODLING, ARE YOU ALL RIGHT?
CLOSE THE PRIESTHOLE... CLOSE THE PRIESTHOLE...

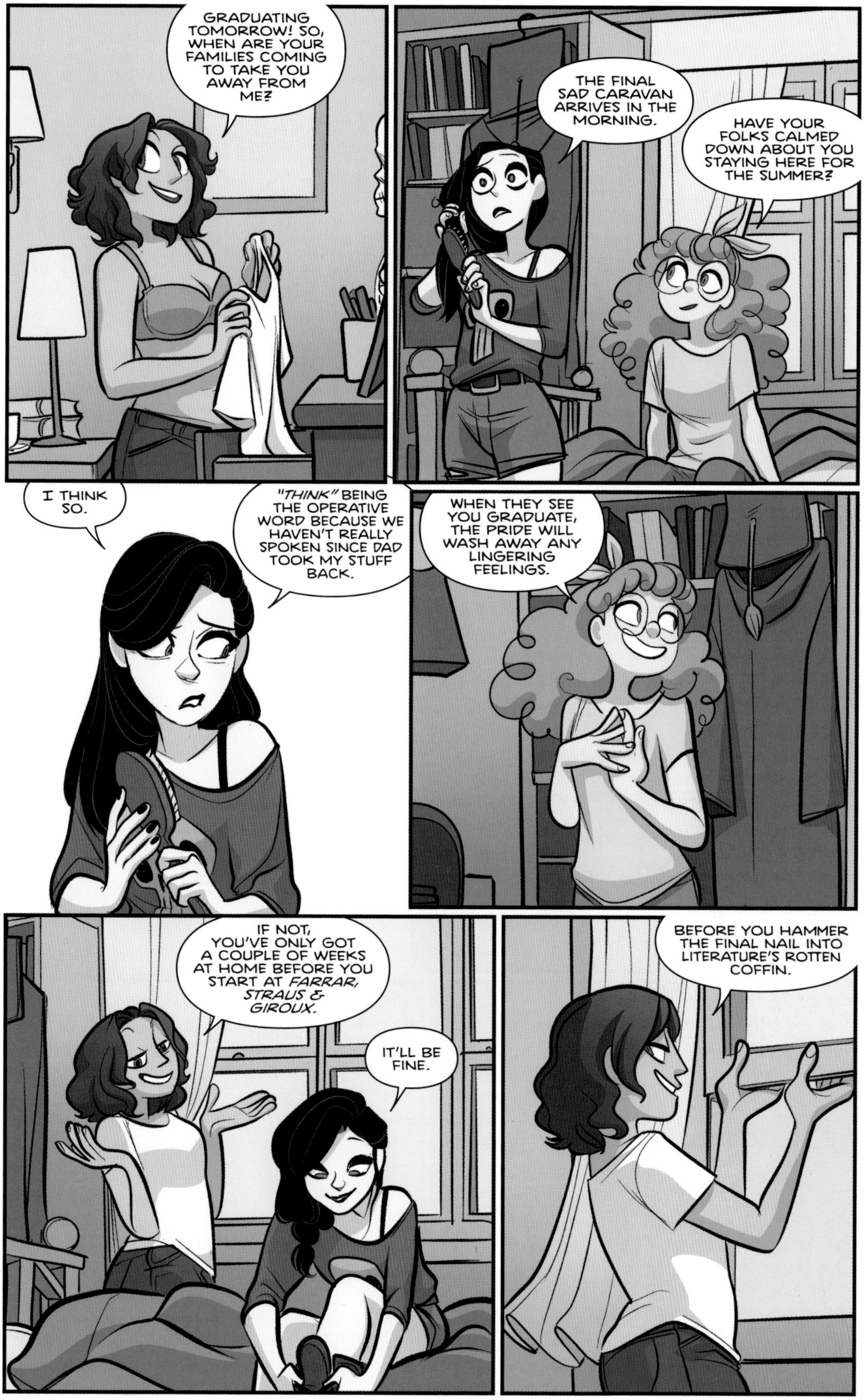
GRADUATING TOMORROW! SO, WHEN ARE YOUR FAMILIES COMING TO TAKE YOU AWAY FROM ME?
THE FINAL SAD CARAVAN ARRIVES IN THE MORNING.
HAVE YOUR FOLKS CALMED DOWN ABOUT YOU STAYING HERE FOR THE SUMMER?
I THINK SO.
*"THINK"* BEING THE OPERATIVE WORD BECAUSE WE HAVEN'T REALLY SPOKEN SINCE DAD TOOK MY STUFF BACK.
WHEN THEY SEE YOU GRADUATE, THE PRIDE WILL WASH AWAY ANY LINGERING FEELINGS.
IF NOT, YOU'VE ONLY GOT A COUPLE OF WEEKS AT HOME BEFORE YOU START AT *FARRAR, STRAUS & GIROUX.*
IT'LL BE FINE.
BEFORE YOU HAMMER THE FINAL NAIL INTO LITERATURE'S ROTTEN COFFIN.

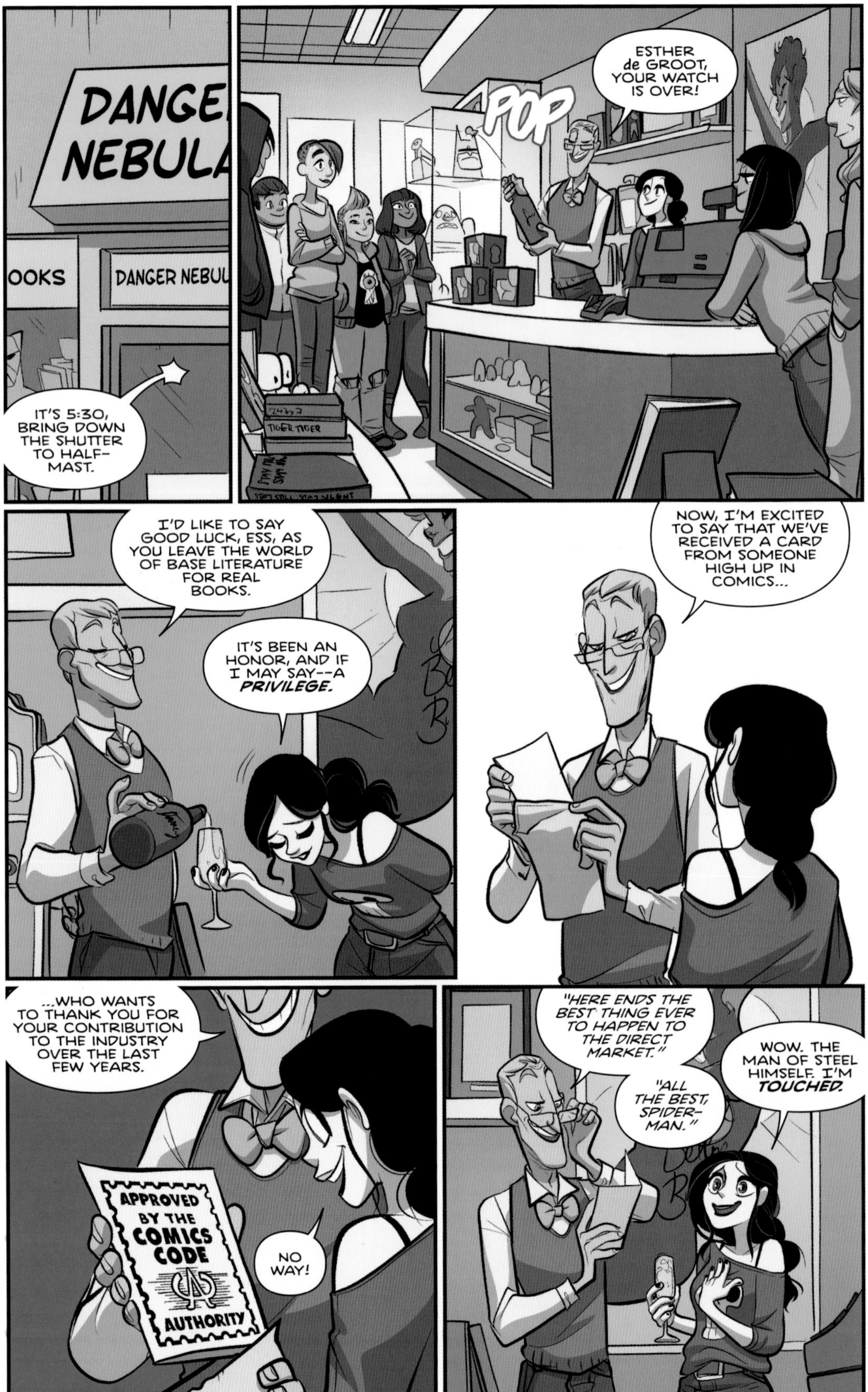
DANGE
NEBULA
OOKS
DANGER NEBUL
IT'S 5:30, BRING DOWN THE SHUTTER TO HALF-MAST.
POP
ESTHER de GROOT, YOUR WATCH IS OVER!
TIGER TIGER
I'D LIKE TO SAY GOOD LUCK, ESS, AS YOU LEAVE THE WORLD OF BASE LITERATURE FOR REAL BOOKS.
IT'S BEEN AN HONOR, AND IF I MAY SAY--A *PRIVILEGE.*
NOW, I'M EXCITED TO SAY THAT WE'VE RECEIVED A CARD FROM SOMEONE HIGH UP IN COMICS...
...WHO WANTS TO THANK YOU FOR YOUR CONTRIBUTION TO THE INDUSTRY OVER THE LAST FEW YEARS.
APPROVED BY THE COMICS CODE AUTHORITY
NO WAY!
*"HERE ENDS THE BEST THING EVER TO HAPPEN TO THE DIRECT MARKET."*
*"ALL THE BEST, SPIDER-MAN."*
WOW. THE MAN OF STEEL HIMSELF. I'M *TOUCHED.*

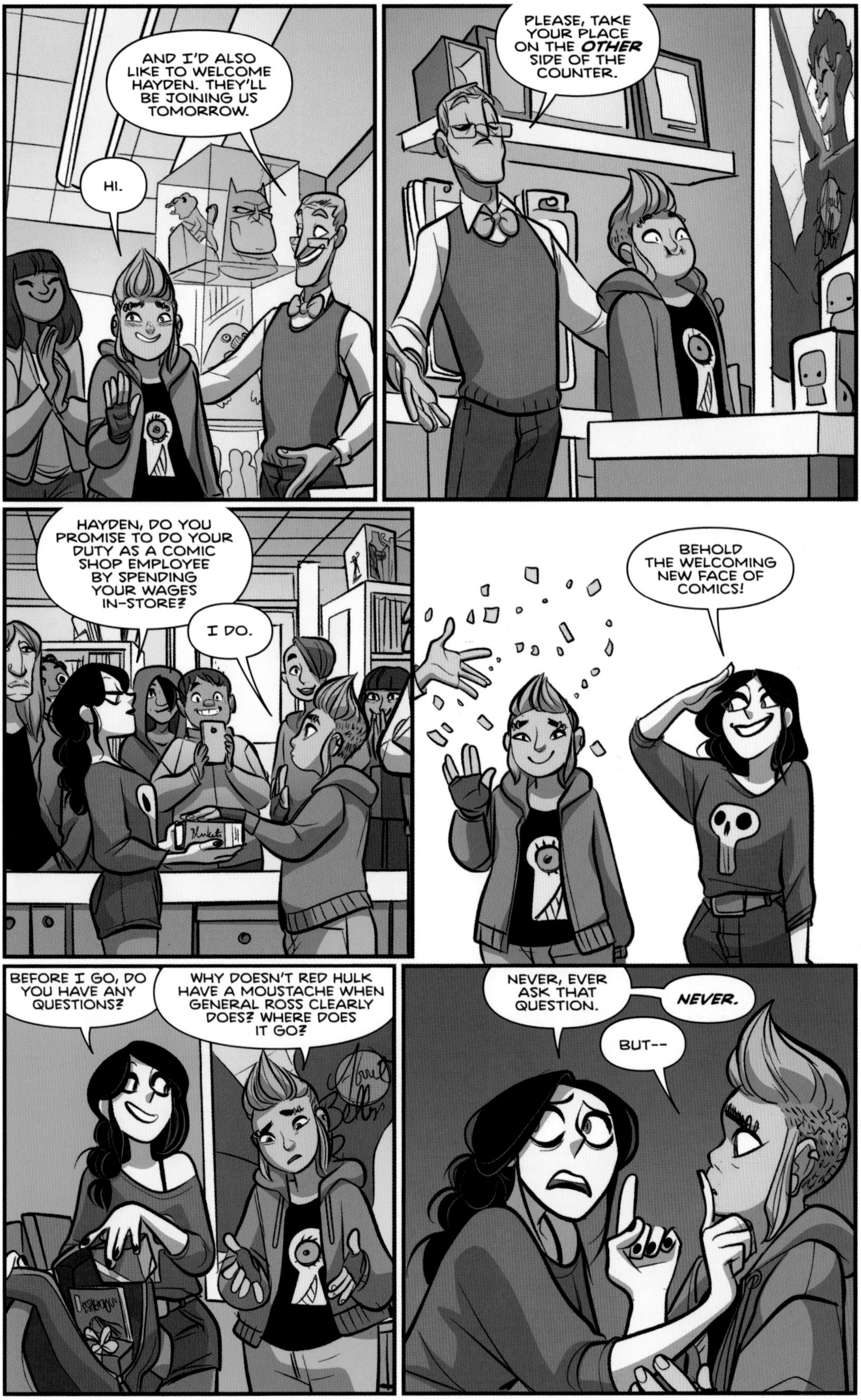
AND I'D ALSO LIKE TO WELCOME HAYDEN. THEY'LL BE JOINING US TOMORROW.
HI.
PLEASE, TAKE YOUR PLACE ON THE *OTHER* SIDE OF THE COUNTER.
HAYDEN, DO YOU PROMISE TO DO YOUR DUTY AS A COMIC SHOP EMPLOYEE BY SPENDING YOUR WAGES IN-STORE?
I DO.
BEHOLD THE WELCOMING NEW FACE OF COMICS!
BEFORE I GO, DO YOU HAVE ANY QUESTIONS?
WHY DOESN'T RED HULK HAVE A MOUSTACHE WHEN GENERAL ROSS CLEARLY DOES? WHERE DOES IT GO?
NEVER, EVER ASK THAT QUESTION.
*NEVER.*
BUT--

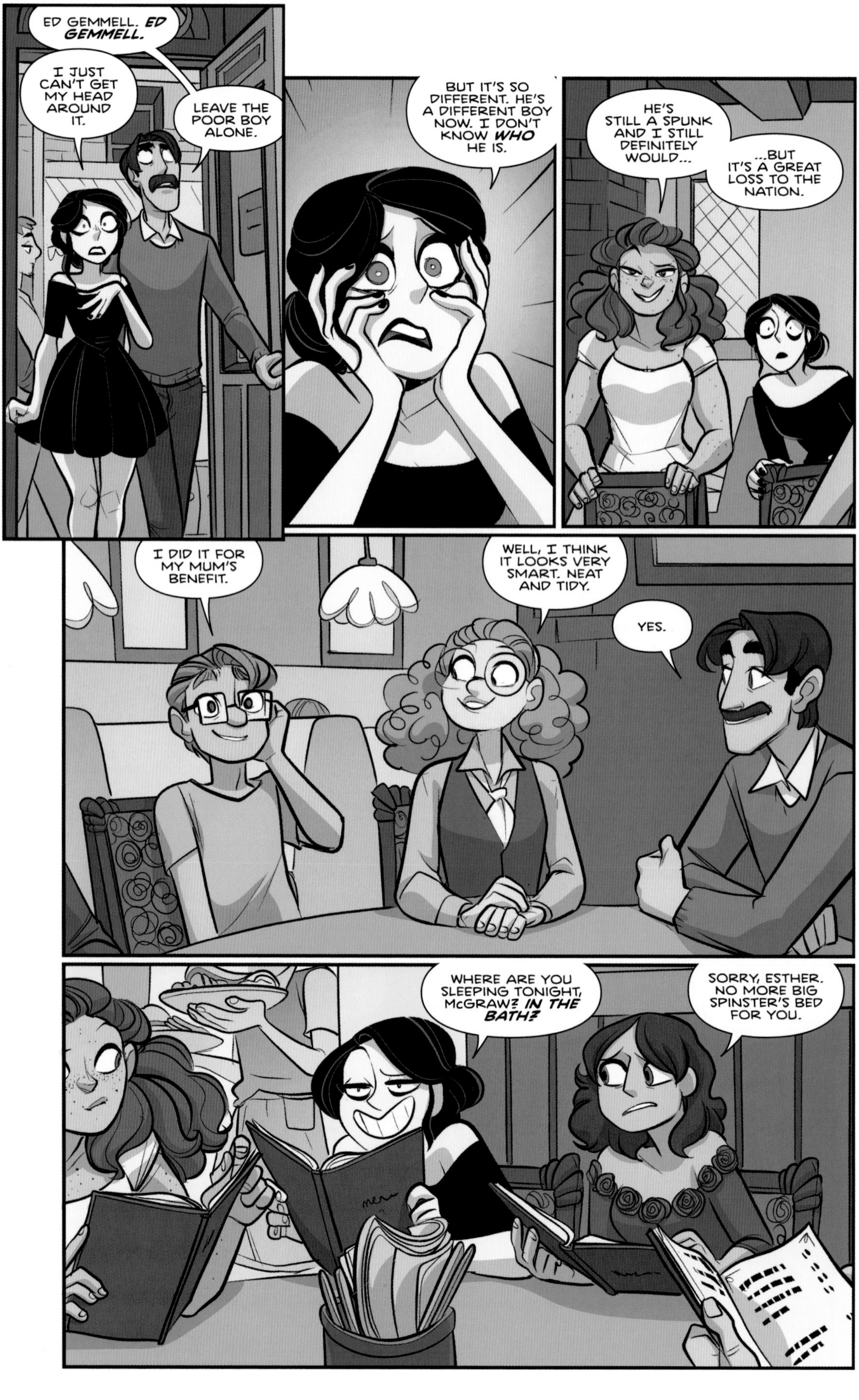
ED GEMMELL. *ED GEMMELL.*
I JUST CAN'T GET MY HEAD AROUND IT.
LEAVE THE POOR BOY ALONE.
BUT IT'S SO DIFFERENT. HE'S A DIFFERENT BOY NOW. I DON'T KNOW *WHO* HE IS.
HE'S STILL A SPUNK AND I STILL DEFINITELY WOULD...
...BUT IT'S A GREAT LOSS TO THE NATION.
I DID IT FOR MY MUM'S BENEFIT.
WELL, I THINK IT LOOKS VERY SMART. NEAT AND TIDY.
YES.
WHERE ARE YOU SLEEPING TONIGHT, McGRAW? *IN THE BATH?*
SORRY, ESTHER. NO MORE BIG SPINSTER'S BED FOR YOU.

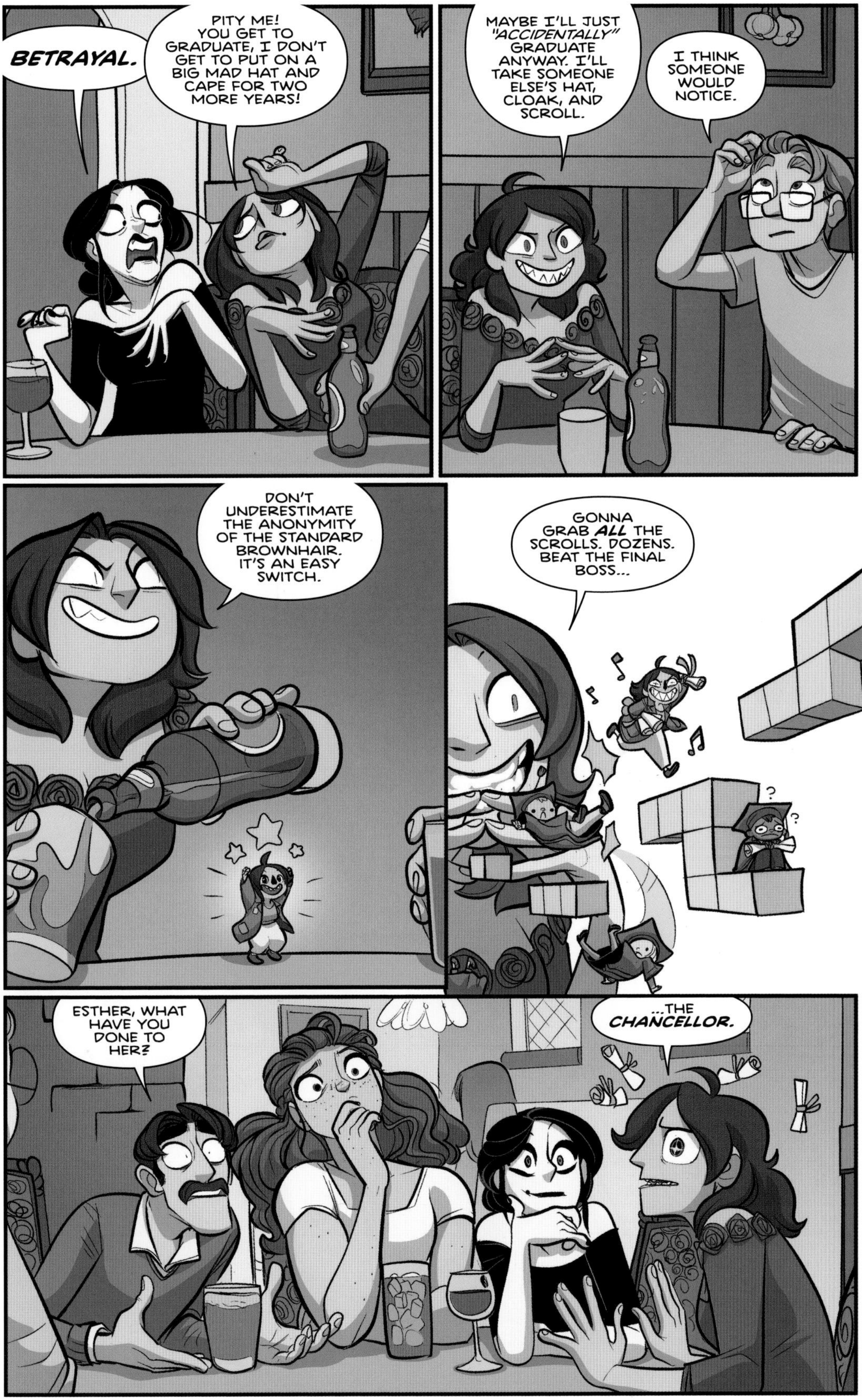
BETRAYAL.
PITY ME! YOU GET TO GRADUATE, I DON'T GET TO PUT ON A BIG MAD HAT AND CAPE FOR TWO MORE YEARS!
MAYBE I'LL JUST "ACCIDENTALLY" GRADUATE ANYWAY. I'LL TAKE SOMEONE ELSE'S HAT, CLOAK, AND SCROLL.
I THINK SOMEONE WOULD NOTICE.
DON'T UNDERESTIMATE THE ANONYMITY OF THE STANDARD BROWNHAIR. IT'S AN EASY SWITCH.
GONNA GRAB ALL THE SCROLLS. DOZENS. BEAT THE FINAL BOSS...
ESTHER, WHAT HAVE YOU DONE TO HER?
...THE CHANCELLOR.

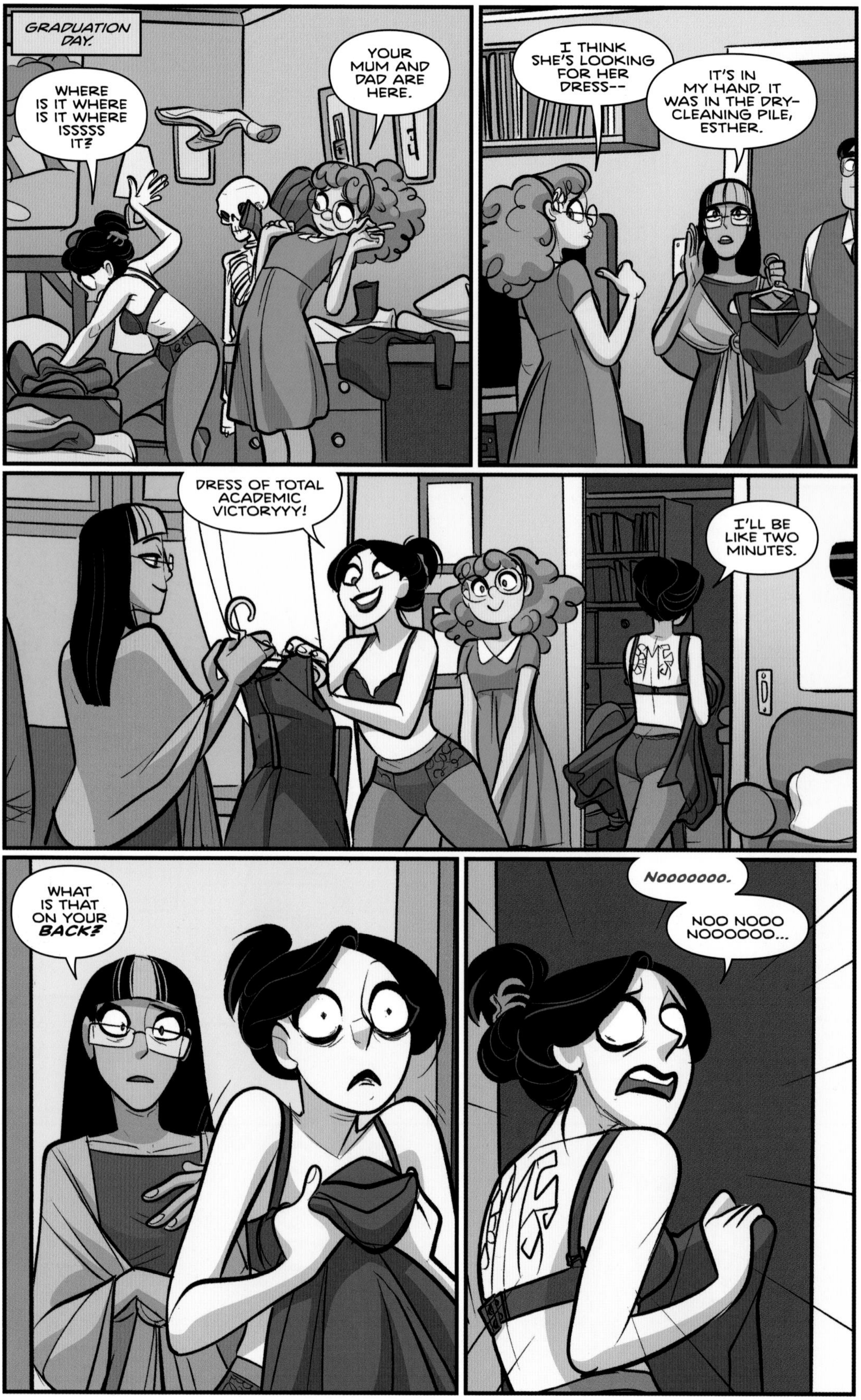
GRADUATION DAY.
WHERE IS IT WHERE IS IT WHERE ISSSSS IT?
YOUR MUM AND DAD ARE HERE.
I THINK SHE'S LOOKING FOR HER DRESS--
IT'S IN MY HAND. IT WAS IN THE DRY-CLEANING PILE, ESTHER.
DRESS OF TOTAL ACADEMIC VICTORYYY!
I'LL BE LIKE TWO MINUTES.
WHAT IS THAT ON YOUR BACK?
Nooooooo.
NOO NOOO NOOOOOO...

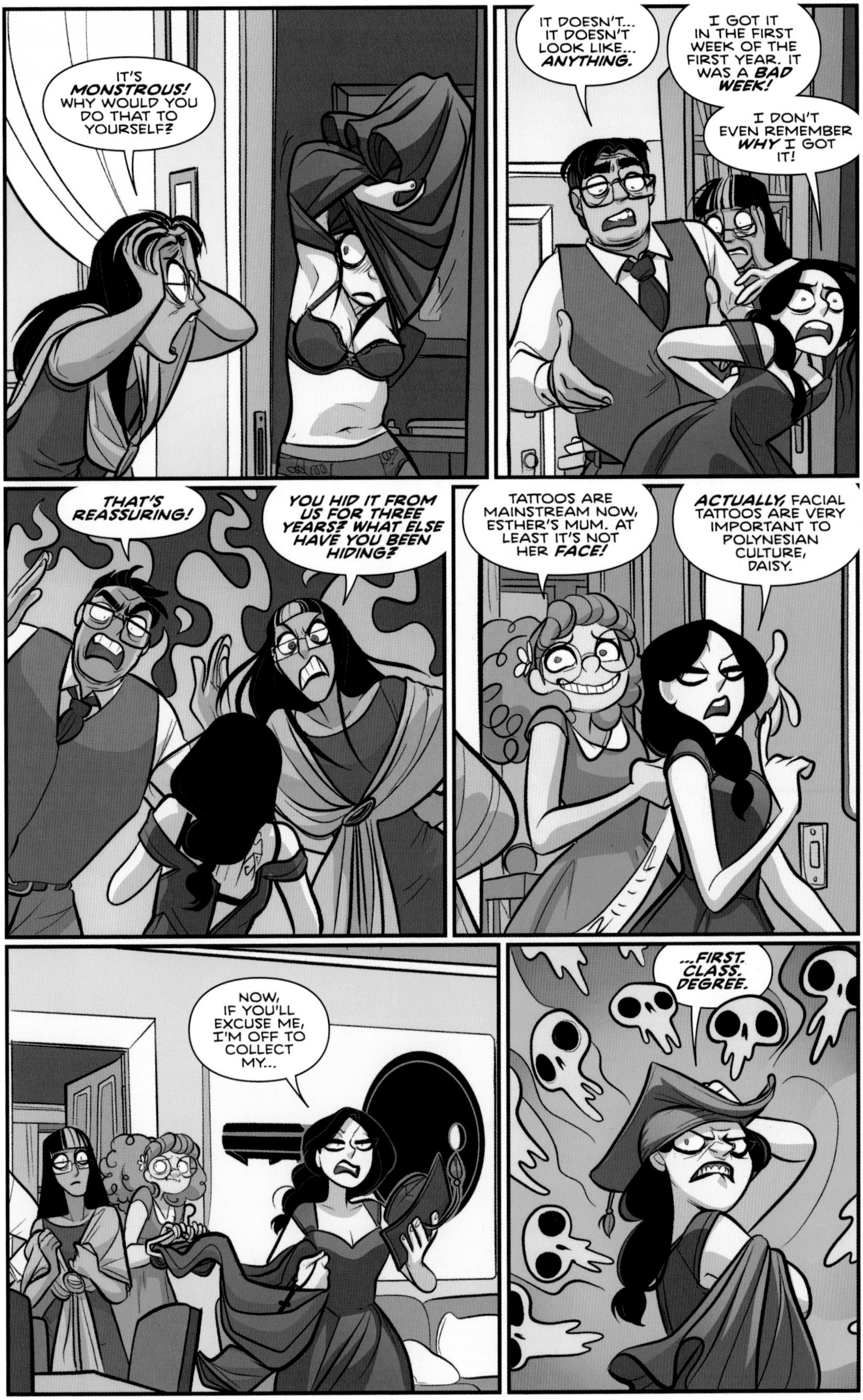
IT'S MONSTROUS! WHY WOULD YOU DO THAT TO YOURSELF?
IT DOESN'T... IT DOESN'T LOOK LIKE... ANYTHING.
I GOT IT IN THE FIRST WEEK OF THE FIRST YEAR. IT WAS A BAD WEEK!
I DON'T EVEN REMEMBER WHY I GOT IT!
THAT'S REASSURING!
YOU HID IT FROM US FOR THREE YEARS? WHAT ELSE HAVE YOU BEEN HIDING?
TATTOOS ARE MAINSTREAM NOW, ESTHER'S MUM. AT LEAST IT'S NOT HER FACE!
ACTUALLY, FACIAL TATTOOS ARE VERY IMPORTANT TO POLYNESIAN CULTURE, DAISY.
NOW, IF YOU'LL EXCUSE ME, I'M OFF TO COLLECT MY...
...FIRST. CLASS. DEGREE.

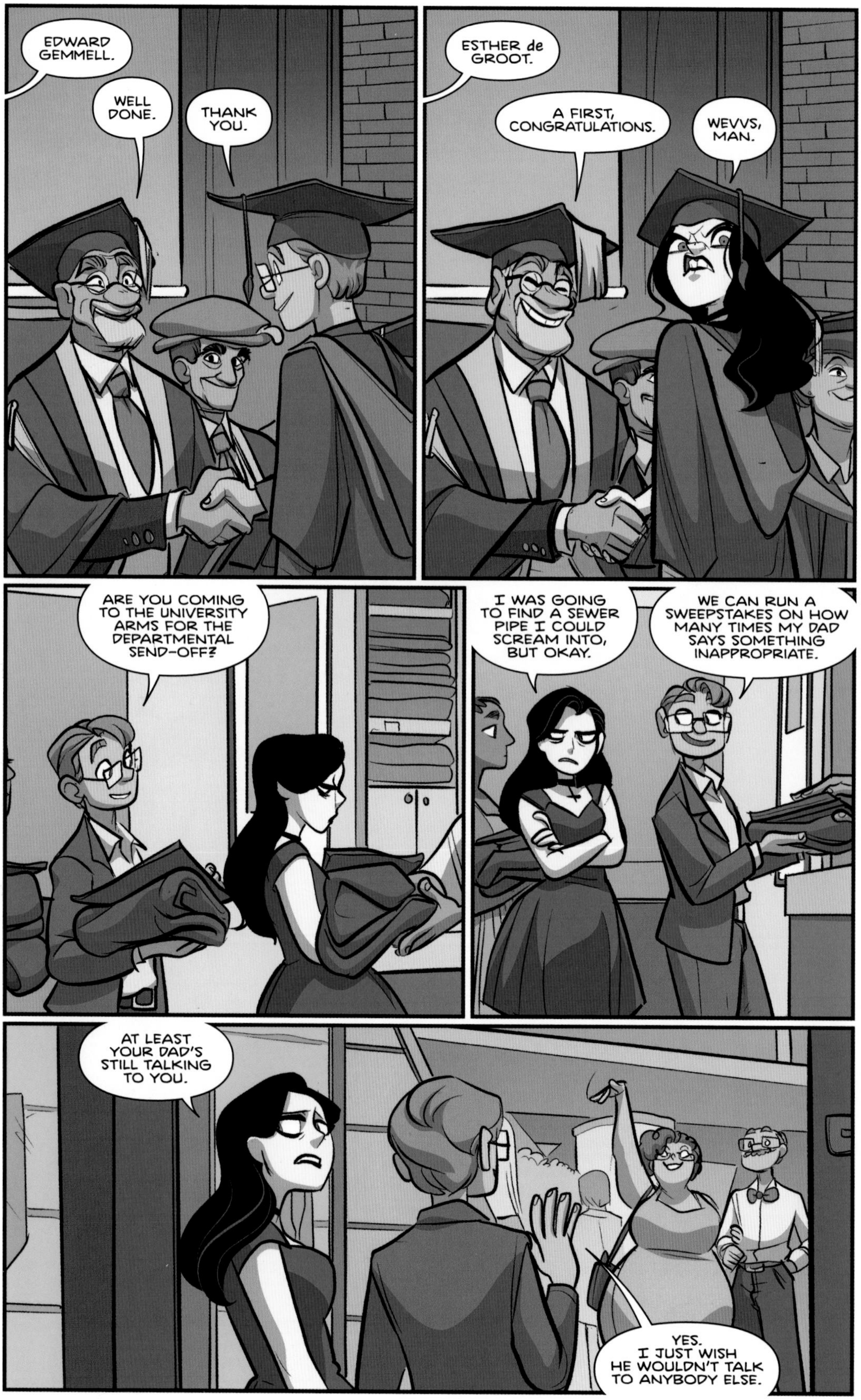
EDWARD GEMMELL.
WELL DONE.
THANK YOU.
ESTHER de GROOT.
A FIRST, CONGRATULATIONS.
WEVVS, MAN.
ARE YOU COMING TO THE UNIVERSITY ARMS FOR THE DEPARTMENTAL SEND-OFF?
I WAS GOING TO FIND A SEWER PIPE I COULD SCREAM INTO, BUT OKAY.
WE CAN RUN A SWEEPSTAKES ON HOW MANY TIMES MY DAD SAYS SOMETHING INAPPROPRIATE.
AT LEAST YOUR DAD'S STILL TALKING TO YOU.
YES. I JUST WISH HE WOULDN'T TALK TO ANYBODY ELSE.

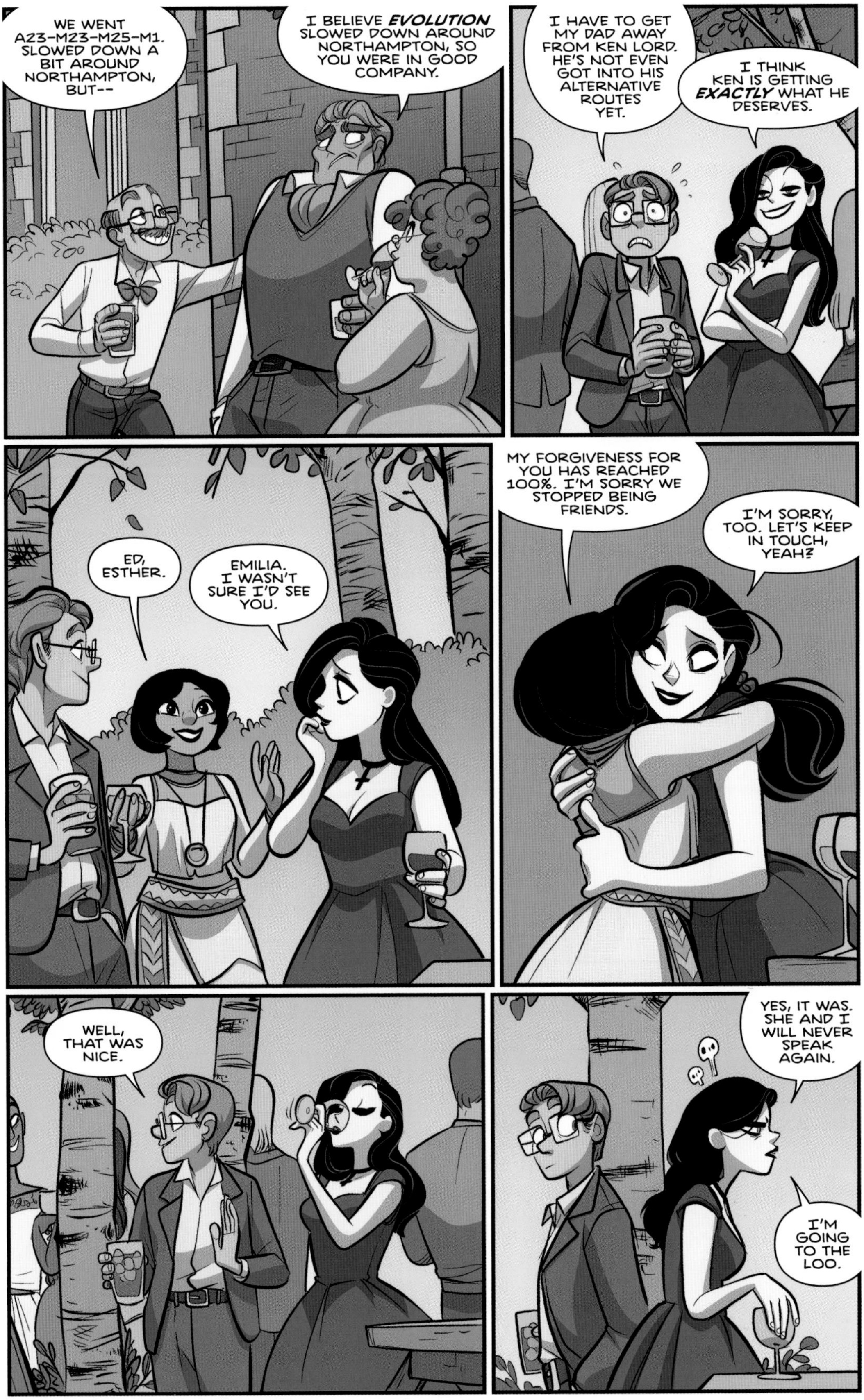
WE WENT A23–M23–M25–M1. SLOWED DOWN A BIT AROUND NORTHAMPTON, BUT--
I BELIEVE EVOLUTION SLOWED DOWN AROUND NORTHAMPTON, SO YOU WERE IN GOOD COMPANY.
I HAVE TO GET MY DAD AWAY FROM KEN LORD. HE'S NOT EVEN GOT INTO HIS ALTERNATIVE ROUTES YET.
I THINK KEN IS GETTING EXACTLY WHAT HE DESERVES.
ED, ESTHER.
EMILIA. I WASN'T SURE I'D SEE YOU.
MY FORGIVENESS FOR YOU HAS REACHED 100%. I'M SORRY WE STOPPED BEING FRIENDS.
I'M SORRY, TOO. LET'S KEEP IN TOUCH, YEAH?
WELL, THAT WAS NICE.
YES, IT WAS. SHE AND I WILL NEVER SPEAK AGAIN.
I'M GOING TO THE LOO.

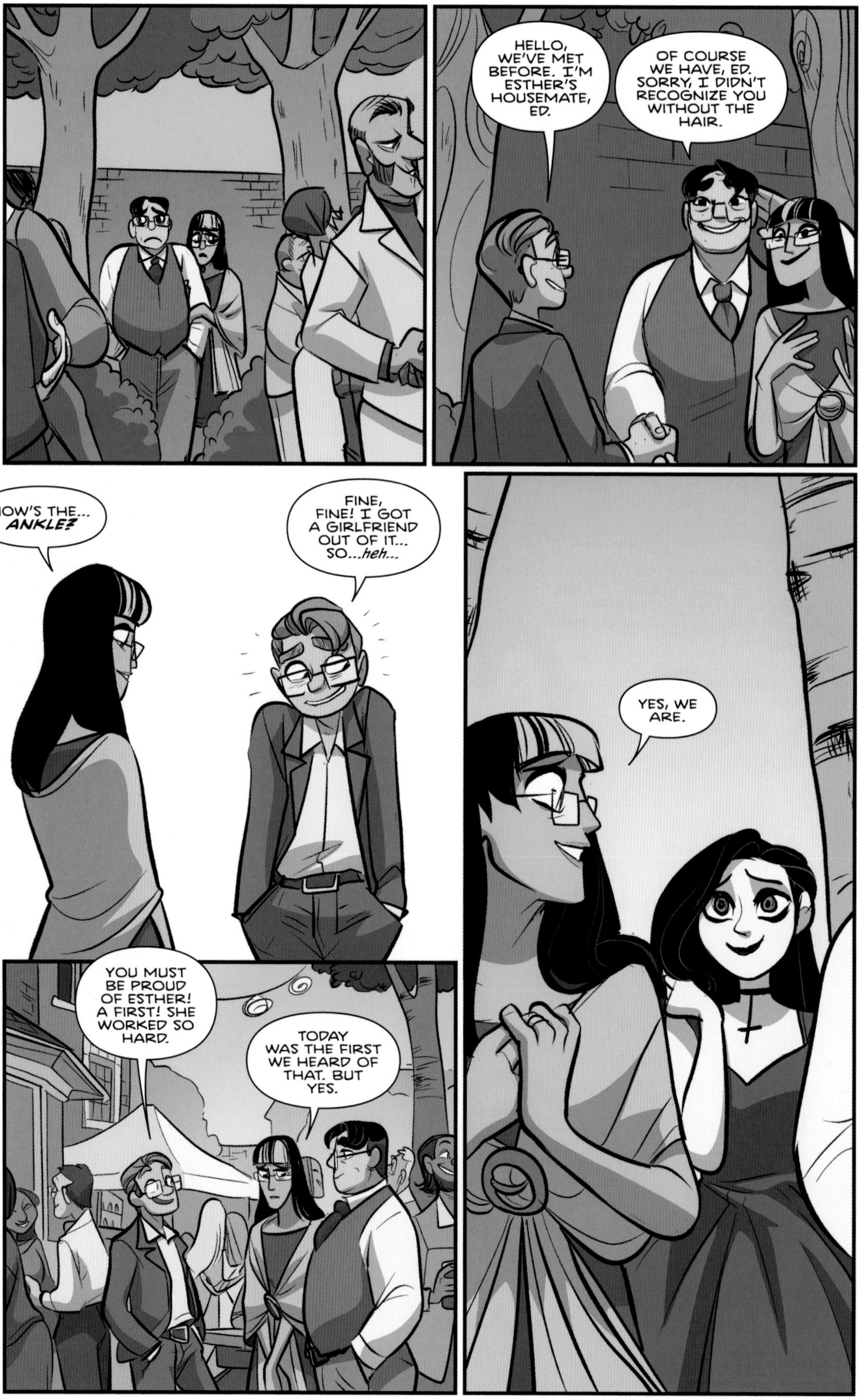
HELLO, WE'VE MET BEFORE. I'M ESTHER'S HOUSEMATE, ED.
OF COURSE WE HAVE, ED. SORRY, I DIDN'T RECOGNIZE YOU WITHOUT THE HAIR.
HOW'S THE... *ANKLE?*
FINE, FINE! I GOT A GIRLFRIEND OUT OF IT... SO...*heh...*
YOU MUST BE PROUD OF ESTHER! A FIRST! SHE WORKED SO HARD.
TODAY WAS THE FIRST WE HEARD OF THAT. BUT YES.
YES, WE ARE.

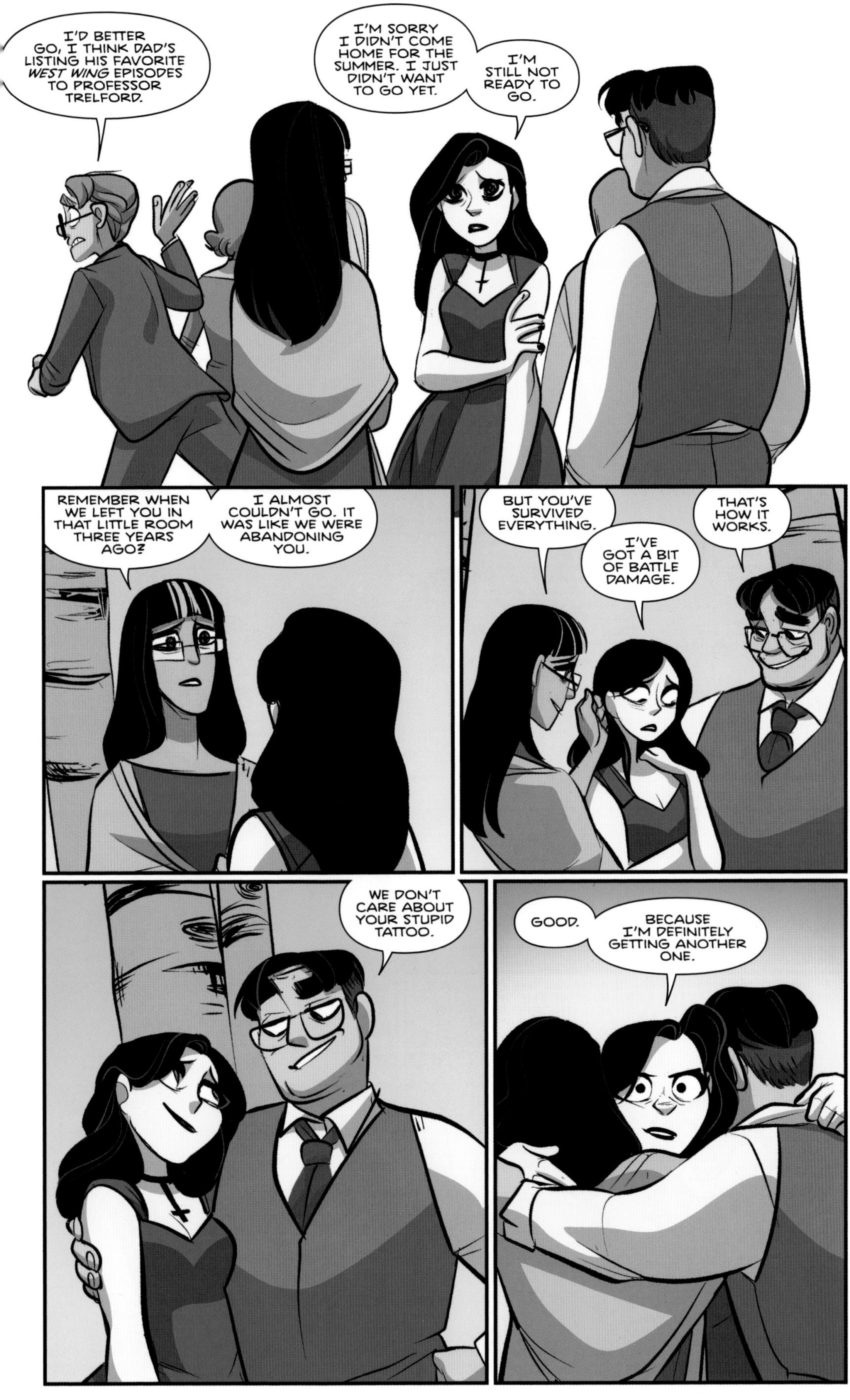
I'D BETTER GO, I THINK DAD'S LISTING HIS FAVORITE *WEST WING* EPISODES TO PROFESSOR TRELFORD.
I'M SORRY I DIDN'T COME HOME FOR THE SUMMER. I JUST DIDN'T WANT TO GO YET.
I'M STILL NOT READY TO GO.
REMEMBER WHEN WE LEFT YOU IN THAT LITTLE ROOM THREE YEARS AGO?
I ALMOST COULDN'T GO. IT WAS LIKE WE WERE ABANDONING YOU.
BUT YOU'VE SURVIVED EVERYTHING.
I'VE GOT A BIT OF BATTLE DAMAGE.
THAT'S HOW IT WORKS.
WE DON'T CARE ABOUT YOUR STUPID TATTOO.
GOOD.
BECAUSE I'M DEFINITELY GETTING ANOTHER ONE.

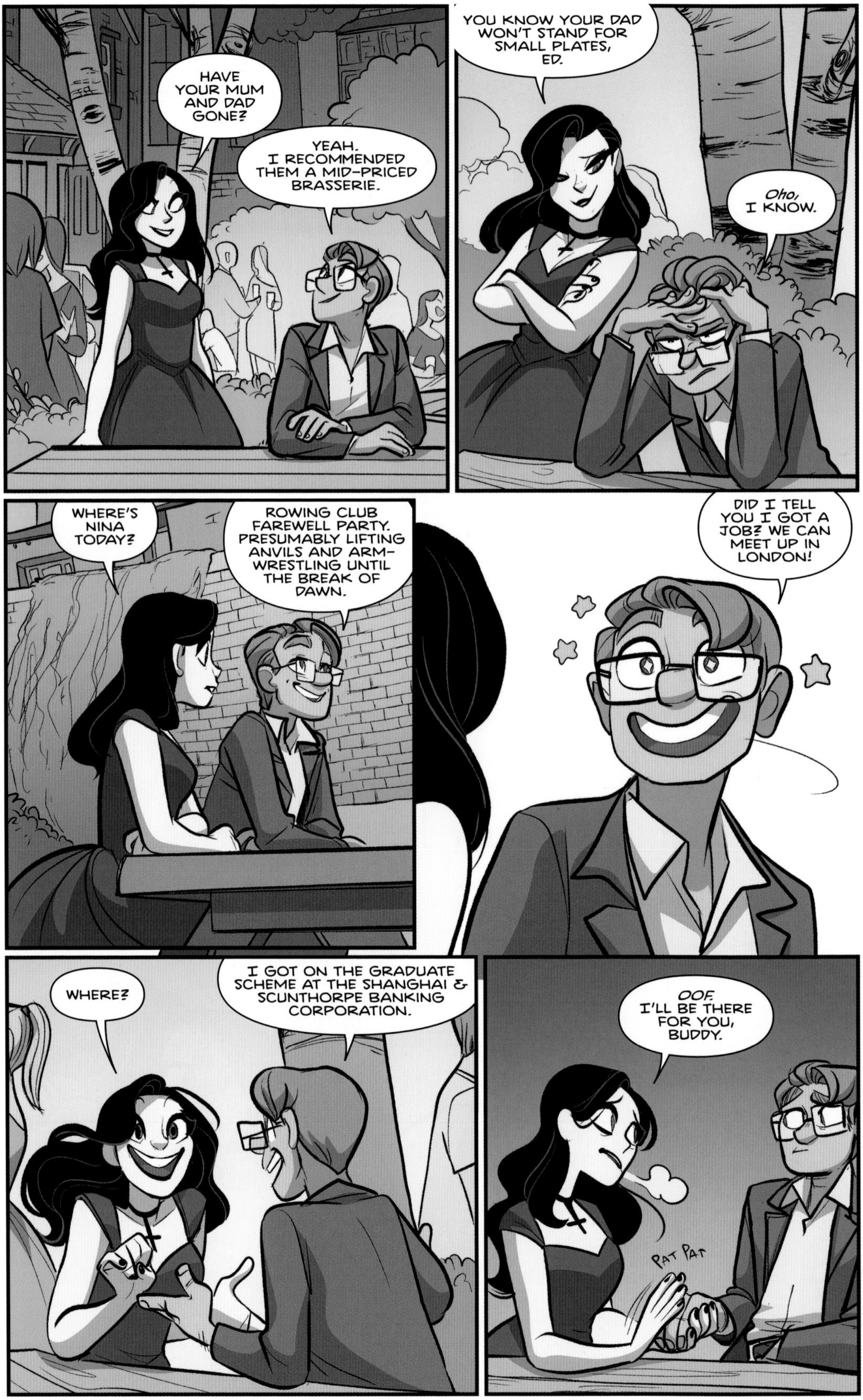
HAVE YOUR MUM AND DAD GONE?
YEAH. I RECOMMENDED THEM A MID-PRICED BRASSERIE.
YOU KNOW YOUR DAD WON'T STAND FOR SMALL PLATES, ED.
*Oho,* I KNOW.
WHERE'S NINA TODAY?
ROWING CLUB FAREWELL PARTY. PRESUMABLY LIFTING ANVILS AND ARM-WRESTLING UNTIL THE BREAK OF DAWN.
DID I TELL YOU I GOT A JOB? WE CAN MEET UP IN LONDON!
WHERE?
I GOT ON THE GRADUATE SCHEME AT THE SHANGHAI & SCUNTHORPE BANKING CORPORATION.
*OOF.* I'LL BE THERE FOR YOU, BUDDY.
PAT PAT

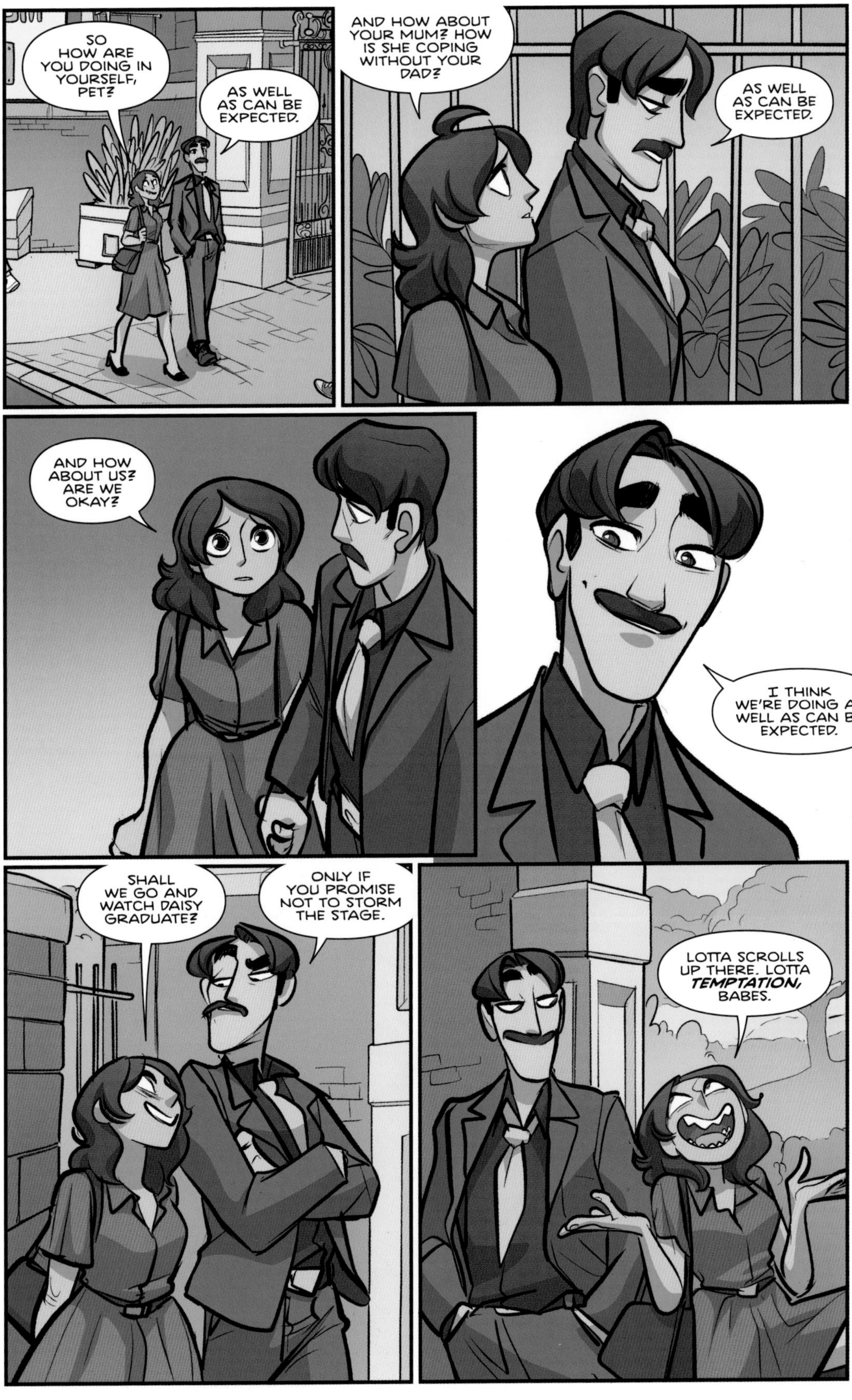
SO HOW ARE YOU DOING IN YOURSELF, PET?
AS WELL AS CAN BE EXPECTED.
AND HOW ABOUT YOUR MUM? HOW IS SHE COPING WITHOUT YOUR DAD?
AS WELL AS CAN BE EXPECTED.
AND HOW ABOUT US? ARE WE OKAY?
I THINK WE'RE DOING AS WELL AS CAN BE EXPECTED.
SHALL WE GO AND WATCH DAISY GRADUATE?
ONLY IF YOU PROMISE NOT TO STORM THE STAGE.
LOTTA SCROLLS UP THERE. LOTTA *TEMPTATION,* BABES.

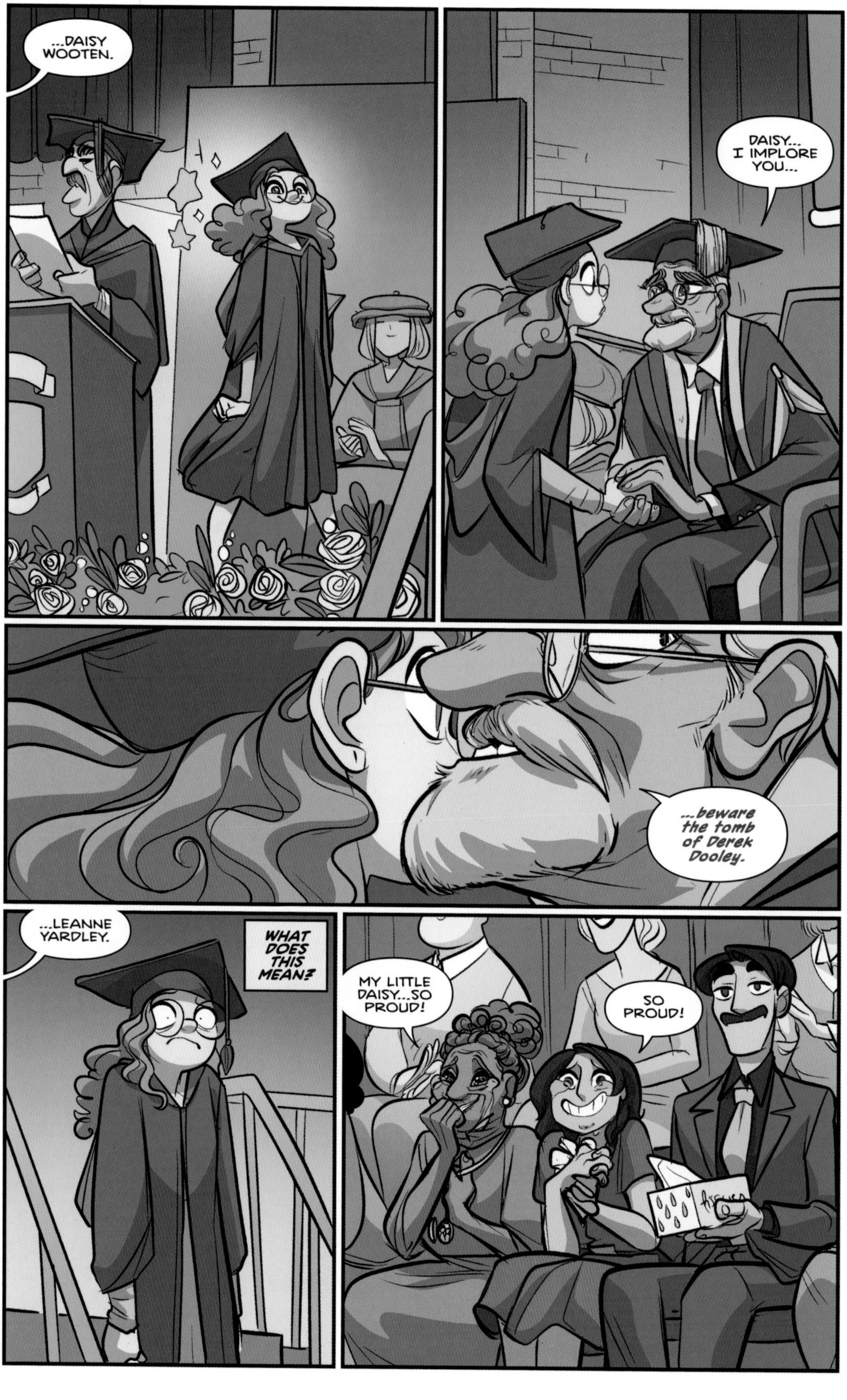
...DAISY WOOTEN.
DAISY... I IMPLORE YOU...
...beware the tomb of Derek Dooley.
...LEANNE YARDLEY.
WHAT DOES THIS MEAN?
MY LITTLE DAISY...SO PROUD!
SO PROUD!

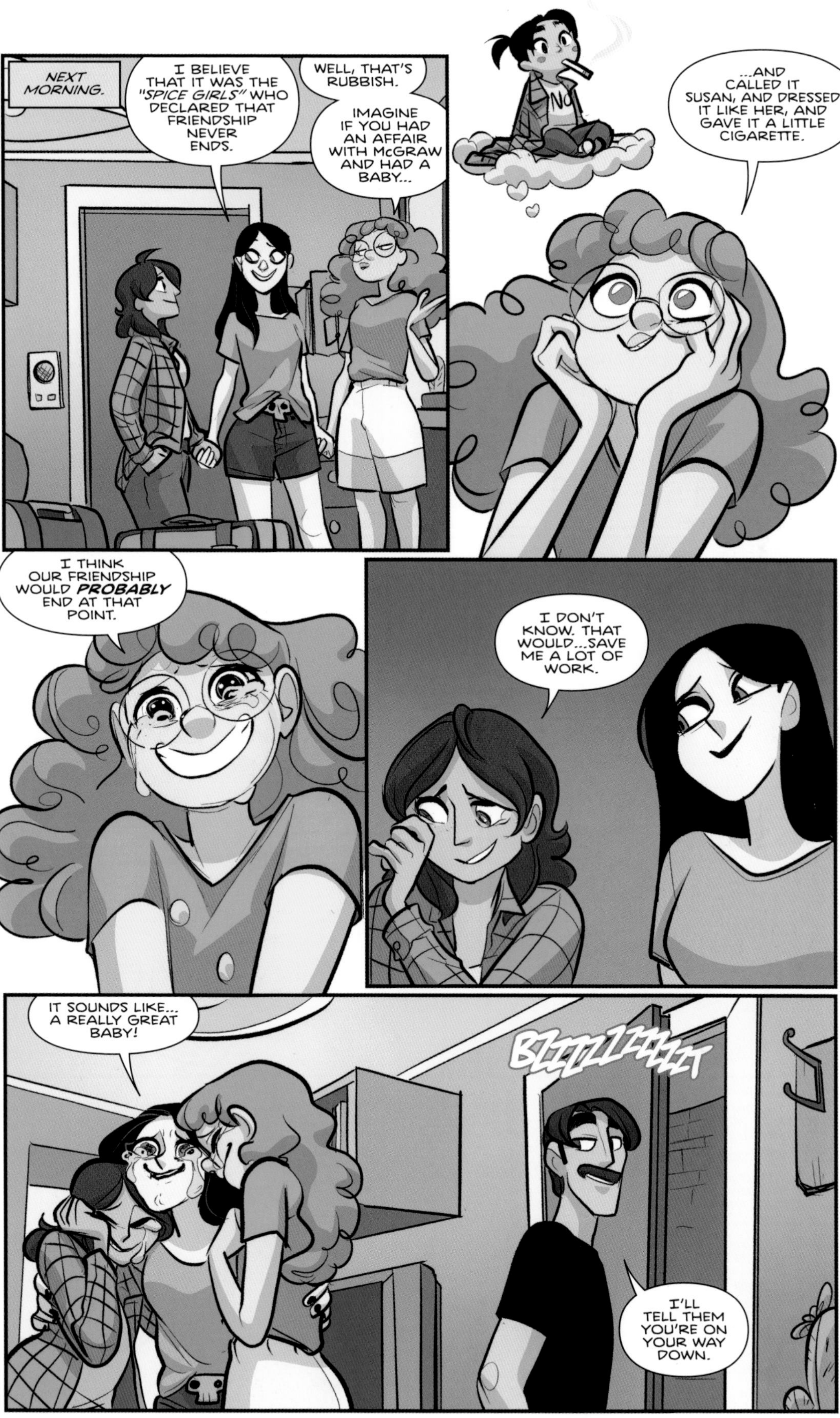
NEXT MORNING.
I BELIEVE THAT IT WAS THE "SPICE GIRLS" WHO DECLARED THAT FRIENDSHIP NEVER ENDS.
WELL, THAT'S RUBBISH.
IMAGINE IF YOU HAD AN AFFAIR WITH McGRAW AND HAD A BABY...
NO
...AND CALLED IT SUSAN, AND DRESSED IT LIKE HER, AND GAVE IT A LITTLE CIGARETTE.
I THINK OUR FRIENDSHIP WOULD PROBABLY END AT THAT POINT.
I DON'T KNOW. THAT WOULD...SAVE ME A LOT OF WORK.
IT SOUNDS LIKE... A REALLY GREAT BABY!
BZZZZZZZT
I'LL TELL THEM YOU'RE ON YOUR WAY DOWN.

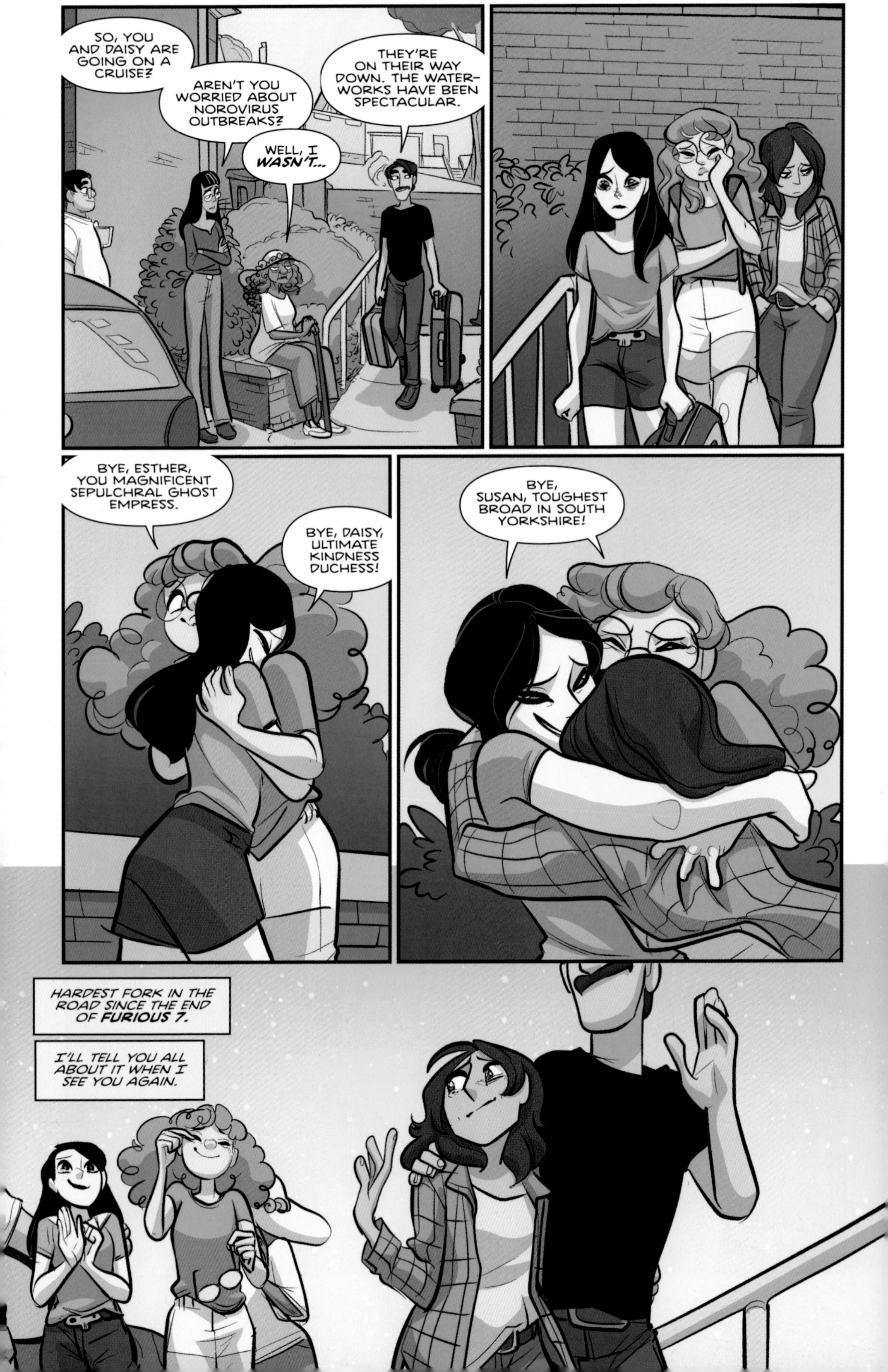
SO, YOU AND DAISY ARE GOING ON A CRUISE?
AREN'T YOU WORRIED ABOUT NOROVIRUS OUTBREAKS?
WELL, I *WASN'T...*
THEY'RE ON THEIR WAY DOWN. THE WATER-WORKS HAVE BEEN SPECTACULAR.
BYE, ESTHER, YOU MAGNIFICENT SEPULCHRAL GHOST EMPRESS.
BYE, DAISY, ULTIMATE KINDNESS DUCHESS!
BYE, SUSAN, TOUGHEST BROAD IN SOUTH YORKSHIRE!
*HARDEST FORK IN THE ROAD SINCE THE END OF **FURIOUS 7.***
*I'LL TELL YOU ALL ABOUT IT WHEN I SEE YOU AGAIN.*

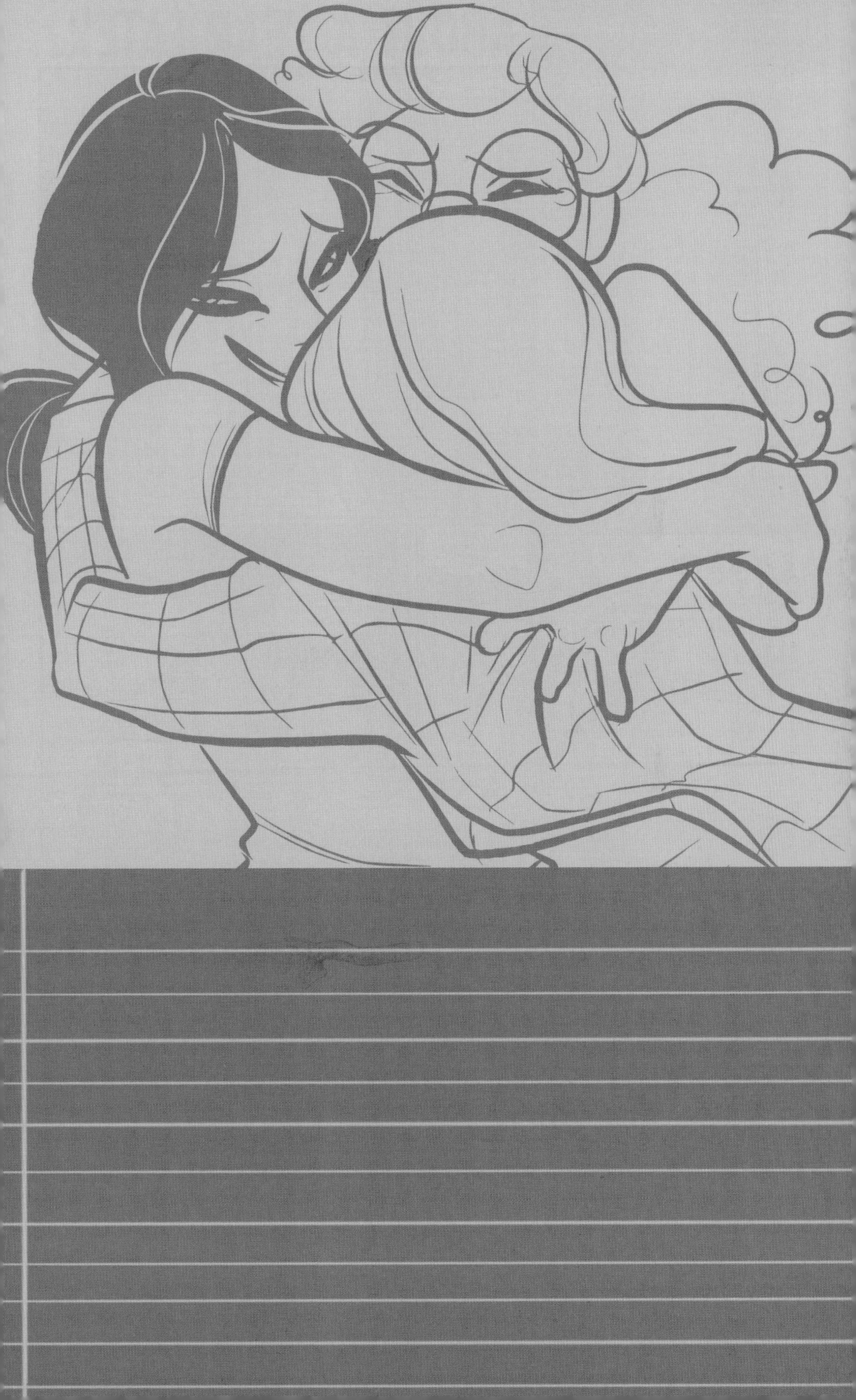

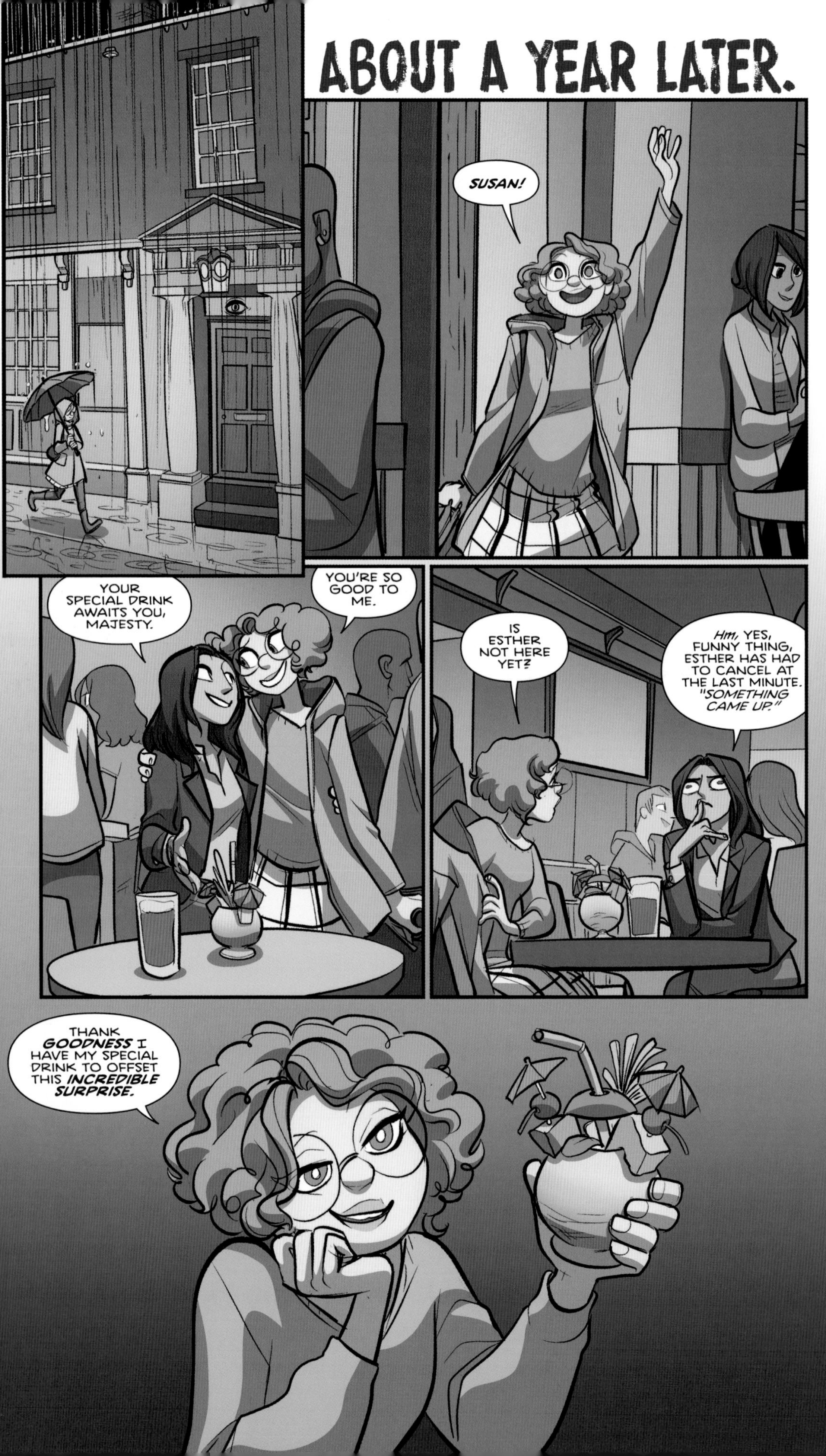
ABOUT A YEAR LATER.
SUSAN!
YOUR SPECIAL DRINK AWAITS YOU, MAJESTY.
YOU'RE SO GOOD TO ME.
IS ESTHER NOT HERE YET?
*Hm*, YES, FUNNY THING, ESTHER HAS HAD TO CANCEL AT THE LAST MINUTE. *"SOMETHING CAME UP."*
THANK ***GOODNESS*** I HAVE MY SPECIAL DRINK TO OFFSET THIS ***INCREDIBLE SURPRISE.***

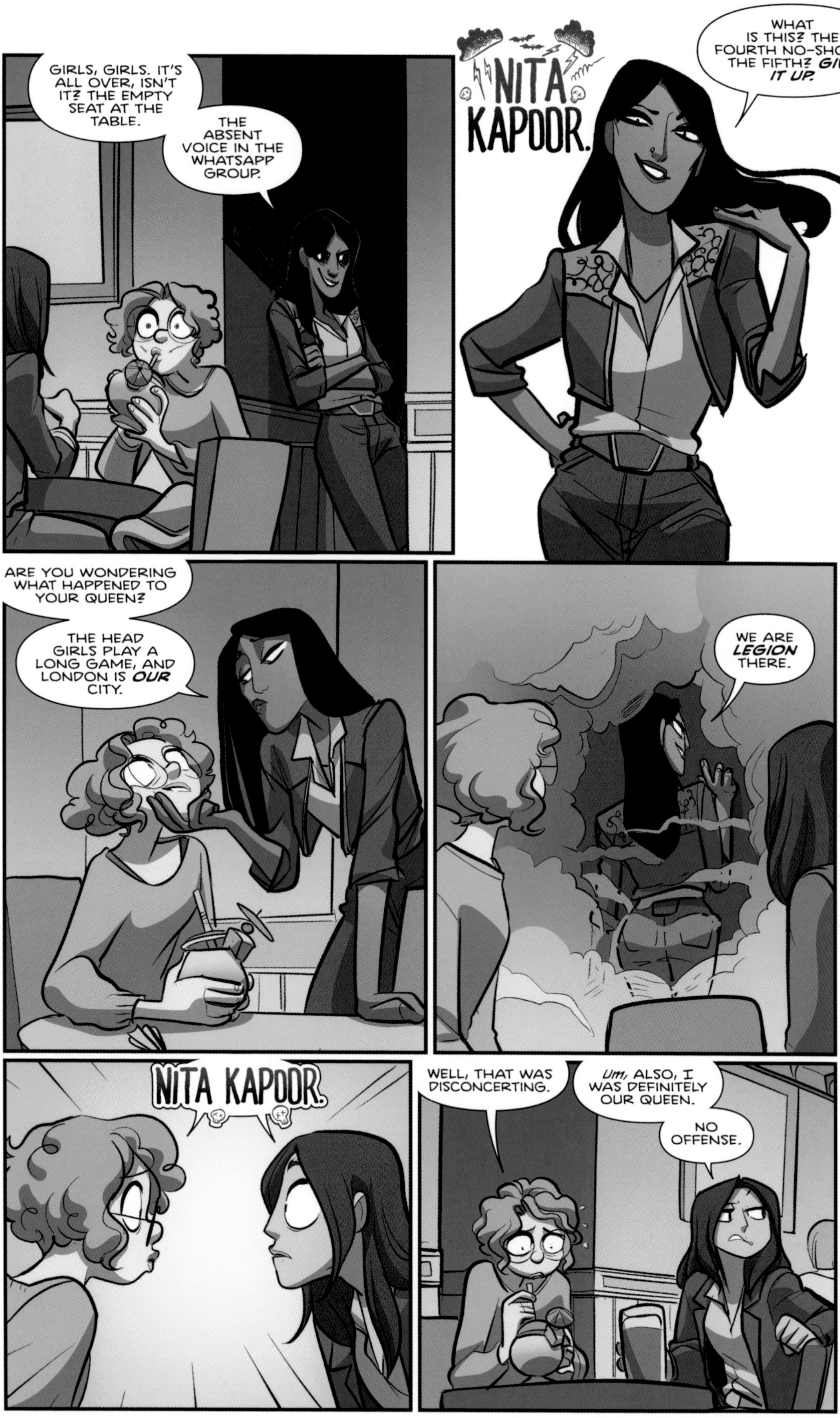
GIRLS, GIRLS. IT'S ALL OVER, ISN'T IT? THE EMPTY SEAT AT THE TABLE.
THE ABSENT VOICE IN THE WHATSAPP GROUP.
NITA KAPOOR.
WHAT IS THIS? THE FOURTH NO-SHOW? THE FIFTH? GIVE IT UP.
ARE YOU WONDERING WHAT HAPPENED TO YOUR QUEEN?
THE HEAD GIRLS PLAY A LONG GAME, AND LONDON IS OUR CITY.
WE ARE LEGION THERE.
NITA KAPOOR.
WELL, THAT WAS DISCONCERTING.
UM, ALSO, I WAS DEFINITELY OUR QUEEN.
NO OFFENSE.

# AS TIME GOES BY

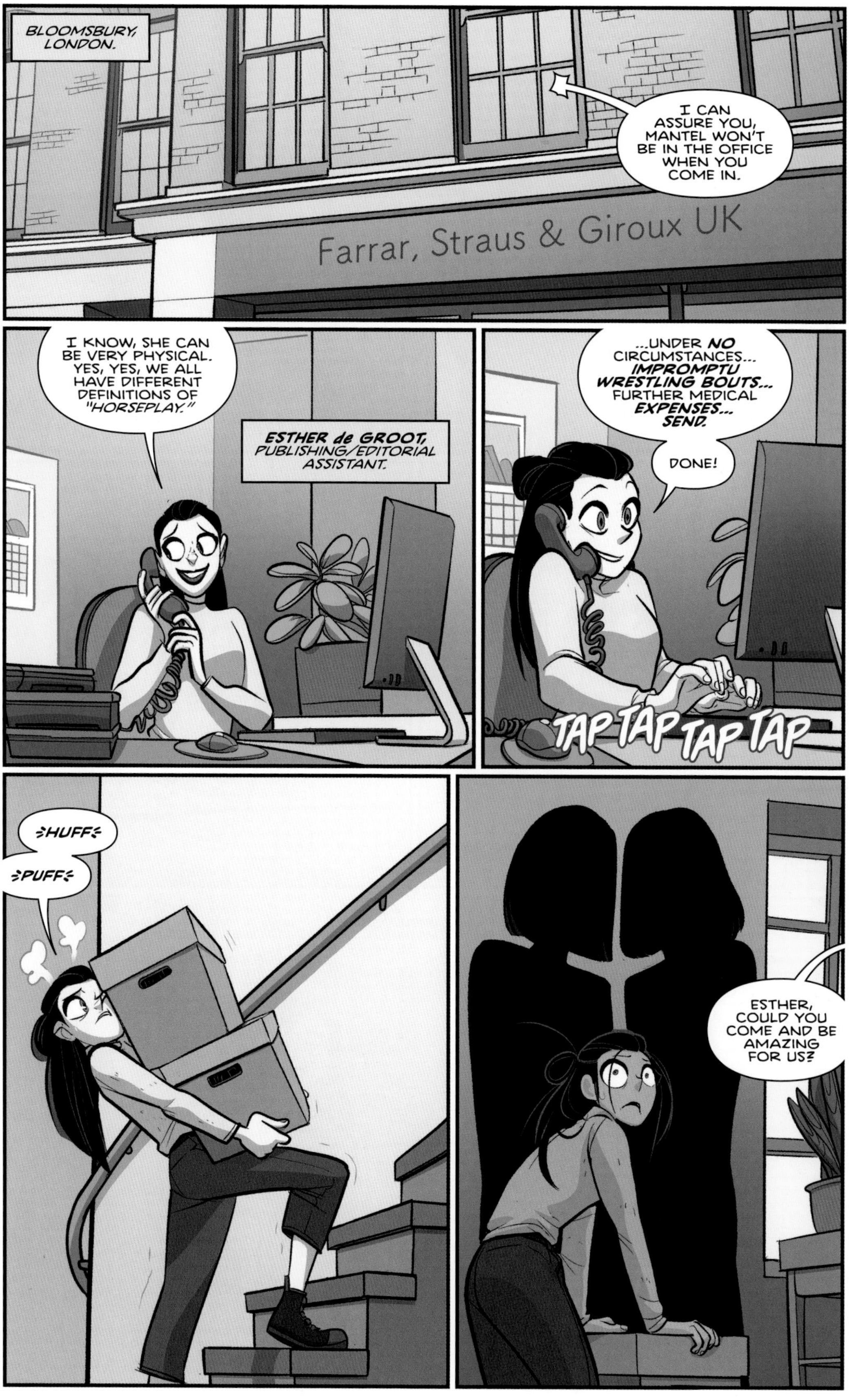
BLOOMSBURY, LONDON.
I CAN ASSURE YOU, MANTEL WON'T BE IN THE OFFICE WHEN YOU COME IN.
Farrar, Straus & Giroux UK
I KNOW, SHE CAN BE VERY PHYSICAL. YES, YES, WE ALL HAVE DIFFERENT DEFINITIONS OF "HORSEPLAY."
ESTHER de GROOT, PUBLISHING/EDITORIAL ASSISTANT.
...UNDER NO CIRCUMSTANCES... IMPROMPTU WRESTLING BOUTS... FURTHER MEDICAL EXPENSES... SEND.
DONE!
TAP TAP TAP TAP
HUFF
PUFF
ESTHER, COULD YOU COME AND BE AMAZING FOR US?

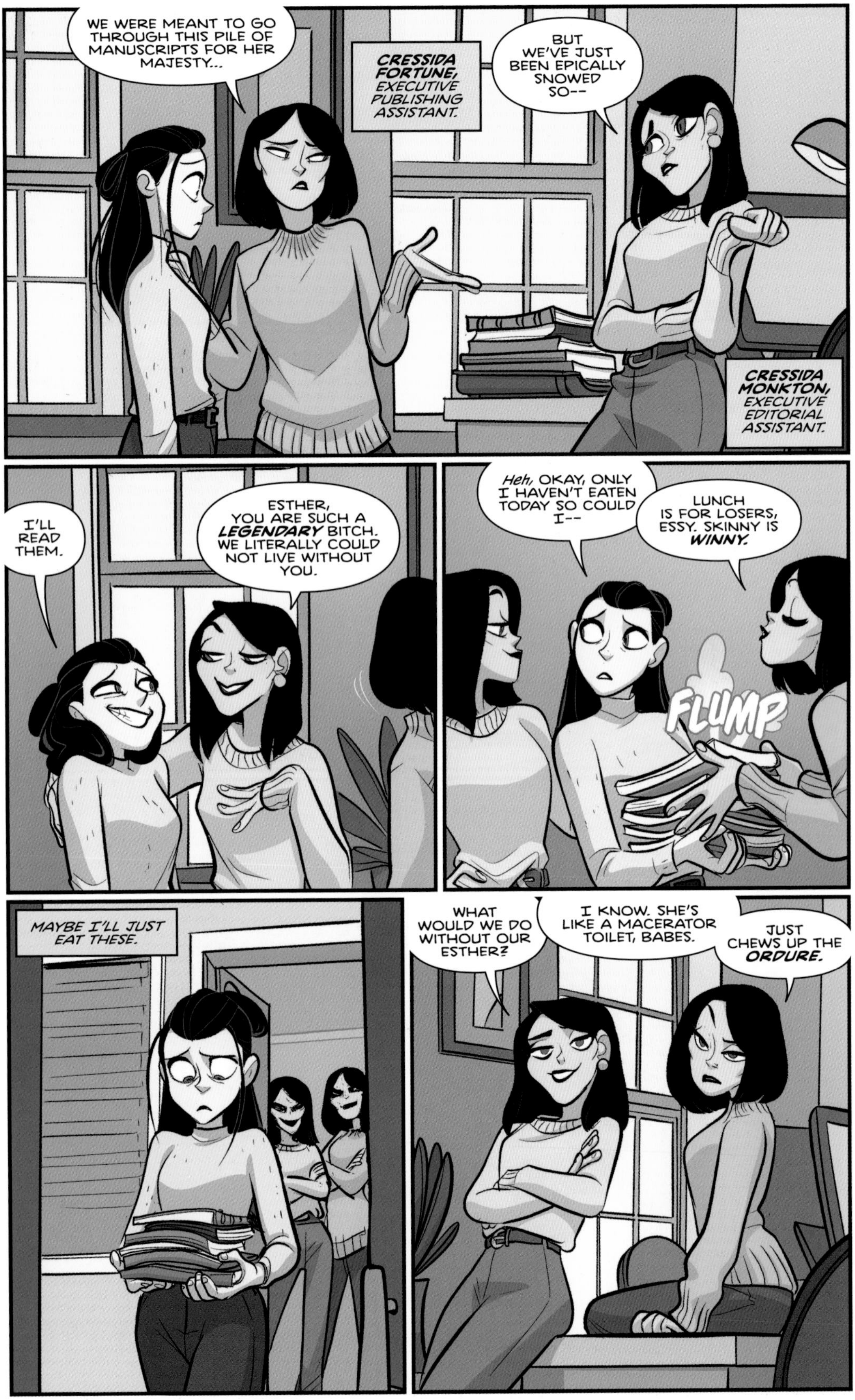
WE WERE MEANT TO GO THROUGH THIS PILE OF MANUSCRIPTS FOR HER MAJESTY...
CRESSIDA FORTUNE, EXECUTIVE PUBLISHING ASSISTANT.
BUT WE'VE JUST BEEN EPICALLY SNOWED SO--
CRESSIDA MONKTON, EXECUTIVE EDITORIAL ASSISTANT.
I'LL READ THEM.
ESTHER, YOU ARE SUCH A LEGENDARY BITCH. WE LITERALLY COULD NOT LIVE WITHOUT YOU.
Heh, OKAY, ONLY I HAVEN'T EATEN TODAY SO COULD I--
LUNCH IS FOR LOSERS, ESSY. SKINNY IS WINNY.
FLUMP
MAYBE I'LL JUST EAT THESE.
WHAT WOULD WE DO WITHOUT OUR ESTHER?
I KNOW. SHE'S LIKE A MACERATOR TOILET, BABES.
JUST CHEWS UP THE ORDURE.

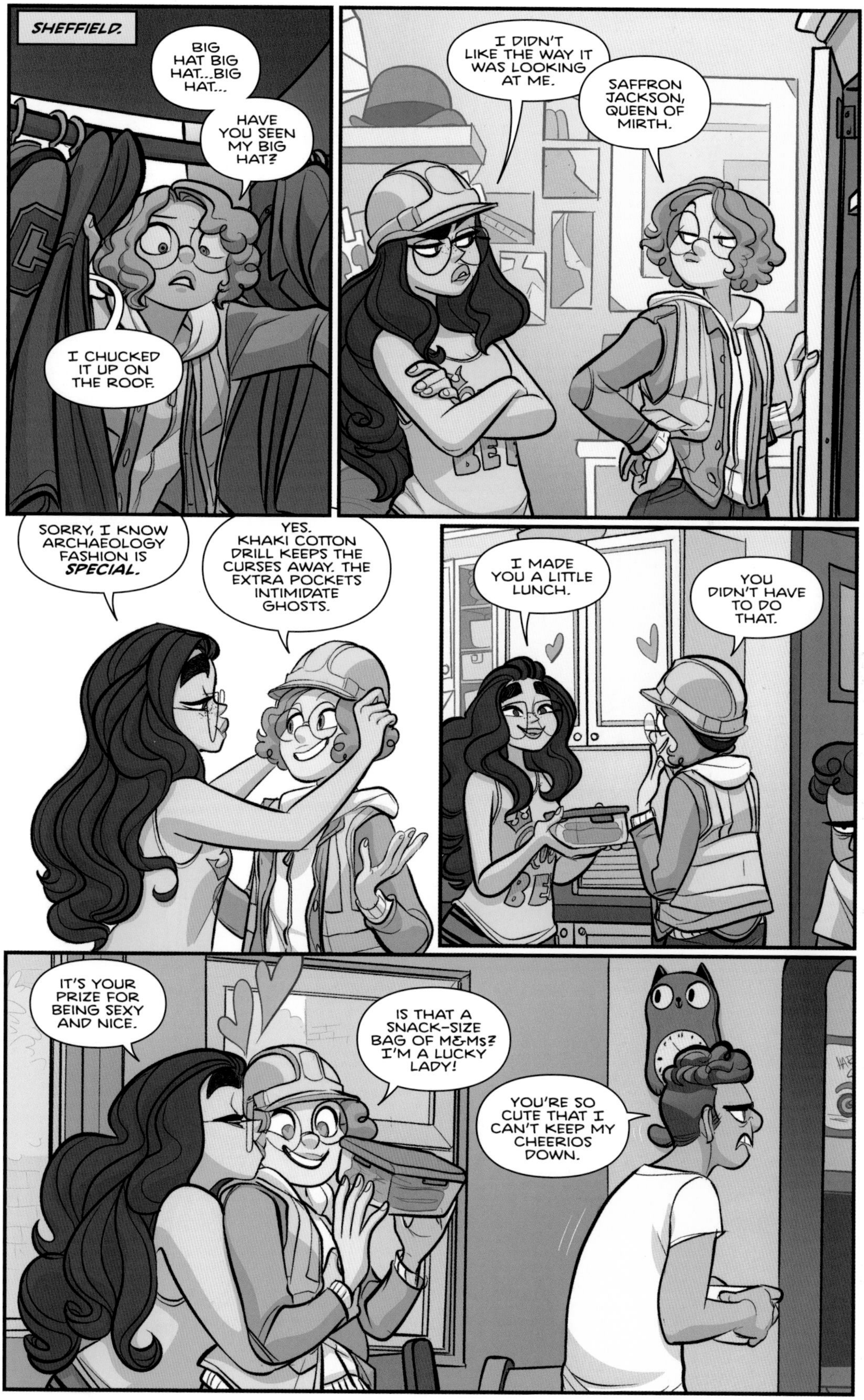
SHEFFIELD.
BIG HAT BIG HAT... BIG HAT...
HAVE YOU SEEN MY BIG HAT?
I CHUCKED IT UP ON THE ROOF.
I DIDN'T LIKE THE WAY IT WAS LOOKING AT ME.
SAFFRON JACKSON, QUEEN OF MIRTH.
SORRY, I KNOW ARCHAEOLOGY FASHION IS *SPECIAL.*
YES. KHAKI COTTON DRILL KEEPS THE CURSES AWAY. THE EXTRA POCKETS INTIMIDATE GHOSTS.
I MADE YOU A LITTLE LUNCH.
YOU DIDN'T HAVE TO DO THAT.
IT'S YOUR PRIZE FOR BEING SEXY AND NICE.
IS THAT A SNACK-SIZE BAG OF M&Ms? I'M A LUCKY LADY!
YOU'RE SO CUTE THAT I CAN'T KEEP MY CHEERIOS DOWN.

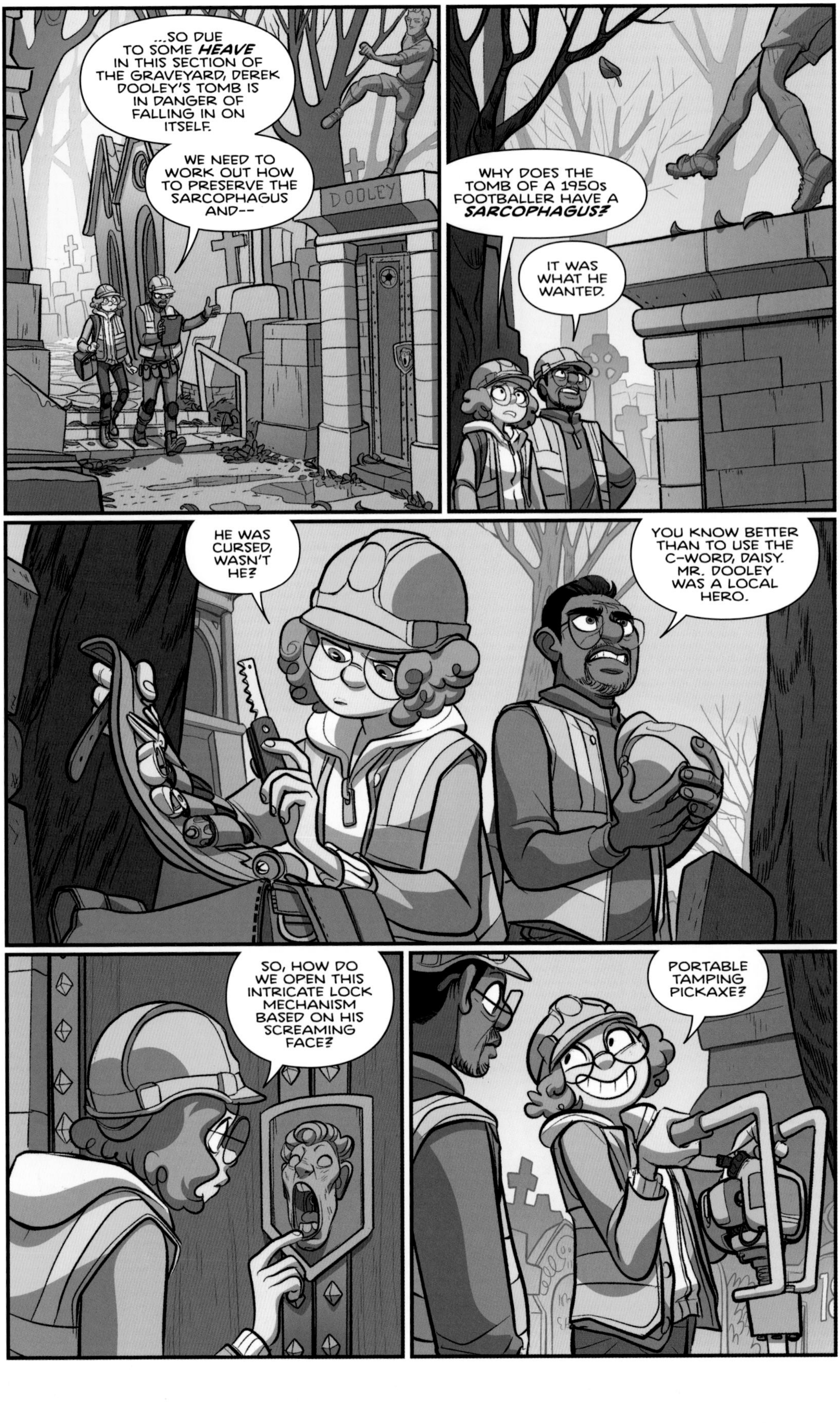
...SO DUE TO SOME *HEAVE* IN THIS SECTION OF THE GRAVEYARD, DEREK DOOLEY'S TOMB IS IN DANGER OF FALLING IN ON ITSELF.
WE NEED TO WORK OUT HOW TO PRESERVE THE SARCOPHAGUS AND--
DOOLEY
WHY DOES THE TOMB OF A 1950s FOOTBALLER HAVE A ***SARCOPHAGUS?***
IT WAS WHAT HE WANTED.
HE WAS CURSED, WASN'T HE?
YOU KNOW BETTER THAN TO USE THE C-WORD, DAISY. MR. DOOLEY WAS A LOCAL HERO.
SO, HOW DO WE OPEN THIS INTRICATE LOCK MECHANISM BASED ON HIS SCREAMING FACE?
PORTABLE TAMPING PICKAXE?

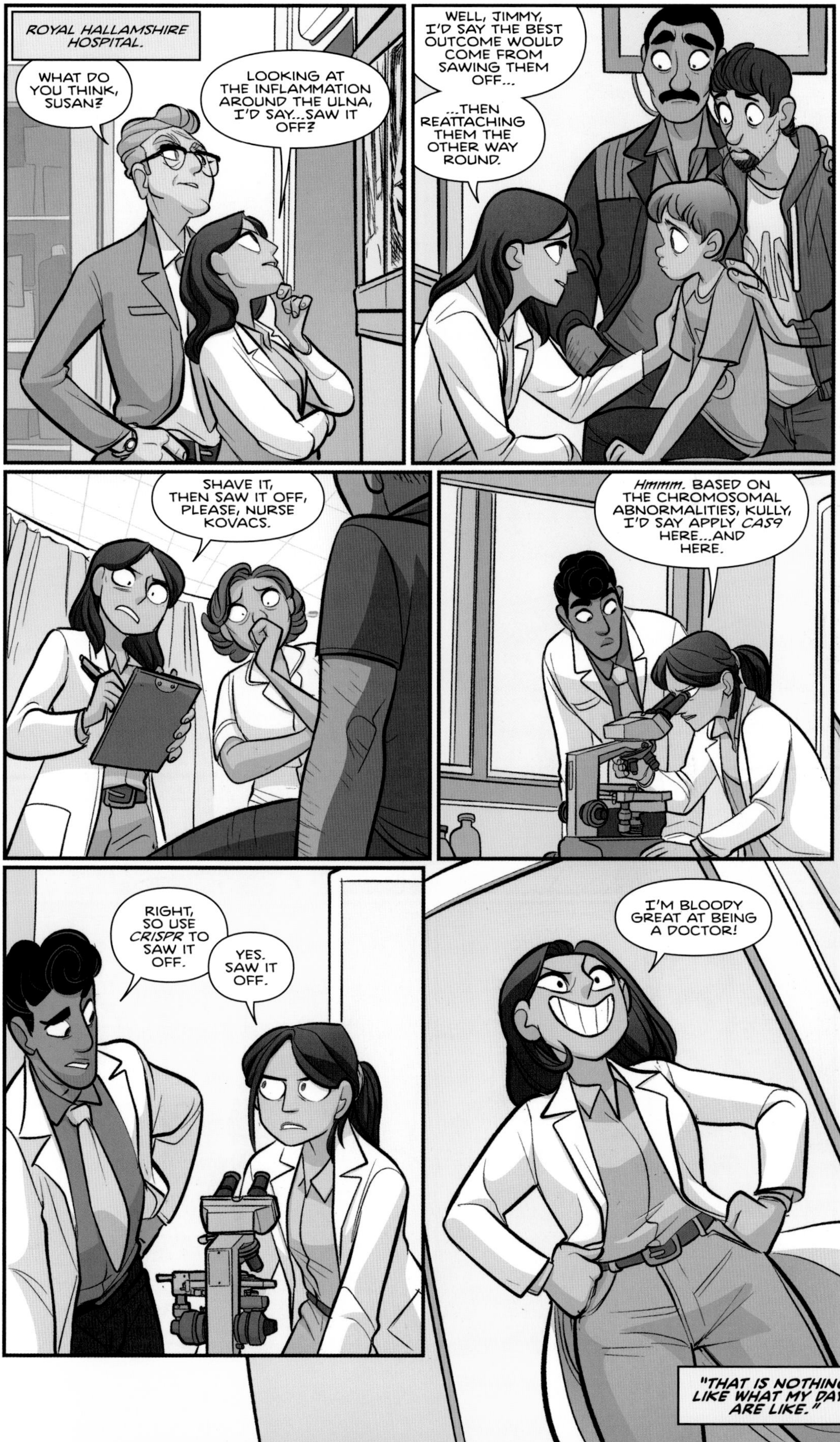
ROYAL HALLAMSHIRE HOSPITAL.
WHAT DO YOU THINK, SUSAN?
LOOKING AT THE INFLAMMATION AROUND THE ULNA, I'D SAY...SAW IT OFF?
WELL, JIMMY, I'D SAY THE BEST OUTCOME WOULD COME FROM SAWING THEM OFF...
...THEN REATTACHING THEM THE OTHER WAY ROUND.
SHAVE IT, THEN SAW IT OFF, PLEASE, NURSE KOVACS.
*Hmmm.* BASED ON THE CHROMOSOMAL ABNORMALITIES, KULLY, I'D SAY APPLY *CAS9* HERE...AND HERE.
RIGHT, SO USE *CRISPR* TO SAW IT OFF.
YES. SAW IT OFF.
I'M BLOODY GREAT AT BEING A DOCTOR!
"THAT IS NOTHING LIKE WHAT MY DAYS ARE LIKE."

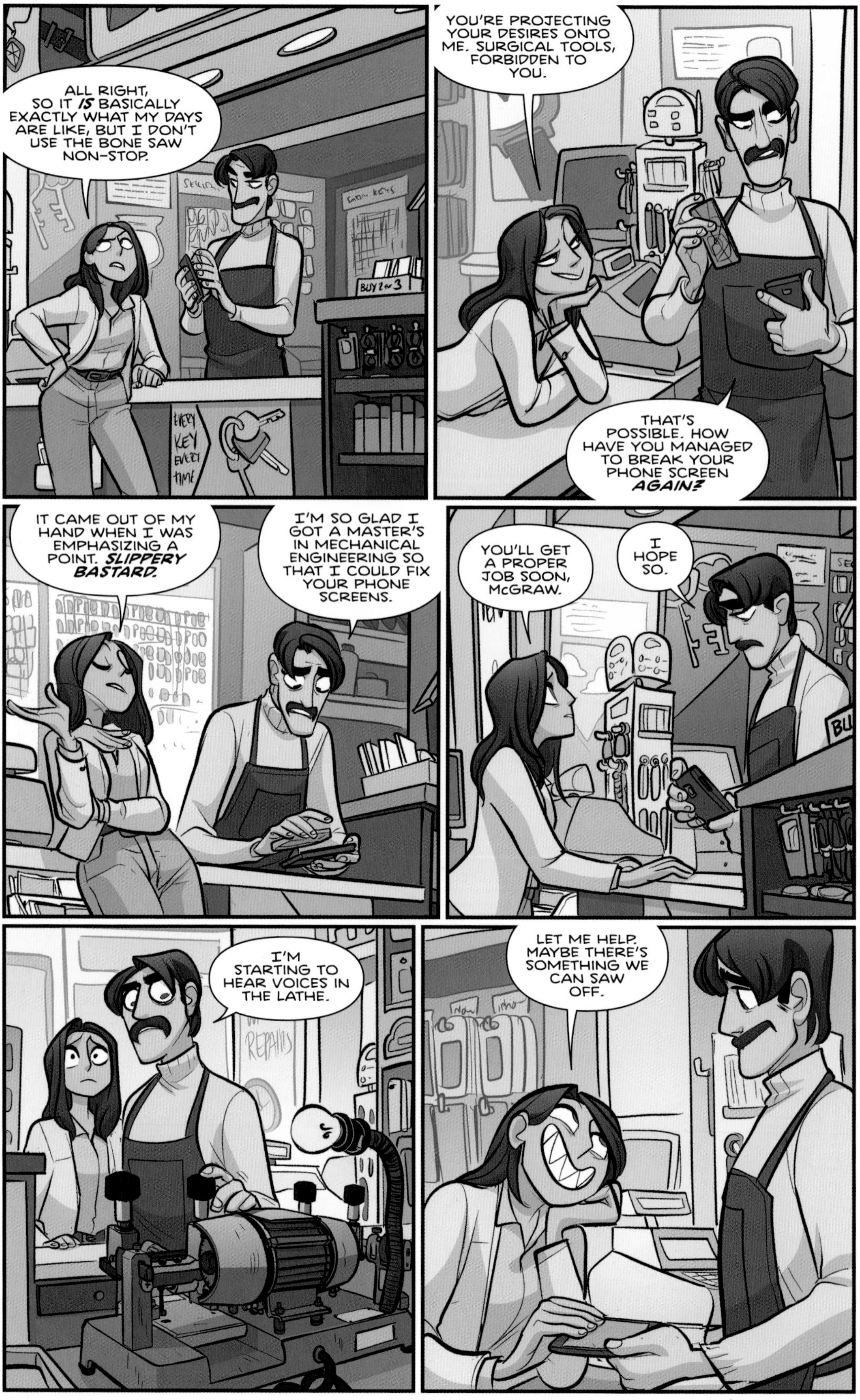
ALL RIGHT, SO IT *IS* BASICALLY EXACTLY WHAT MY DAYS ARE LIKE, BUT I DON'T USE THE BONE SAW NON-STOP.
YOU'RE PROJECTING YOUR DESIRES ONTO ME. SURGICAL TOOLS, FORBIDDEN TO YOU.
THAT'S POSSIBLE. HOW HAVE YOU MANAGED TO BREAK YOUR PHONE SCREEN ***AGAIN?***
IT CAME OUT OF MY HAND WHEN I WAS EMPHASIZING A POINT. ***SLIPPERY BASTARD.***
I'M SO GLAD I GOT A MASTER'S IN MECHANICAL ENGINEERING SO THAT I COULD FIX YOUR PHONE SCREENS.
YOU'LL GET A PROPER JOB SOON, McGRAW.
I HOPE SO.
I'M STARTING TO HEAR VOICES IN THE LATHE.
LET ME HELP. MAYBE THERE'S SOMETHING WE CAN SAW OFF.

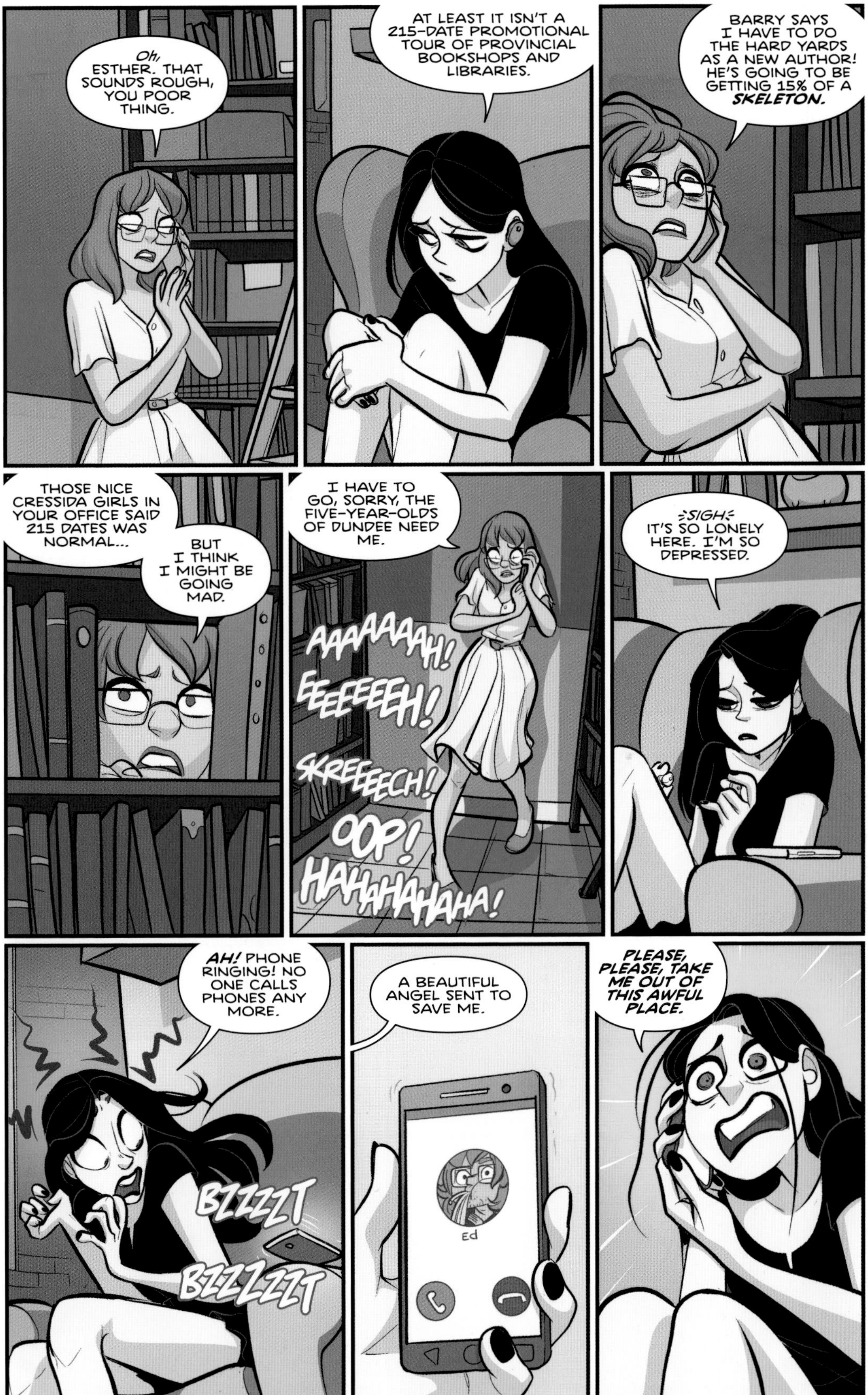

Oh, ESTHER. THAT SOUNDS ROUGH, YOU POOR THING.
AT LEAST IT ISN'T A 215-DATE PROMOTIONAL TOUR OF PROVINCIAL BOOKSHOPS AND LIBRARIES.
BARRY SAYS I HAVE TO DO THE HARD YARDS AS A NEW AUTHOR! HE'S GOING TO BE GETTING 15% OF A SKELETON.
THOSE NICE CRESSIDA GIRLS IN YOUR OFFICE SAID 215 DATES WAS NORMAL...
BUT I THINK I MIGHT BE GOING MAD.
I HAVE TO GO, SORRY, THE FIVE-YEAR-OLDS OF DUNDEE NEED ME.
AAAAAAAH!
EEEEEEEH!
SKREEEEECH!
OOP!
HAHAHAHAHAHA!
SIGH
IT'S SO LONELY HERE. I'M SO DEPRESSED.
AH! PHONE RINGING! NO ONE CALLS PHONES ANY MORE.
BZZZZT
BZZZZZT
A BEAUTIFUL ANGEL SENT TO SAVE ME.
Ed
PLEASE, PLEASE, TAKE ME OUT OF THIS AWFUL PLACE.

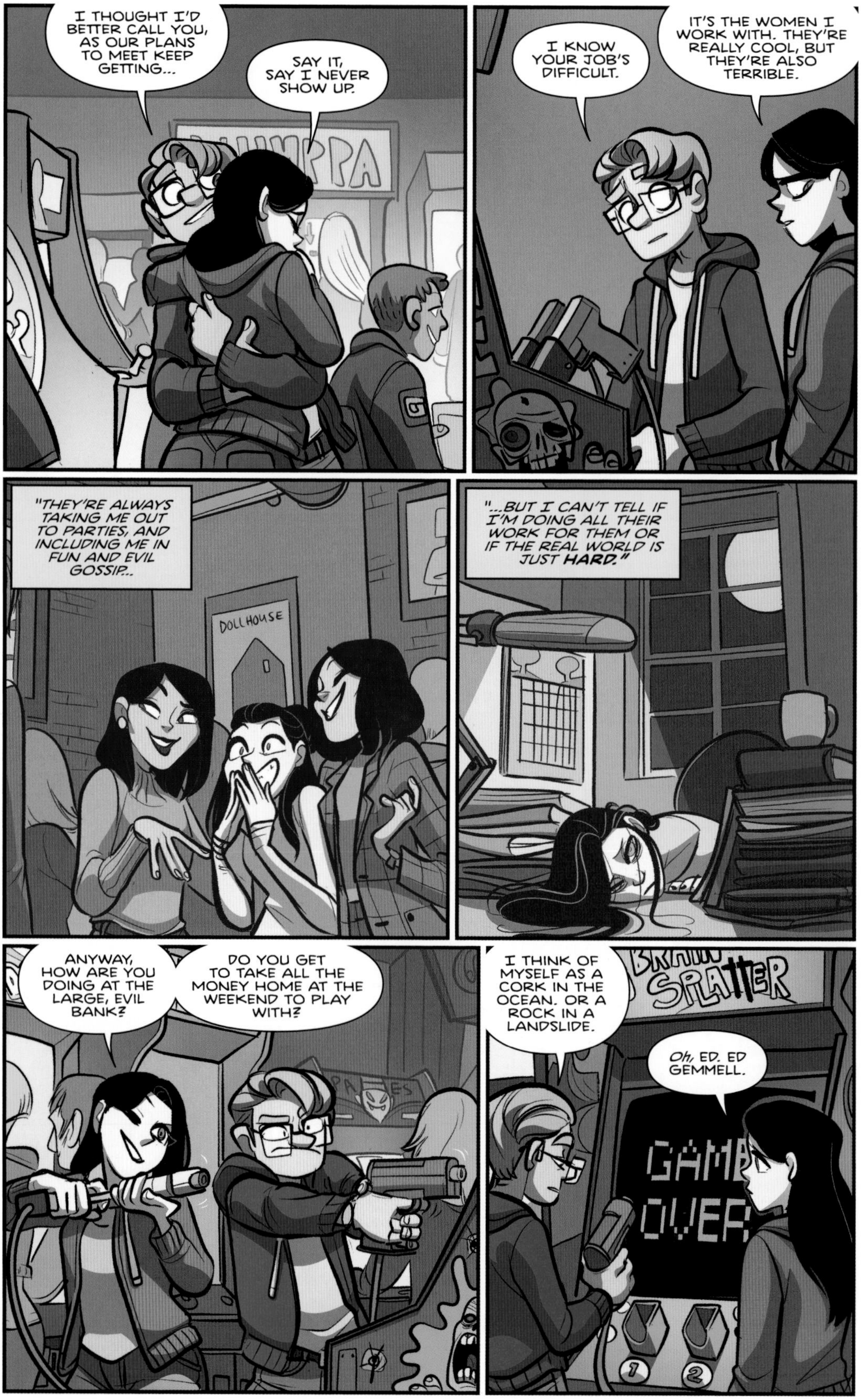
I THOUGHT I'D BETTER CALL YOU, AS OUR PLANS TO MEET KEEP GETTING...
SAY IT, SAY I NEVER SHOW UP.
I KNOW YOUR JOB'S DIFFICULT.
IT'S THE WOMEN I WORK WITH. THEY'RE REALLY COOL, BUT THEY'RE ALSO TERRIBLE.
"THEY'RE ALWAYS TAKING ME OUT TO PARTIES, AND INCLUDING ME IN FUN AND EVIL GOSSIP...
DOLLHOUSE
"...BUT I CAN'T TELL IF I'M DOING ALL THEIR WORK FOR THEM OR IF THE REAL WORLD IS JUST **HARD.**"
ANYWAY, HOW ARE YOU DOING AT THE LARGE, EVIL BANK?
DO YOU GET TO TAKE ALL THE MONEY HOME AT THE WEEKEND TO PLAY WITH?
SPLATTER
I THINK OF MYSELF AS A CORK IN THE OCEAN. OR A ROCK IN A LANDSLIDE.
*Oh,* ED. ED GEMMELL.

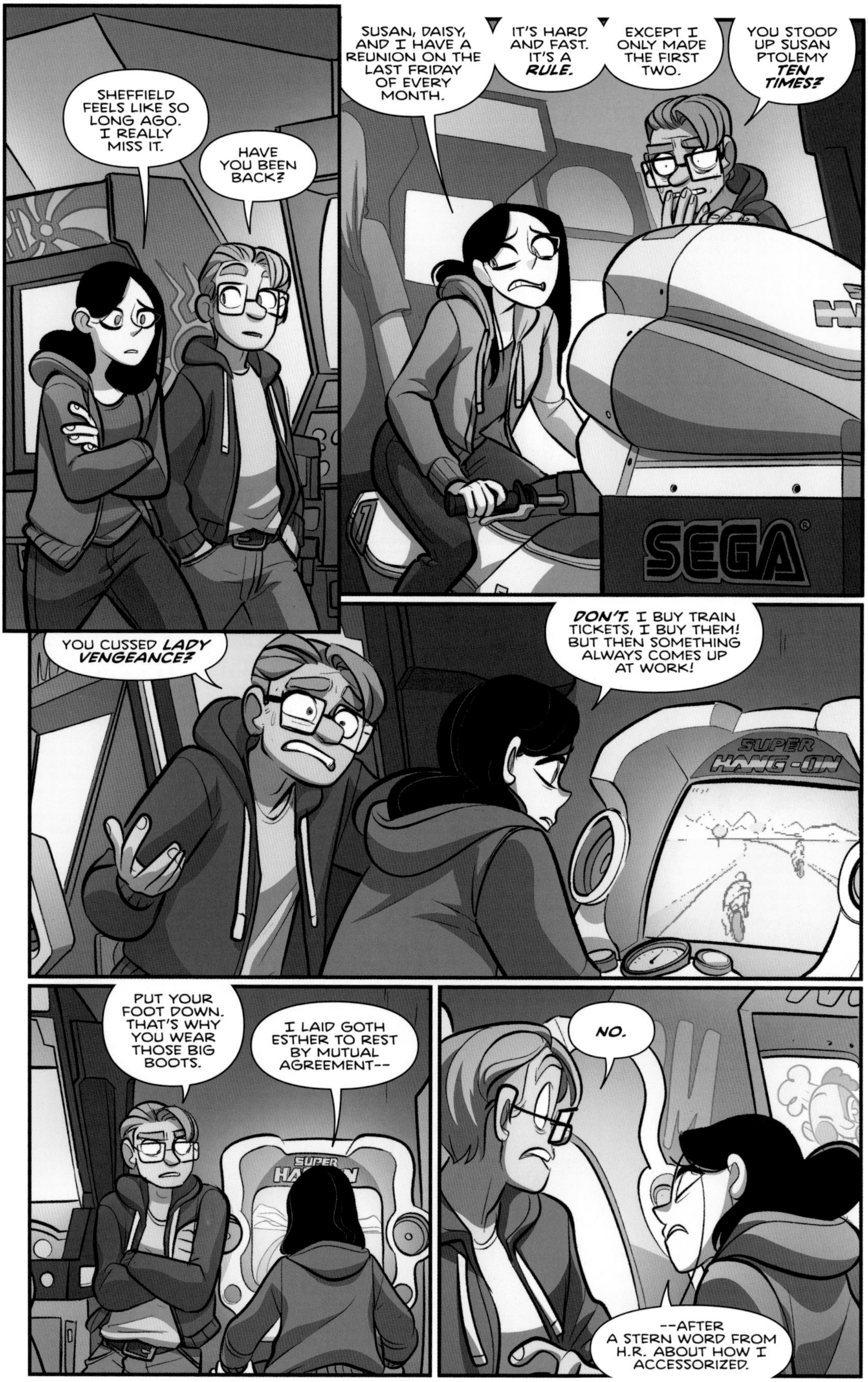
SHEFFIELD FEELS LIKE SO LONG AGO. I REALLY MISS IT.
HAVE YOU BEEN BACK?
SUSAN, DAISY, AND I HAVE A REUNION ON THE LAST FRIDAY OF EVERY MONTH.
IT'S HARD AND FAST. IT'S A *RULE.*
EXCEPT I ONLY MADE THE FIRST TWO.
YOU STOOD UP SUSAN PTOLEMY *TEN TIMES?*
SEGA
YOU CUSSED *LADY VENGEANCE?*
*DON'T.* I BUY TRAIN TICKETS, I BUY THEM! BUT THEN SOMETHING ALWAYS COMES UP AT WORK!
SUPER HANG-ON
PUT YOUR FOOT DOWN. THAT'S WHY YOU WEAR THOSE BIG BOOTS.
I LAID GOTH ESTHER TO REST BY MUTUAL AGREEMENT--
*NO.*
--AFTER A STERN WORD FROM H.R. ABOUT HOW I ACCESSORIZED.

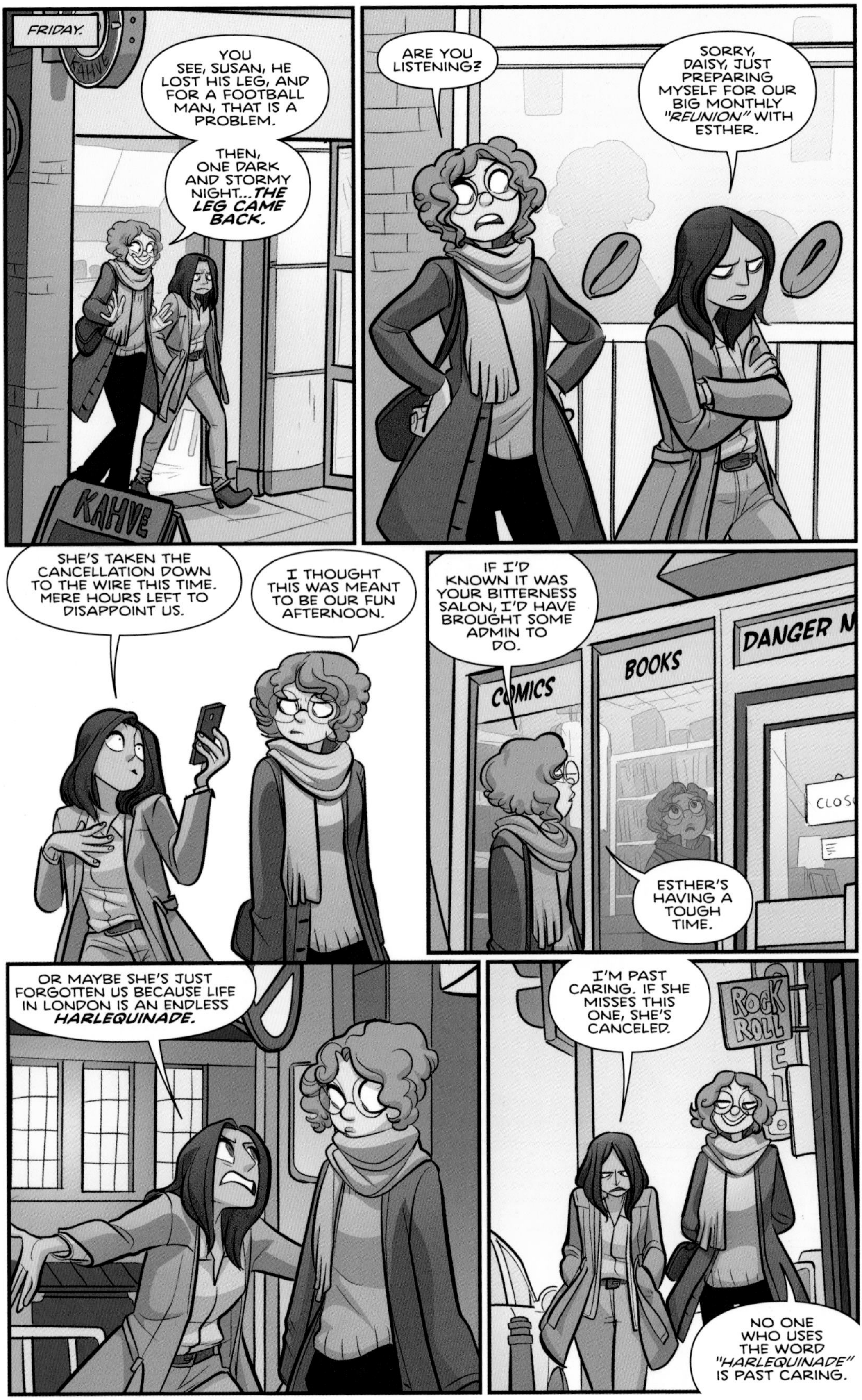
FRIDAY.
KAHVE
YOU SEE, SUSAN, HE LOST HIS LEG, AND FOR A FOOTBALL MAN, THAT IS A PROBLEM.
THEN, ONE DARK AND STORMY NIGHT... THE LEG CAME BACK.
KAHVE
ARE YOU LISTENING?
SORRY, DAISY, JUST PREPARING MYSELF FOR OUR BIG MONTHLY "REUNION" WITH ESTHER.
SHE'S TAKEN THE CANCELLATION DOWN TO THE WIRE THIS TIME. MERE HOURS LEFT TO DISAPPOINT US.
I THOUGHT THIS WAS MEANT TO BE OUR FUN AFTERNOON.
IF I'D KNOWN IT WAS YOUR BITTERNESS SALON, I'D HAVE BROUGHT SOME ADMIN TO DO.
COMICS
BOOKS
DANGER M
ESTHER'S HAVING A TOUGH TIME.
OR MAYBE SHE'S JUST FORGOTTEN US BECAUSE LIFE IN LONDON IS AN ENDLESS HARLEQUINADE.
I'M PAST CARING. IF SHE MISSES THIS ONE, SHE'S CANCELED.
ROCK ROLL
NO ONE WHO USES THE WORD "HARLEQUINADE" IS PAST CARING.

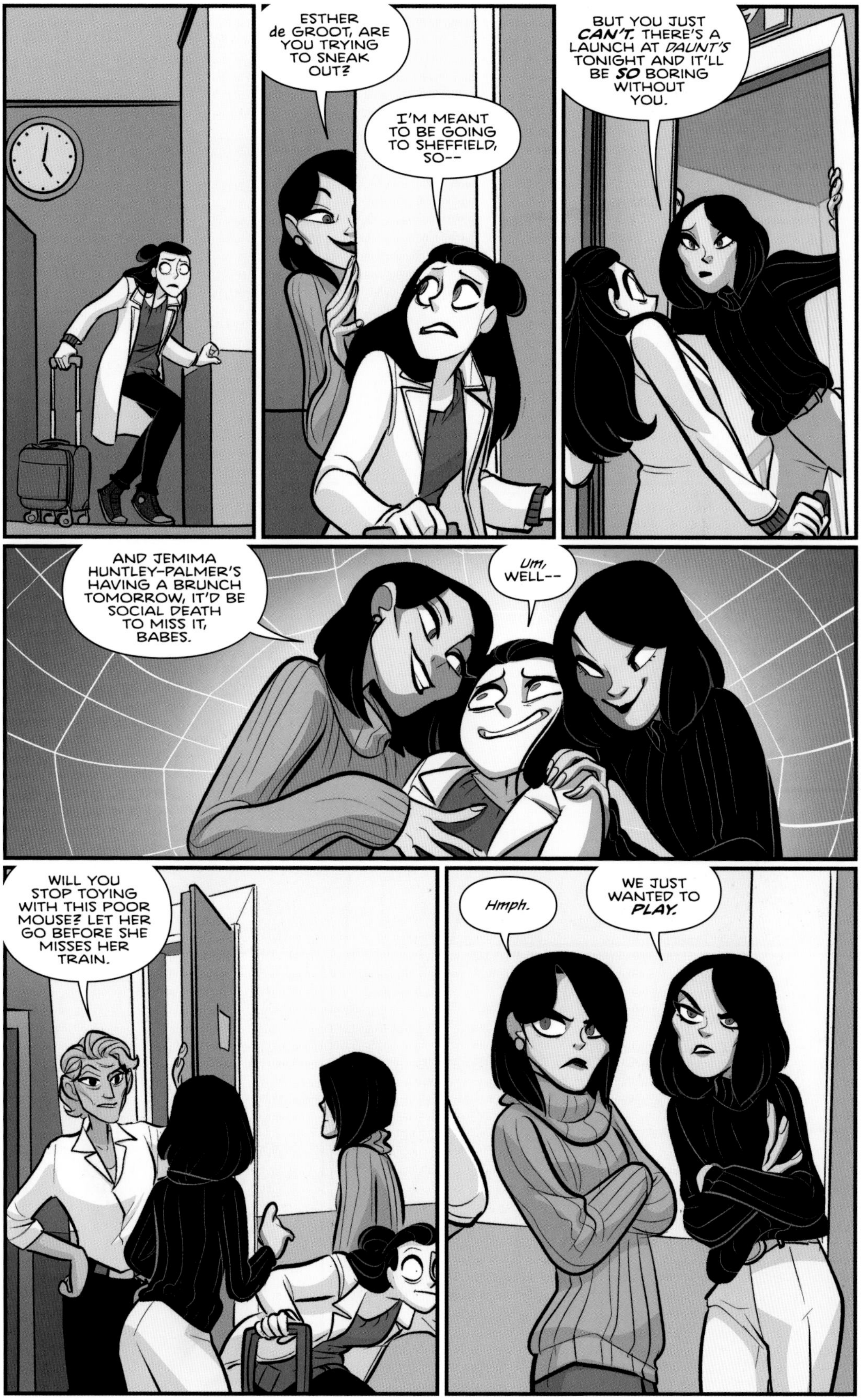
ESTHER de GROOT, ARE YOU TRYING TO SNEAK OUT?
I'M MEANT TO BE GOING TO SHEFFIELD, SO--
BUT YOU JUST *CAN'T.* THERE'S A LAUNCH AT *DAUNT'S* TONIGHT AND IT'LL BE *SO* BORING WITHOUT YOU.
AND JEMIMA HUNTLEY-PALMER'S HAVING A BRUNCH TOMORROW, IT'D BE SOCIAL DEATH TO MISS IT, BABES.
*Um,* WELL--
WILL YOU STOP TOYING WITH THIS POOR MOUSE? LET HER GO BEFORE SHE MISSES HER TRAIN.
*Hmph.*
WE JUST WANTED TO *PLAY.*

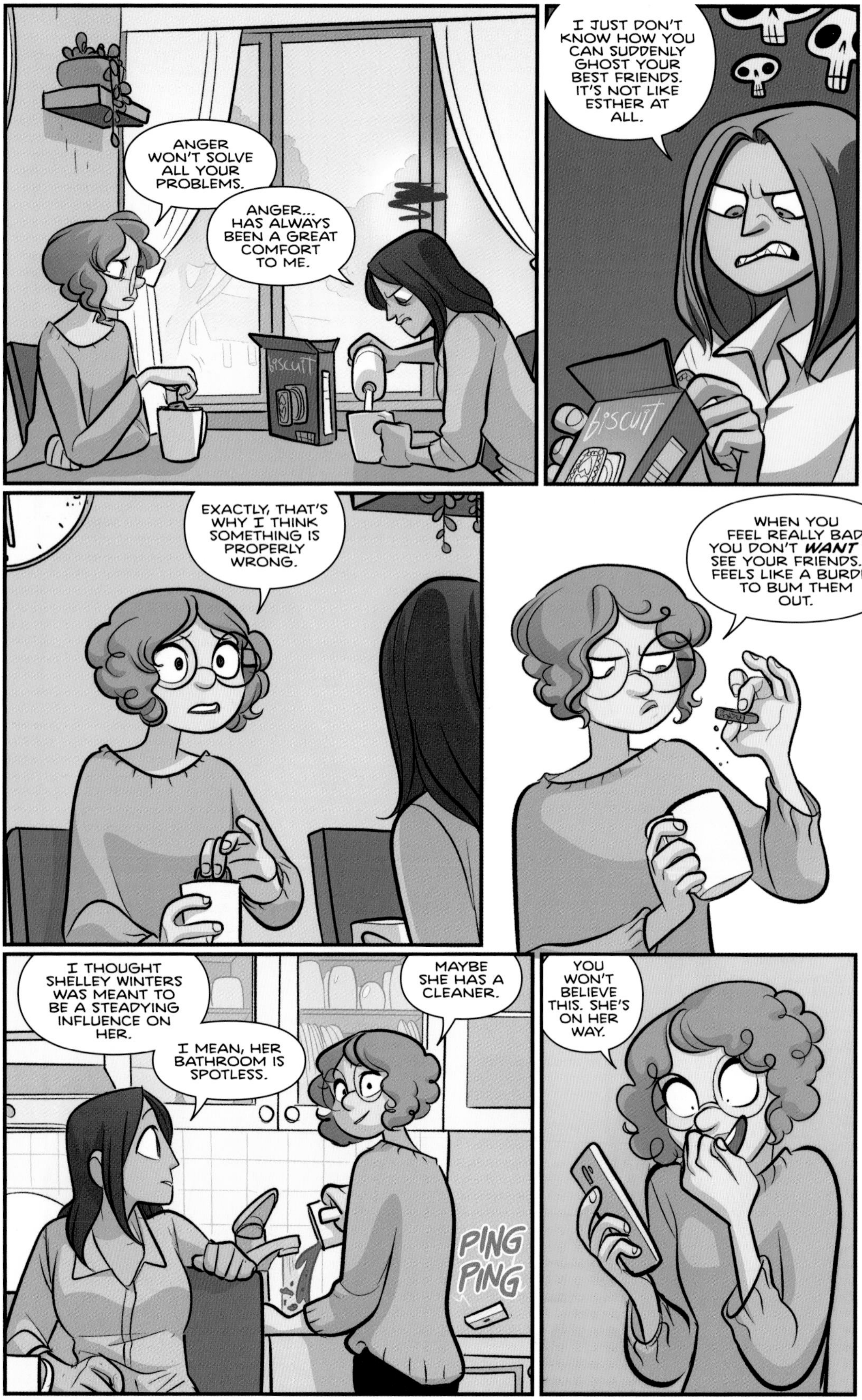
ANGER WON'T SOLVE ALL YOUR PROBLEMS.
ANGER... HAS ALWAYS BEEN A GREAT COMFORT TO ME.
biscuit
I JUST DON'T KNOW HOW YOU CAN SUDDENLY GHOST YOUR BEST FRIENDS. IT'S NOT LIKE ESTHER AT ALL.
biscuit
EXACTLY, THAT'S WHY I THINK SOMETHING IS PROPERLY WRONG.
WHEN YOU FEEL REALLY BAD, YOU DON'T **WANT** TO SEE YOUR FRIENDS. IT FEELS LIKE A BURDEN TO BUM THEM OUT.
I THOUGHT SHELLEY WINTERS WAS MEANT TO BE A STEADYING INFLUENCE ON HER.
I MEAN, HER BATHROOM IS SPOTLESS.
MAYBE SHE HAS A CLEANER.
PING PING
YOU WON'T BELIEVE THIS. SHE'S ON HER WAY.

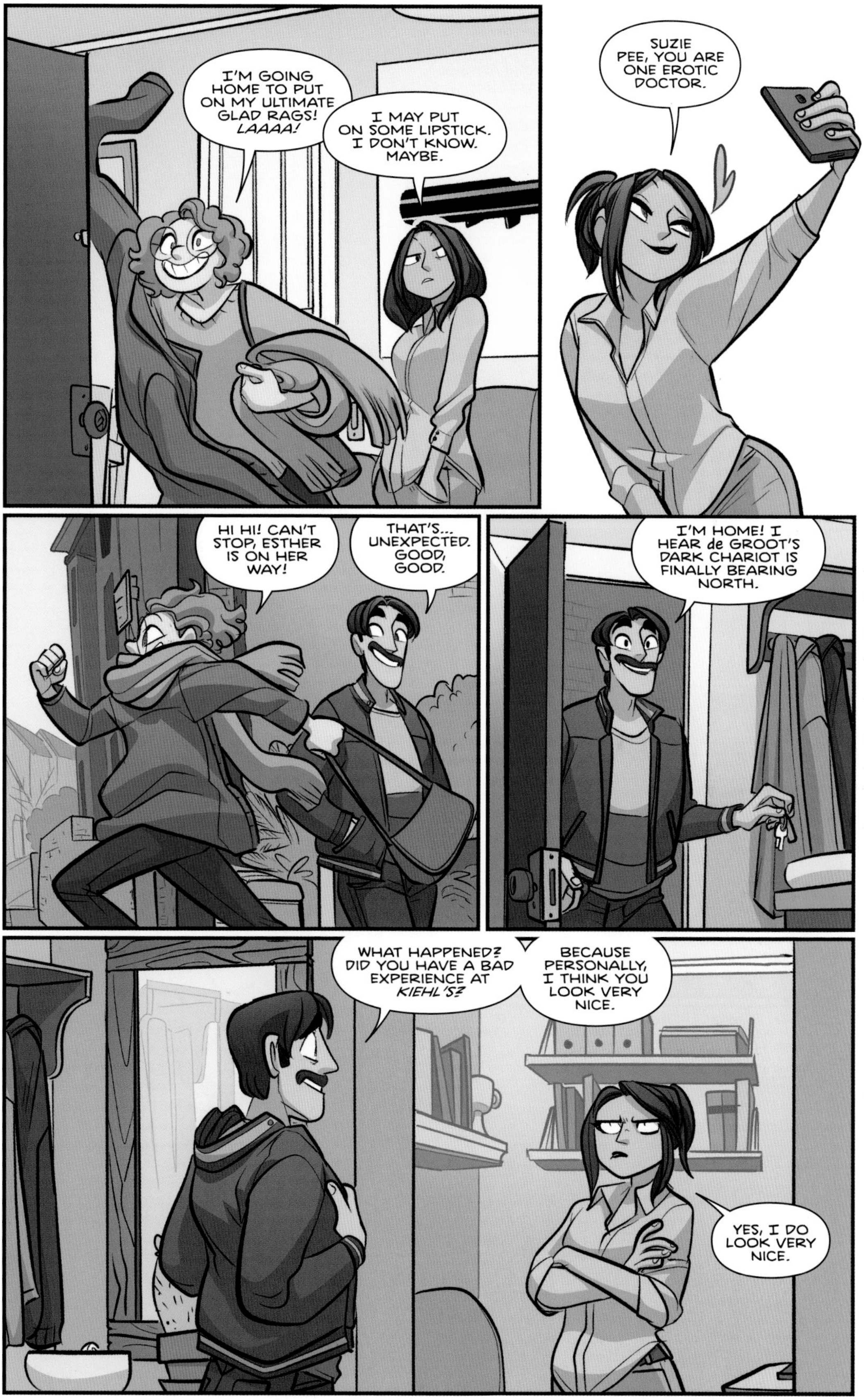
I'M GOING HOME TO PUT ON MY ULTIMATE GLAD RAGS! LAAAA!
I MAY PUT ON SOME LIPSTICK. I DON'T KNOW. MAYBE.
SUZIE PEE, YOU ARE ONE EROTIC DOCTOR.
HI HI! CAN'T STOP, ESTHER IS ON HER WAY!
THAT'S... UNEXPECTED. GOOD, GOOD.
I'M HOME! I HEAR de GROOT'S DARK CHARIOT IS FINALLY BEARING NORTH.
WHAT HAPPENED? DID YOU HAVE A BAD EXPERIENCE AT KIEHL'S?
BECAUSE PERSONALLY, I THINK YOU LOOK VERY NICE.
YES, I DO LOOK VERY NICE.

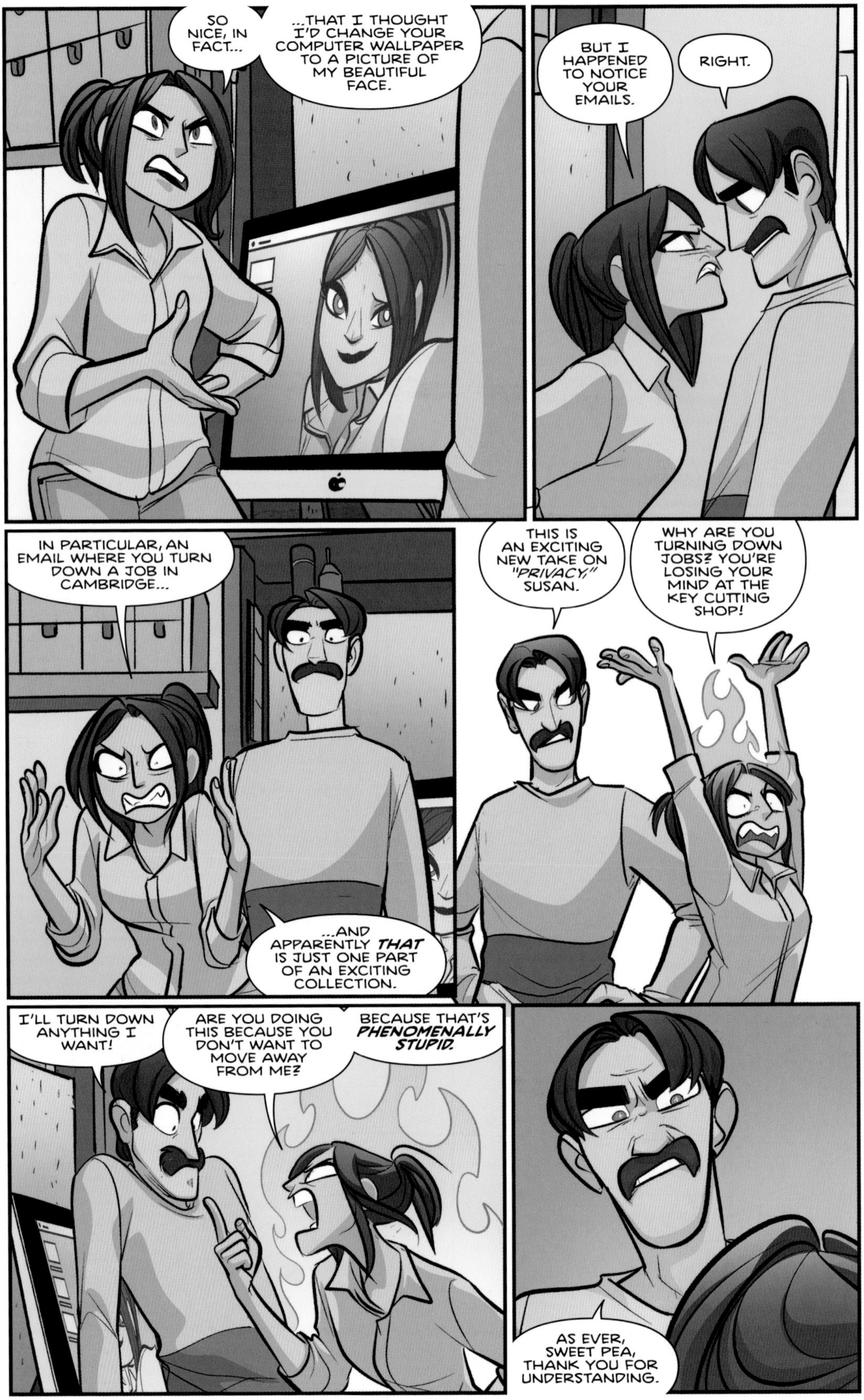
SO NICE, IN FACT...
...THAT I THOUGHT I'D CHANGE YOUR COMPUTER WALLPAPER TO A PICTURE OF MY BEAUTIFUL FACE.
BUT I HAPPENED TO NOTICE YOUR EMAILS.
RIGHT.
IN PARTICULAR, AN EMAIL WHERE YOU TURN DOWN A JOB IN CAMBRIDGE...
...AND APPARENTLY *THAT* IS JUST ONE PART OF AN EXCITING COLLECTION.
THIS IS AN EXCITING NEW TAKE ON *"PRIVACY,"* SUSAN.
WHY ARE YOU TURNING DOWN JOBS? YOU'RE LOSING YOUR MIND AT THE KEY CUTTING SHOP!
I'LL TURN DOWN ANYTHING I WANT!
ARE YOU DOING THIS BECAUSE YOU DON'T WANT TO MOVE AWAY FROM ME?
BECAUSE THAT'S ***PHENOMENALLY STUPID.***
AS EVER, SWEET PEA, THANK YOU FOR UNDERSTANDING.

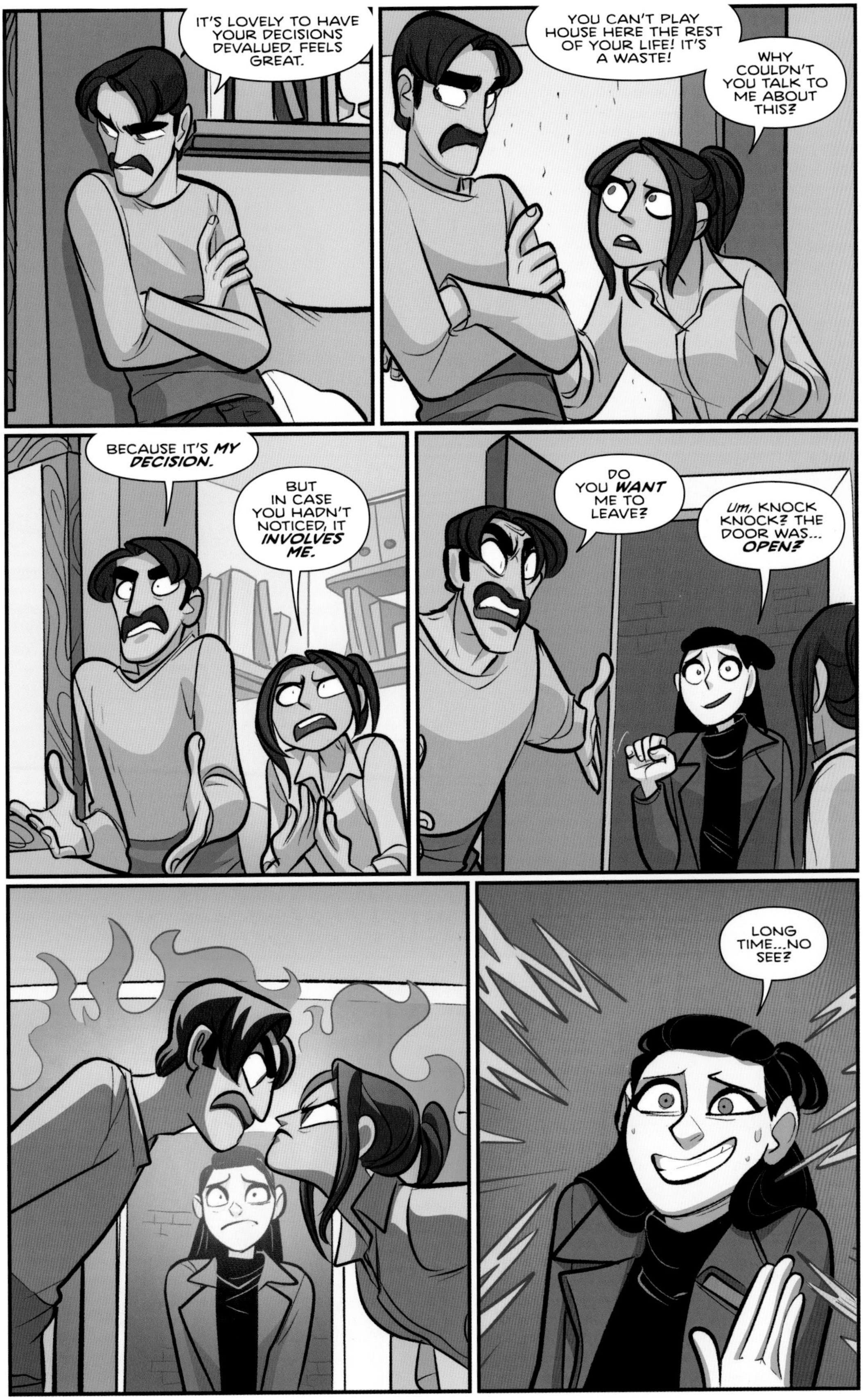
IT'S LOVELY TO HAVE YOUR DECISIONS DEVALUED. FEELS GREAT.
YOU CAN'T PLAY HOUSE HERE THE REST OF YOUR LIFE! IT'S A WASTE!
WHY COULDN'T YOU TALK TO ME ABOUT THIS?
BECAUSE IT'S *MY DECISION.*
BUT IN CASE YOU HADN'T NOTICED, IT *INVOLVES ME.*
DO YOU *WANT* ME TO LEAVE?
*Um,* KNOCK KNOCK? THE DOOR WAS... *OPEN?*
LONG TIME...NO SEE?

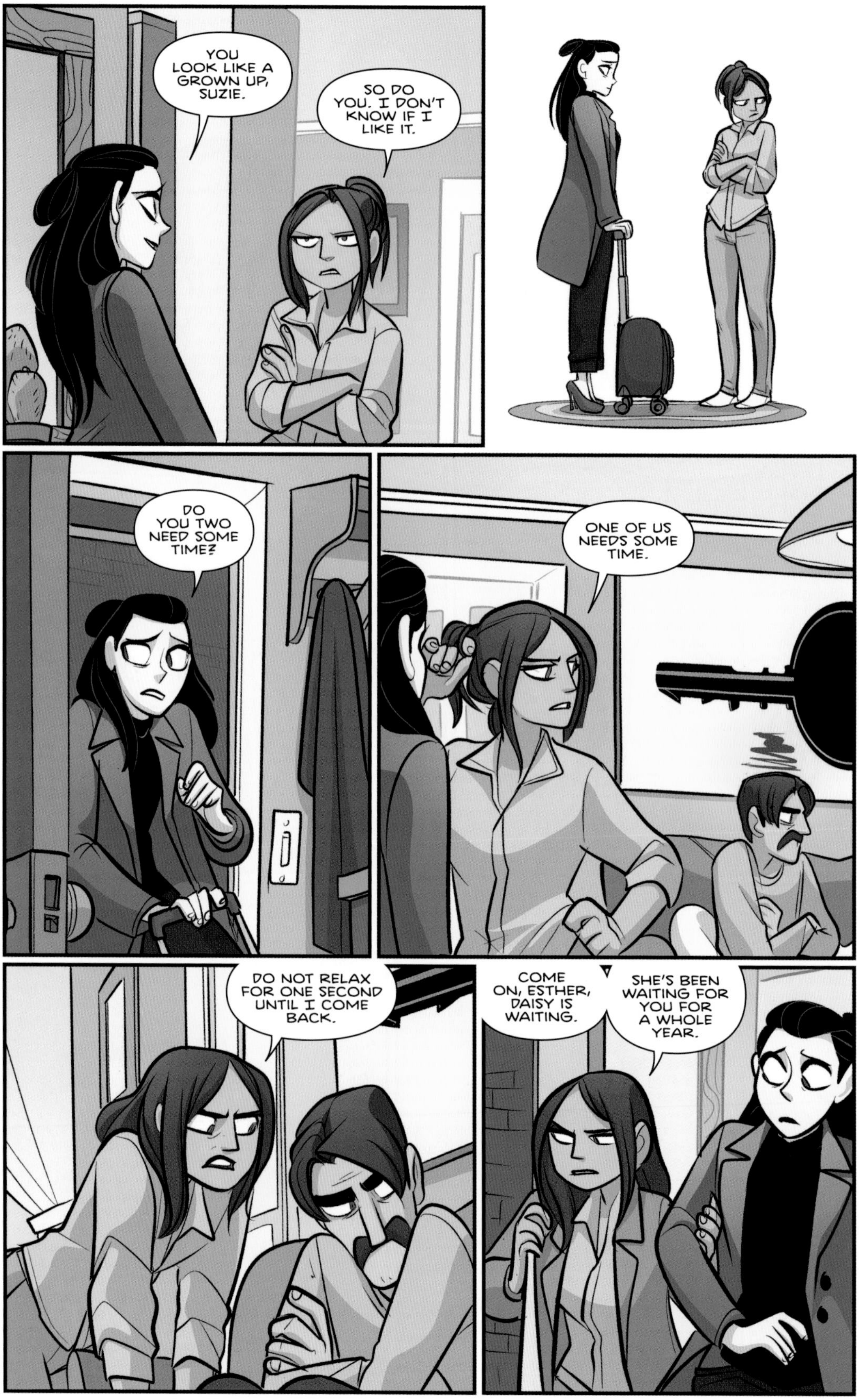
YOU LOOK LIKE A GROWN UP, SUZIE.
SO DO YOU. I DON'T KNOW IF I LIKE IT.
DO YOU TWO NEED SOME TIME?
ONE OF US NEEDS SOME TIME.
DO NOT RELAX FOR ONE SECOND UNTIL I COME BACK.
COME ON, ESTHER, DAISY IS WAITING.
SHE'S BEEN WAITING FOR YOU FOR A WHOLE YEAR.

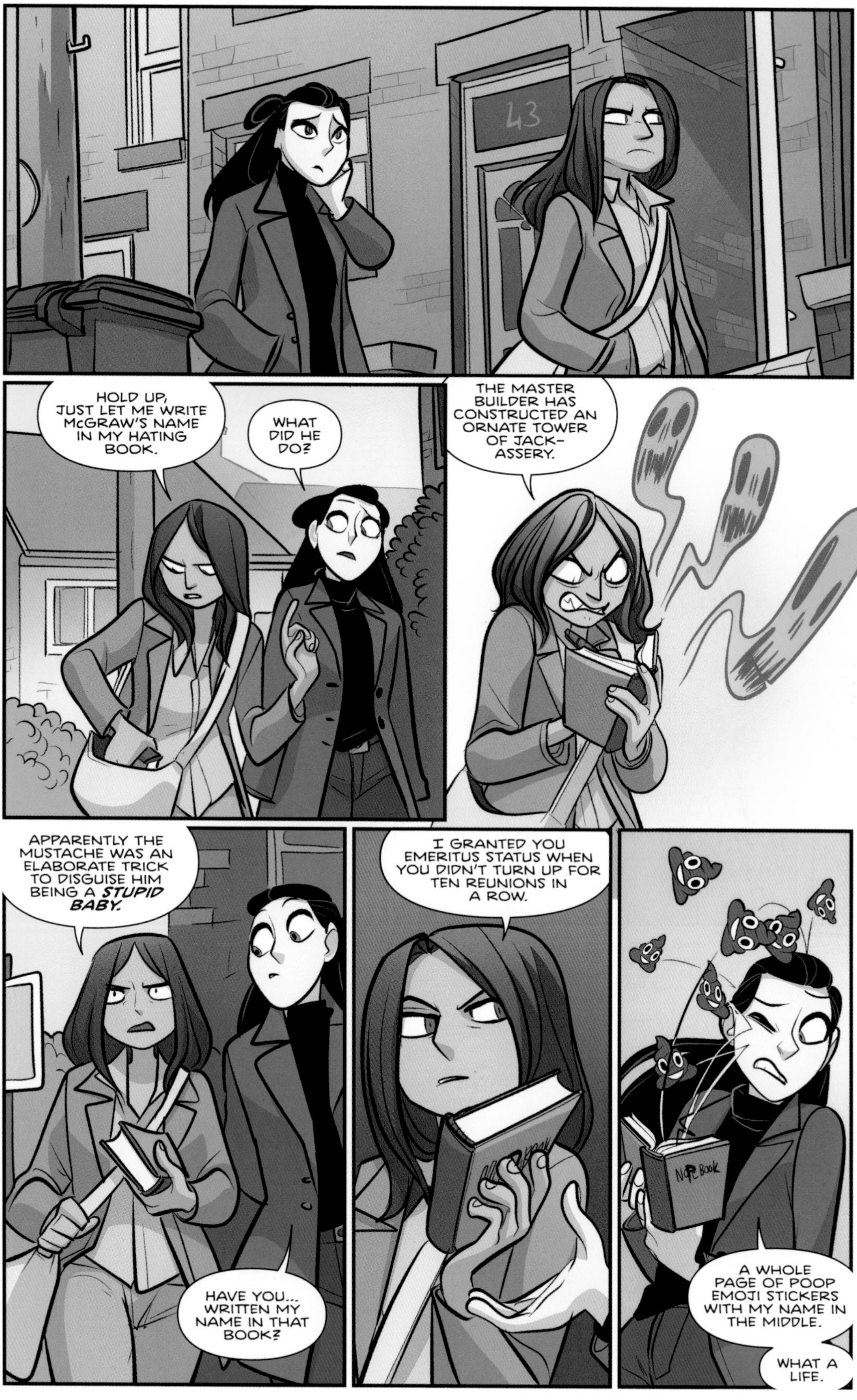
HOLD UP, JUST LET ME WRITE McGRAW'S NAME IN MY HATING BOOK.
WHAT DID HE DO?
THE MASTER BUILDER HAS CONSTRUCTED AN ORNATE TOWER OF JACK-ASSERY.
APPARENTLY THE MUSTACHE WAS AN ELABORATE TRICK TO DISGUISE HIM BEING A *STUPID BABY.*
HAVE YOU... WRITTEN MY NAME IN THAT BOOK?
I GRANTED YOU EMERITUS STATUS WHEN YOU DIDN'T TURN UP FOR TEN REUNIONS IN A ROW.
A WHOLE PAGE OF POOP EMOJI STICKERS WITH MY NAME IN THE MIDDLE.
WHAT A LIFE.

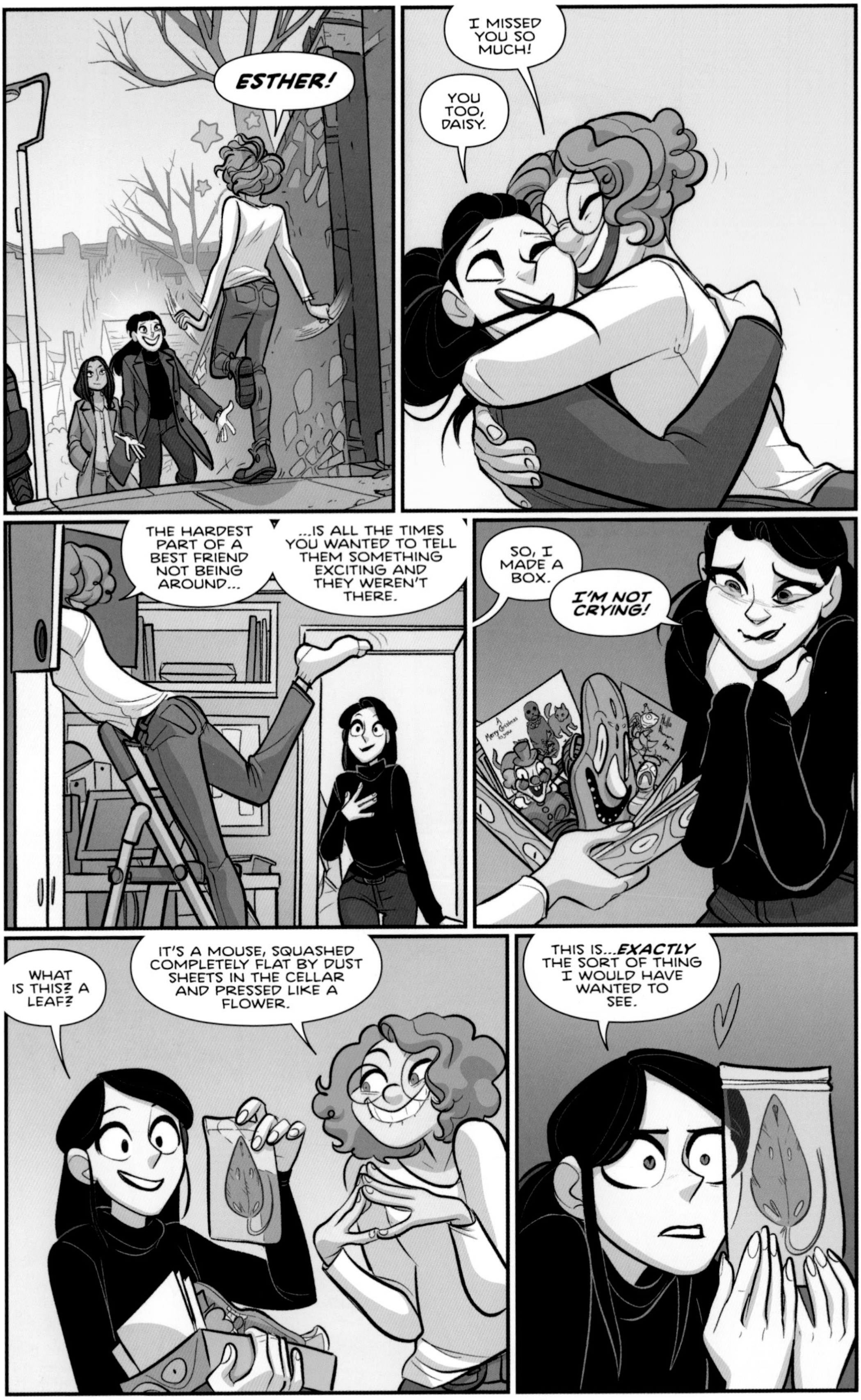
ESTHER!
I MISSED YOU SO MUCH!
YOU TOO, DAISY.
THE HARDEST PART OF A BEST FRIEND NOT BEING AROUND...
...IS ALL THE TIMES YOU WANTED TO TELL THEM SOMETHING EXCITING AND THEY WEREN'T THERE.
SO, I MADE A BOX.
I'M NOT CRYING!
WHAT IS THIS? A LEAF?
IT'S A MOUSE, SQUASHED COMPLETELY FLAT BY DUST SHEETS IN THE CELLAR AND PRESSED LIKE A FLOWER.
THIS IS...EXACTLY THE SORT OF THING I WOULD HAVE WANTED TO SEE.

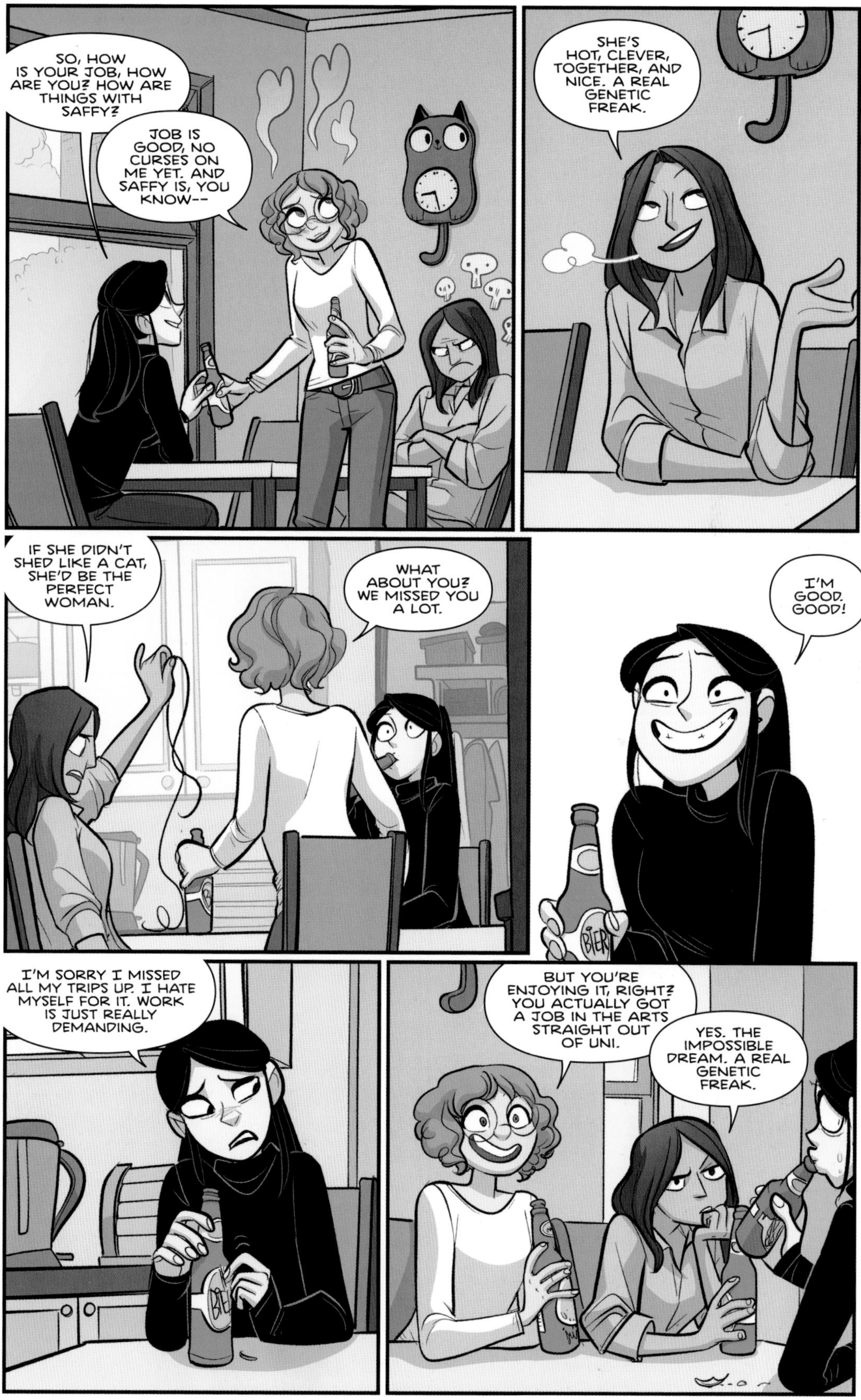
SO, HOW IS YOUR JOB, HOW ARE YOU? HOW ARE THINGS WITH SAFFY?
JOB IS GOOD, NO CURSES ON ME YET. AND SAFFY IS, YOU KNOW--
SHE'S HOT, CLEVER, TOGETHER, AND NICE. A REAL GENETIC FREAK.
IF SHE DIDN'T SHED LIKE A CAT, SHE'D BE THE PERFECT WOMAN.
WHAT ABOUT YOU? WE MISSED YOU A LOT.
I'M GOOD. GOOD!
BIER
I'M SORRY I MISSED ALL MY TRIPS UP. I HATE MYSELF FOR IT. WORK IS JUST REALLY DEMANDING.
BUT YOU'RE ENJOYING IT, RIGHT? YOU ACTUALLY GOT A JOB IN THE ARTS STRAIGHT OUT OF UNI.
YES. THE IMPOSSIBLE DREAM. A REAL GENETIC FREAK.

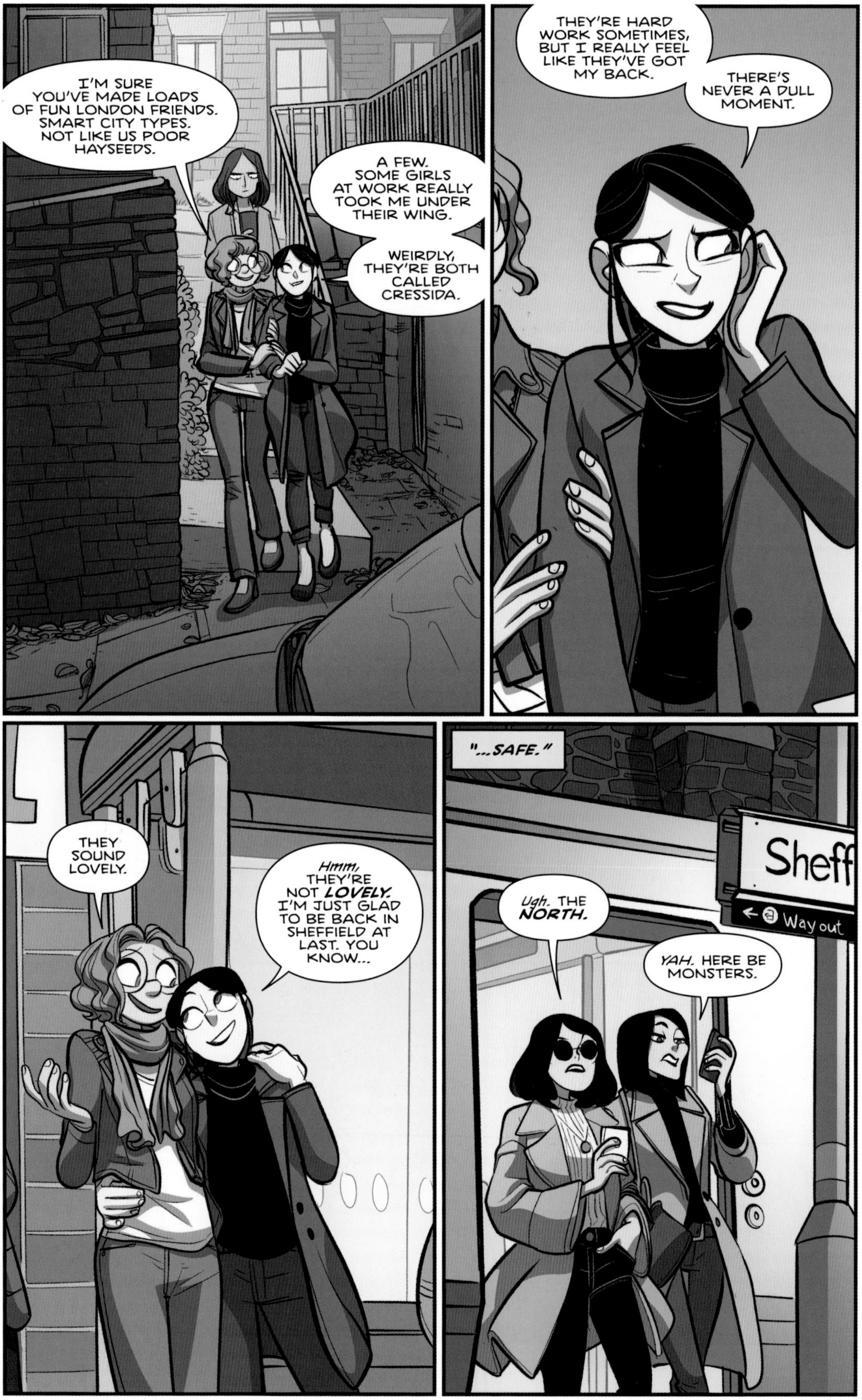

I'M SURE YOU'VE MADE LOADS OF FUN LONDON FRIENDS. SMART CITY TYPES. NOT LIKE US POOR HAYSEEDS.
A FEW. SOME GIRLS AT WORK REALLY TOOK ME UNDER THEIR WING.
WEIRDLY, THEY'RE BOTH CALLED CRESSIDA.
THEY'RE HARD WORK SOMETIMES, BUT I REALLY FEEL LIKE THEY'VE GOT MY BACK.
THERE'S NEVER A DULL MOMENT.
THEY SOUND LOVELY.
*Hmm,* THEY'RE NOT ***LOVELY.*** I'M JUST GLAD TO BE BACK IN SHEFFIELD AT LAST. YOU KNOW...
"...SAFE."
Sheff
Way out
*Ugh.* THE ***NORTH.***
*YAH.* HERE BE MONSTERS.

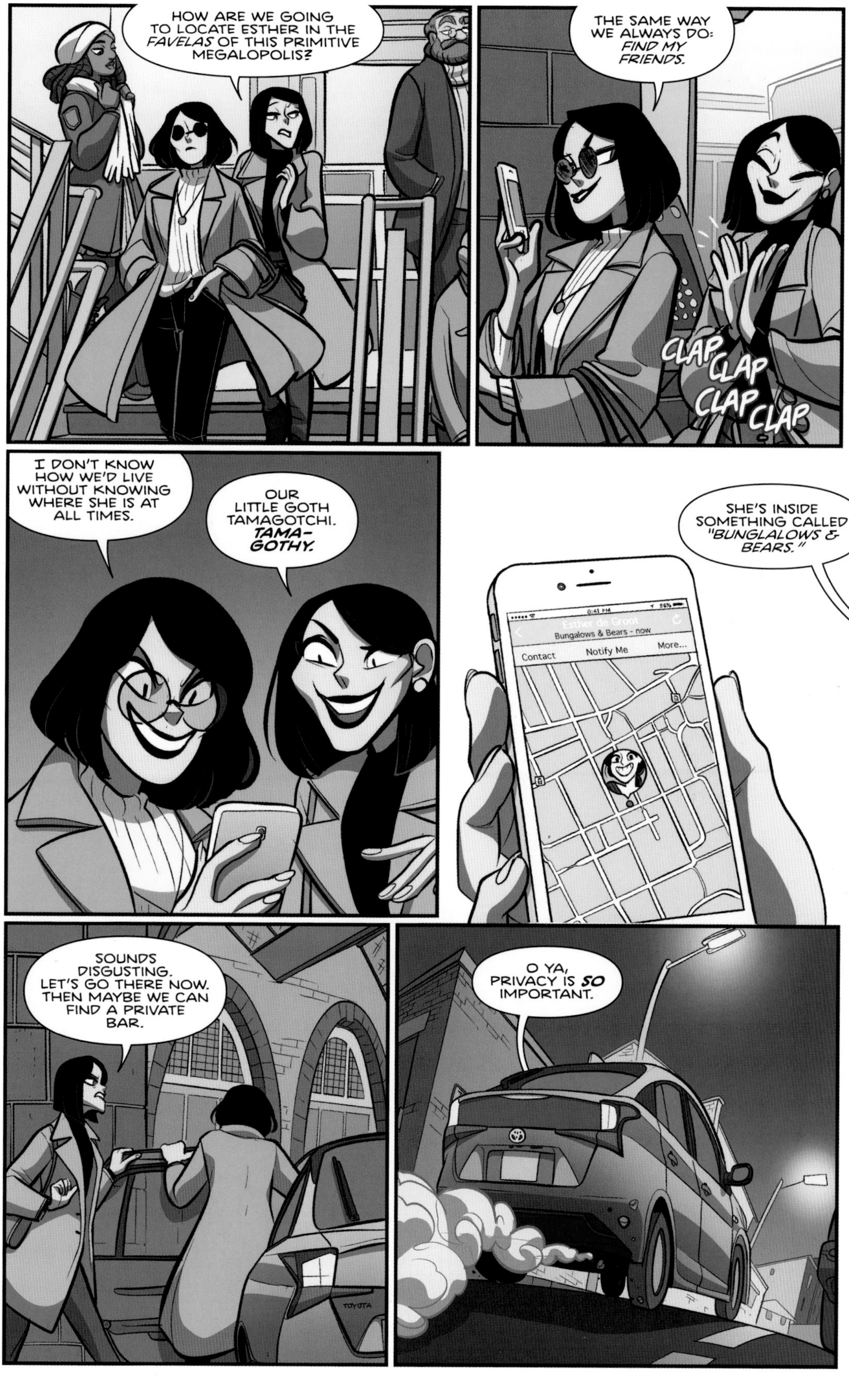
HOW ARE WE GOING TO LOCATE ESTHER IN THE *FAVELAS* OF THIS PRIMITIVE MEGALOPOLIS?
THE SAME WAY WE ALWAYS DO: *FIND MY FRIENDS.*
CLAP CLAP CLAP CLAP
I DON'T KNOW HOW WE'D LIVE WITHOUT KNOWING WHERE SHE IS AT ALL TIMES.
OUR LITTLE GOTH TAMAGOTCHI. ***TAMA-GOTHY.***
SHE'S INSIDE SOMETHING CALLED *"BUNGLALOWS & BEARS."*
8:41 PM
Esther de Groot
Bungalows & Bears - now
Contact
Notify Me
More...
SOUNDS DISGUSTING. LET'S GO THERE NOW. THEN MAYBE WE CAN FIND A PRIVATE BAR.
TOYOTA
O YA, PRIVACY IS ***SO*** IMPORTANT.

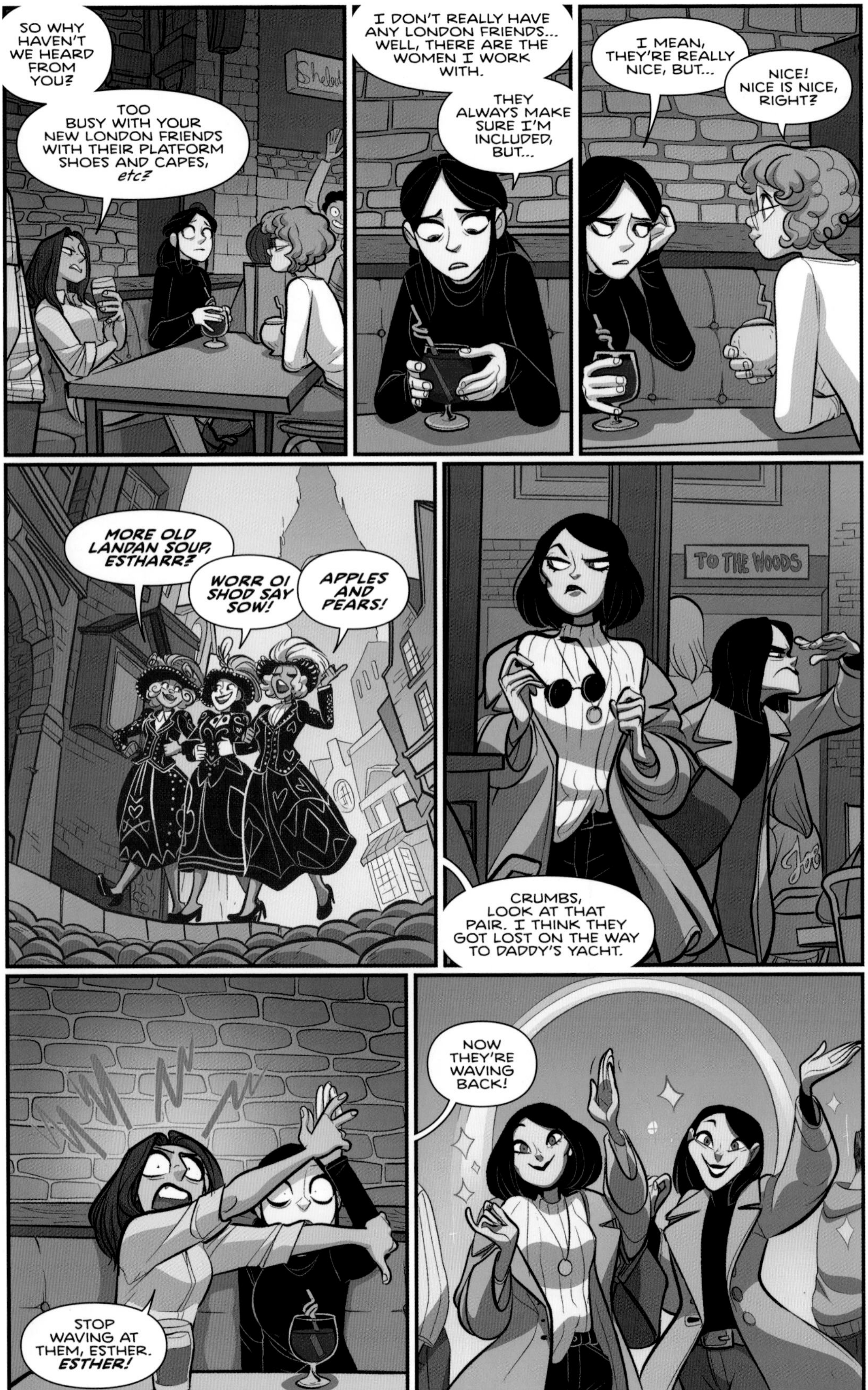
SO WHY HAVEN'T WE HEARD FROM YOU?
TOO BUSY WITH YOUR NEW LONDON FRIENDS WITH THEIR PLATFORM SHOES AND CAPES, *etc?*
I DON'T REALLY HAVE ANY LONDON FRIENDS... WELL, THERE ARE THE WOMEN I WORK WITH.
THEY ALWAYS MAKE SURE I'M INCLUDED, BUT...
I MEAN, THEY'RE REALLY NICE, BUT...
NICE! NICE IS NICE, RIGHT?
*MORE OLD LANDAN SOUP, ESTHARR?*
*WORR OI SHOD SAY SOW!*
*APPLES AND PEARS!*
TO THE WOODS
CRUMBS, LOOK AT THAT PAIR. I THINK THEY GOT LOST ON THE WAY TO DADDY'S YACHT.
STOP WAVING AT THEM, ESTHER. ***ESTHER!***
NOW THEY'RE WAVING BACK!

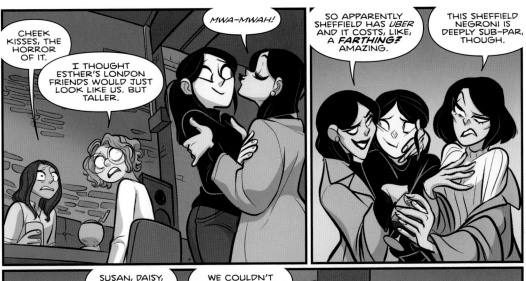

CHEEK KISSES, THE HORROR OF IT.

I THOUGHT ESTHER'S LONDON FRIENDS WOULD JUST LOOK LIKE US. BUT TALLER.

MWA-MWAH!

SO APPARENTLY SHEFFIELD HAS *UBER* AND IT COSTS, LIKE, A *FARTHING?* AMAZING.

THIS SHEFFIELD NEGRONI IS DEEPLY SUB-PAR, THOUGH.

SUSAN, DAISY, THESE ARE THE CRESSIDAS.

WE COULDN'T SURVIVE WITHOUT THIS ONE.

THAT IS...SELF-EVIDENT.

SHE'S SUCH A CRAZY BITCH. ESTHER WILL DO ANYTHING. AND *ANYONE.*

Eh heh heh heh. I DON'T--

CAN WE GET OUT OF HERE, ESSY-BOBS? IT'S FULL OF STUDENTS LOOKING AT ME WITH THEIR DIRTY EYES.

*Oh,* SURE--

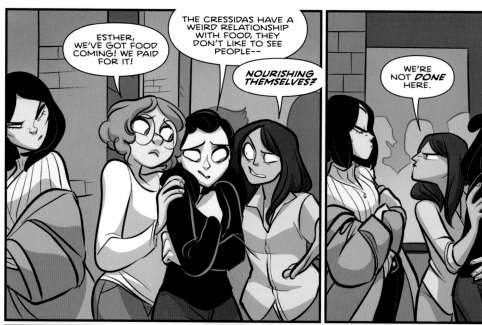

ESTHER, WE'VE GOT FOOD COMING! WE PAID FOR IT!

THE CRESSIDAS HAVE A WEIRD RELATIONSHIP WITH FOOD, THEY DON'T LIKE TO SEE PEOPLE--

NOURISHING THEMSELVES?

WE'RE NOT *DONE* HERE.

WE'RE GOING TO FRESHEN UP, THEN WE'RE BLOWING THIS PLACE. YOU COMING, ESTHER?

WHAT... IS GOING ON?

MAYBE THEY'LL CALM DOWN AFTER A FEW DRINKS.

I CAN THINK OF OTHER WAYS OF CALMING THEM DOWN.

CALMING THEM DOWN *PERMANENTLY*.

THESE ARE *HEALING* HANDS NOW, SUSAN.

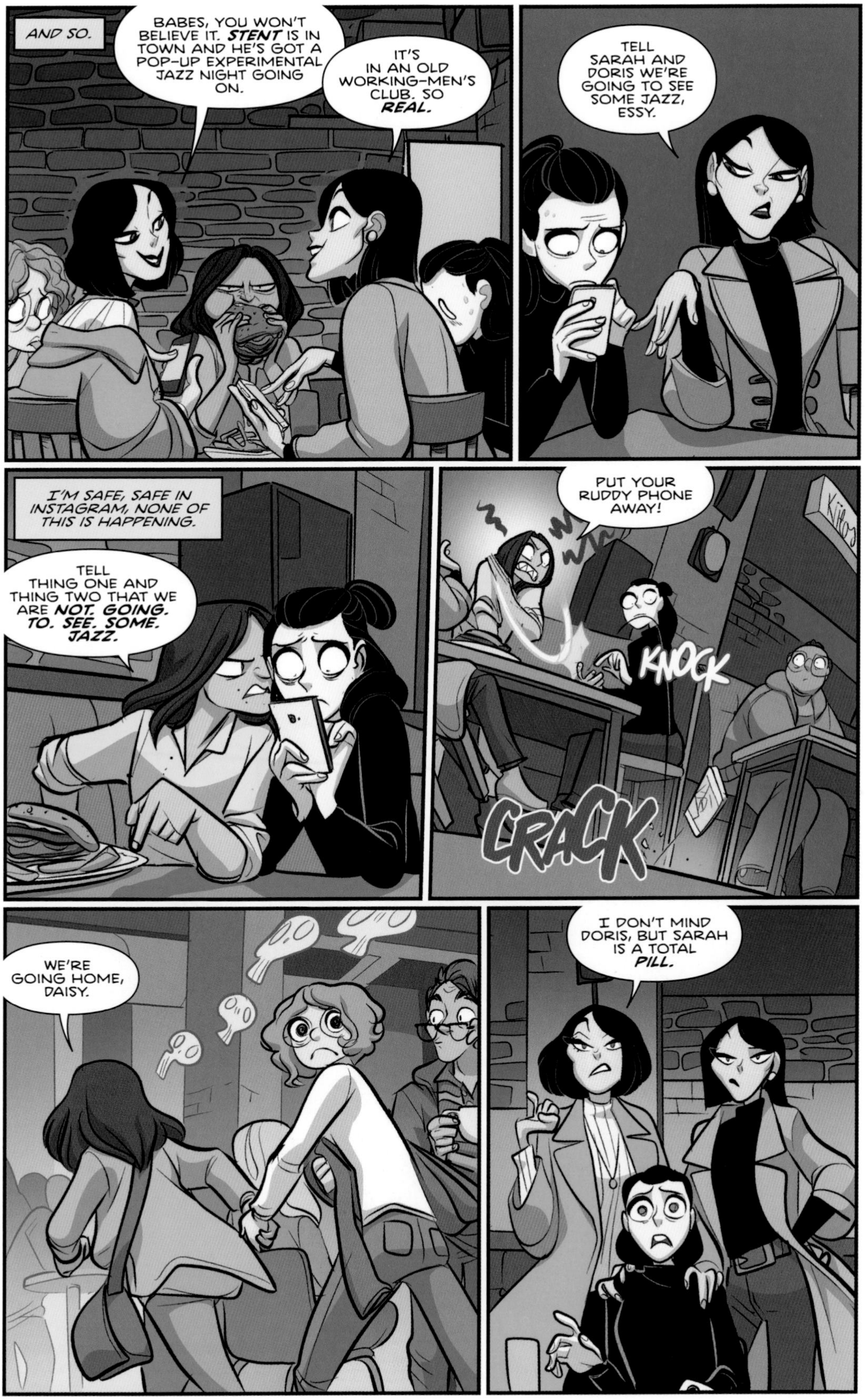
AND SO.
BABES, YOU WON'T BELIEVE IT. STENT IS IN TOWN AND HE'S GOT A POP-UP EXPERIMENTAL JAZZ NIGHT GOING ON.
IT'S IN AN OLD WORKING-MEN'S CLUB. SO REAL.
TELL SARAH AND DORIS WE'RE GOING TO SEE SOME JAZZ, ESSY.
I'M SAFE, SAFE IN INSTAGRAM, NONE OF THIS IS HAPPENING.
TELL THING ONE AND THING TWO THAT WE ARE NOT. GOING. TO. SEE. SOME. JAZZ.
PUT YOUR RUDDY PHONE AWAY!
KNOCK
CRACK
WE'RE GOING HOME, DAISY.
I DON'T MIND DORIS, BUT SARAH IS A TOTAL PILL.

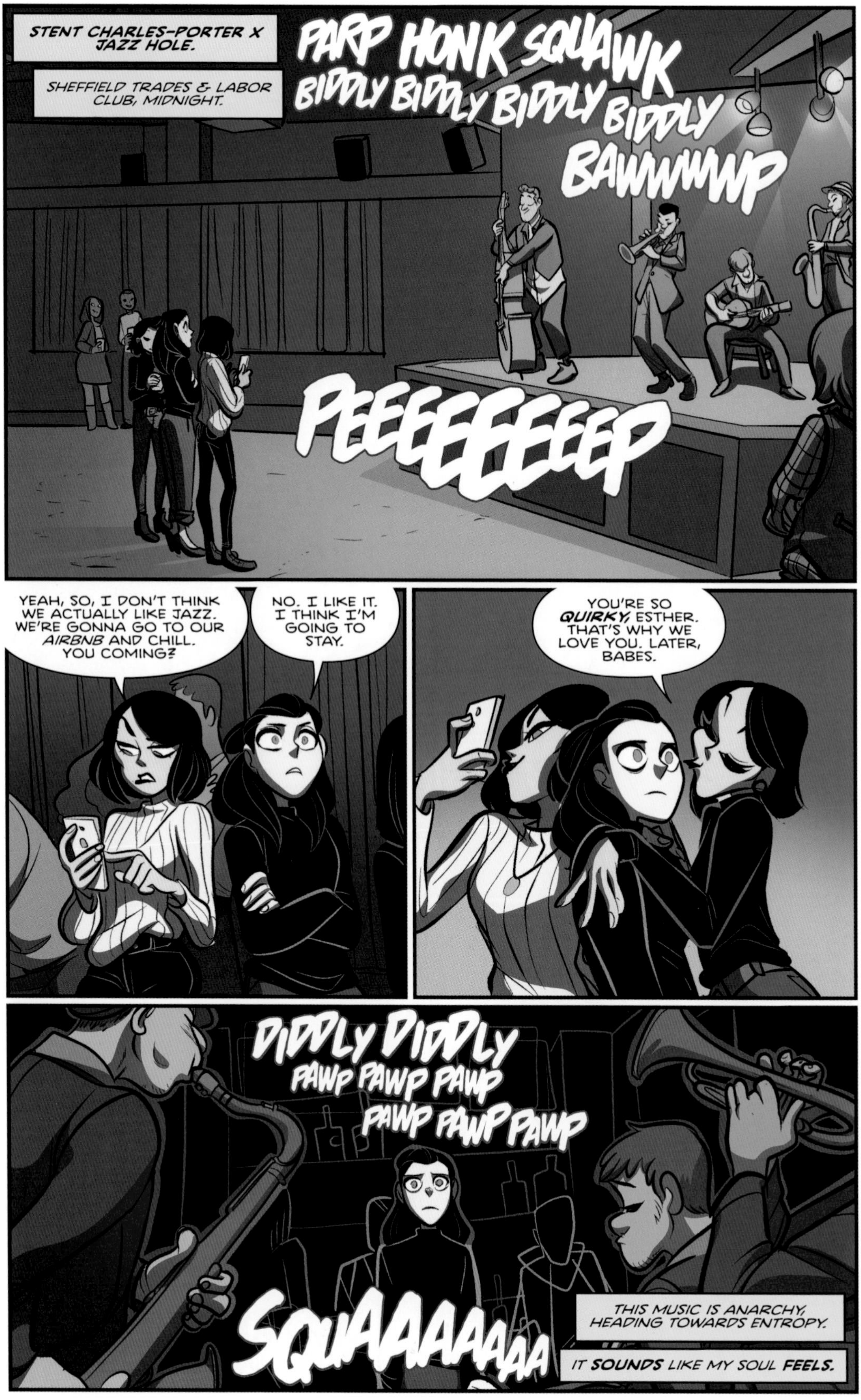
STENT CHARLES-PORTER X JAZZ HOLE.
SHEFFIELD TRADES & LABOR CLUB, MIDNIGHT.
PARP HONK SQUAWK
BIDDLY BIDDLY BIDDLY BIDDLY
BAWWWWP
PEEEEEEEEEP
YEAH, SO, I DON'T THINK WE ACTUALLY LIKE JAZZ. WE'RE GONNA GO TO OUR AIRBNB AND CHILL. YOU COMING?
NO. I LIKE IT. I THINK I'M GOING TO STAY.
YOU'RE SO QUIRKY, ESTHER. THAT'S WHY WE LOVE YOU. LATER, BABES.
DIDDLY DIDDLY
PAWP PAWP PAWP
PAWP PAWP PAWP
SQUAAAAAAAA
THIS MUSIC IS ANARCHY, HEADING TOWARDS ENTROPY.
IT SOUNDS LIKE MY SOUL FEELS.

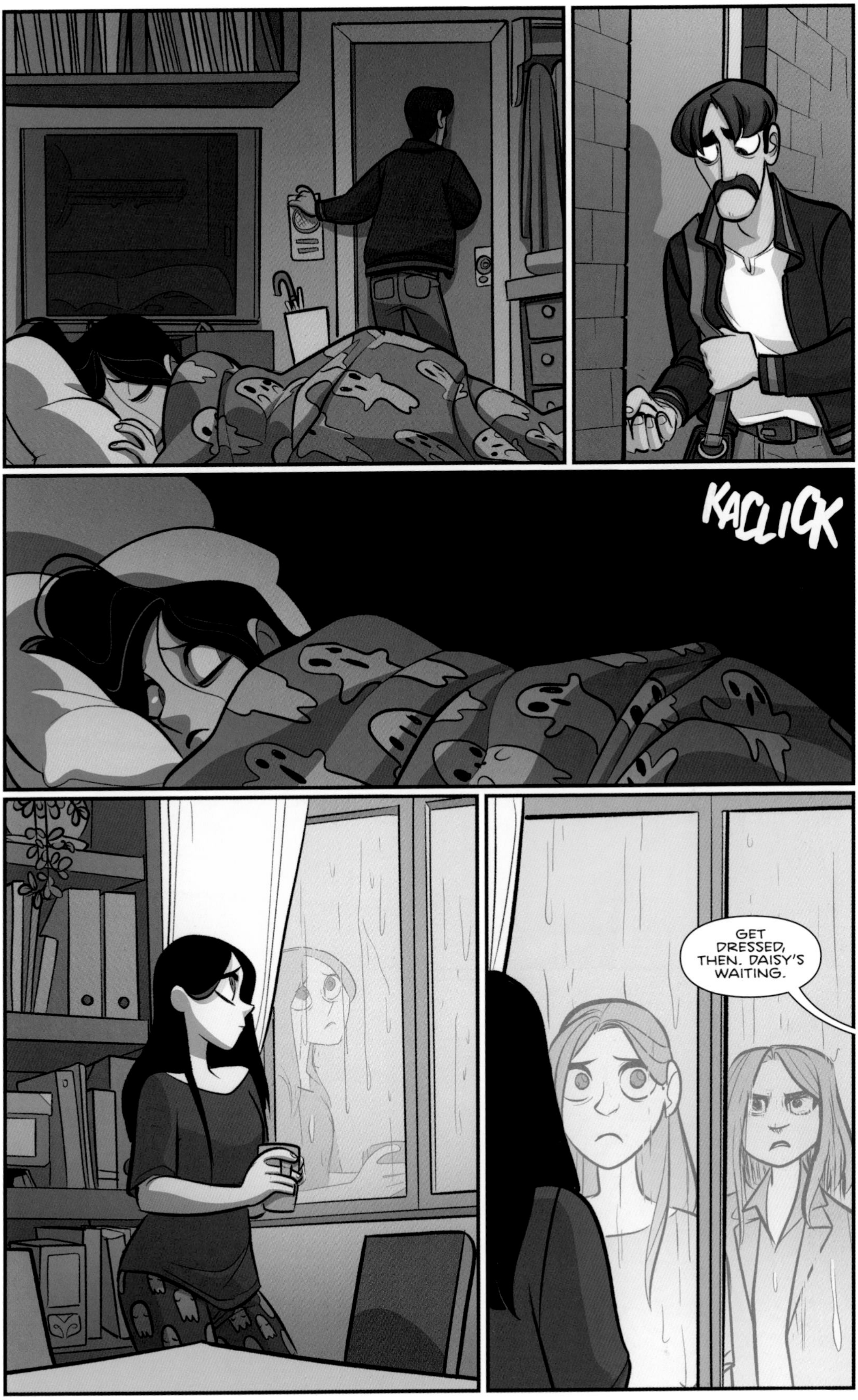
KACLICK
GET DRESSED, THEN. DAISY'S WAITING.

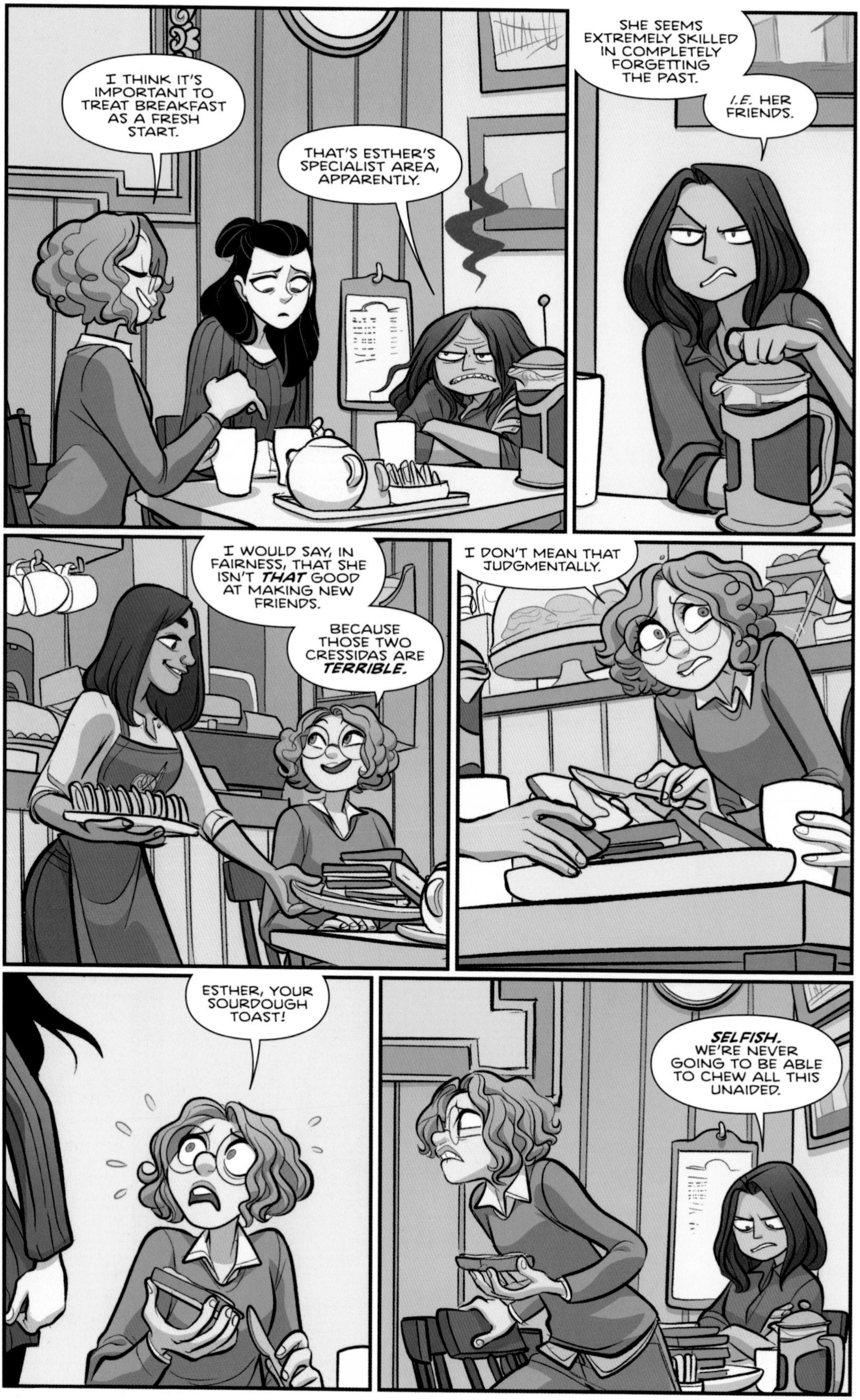
I THINK IT'S IMPORTANT TO TREAT BREAKFAST AS A FRESH START.
THAT'S ESTHER'S SPECIALIST AREA, APPARENTLY.
SHE SEEMS EXTREMELY SKILLED IN COMPLETELY FORGETTING THE PAST.
I.E. HER FRIENDS.
I WOULD SAY, IN FAIRNESS, THAT SHE ISN'T THAT GOOD AT MAKING NEW FRIENDS.
BECAUSE THOSE TWO CRESSIDAS ARE TERRIBLE.
I DON'T MEAN THAT JUDGMENTALLY.
ESTHER, YOUR SOURDOUGH TOAST!
SELFISH. WE'RE NEVER GOING TO BE ABLE TO CHEW ALL THIS UNAIDED.

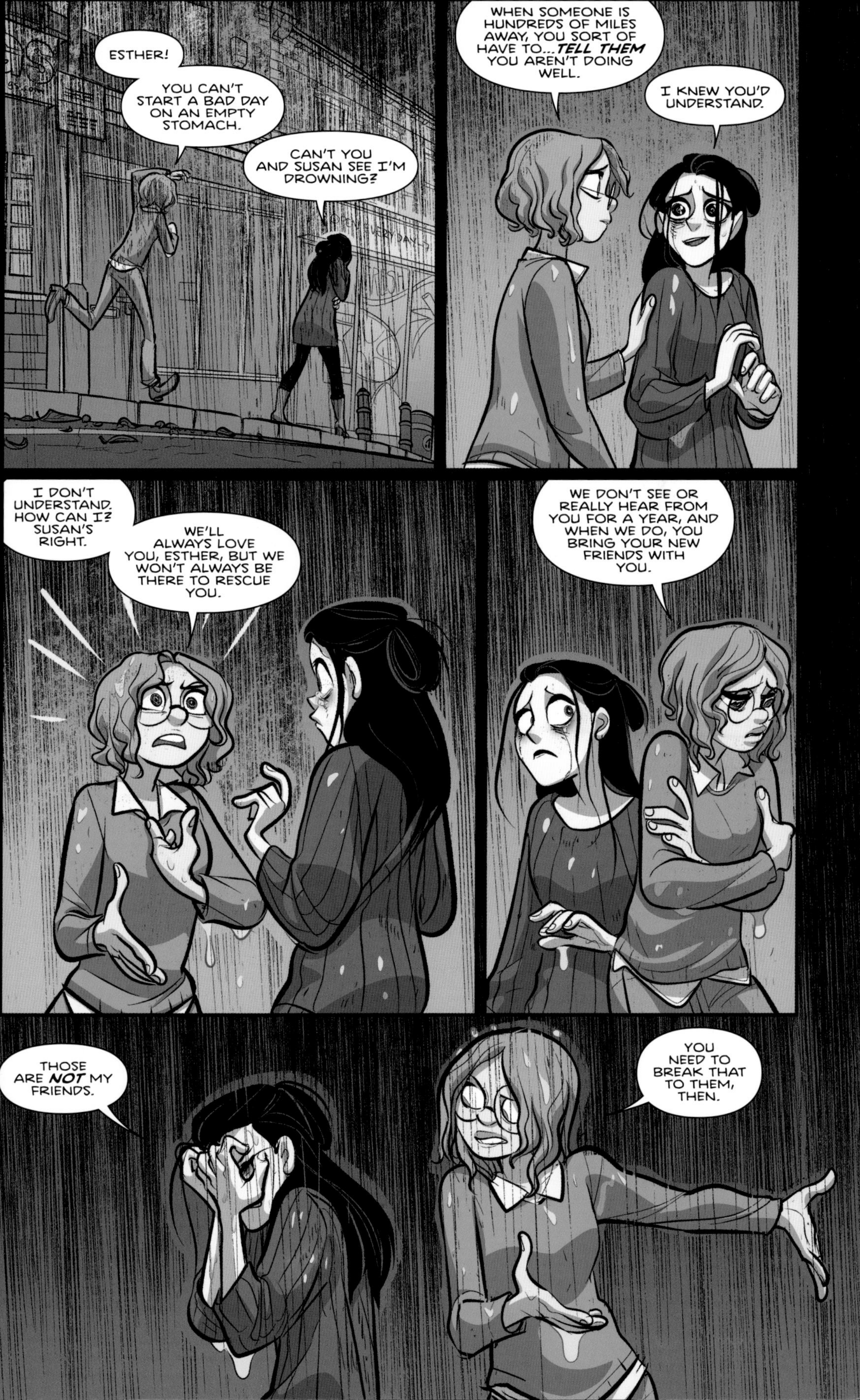
ESTHER!
YOU CAN'T START A BAD DAY ON AN EMPTY STOMACH.
CAN'T YOU AND SUSAN SEE I'M DROWNING?
WHEN SOMEONE IS HUNDREDS OF MILES AWAY, YOU SORT OF HAVE TO...*TELL THEM* YOU AREN'T DOING WELL.
I KNEW YOU'D UNDERSTAND.
I DON'T UNDERSTAND. HOW CAN I? SUSAN'S RIGHT.
WE'LL ALWAYS LOVE YOU, ESTHER, BUT WE WON'T ALWAYS BE THERE TO RESCUE YOU.
WE DON'T SEE OR REALLY HEAR FROM YOU FOR A YEAR, AND WHEN WE DO, YOU BRING YOUR NEW FRIENDS WITH YOU.
THOSE ARE *NOT* MY FRIENDS.
YOU NEED TO BREAK THAT TO THEM, THEN.

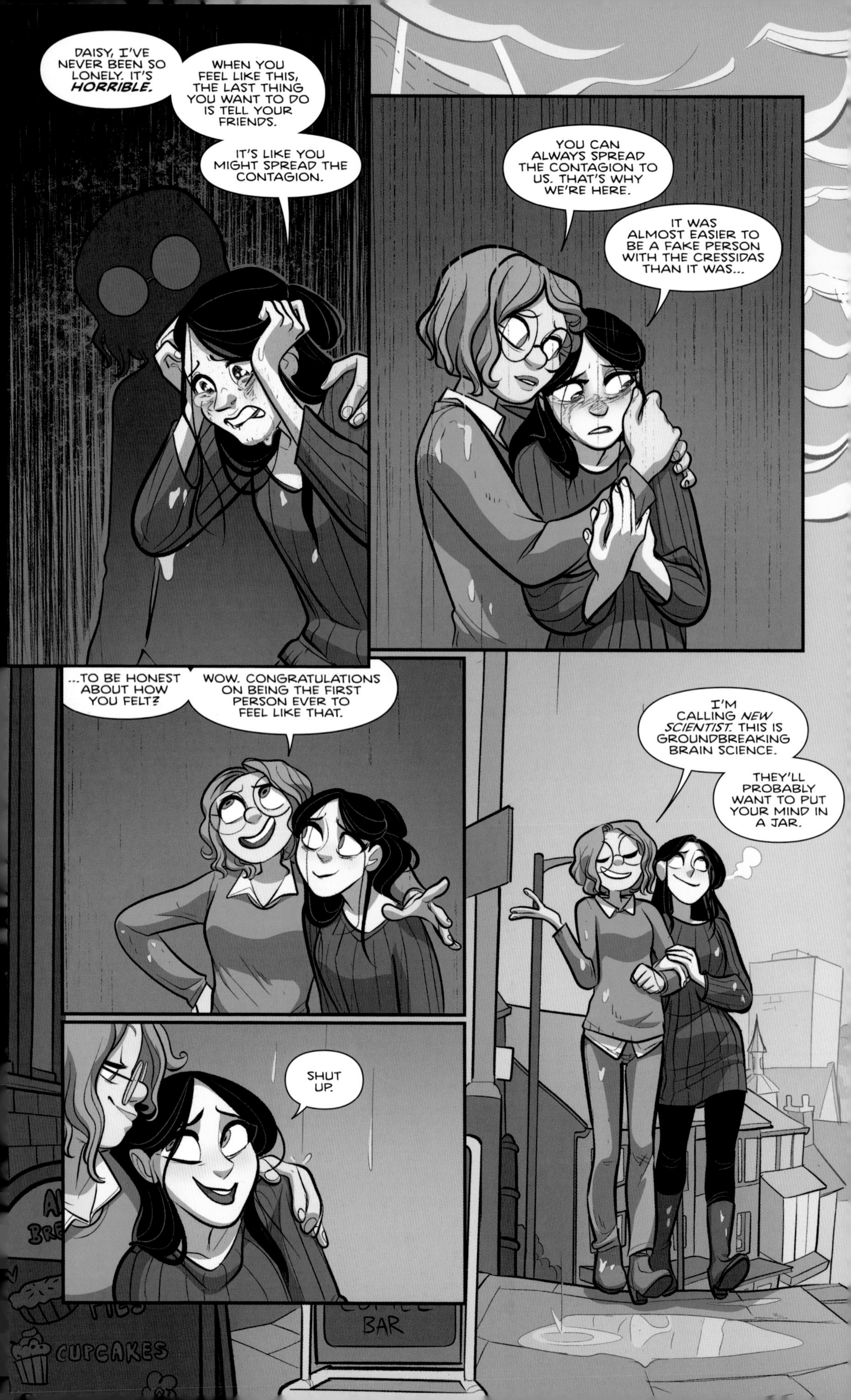
DAISY, I'VE NEVER BEEN SO LONELY. IT'S **HORRIBLE.**
WHEN YOU FEEL LIKE THIS, THE LAST THING YOU WANT TO DO IS TELL YOUR FRIENDS.
IT'S LIKE YOU MIGHT SPREAD THE CONTAGION.
YOU CAN ALWAYS SPREAD THE CONTAGION TO US. THAT'S WHY WE'RE HERE.
IT WAS ALMOST EASIER TO BE A FAKE PERSON WITH THE CRESSIDAS THAN IT WAS...
...TO BE HONEST ABOUT HOW YOU FELT?
WOW. CONGRATULATIONS ON BEING THE FIRST PERSON EVER TO FEEL LIKE THAT.
SHUT UP.
I'M CALLING *NEW SCIENTIST.* THIS IS GROUNDBREAKING BRAIN SCIENCE.
THEY'LL PROBABLY WANT TO PUT YOUR MIND IN A JAR.
BAR
CUPCAKES

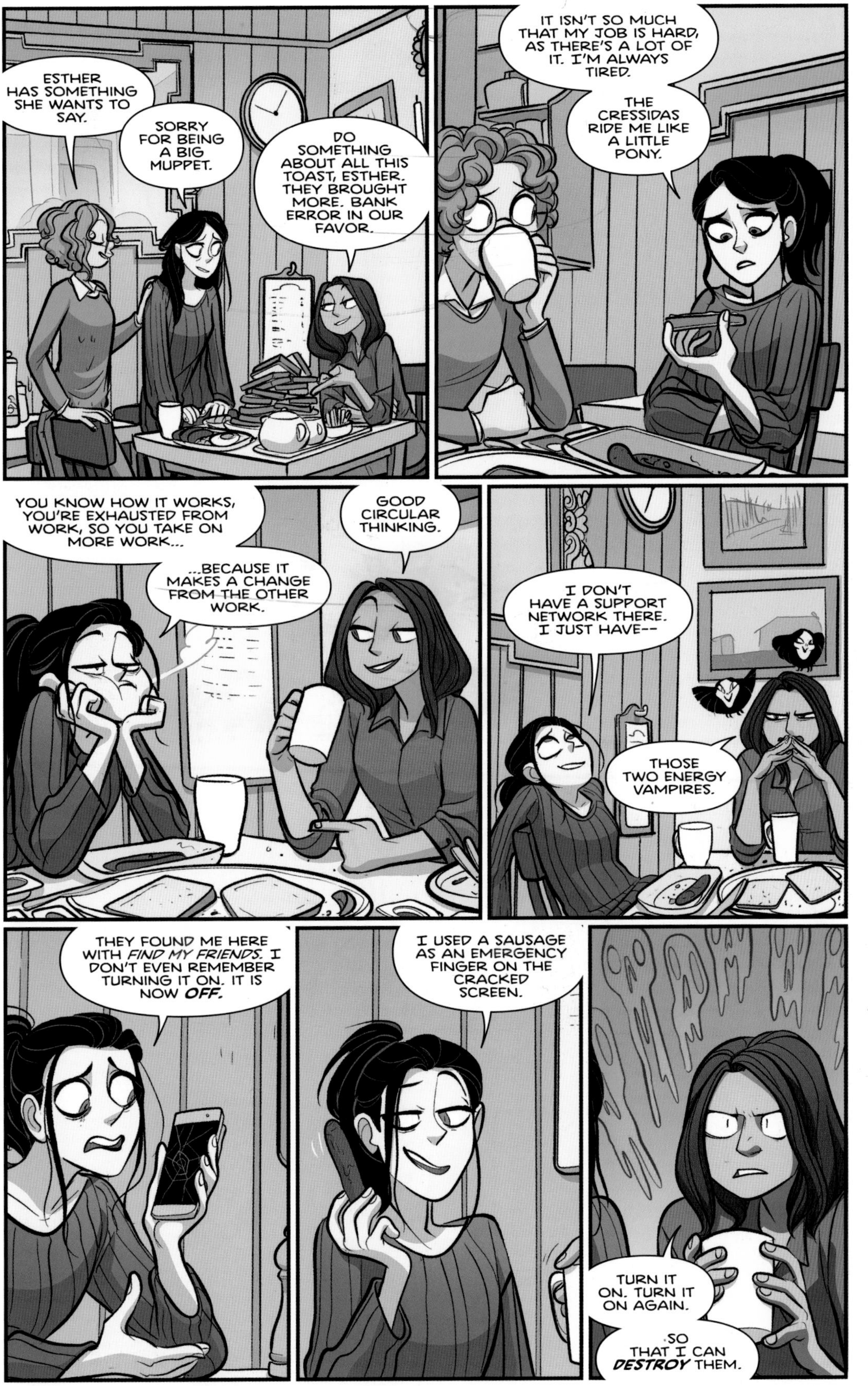

ESTHER HAS SOMETHING SHE WANTS TO SAY.
SORRY FOR BEING A BIG MUPPET.
DO SOMETHING ABOUT ALL THIS TOAST, ESTHER. THEY BROUGHT MORE. BANK ERROR IN OUR FAVOR.
IT ISN'T SO MUCH THAT MY JOB IS HARD, AS THERE'S A LOT OF IT. I'M ALWAYS TIRED.
THE CRESSIDAS RIDE ME LIKE A LITTLE PONY.
YOU KNOW HOW IT WORKS, YOU'RE EXHAUSTED FROM WORK, SO YOU TAKE ON MORE WORK...
...BECAUSE IT MAKES A CHANGE FROM THE OTHER WORK.
GOOD CIRCULAR THINKING.
I DON'T HAVE A SUPPORT NETWORK THERE. I JUST HAVE--
THOSE TWO ENERGY VAMPIRES.
THEY FOUND ME HERE WITH *FIND MY FRIENDS*. I DON'T EVEN REMEMBER TURNING IT ON. IT IS NOW ***OFF.***
I USED A SAUSAGE AS AN EMERGENCY FINGER ON THE CRACKED SCREEN.
TURN IT ON. TURN IT ON AGAIN.
...SO THAT I CAN ***DESTROY*** THEM.

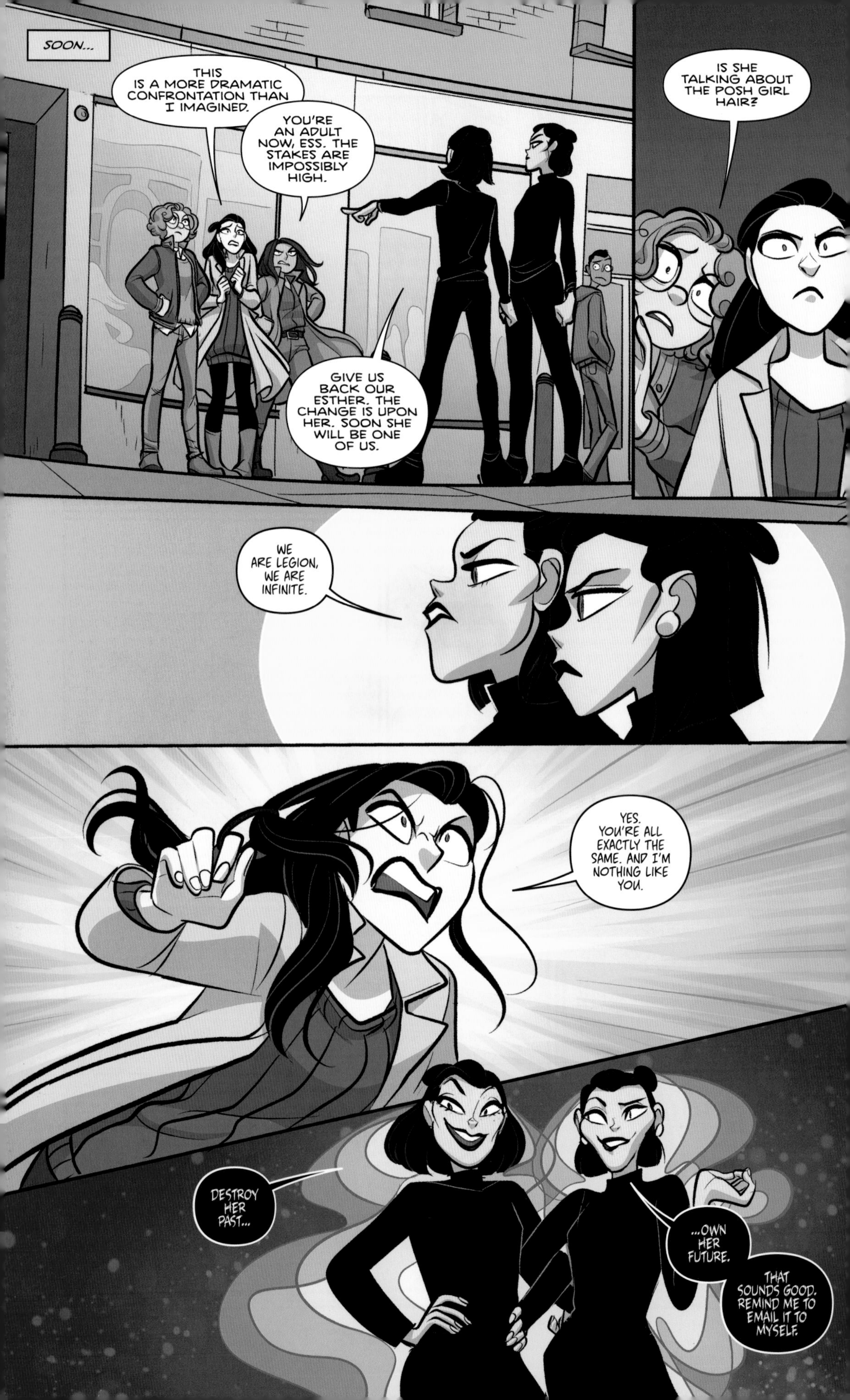
SOON...
THIS IS A MORE DRAMATIC CONFRONTATION THAN I IMAGINED.
YOU'RE AN ADULT NOW, ESS. THE STAKES ARE IMPOSSIBLY HIGH.
GIVE US BACK OUR ESTHER. THE CHANGE IS UPON HER. SOON SHE WILL BE ONE OF US.
IS SHE TALKING ABOUT THE POSH GIRL HAIR?
WE ARE LEGION, WE ARE INFINITE.
YES. YOU'RE ALL EXACTLY THE SAME. AND I'M NOTHING LIKE YOU.
DESTROY HER PAST...
...OWN HER FUTURE.
THAT SOUNDS GOOD. REMIND ME TO EMAIL IT TO MYSELF.

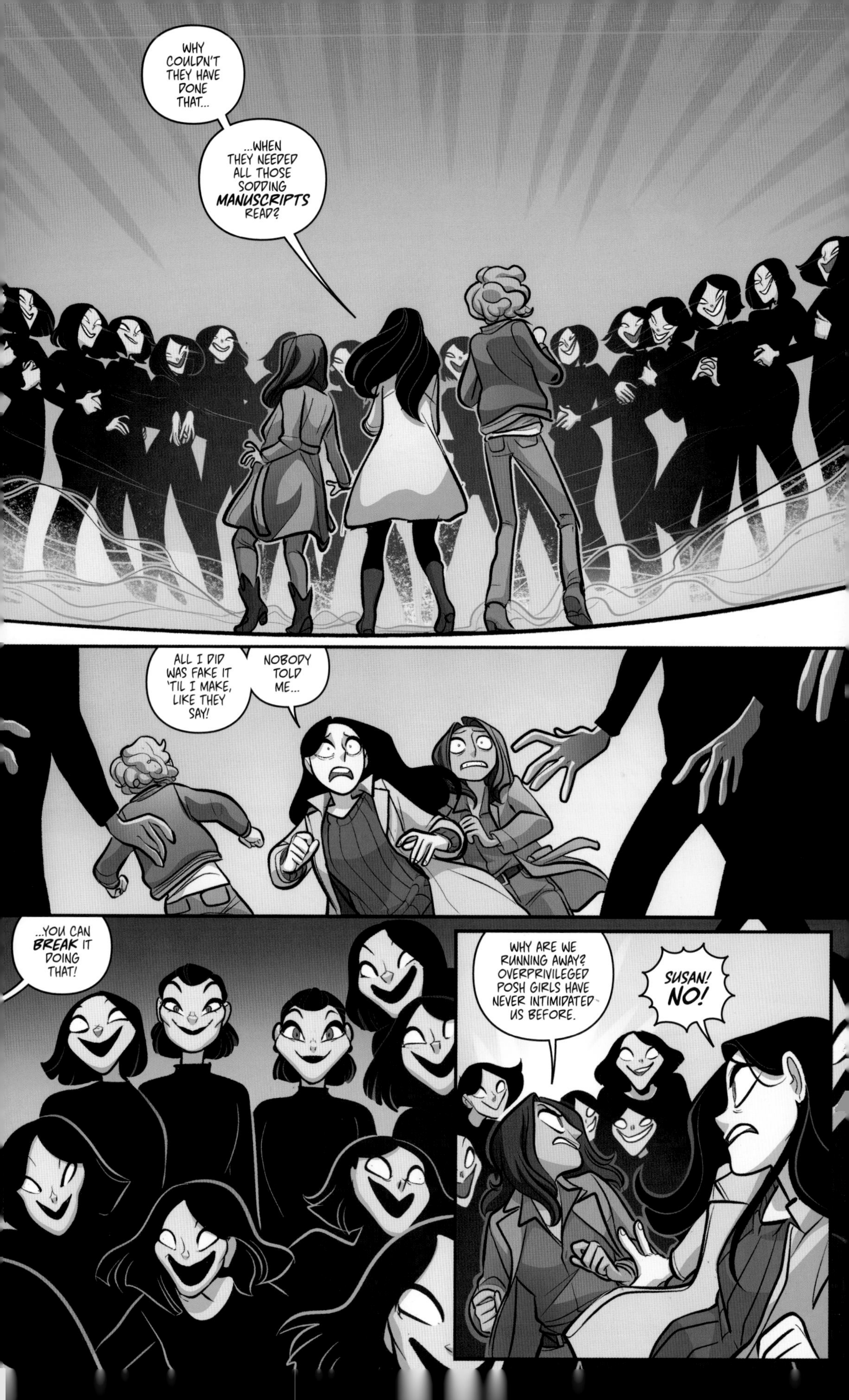
WHY COULDN'T THEY HAVE DONE THAT...
...WHEN THEY NEEDED ALL THOSE SODDING MANUSCRIPTS READ?
ALL I DID WAS FAKE IT 'TIL I MAKE, LIKE THEY SAY!
NOBODY TOLD ME...
...YOU CAN BREAK IT DOING THAT!
WHY ARE WE RUNNING AWAY? OVERPRIVILEGED POSH GIRLS HAVE NEVER INTIMIDATED US BEFORE.
SUSAN! NO!

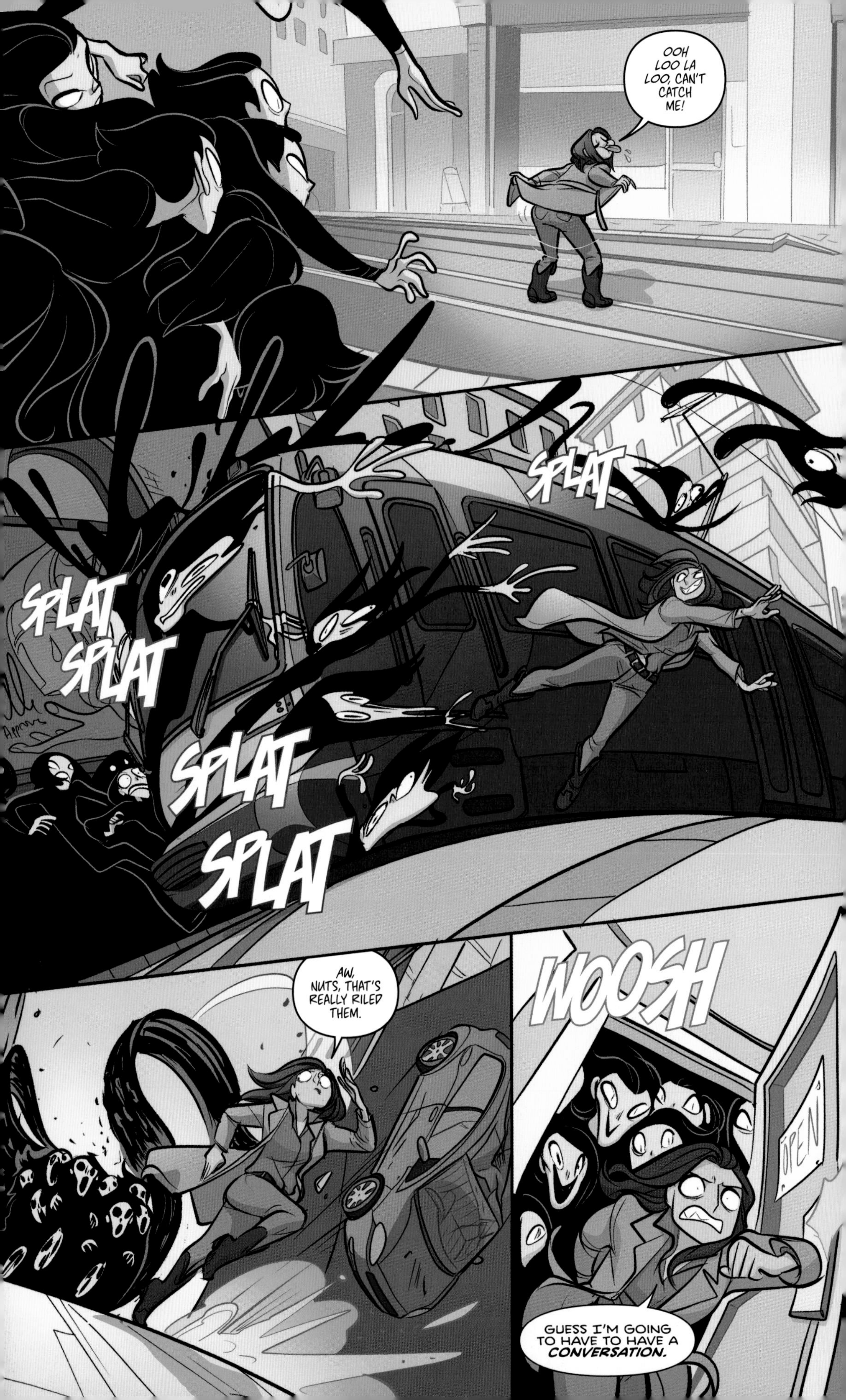
OOH LOO LA LOO, CAN'T CATCH ME!
SPLAT
SPLAT
SPLAT
SPLAT
SPLAT
AW, NUTS, THAT'S REALLY RILED THEM.
WOOSH
OPEN
GUESS I'M GOING TO HAVE TO HAVE A *CONVERSATION.*

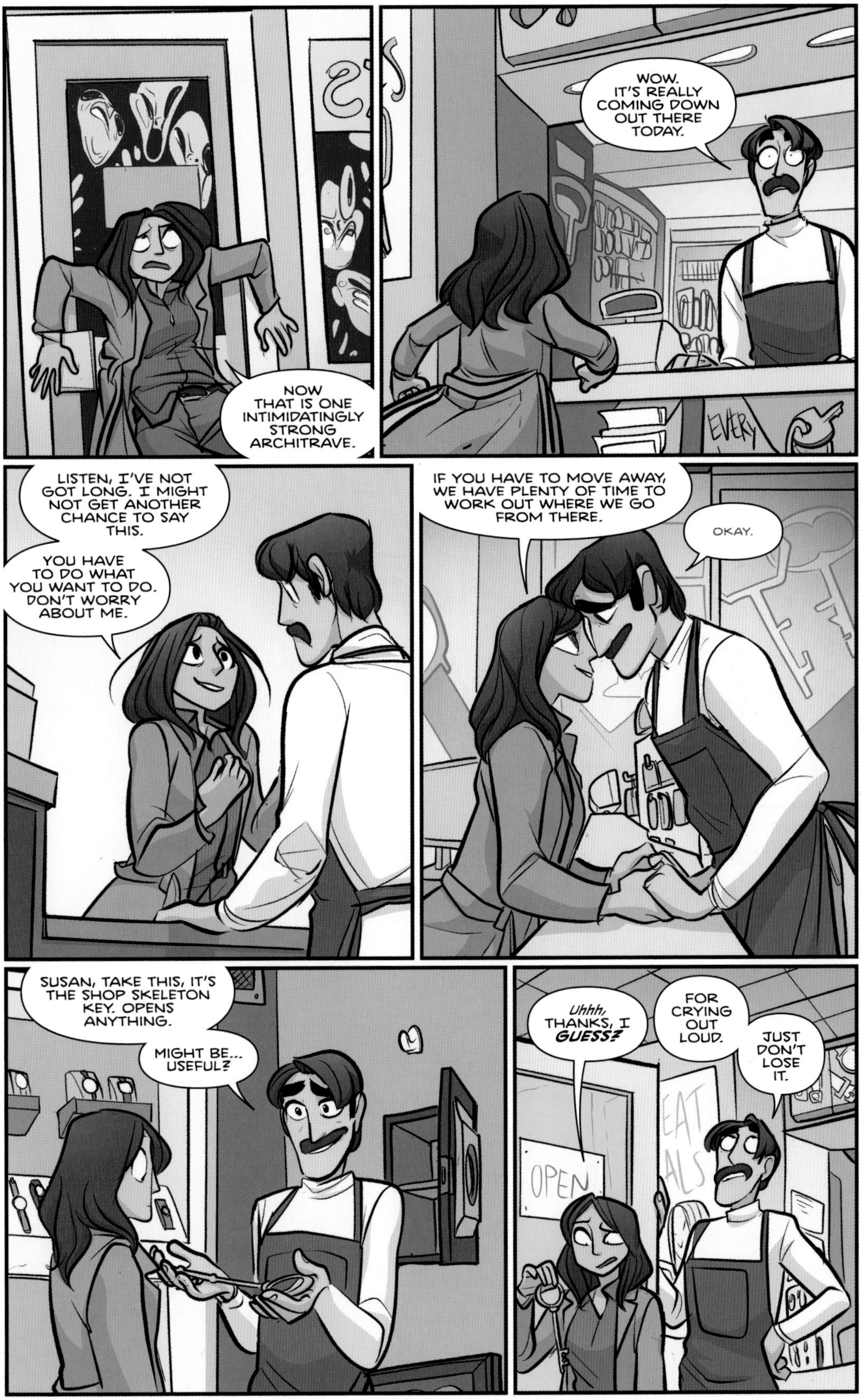
NOW THAT IS ONE INTIMIDATINGLY STRONG ARCHITRAVE.
WOW. IT'S REALLY COMING DOWN OUT THERE TODAY.
EVERY
LISTEN, I'VE NOT GOT LONG. I MIGHT NOT GET ANOTHER CHANCE TO SAY THIS.
YOU HAVE TO DO WHAT YOU WANT TO DO. DON'T WORRY ABOUT ME.
IF YOU HAVE TO MOVE AWAY, WE HAVE PLENTY OF TIME TO WORK OUT WHERE WE GO FROM THERE.
OKAY.
SUSAN, TAKE THIS, IT'S THE SHOP SKELETON KEY. OPENS ANYTHING.
MIGHT BE... USEFUL?
*Uhhh,* THANKS, I ***GUESS?***
FOR CRYING OUT LOUD.
JUST DON'T LOSE IT.
OPEN

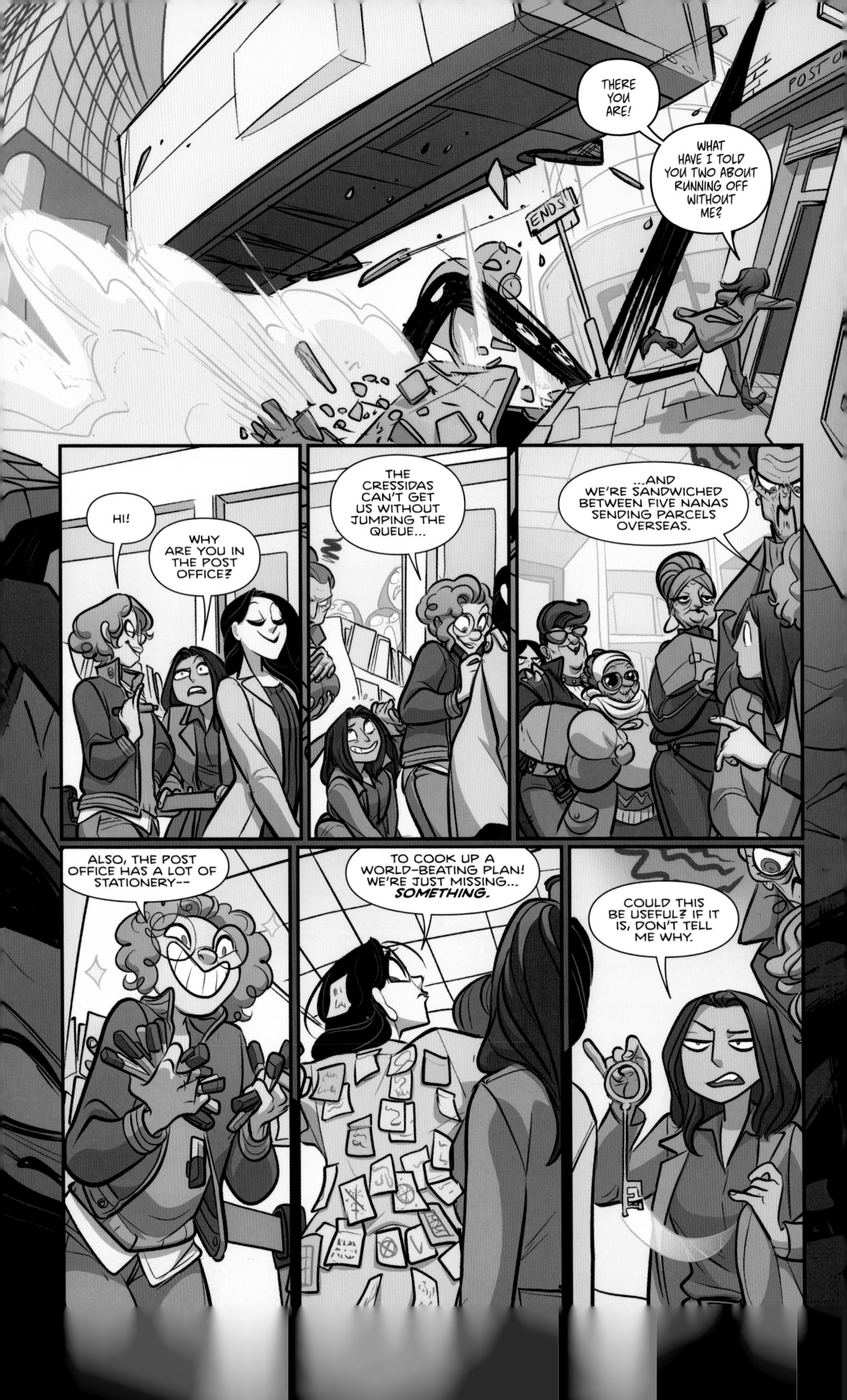
THERE YOU ARE!
WHAT HAVE I TOLD YOU TWO ABOUT RUNNING OFF WITHOUT ME?
ENDS
POST O
HI!
WHY ARE YOU IN THE POST OFFICE?
THE CRESSIDAS CAN'T GET US WITHOUT JUMPING THE QUEUE...
...AND WE'RE SANDWICHED BETWEEN FIVE NANAS SENDING PARCELS OVERSEAS.
ALSO, THE POST OFFICE HAS A LOT OF STATIONERY--
TO COOK UP A WORLD-BEATING PLAN! WE'RE JUST MISSING... *SOMETHING.*
COULD THIS BE USEFUL? IF IT IS, DON'T TELL ME WHY.

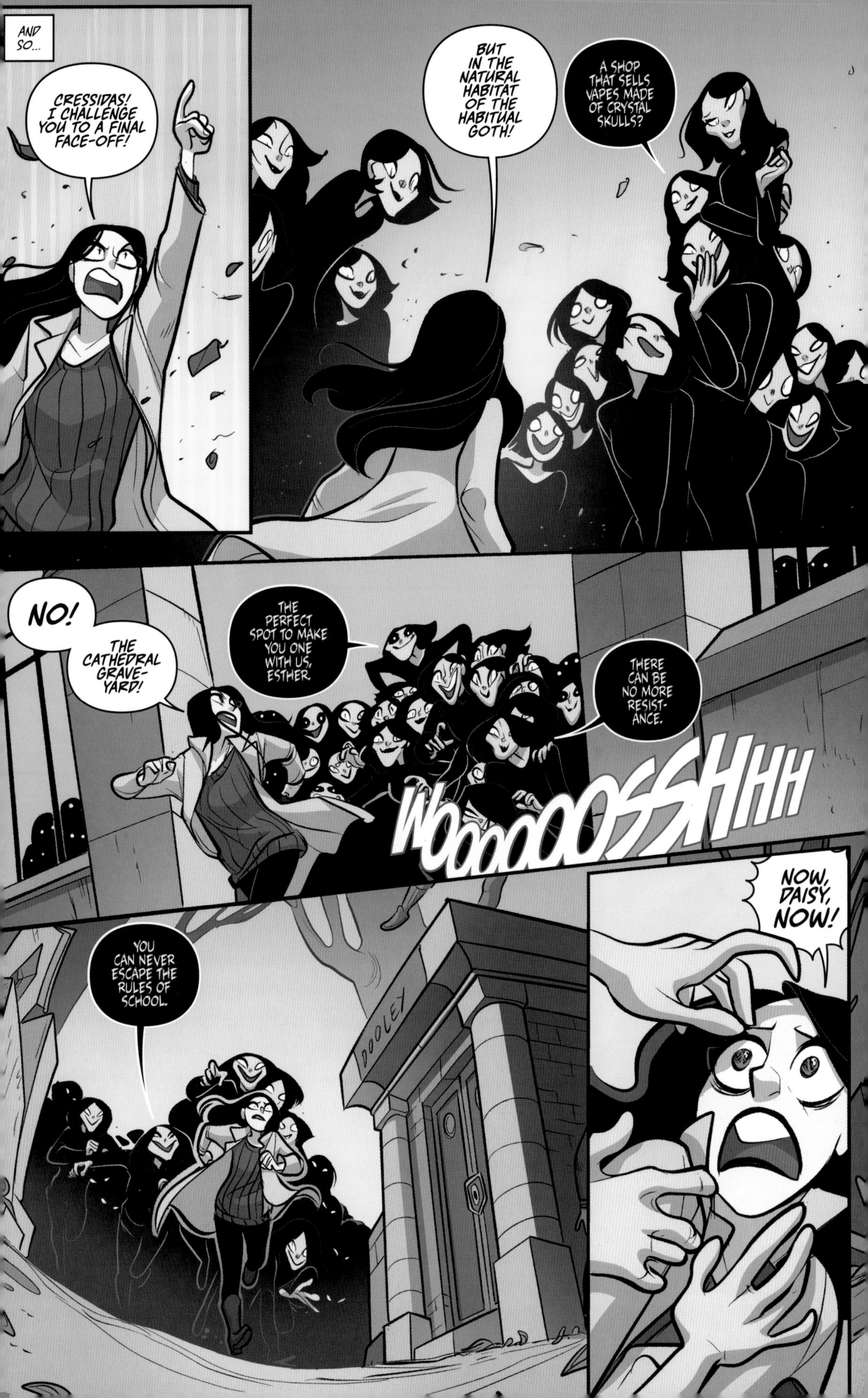
AND SO...
CRESSIDAS! I CHALLENGE YOU TO A FINAL FACE-OFF!
BUT IN THE NATURAL HABITAT OF THE HABITUAL GOTH!
A SHOP THAT SELLS VAPES MADE OF CRYSTAL SKULLS?
NO! THE CATHEDRAL GRAVE-YARD!
THE PERFECT SPOT TO MAKE YOU ONE WITH US, ESTHER.
THERE CAN BE NO MORE RESIST-ANCE.
WOOOOOOOSSHHH
YOU CAN NEVER ESCAPE THE RULES OF SCHOOL.
DOOLEY
NOW, DAISY, NOW!

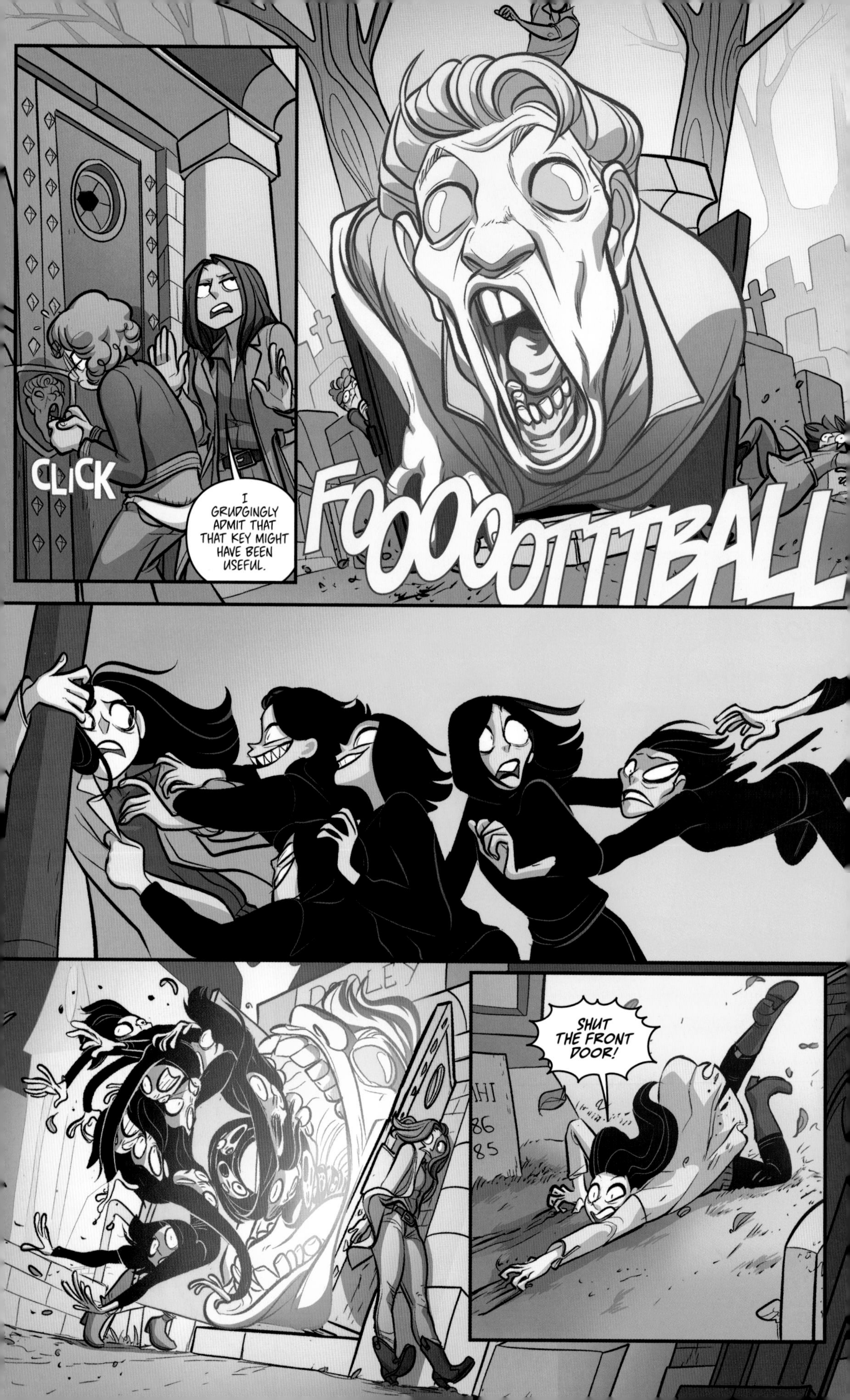
CLICK
I GRUDGINGLY ADMIT THAT THAT KEY MIGHT HAVE BEEN USEFUL.
FOOOOOTTTBALL
SHUT THE FRONT DOOR!

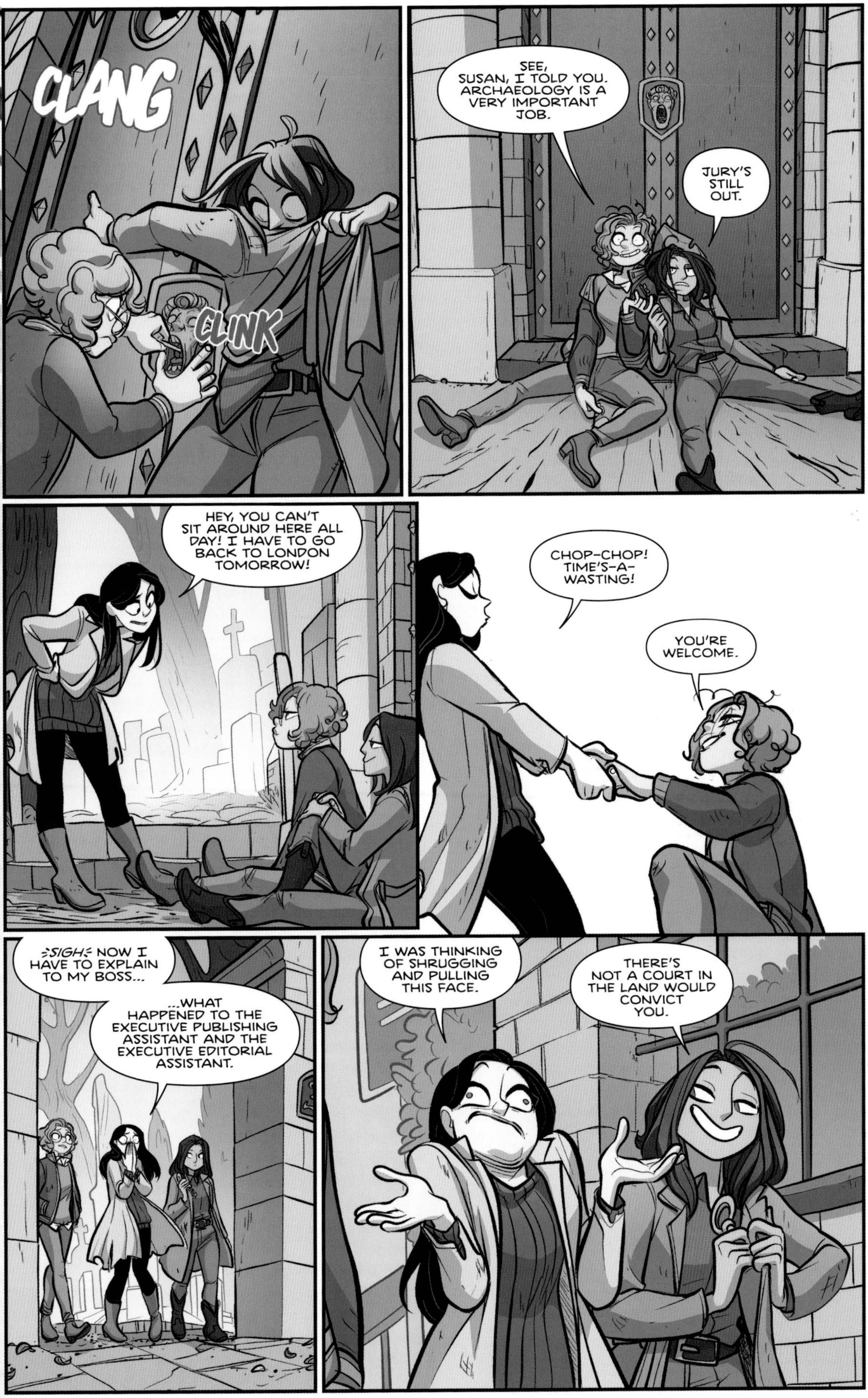
CLANG
CLINK
SEE, SUSAN, I TOLD YOU. ARCHAEOLOGY IS A VERY IMPORTANT JOB.
JURY'S STILL OUT.
HEY, YOU CAN'T SIT AROUND HERE ALL DAY! I HAVE TO GO BACK TO LONDON TOMORROW!
CHOP-CHOP! TIME'S-A-WASTING!
YOU'RE WELCOME.
SIGH NOW I HAVE TO EXPLAIN TO MY BOSS...
...WHAT HAPPENED TO THE EXECUTIVE PUBLISHING ASSISTANT AND THE EXECUTIVE EDITORIAL ASSISTANT.
I WAS THINKING OF SHRUGGING AND PULLING THIS FACE.
THERE'S NOT A COURT IN THE LAND WOULD CONVICT YOU.

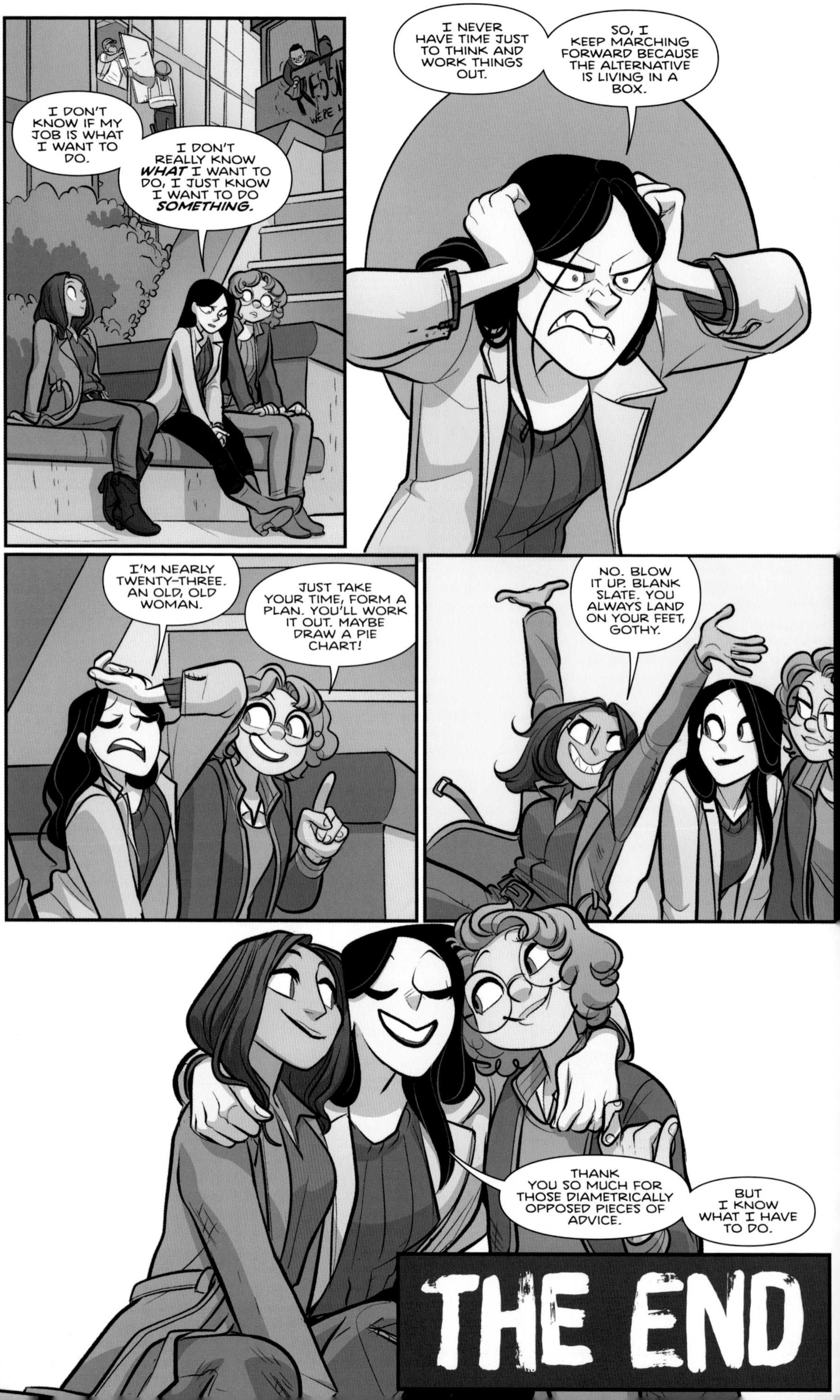
I DON'T KNOW IF MY JOB IS WHAT I WANT TO DO.
I DON'T REALLY KNOW *WHAT* I WANT TO DO, I JUST KNOW I WANT TO DO *SOMETHING.*
I NEVER HAVE TIME JUST TO THINK AND WORK THINGS OUT.
SO, I KEEP MARCHING FORWARD BECAUSE THE ALTERNATIVE IS LIVING IN A BOX.
I'M NEARLY TWENTY-THREE. AN OLD, OLD WOMAN.
JUST TAKE YOUR TIME, FORM A PLAN. YOU'LL WORK IT OUT. MAYBE DRAW A PIE CHART!
NO. BLOW IT UP. BLANK SLATE. YOU ALWAYS LAND ON YOUR FEET, GOTHY.
THANK YOU SO MUCH FOR THOSE DIAMETRICALLY OPPOSED PIECES OF ADVICE.
BUT I KNOW WHAT I HAVE TO DO.
THE END

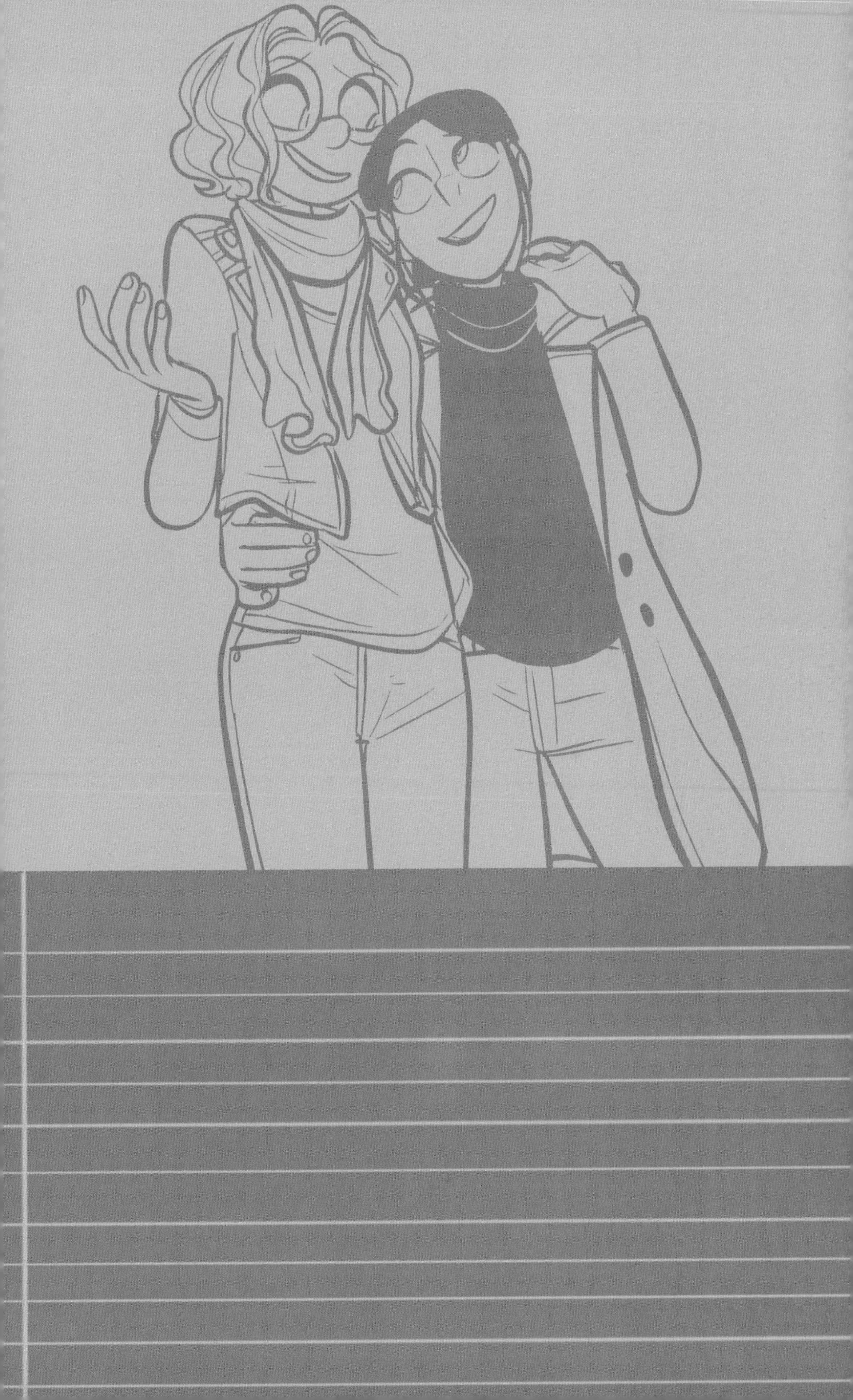

COVER GALLERY

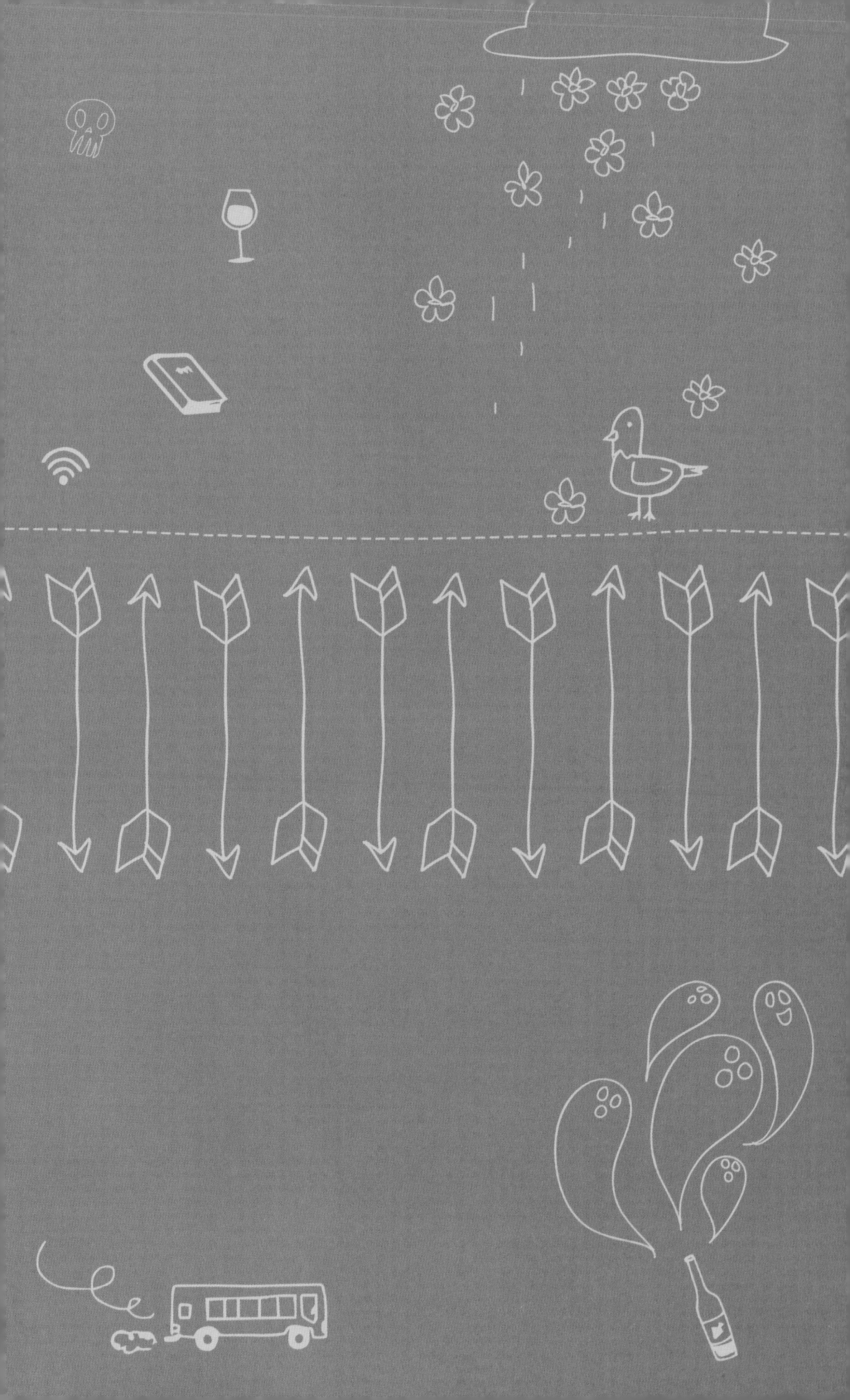

ISSUE #53 COVER
**MAX SARIN**

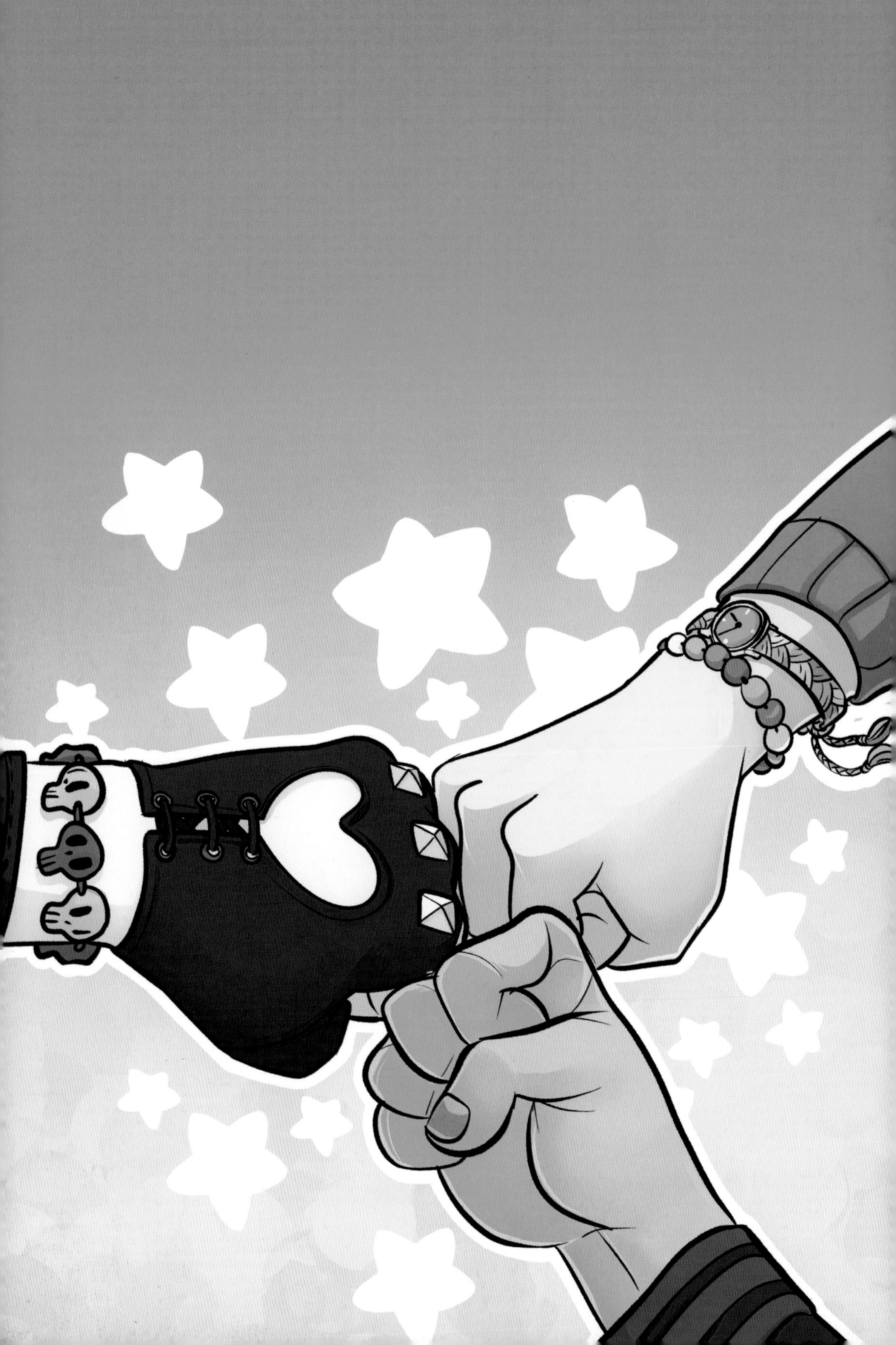

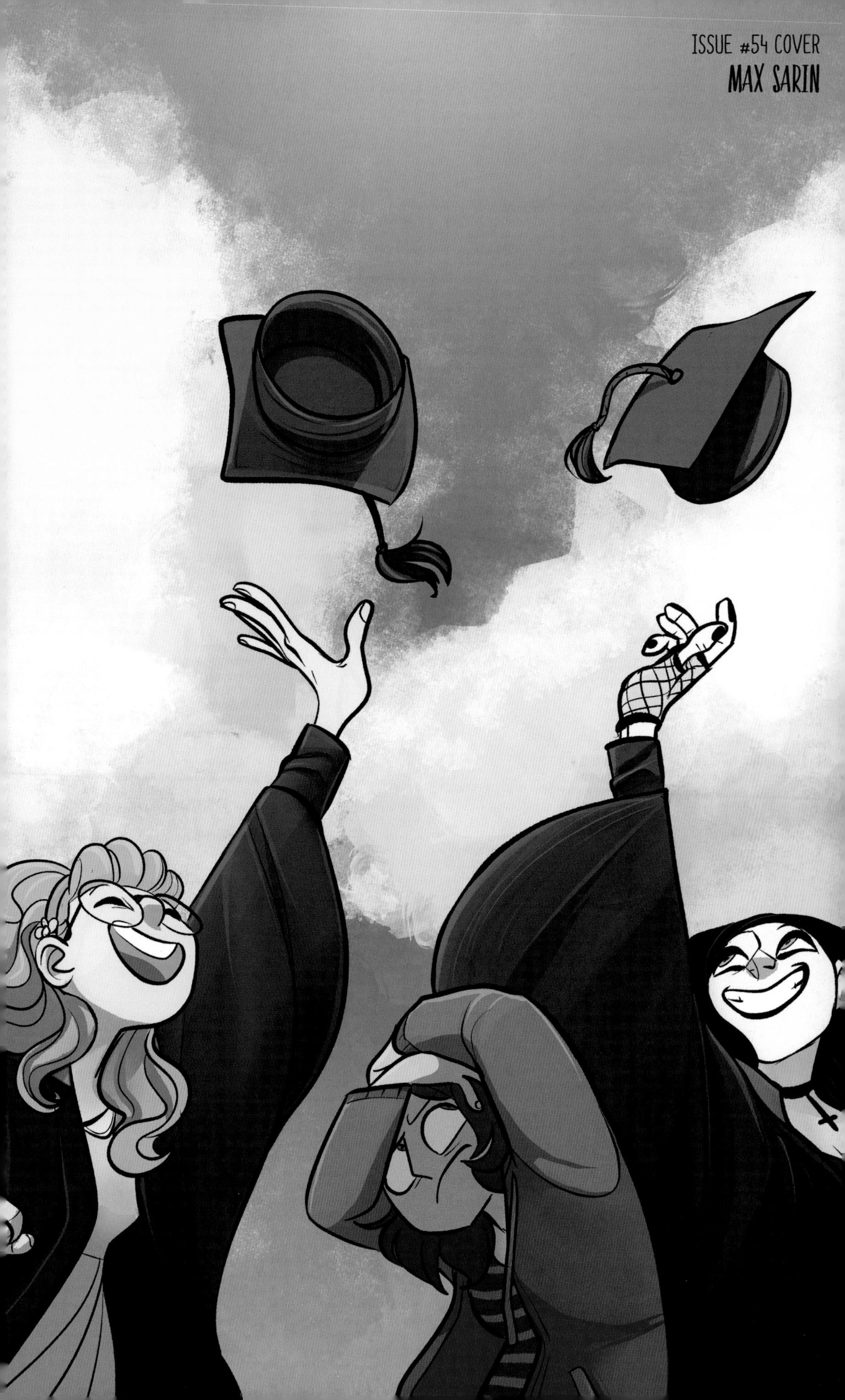

ISSUE #54 COVER
**MAX SARIN**

AS TIME GOES BY COVER
**MAX SARIN**

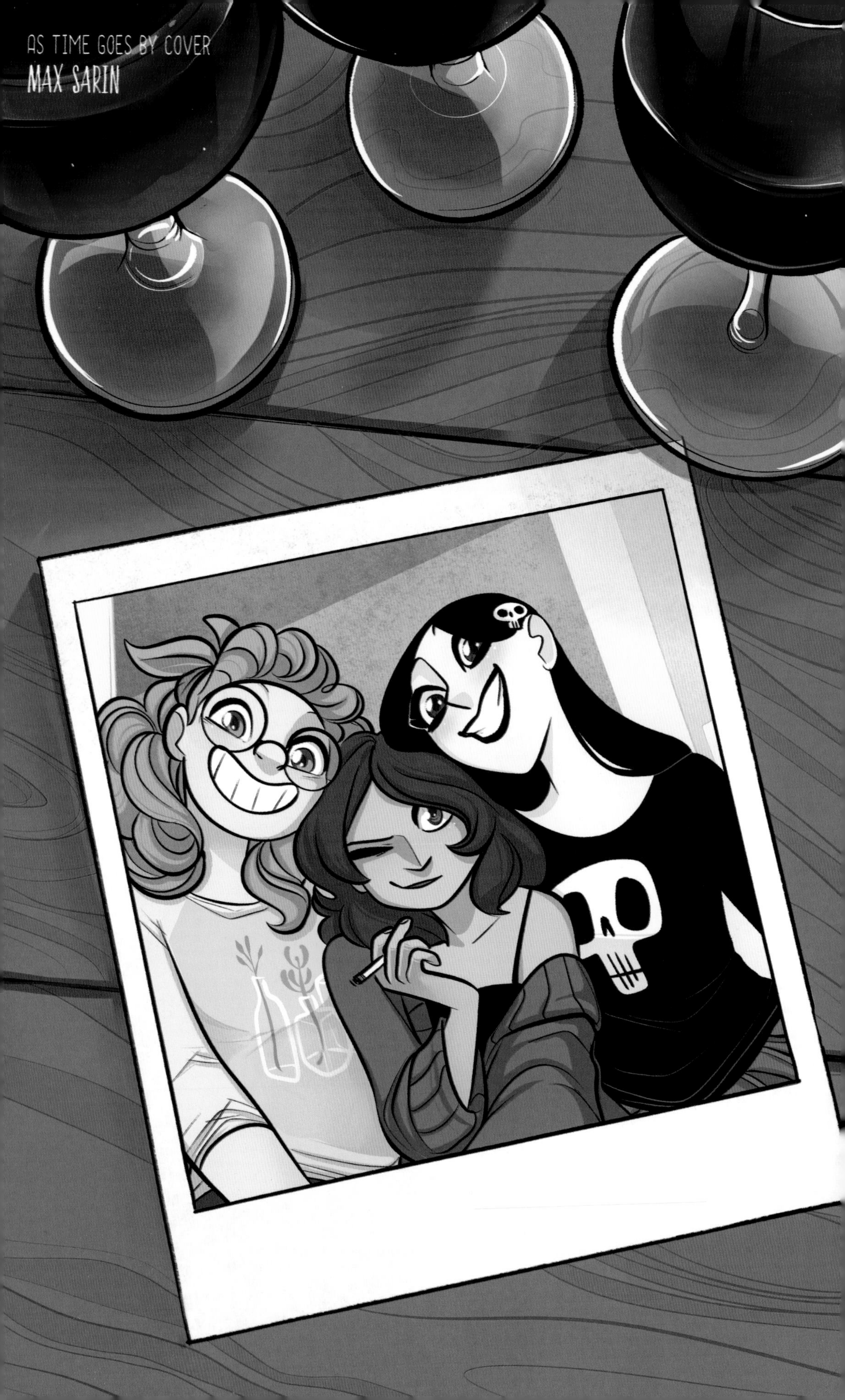

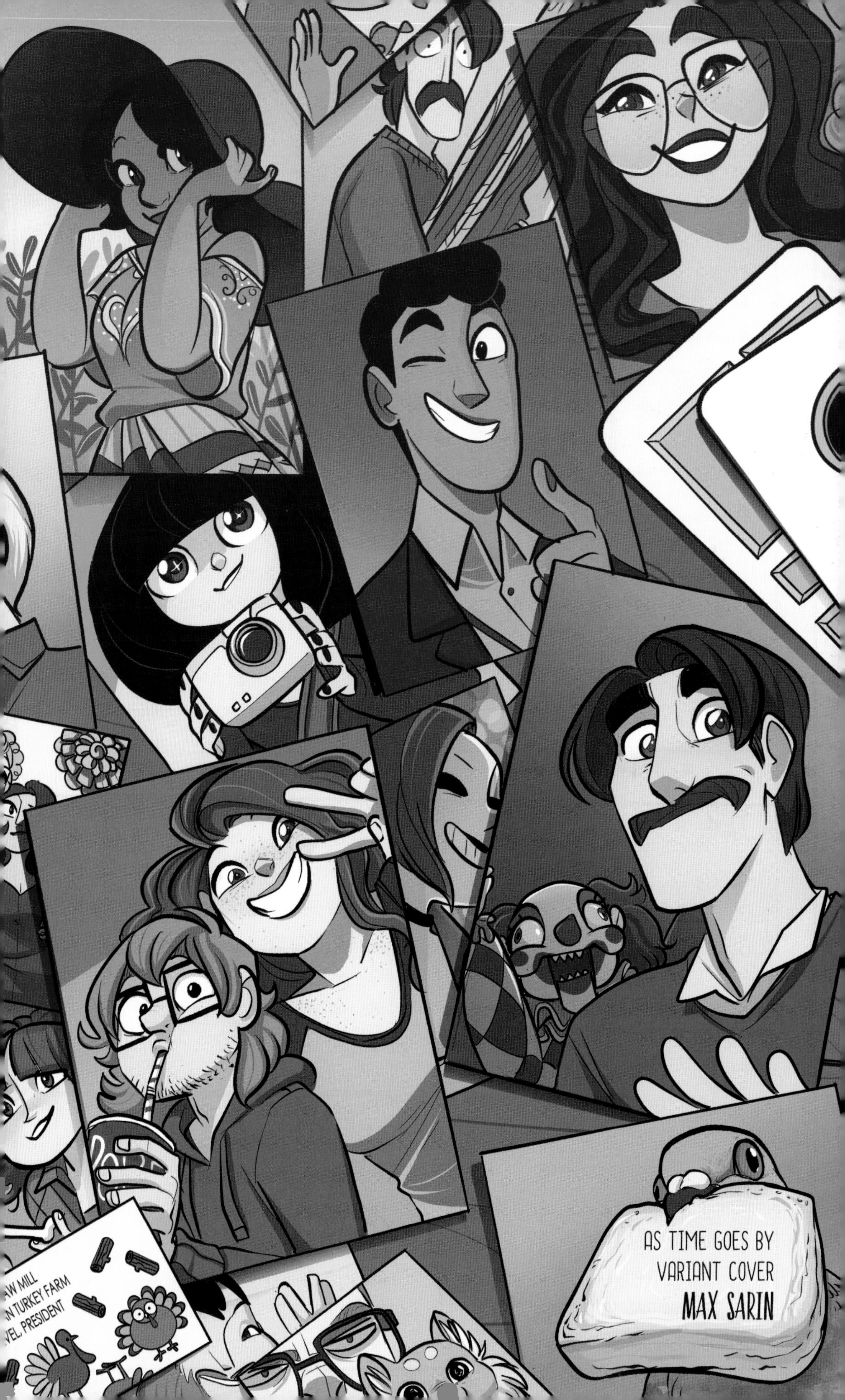
AS TIME GOES BY
VARIANT COVER
MAX SARIN

# PENCILS FOR #53 BY MAX SARIN

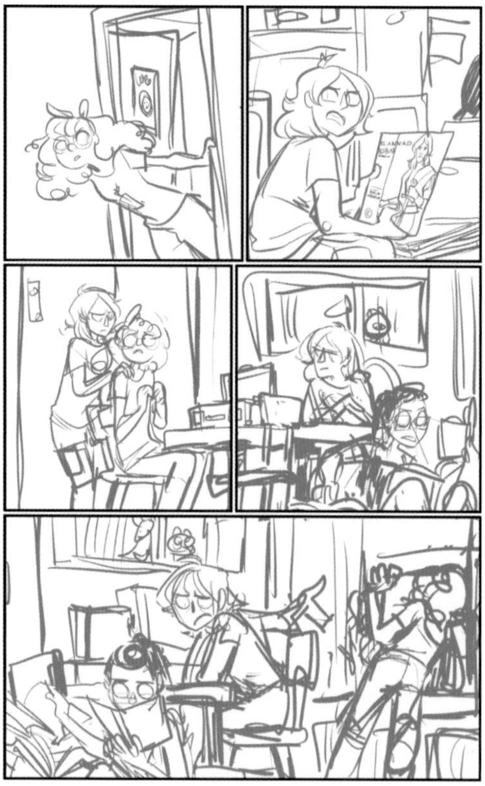

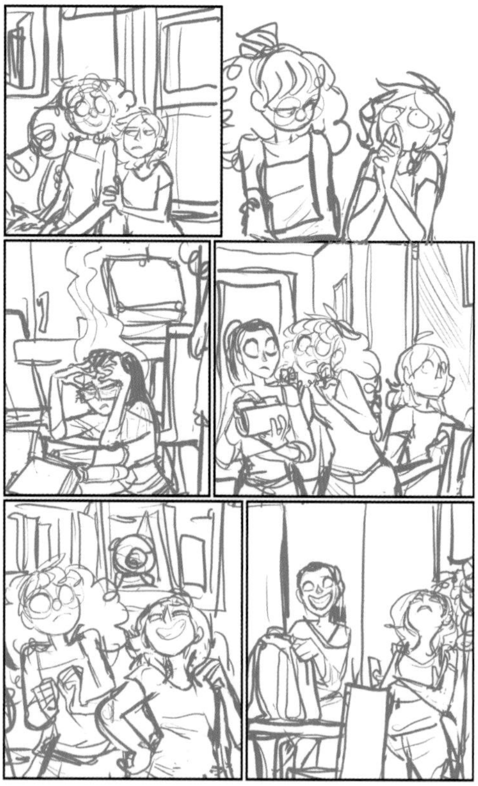

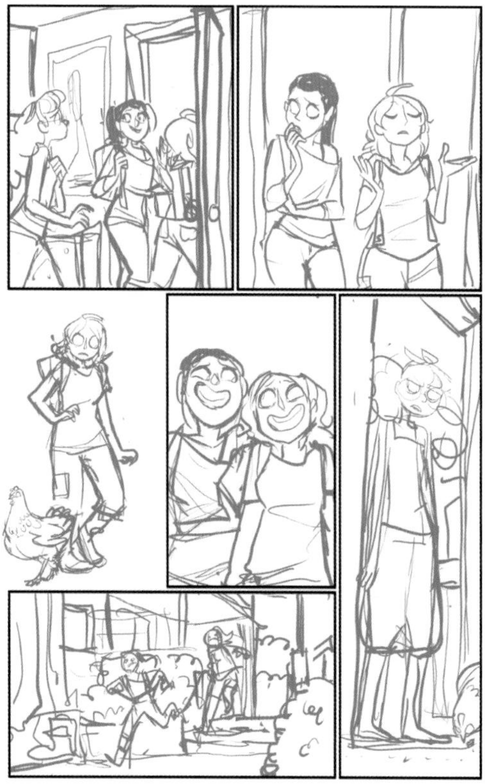

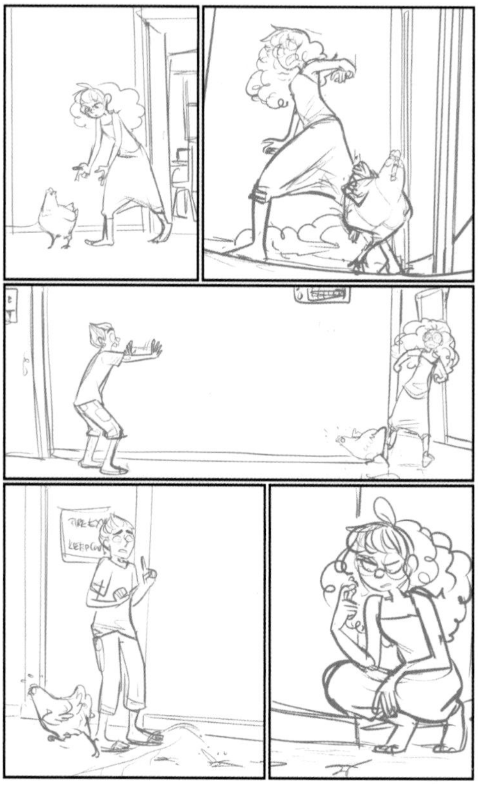

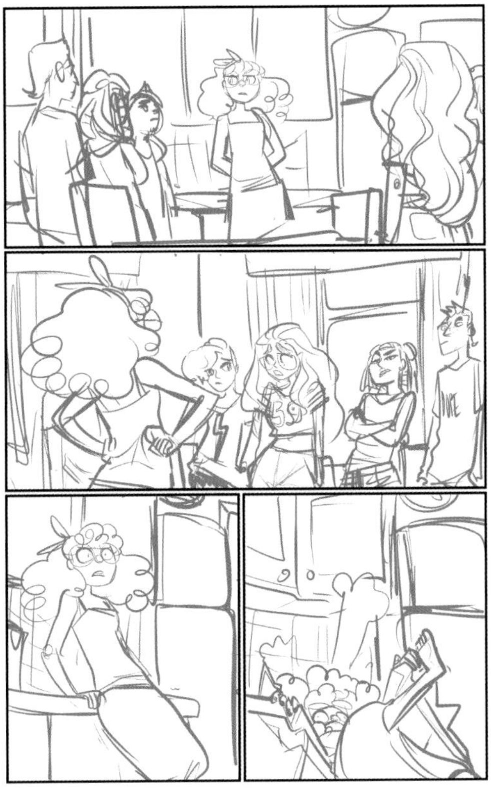

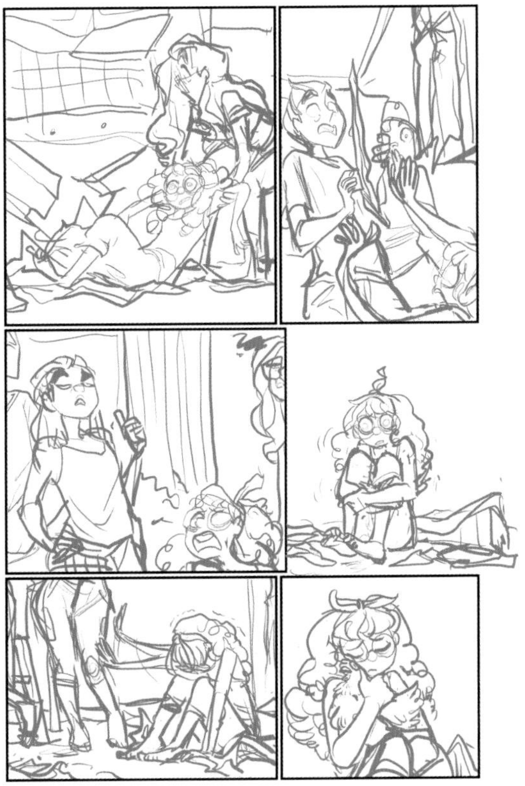

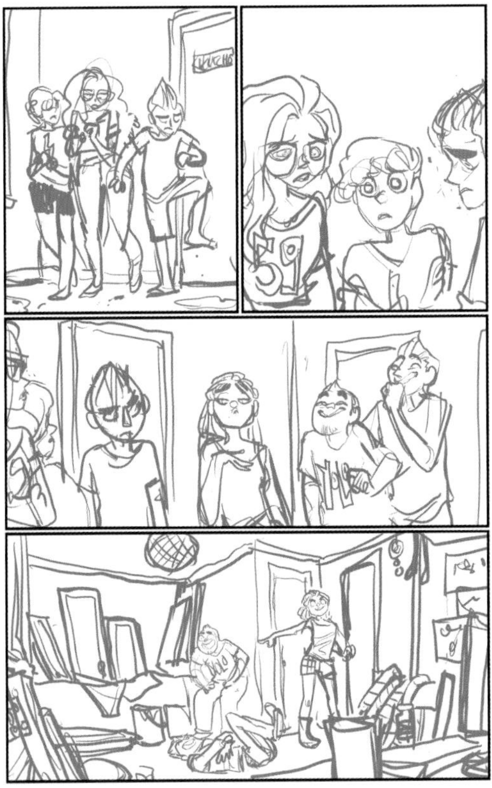

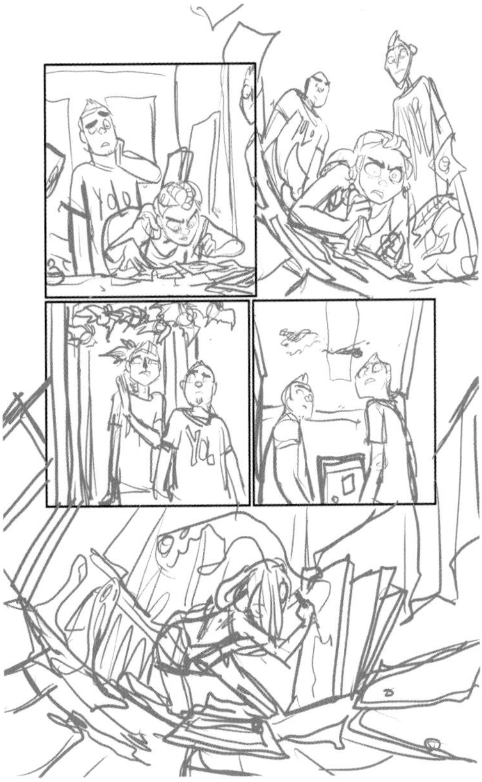

# PENCILS FOR #54 BY MAX SARIN

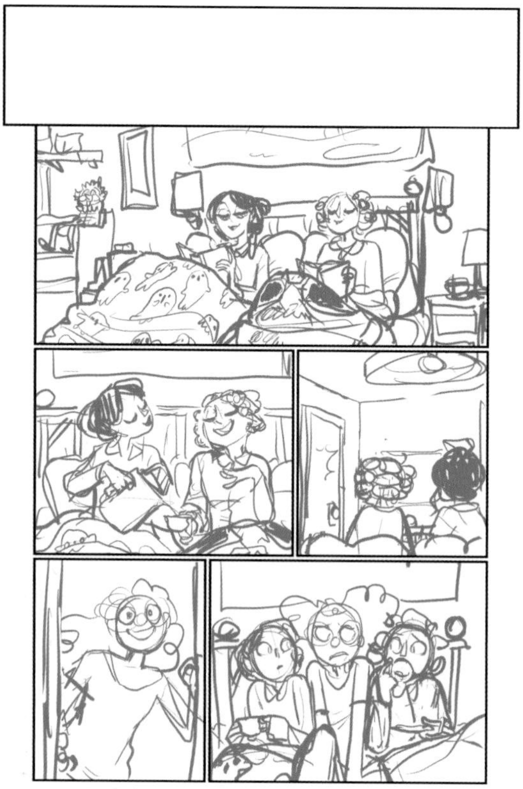

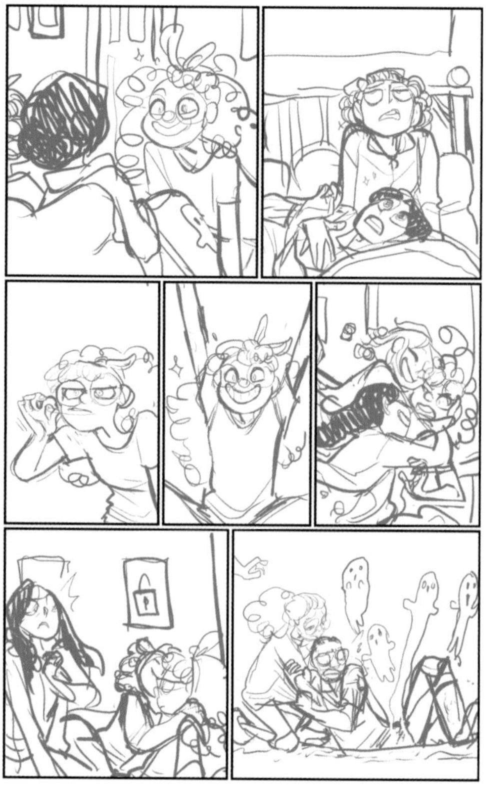

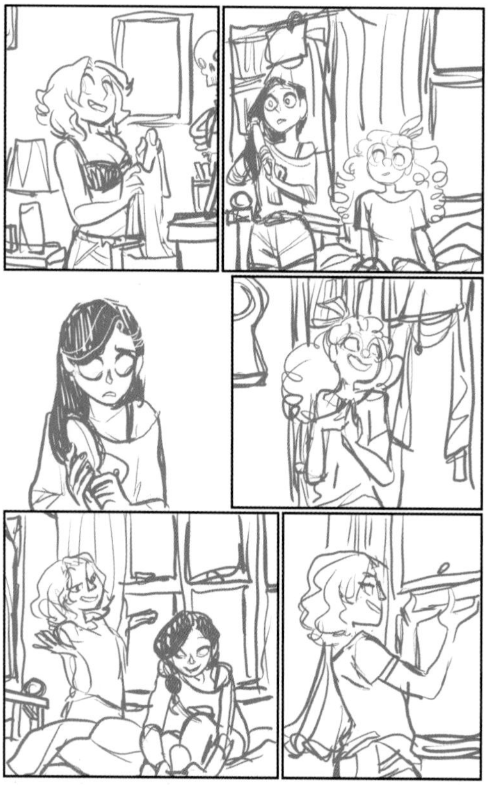

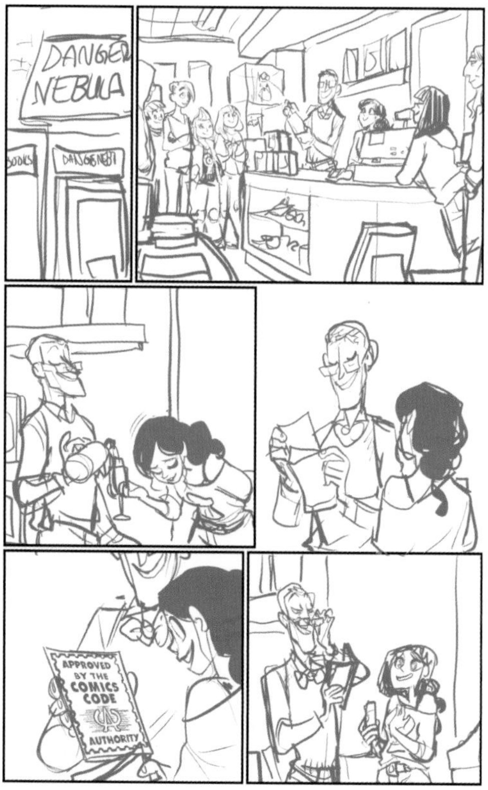
DANGER
NEBULA
APPROVED BY THE COMICS CODE AUTHORITY

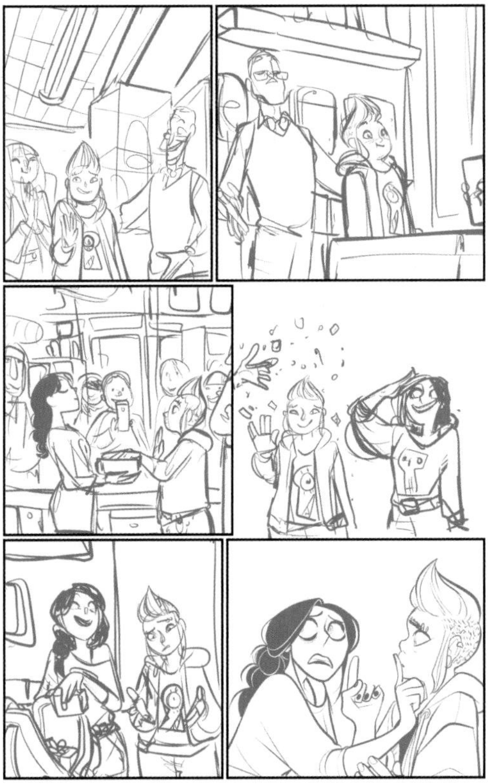

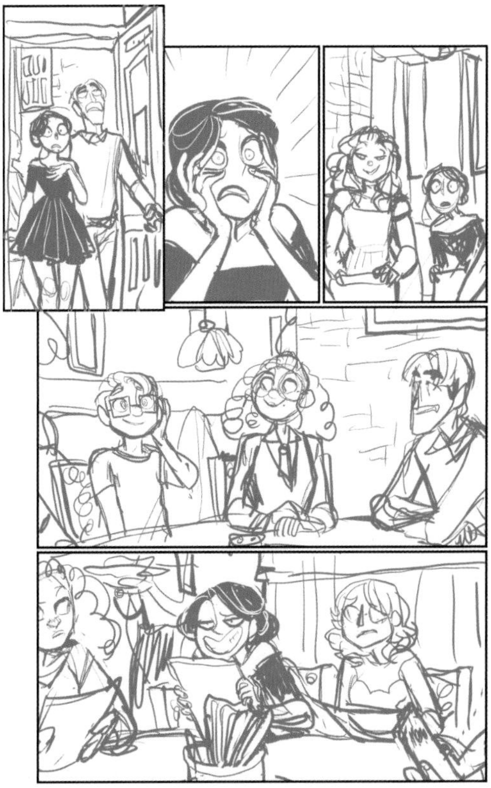

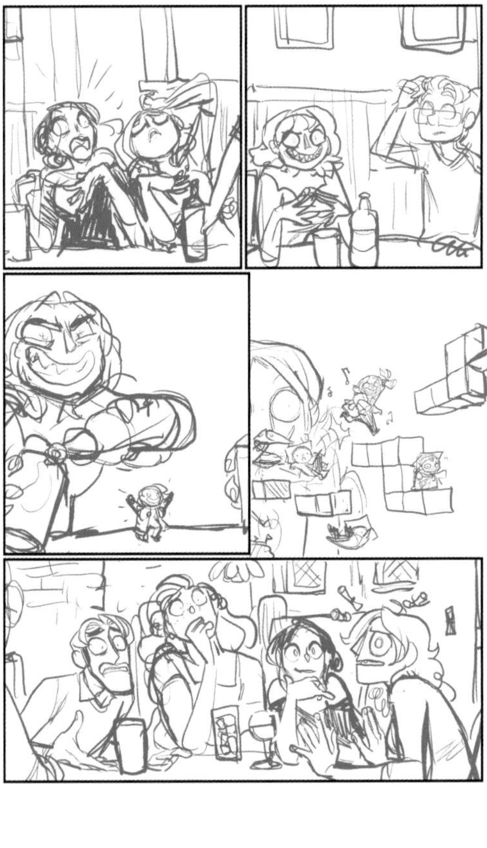

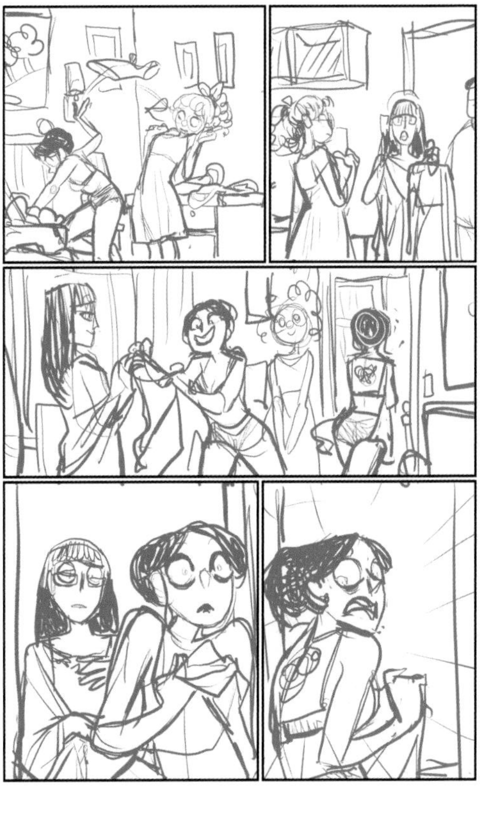

PENCILS FOR #55 (AS TIME GOES BY) BY MAX SARIN

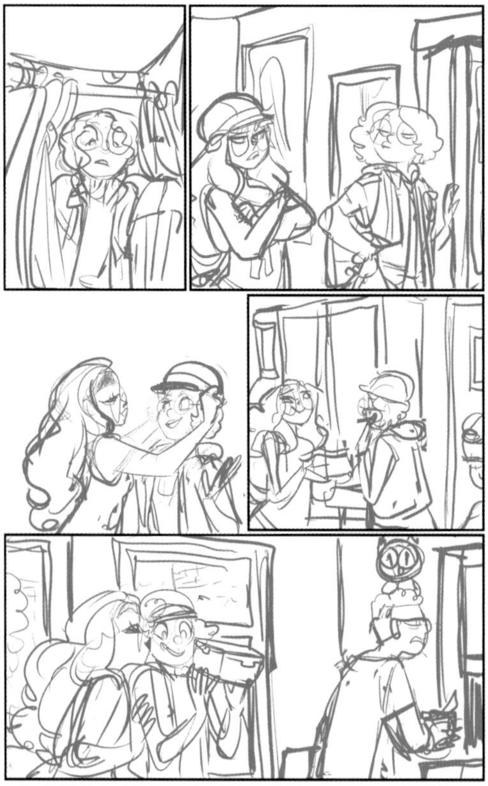

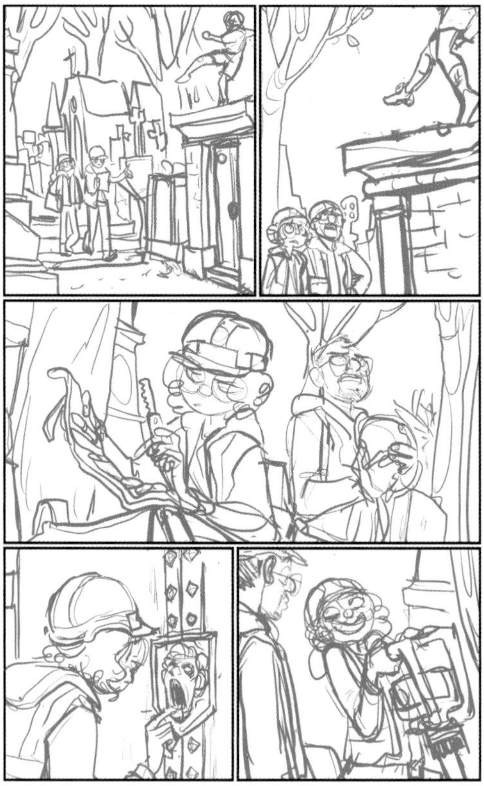

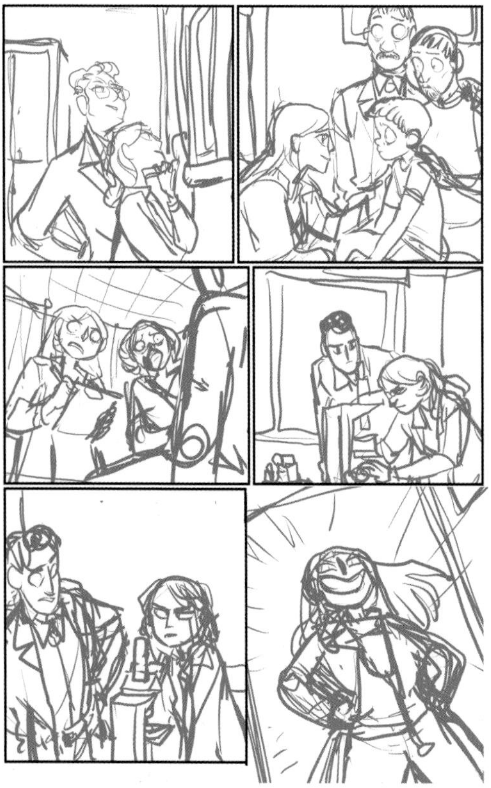

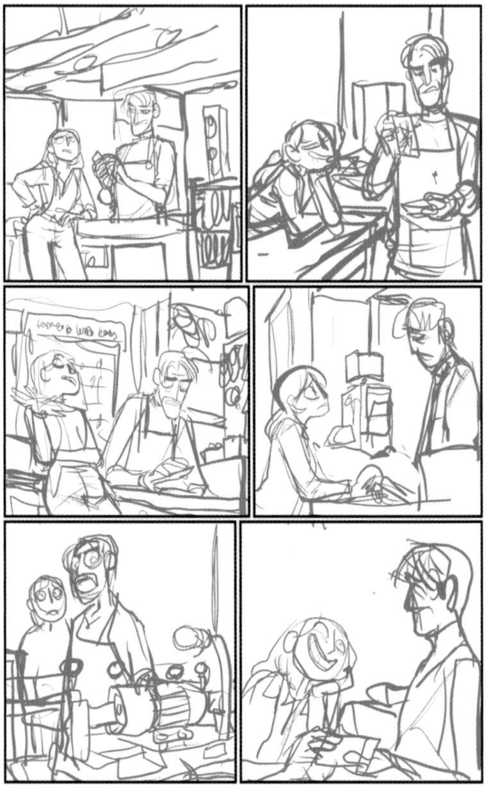

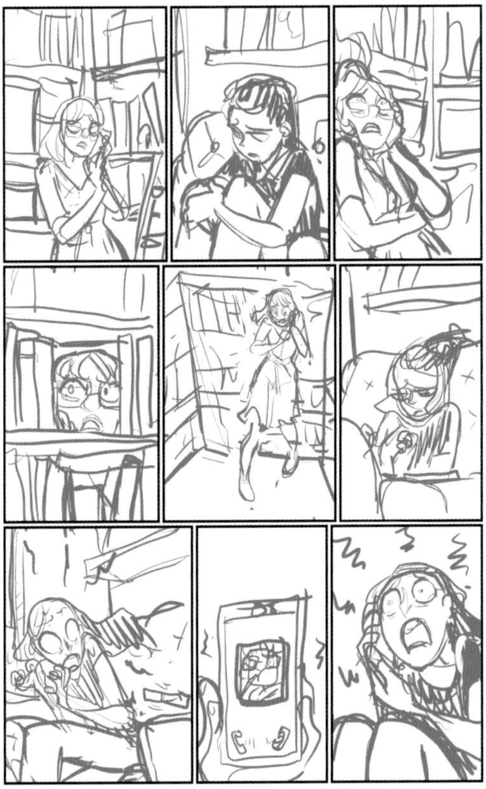

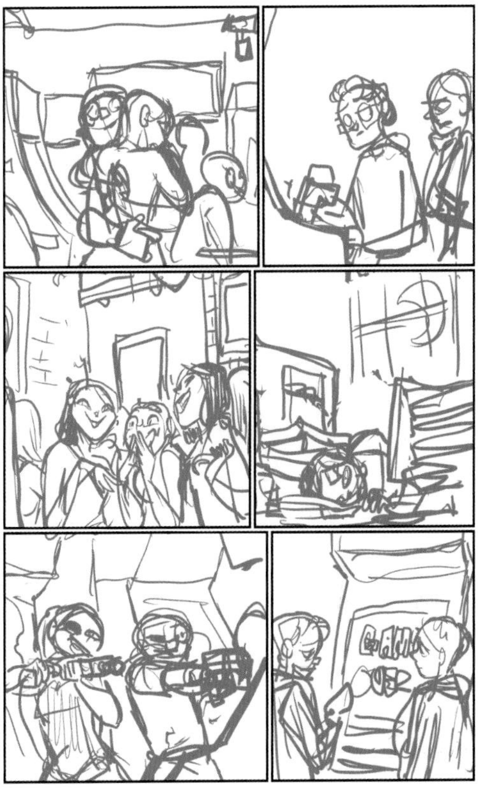

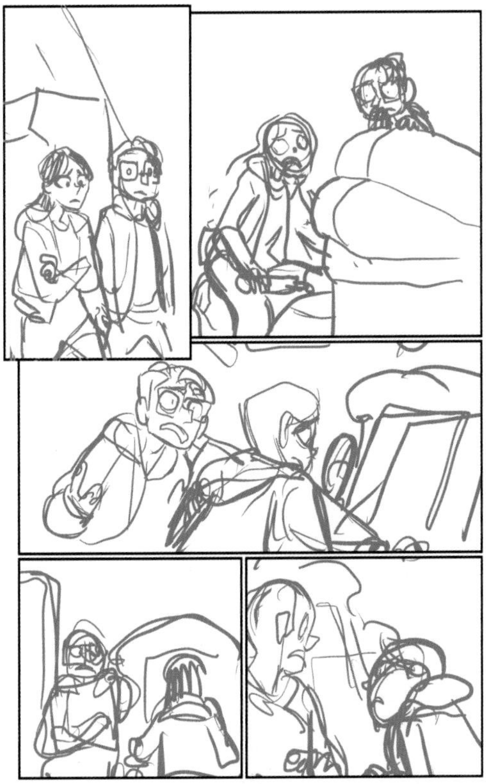

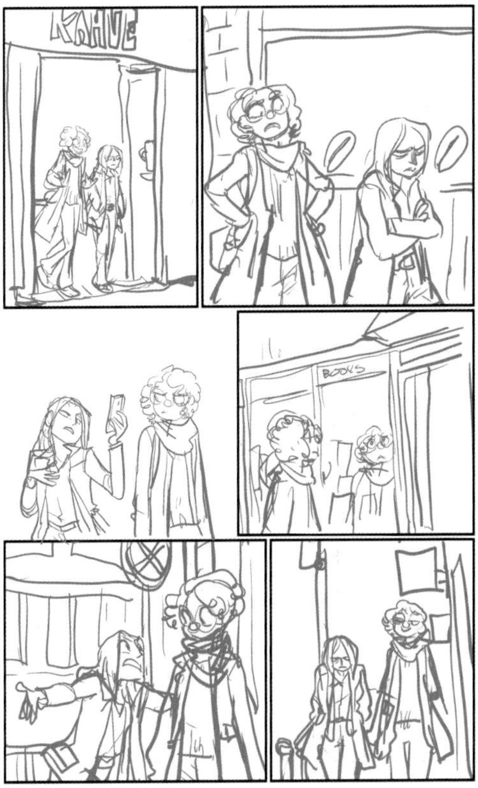
BOOKS

SKETCHES AND DESIGNS BY MAX SARIN

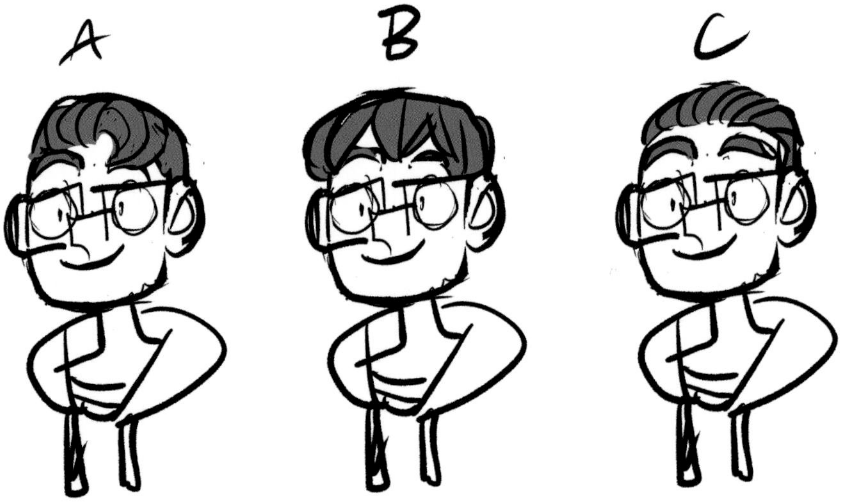
A
B
C

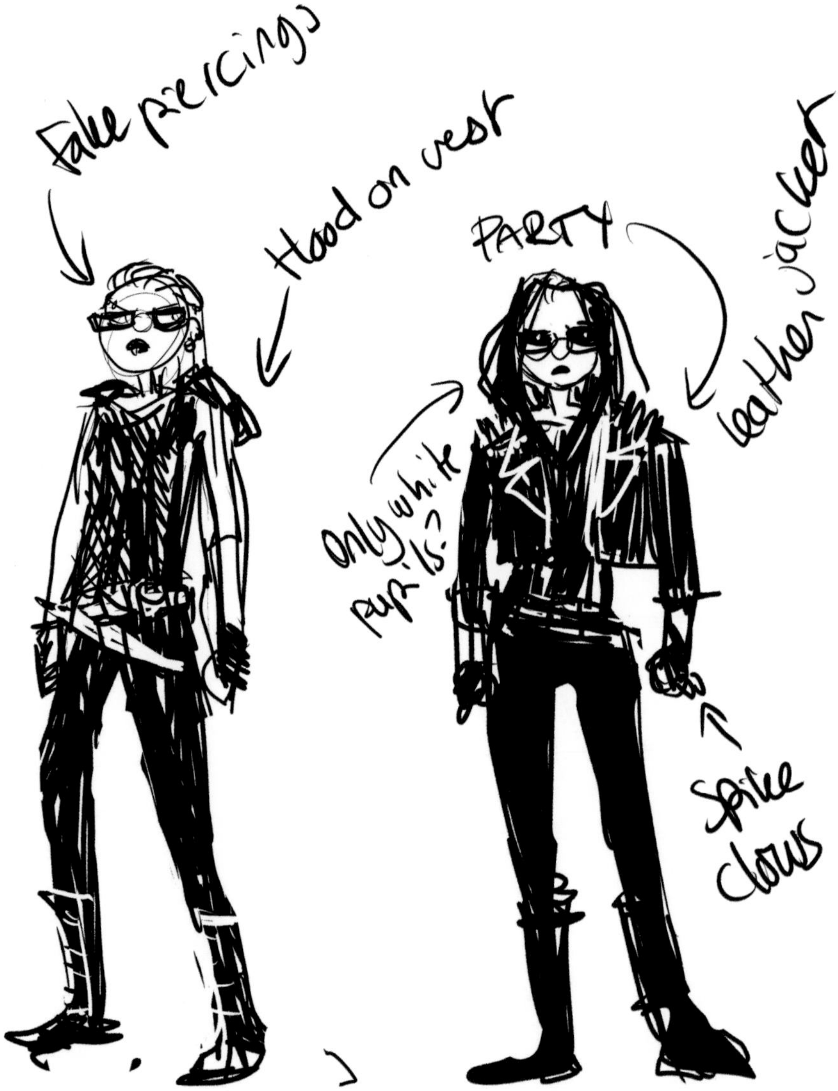
Fake piercings
Hood on vest
PARTY
leather jacket
Only white pupils?
Spike claws

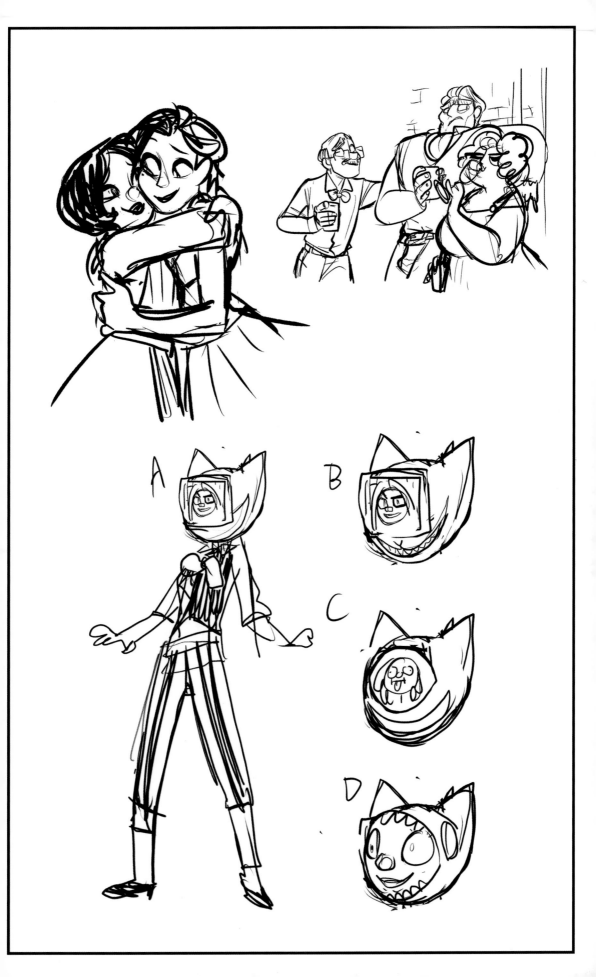

A

B

C

D

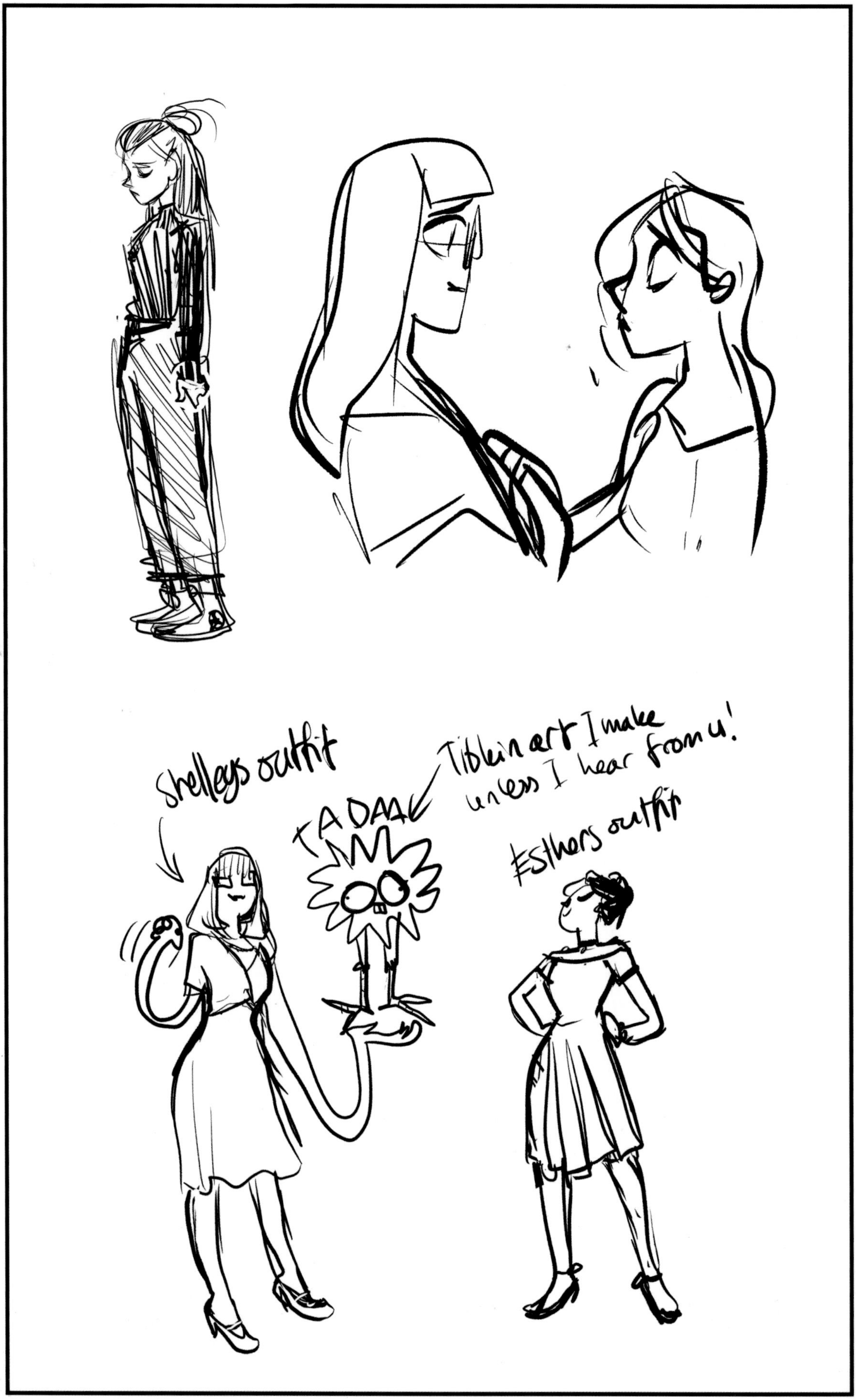

Shelleys outfit
TADAA
Tiblein art I make unless I hear from u!
Esthers outfit

# DISCOVER
# ALL THE HITS

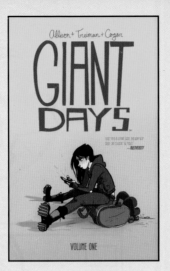

## Lumberjanes
*Noelle Stevenson, Shannon Watters, Grace Ellis, Brooklyn Allen, and Others*
**Volume 1: Beware the Kitten Holy**
ISBN: 978-1-60886-687-8 | $14.99 US
**Volume 2: Friendship to the Max**
ISBN: 978-1-60886-737-0 | $14.99 US
**Volume 3: A Terrible Plan**
ISBN: 978-1-60886-803-2 | $14.99 US
**Volume 4: Out of Time**
ISBN: 978-1-60886-860-5 | $14.99 US
**Volume 5: Band Together**
ISBN: 978-1-60886-919-0 | $14.99 US

## Giant Days
*John Allison, Lissa Treiman, Max Sarin*
**Volume 1**
ISBN: 978-1-60886-789-9 | $9.99 US
**Volume 2**
ISBN: 978-1-60886-804-9 | $14.99 US
**Volume 3**
ISBN: 978-1-60886-851-3 | $14.99 US

## Jonesy
*Sam Humphries, Caitlin Rose Boyle*
**Volume 1**
ISBN: 978-1-60886-883-4 | $9.99 US
**Volume 2**
ISBN: 978-1-60886-999-2 | $14.99 US

## Slam!
*Pamela Ribon, Veronica Fish, Brittany Peer*
**Volume 1**
ISBN: 978-1-68415-004-5 | $14.99 US

## Goldie Vance
*Hope Larson, Brittney Williams*
**Volume 1**
ISBN: 978-1-60886-898-8 | $9.99 US
**Volume 2**
ISBN: 978-1-60886-974-9 | $14.99 US

## The Backstagers
*James Tynion IV, Rian Sygh*
**Volume 1**
ISBN: 978-1-60886-993-0 | $14.99 US

## Tyson Hesse's Diesel: Ignition
*Tyson Hesse*
ISBN: 978-1-60886-907-7 | $14.99 US

## Coady & The Creepies
*Liz Prince, Amanda Kirk, Hannah Fisher*
ISBN: 978-1-68415-029-8 | $14.99 US

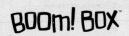

**AVAILABLE AT YOUR LOCAL COMICS SHOP AND BOOKSTORE**
To find a comics shop in your area, visit www.comicshoplocator.com
WWW.**BOOM-STUDIOS**.COM

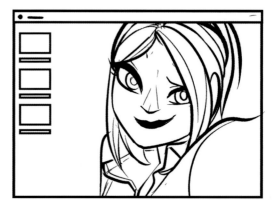